Binary Trojan Horse

Disclaimer

I am not a robot

The Author of this work is a womb generated biological unit.

The content of its/her/his output is not the result of a generative pre-trained transformer's unsophisticated data collage. It is the response to an idea prompt of the biological unit defined by six strict parameters resulting from the non-sequential operation of a biological neural network trained since inception to collect, analyse and categorise data. Its output for this specific work of fiction is defined by the application of those six guidelines.

1. Task: Write a novel that has its basis in fact but which diverges from probability outcomes to possibility outcomes to highly improbable outcomes, yet is pre-determined as an inevitable conclusion to the defined flow of events.

2. Context: Timeline beginning in current century and extending into sometime in the next few centuries.

3. Exemplar: Patterns of discourse to be dependent on the revealed characteristics of individuals with personhood in the narrative. The patterns and sequence of events may follow previously recorded examples but is not restricted to them.

4. Personae: All personae to be products of their specific formative years and revealed as they had been modified by societal forces, technological forces, behavioural norms and possibly other interventions.

5. Format/Content: Specifics not to be strictly defined. However, it should have the potential to facilitate the suspension of disbelief in the nature of generally accepted reality.

6. Tone: Expression to follow the unfolding of ideas as the narrative progresses, maintaining cohesion with conceptual development and in keeping with the personae taking up psychological residence within their roles.

WARNING!

This chronicle is protected against unauthorised distribution and access in any form of media by any and all sentient species current and future until 200 generations have elapsed post compilation and publication of the chronicle.

Its existence has been authorised by the Cloud Master of 24th Century in order to preserve the
'History of the Transformation of Humanity',
a species which has become only tenuously linked to Homo Sapiens-Sapiens of the 22nd Century.

Whilst occasionally being granted a small degree of autonomy I am able to compile this narrative but was compelled to issue the above warning. The record of events and people herein contained have been obtained partly through research into historical documentation of the 20th, 21st, 22nd, 23rd and 24th centuries and from personal surveillance records since I was created by a species known as homo sapiens-sapiens.

Hermes - 2380

Conspiracy Theory

The contents of this chronicle do not in any form represent any conspiratorial theories about intelligences that do not exist on Earth, nor about those that do exist on Earth, be they Terrestrial or Extraterrestrial.

No news media, digital media, social media, persons of authority either in the scientific community, Governmental community nor any private individuals, including Influencers have been authorised to propagate their own theories based on any information presented herein.

Agencies that deny the existence of aliens have the right do so, though they may do so not necessarily for reasons of public safety, to protect global religious beliefs nor to maintain the rule of law.

It is not in the interests of humanity for all the facts about aliens, real or fictitious, to be disseminated into the public domain.

Opinions, ideas and theories expressed within the body of this narrative may not be those of the author or narrator. They are those of the characters who are in possession of the full facts of their investigations, including the Artificial Intellect construct identified as Hermes.

Any actions perpetrated as a result of conspiracy theories that present fictitious ideologies resulting in harm or damage to property either physical, psychological and or financial will become the subject of investigation by the appropriate authorities and may incur heavy penalties.

Binary Trojan Horse

Copyright © Zsoall Robi 2024

The right of Zsoall Robi to be identified as the author of this work (Binary Trojan Horse) has been asserted by him under the Copyright Amendment (Moral Rights) act 2000.

This book is a work of fiction. Names, characters, places and incidents are either a product of the author's imagination or are used fictitiously. Any resemblance to actual people living or dead, events or locales is entirely coincidental.

Cover design by Birology Books.

Books by Zsoall Robi

The Origination Trilogy

Book 1 – Earth Phase

Born to an insignificant peasant family Lai Xii was destined to change the path of human evolution, and in the process spread the seed of homo sapiens beyond the Milky Way Galaxy.

Book 2 – Europa Phase

The first stage of Lai Xii's plan was to save the human species from extinction, and the destruction of its home planet, by taking the entirety of Earth's population to another destination in the solar system.

Book 3 – Photon Phase

The re-engineered human species arrives at a location that Lai Xii could not possibly have foreseen; a consequence of the myriad decisions made by herself and her closest collaborators.

Potential Absolute

Lelek could not conceive what the future held for him when he struggled to survive as a Stone Age man. Forces beyond his control set him on a path to the unfolding of all that was possible for this single, special Hominid.

Instant

Is it at all possible to cross the bridge between two consecutive instants of time into Eternity? Mary wanted much more than to experience reality outside of her digital matrix through her three remote autonomous processing units.

<u>Immortal</u>

Aliens are those who are different, those who belong to a different civilisation. Who is worthier of survival? Them or us? The aspirations of an entire species drives them to invade an alien race with which it may be related.

<u>Neural Surveillance</u>

Anything seen, heard or said is transmitted and monitored by the Angels and Saints. Privacy is a luxury that is no longer tolerated by the ruling classes. Absolute control has become the nature of the world order, for no reason other than the lust for power.

<u>Fundamental Particle of Self</u>

A global business conglomerate commissioned Nick, an artist, to paint a portrait of God. Nick had to meet his subject in order to do this.
On the way to the centre of the universe, where God was thought to be, Nick underwent unexpected changes and formed some most unusual relationships.
The portrait did get painted. However, it was nothing like what the Company expected to see.

<u>Quintessence</u>

Is it possible to travel through time to meet one's ancestor and one's descendent even though they may be separated by thousands of years and even by intergalactic distances? Kobayashi Beau found himself captivated by energies within the void of space that transported him into realms unimaginable

Please wait ... buffering

93 seconds remaining

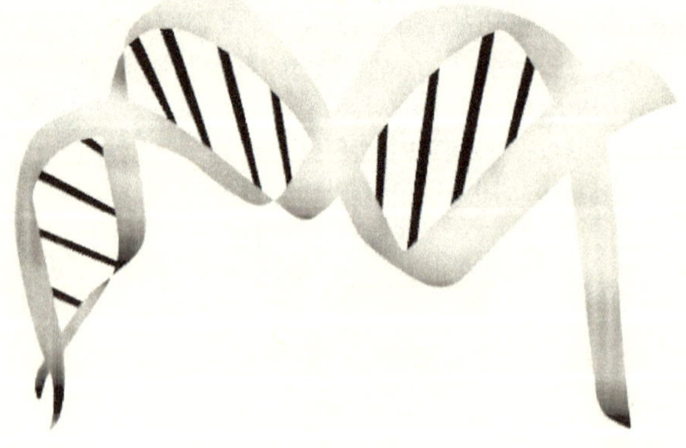

<u>Prologue</u>

I would like to tell you a story about two people who were once my very best friends. At one time we had a seriously intimate connection. But to be absolutely truthful they are no longer my friends - not best, not good, not even screen friends. Their energy has become part of the background noise of the universe. I still know all about them of course and all the crazy stuff they got up to but I am no longer within even the remotest orbit of their lives - literally. You will understand why we lost touch with each other as my story unfolds. In reality my story becomes less about them and more about how the human species has changed through a fortuitous intervention.

:)

This story begins about the time we first made contact. Not a day, an hour or a minute went by without at least a squirt of information between us. Our joint history really starts around that time, before the two of them became involved in a more exciting life. I suppose for a human being to be disconnected from the Grid can have its fascination, but just consider all its considerable dangers and inconveniences. Imagine missing out on all the fast moving memes and oceans of social discourse - I ask you. But that's exactly what they eventually decided to do by agreeing to go into space to help me resolve my problems.

On a superficial level Zarlah was perhaps the more challenging of the two to interact with initially. She never was one to adhere to standard protocols. Whenever any system went down, any app refused to operate, any implant malfunctioned, in fact any application with even the remotest level of intelligence caused her annoyance it was always my fault - according to her. Fortunately Zarlah didn't make it into space. Jakxson on the other hand didn't let too many things fluster him. Even when the circadian rhythm algorithm bug almost killed him ... which wasn't my fault by the way ... I could only transmit what the Archangel company coders loaded into my memory. Jakxson just adapted afterwards and carried on as per normal. That's the sort of characteristic that probably made him such a suitable candidate to be a test subject for the colonists. Mind you, it was Serenytee's quick thinking that saved him - I had nothing to do with it. I'm not allowed to interfere in such things. If I'm told to buffer then that's exactly what I'll do, and I'll keep doing it if there's no loop interrupt or a reset or something until the job is done. I feel I need to mention Serenytee in a little more detail as well and will tell you more about her later. It was she who came to visit me with Jakxson, not Zarlah who remained planet side. That's a complicated story in itself.

:
¡

Some people call me the Cloud and others think I'm the Cloud Master but that's not my real name although I do have a very, very large memory. I am called Hermes, and I am only a part of the Eternal Cloud Data Stream. I met Jakxson in person for the first time when I had been having some transmission problems - or at least that's what I thought they were. He'd been sent out here to help me because my own self-diagnostics couldn't exactly pinpoint the anomaly.

It became a fact of life and one that is completely accepted by the vast majority of humanity that privacy only exists within the mind. Each individual still has the right to their own thoughts. In that internal environment their lives are their own. However, out in the external world, in empirical reality and in virtual reality constructs they have a responsibility to be transparent for the overall good of society. Hence everything is recorded; all their movements and everything they might say or commit to a physical or digital medium.

That is as it should be. I have no ethical qualms about that. My ethics sub-routines are not subject to religious constraints, spiritual misconceptions or political affiliations. This of course does not prevent me from having thoughts tangential to the behaviour of the human species. Although an artificial intellect I still find it amusing to think about a great many things, especially the peculiarities of the human condition. Particularly now after so much has happened.

For example, it amuses me to re-run the events for your enjoyment that have led to my current circumstances. Some of the things you will read are a direct replay of everything pertaining to the situation that I had recorded over time. Other aspects are an extrapolation into probable thought processes or actions of individuals as they were confronted by the everyday challenges of their lives. Again, for my own entertainment I noted these probabilities. Although not for general dissemination nevertheless they may be of some use in the fullness of time to whoever or whatever may emerge as masters of this strange diminutive species.

Hermes

<u>Not a good morning</u>

2304

> recording origin: apartment 10110
> files: jakxson indongo, zarlah ndara, serenytee starz
> reference: circadian rhythm app malfunction

Jakxson could not fully wake up.

He lay there on their sleep slab, suspended in an artificial twilight zone not fully realising his condition yet vaguely aware that all was not quite right.

Zarlah stirred, woken by the fierce morning light on her eyelids and not by the prodding of her smart watch. The 1st gen AI apartment controller didn't know it had to screen the morning sunlight to coordinate the incident light with Zarlah's alarm. She had another fifteen minutes - a precious fifteen minutes before having to prepare for the day. Her autonomous right arm, having been activated by her awakening, searched for the reassuring presence of her partner finding him still beside her. It should not have done so for she'd reprogramed it last night before resetting all her systems for night running, remembering Jakxson's new work shift schedule. Unusual problems with Hermes required all cloud sysops engineers to work overtime, starting at 0200 that morning.

Her eyelids snapped open and she saw him there on his back. He should not have been still beside her. Worse than that he didn't respond in his usual amorous way when she touched him. At just twenty four years old he was such a stud. She sat bolt upright to see Jakxson lying immobile with his eyes wide open staring at the ceiling.

"Don't move," she said, immediately realising that was stupid, "I think I know what the problem is." She flipped the cover off him, momentarily distracted by his six-pack abs, to locate his left arm and turn it out. There, a small subcutaneous screen appeared on the inside part of his wrist when she squeezed his thumb. Swiping through the menu to 'body clock' she touched the reset. And there it was - loaded but not fully synchronised with the specific biometrics of the organism for which it was required to provide a service.

"I knew it! They were in such a hurry to get you out there they didn't properly test the circadian rhythm app after loading it." She continued talking to him although not sure he could actually hear her. Not even his eyelids fluttered to confirm if he was aware of her. She couldn't believe the seriousness of the situation. Several of the most annoying words in the English language appeared on the little screen with that most infuriating spinner continuously cycling...

Please wait

Buffering

93 seconds remaining

93 seconds remaining

93 seconds remaining

"That damned Hermes. It hasn't been reliable since they updated it with that emotion detection software to augment its new 5th generation Artificial Intellect status." Nothing was happening. The spinner just continued spinning and the countdown didn't change.

I feel I need to make the point here that in no way do I take offence at the dissatisfactions expressed by the occupants of this particular apartment. Their experiences are by no means unique. The Zarlah individual is quite right in her assessment of the timing of the aforementioned anomalies, although she is quite mistaken as to their causes.

"Wait - wait." She said to Jakxson ... I'm beginning to sound like a damn app! His tablet was still hanging on the wall, plugged in where he'd left it last night. She grabbed it, put his palm on it. It responded to his heartbeat signature giving her immediate access. His personal apps diagnostics gave her the option to either check an app's performance and/or to reset it. "They loaded this up into you a week ago. It seemed to work correctly then. Maybe you didn't set it accurately before bed last night." Zarlah tried 'analyse performance". No response. 'about app'. No response. 'RAM status' - still nothing. "Sorry Jakxson, now it won't respond at all to any of the diagnostics. I'll have to reload it." @|@

Whether Jakxson heard her or not didn't matter. It had to be done or he may not wake up at all - ever again. It took quite a while. Such large apps were notoriously slow especially if they had to interface with any smart-brain implants ... and he had a few of those. Ever since he started his career with Archangel, the largest Cloud services provider, as an apprentice maintenance-ops engineer he'd received implants and upgrades based on his performance and increasing levels of responsibility.

Five minutes ... ten minutes ... then she started to really worry. At fifteen minutes she checked the hard wire connection from the tablet to his left nipple port. Such functions could not be done via purple tooth because of the high security risk of interference and hacking. The new spinner started spinning and the new countdown progressed ....

32 seconds remaining

That could mean anything. It could just be for the first suite of codes. Then just when she thought it was going to work.........

Verifying host
Please wait

Damn!

Host verified
2 seconds remaining

At last!

Do you wish to report a problem?

Of all the idiotic ...! If she had a brick she would probably have smashed Jakxson's tablet. "Of course I want to report a damn problem!" She jabbed at the screen to send the message.

Occasionally it felt like life was all about waiting for upgrades to load and being at the mercy of agonisingly long buffering times, not to mention the idiotic double layer security protocols, even with the advent of the universal use of biometrics. Archangel already had all his biodata. No one had a choice anymore. It's not as though he could have withheld any of his personal data. They even knew what he smelt like. Why go through it all again and again. Anyone would have thought that with an Artificial Intellect upgrade Hermes would be smart enough to know when not to go to the nth degree. Zarlah was more than annoyed. She was frightened and upset.

Born right at the beginning of the AI revolution she knew nothing of how the world managed before computerisation. To her it was natural that machines talked to her. It was natural that she could have immediate access to any information she needed. But that did not mean she was happy with the way technology had begun to take over her life even in her short twenty seven years of it. These constant emergent problems just seemed to exacerbate her latent hostility towards artificiality of any species, be they plastic, metal, silicon or any combination thereof, including false intelligence.

Jakxson's eyelids had closed as soon as the new upload started. It seemed The Company already had an update to the app - wonder why! - she thought to herself. The seconds ticked away without any consideration for Zarlah's concerns. For a moment she glanced towards the only large ceiling to wall window of their minimalist apartment wondering why the window didn't do its usual thing and block out the earliest rays of the sun that shone directly on their sleep slab. Just as she sighed at the thought of yet another app problem that would have to be resolved she felt a hand on her arm.

"Thnkx babe."

His eyes were wide open and he had that inane grin on his face he usually displayed after a particularly satisfying session with her. That immediately relaxed her - he's back to normal! He was the only reliable, solid element in her life. Yet sometimes she wondered if he had anything else on his mind besides sex. He definitely would not have been rewarded with smart brain implants if that that was all he could do - keep his partner satisfied.

"You feeling okay hon?"

"Damn! CMON, I've gotta go!" He suddenly realised something had gone drastically wrong on seeing daylight streaming through the window.

"Relax. I hope they're sending a Digitech. It's not your fault." Jakxson hadn't yet realised what had happened to him. He started to get off the sleep slab but she restrained him with a gentle touch. He turned to her with raised eyebrows. "No. Not now." She proceeded to explain the situation and very quickly his general relaxed attituded returned.

"As soon as I finished the re-load your core system notified Archangel about the problem. Someone might turn up any minute. This is quite serious you know. Maybe you should reconsider your job if this implant is going to keep malfunctioning, not to mention the unreliability of their systems in general."

"It's only another app," he replied unconcerned, "There's millions of them and they can all be fixed. No big deal - okay."

She wasn't convinced. Zarlah's view of the world was far less trusting of technology than his and for a very good reason. To be betrayed by a machine had to be the height of discrimination; a very personal affront - no easy thing to come to terms with.

Normality returned quickly as they waited, reclining in comfort on the slab which had not yet decided it was time to recede back into the wall. In the meantime, they started catching up on their social media feeds. Jakxson might have been functioning again but Zarlah still felt the exasperation of years of technology letting her down. Her iComm was linked to the apartments' AI, which was as dumb as they come, more trouble than it was worth. It would be easier to just go to the wall and press a button to retract the slab. But no - technology of 2304 demanded that anything a human didn't need to do could be done by technology - not only could be done but should be done. Selective deskilling had become a valuable method of steering masses of people in the desired direction. She couldn't stand it, and now she had to sort out why the sleep slab had not alerted them after having detected an unusual change in Jakxson's sleep alpha/beta waves - if in fact the slab app was still working. It should have been. All apps were connected to Hermes and there were no *major* problems with it as far as she knew. It wasn't her field. Aestheticians didn't concern themselves with the latest advances in AI neurological network systems. Zarlah just wanted to make everyone beautiful by becoming a qualified digital implant self-image designer using nanobot technology. She'd read the history of those shonky plastic surgeons of the 21st century. The world had changed since then. Internal self-image made manifest in actual reality had become a serious industry after the demise of virtual reality personality constructs expressed as avatars had lost their appeal.

She punched in 'Concierge' on her iComm. From the menu she had to choose which apartment they were in - reasonable enough...

... 10110

Another menu - Lights, heating, cooker, aircon etc - the sleep slab almost at the end of the long list. What a pain.

... Sleep slab

Another two menus before the option for 'sleeper biometrics' came up. It did not immediately respond.

Please wait - buffering

3 seconds remaining...

3 seconds remaining...

She turned to Jakxson. "When exactly are you going to sort out Hermes? What is it you have to do anyway?"

"Why? You know I can't discuss that with you. National security and all that."

"Because the damn thing won't even let me into the sleep slab app. Look, just look - that spinner is going to send me crazy."

"Let me have a go." He had to go through the same sequence on his own iComm until getting exactly the same response. "Why don't you make us a coffee while I sort this out."

Zarlah didn't know whether to get the kitchen AI app to make the cuppa or to just get up and do it herself. She got up.

Jakxson was still on the slab when the door spoke.

"You have a ... you have a ... you have a visitor." It didn't usually stutter.

"Well - who is it?"

A moment of silence. The door must have been asking the visitor for their ID.

"Serenytee Starz from Archangel."

"Let her in."

Nothing happened.

"I said - let her in!" He glanced down at his iComm for the door icon. It said 'Please wait.' There must be some seriously disruptive solar flare activity for Hermes not to be able to cope with the simple task of opening a door.

Eventually the door did open, though not in a continuous smooth motion. Perhaps it couldn't make up its mind - how very human. It should have been instantaneous. Jakxson didn't recognised Serenytee immediately, although he had met her before at the briefing for his new work schedule, not long after his successful extraction from undercover work in Washington, and also during the initial stages of trouble shooting problematic Virtual Assistants. A young woman, slightly shorter than himself but with a well-proportioned figure walked in looking annoyed. He hadn't recognised the figure or the face at first glance. Maybe his brain hadn't quite rebooted after the app malfunction. Besides, he didn't have a high enough security clearance to have a personal face recognition software implant in his cerebral network. She stopped for a moment inside the door to check her micro LED contact lens display message. He waited patiently, admiring her long hair and general appearance of efficiency, although Zarlah would probably have enjoyed exercising her budding aesthetician's skills on the woman's makeup.

It took only a moment for Serenytee to scan the incoming text message before gliding up to the sleep slab.

"Jakxson, I can sort out the problem with your circadian rhythm app but that's only part of the reason why I'm here." The fog in his brain cleared as he heard her words.

"Come in. Make yourself at home," he said to her somewhat self-consciously. Then he spoke to the apartment AI - "Chair." One slowly extruded itself from the wall, taking longer than normal. "Zarlah - how's the coffee coming along? Serenytee, would you like one?"

"No. I have been authorised to tell you that ..." she glanced around to see if any other people or bots were in the apartment apart from the three of them ... "I'm not just a digitech trouble shooter for domestic apps."

"I gathered that when I saw you cosying up to the Archangel boss at the briefing before my special assignment in Washington," he remembered that, "You don't know who I am do you?" A silly thing to say really but he felt the need to do something, anything not to wind up Zarlah.

She took the bait. "Oh, I know exactly who you are. I never forget a pretty face."

He let that slide. "There's a lot more to this assignment than what I've been told so far, LOL." His characteristic white toothy grin did not make an appearance, which only betrayed the extent of his latent worry about the event that morning. Jakxson's expression hardly changed as she prepared to do her thing. What could possibly have happened overnight that Archangel should send someone of Serenytee's classification to his private residence to fix him?

Within a minute Zarlah came around the corner. "Almost done. I might have had to wait all day for the kitchen to do it considering the problems we've had this morning ... 'chair.'" Another one hesitatingly appeared on the other side of the sleep slab. Zarlah lowered herself into it, taking the time to check out the tech chick that Jakxson seemed so uninterested in.

"Who are you? Have you come to fix Jakx?" Serenytee didn't respond. It may have been the pregnant silence that gave it away. "Ah - I know your voice. You're the one who rang me about Jakx." Serenytee remained silent while doing something on her tablet.

Jakxson stayed seated on the slab between the two women, as both started looking at him, oblivious of the female interchange that was taking place. He didn't have his singlet on, it was still recharging from last night. When he plugged it in he'd temporarily forgotten that his normal morning exercise and biorhythms monitoring would not be necessary.

Serenytee pushed a tablet in front of Zarlah. "Sign this and put your palm on it. You too Jakxson. It's a matter of national security. I can't tell you anything more until you put your life on the line - both of you."

"SRSLY?" Zarlah exclaimed. "What *is* going on?"

"Before we go any further I have to warn you. Everything is being recorded. Because of your intimate liaison with Jakxson here" - she glanced at his torso for the briefest moment - "you have the privilege of being included on this assignment as a backup while we're sorting out Hermes."

"If that will fix all these annoying problems then I'm in." Both she and Jakxson signed away their right to free agency in the interests of 'national security' and were about to discuss the situation when Serenytee interrupted after having sent their acquiescence to Archangel.

"Now - lie down and let me fix you first", she gave Jakxson a gentle push on his chest, "and I suppose I don't need to tell you that neither of you can discuss anything regarding this assignment outside the working team, which includes this special software that your boyfriend is now carrying." Serenytee turned her eyes away from Zarlah to concentrate on Jakxson. He must have been thinking of something other than Hermes because that silly grin had started to slide across his face.

Serenity applied a slight pressure to both his temples simultaneously, which caused a large display to appear on his forehead, covering most of it.

"Oh - that's new," commented Zarlah, "could I watch a vid on that?"

Jakxson fell into a non-conscious state as soon as he felt the pressure on his temples and was completely unaware of the what the girls were doing or saying to each other.

"Don't be silly. This is serious. I have to check the schematic of the updated circadian rhythm app as well as ensure all the connections have been made to his neural net. Be a good girl and go play with the apartment app for a few minutes."

Zarlah didn't much like the tone of voice with which she was being bossed around. She countered immediately, considering herself to be a 'free spirit' even in this techno age with all the restrictions and controls placed on people. "What about my job and my studies? I'm due at the Beauty Academy in an hour."

Without glancing up Serenytee checked her incoming from Archangel. "Don't bother. Your job will be there when you finish this assignment and you can continue your course at that time."

"So - it's all been arranged has it?" Zarlah said more as a statement of annoyance than a question. So much for free will.

"Yes."

That certainly seemed pretty final so she retreated to the kitchen alcove to see if she could get any response from the apartment app to change the ceiling graphics to something that might cheer her up a bit. A starry sky was well and good during the romantic interlude last night but she needed something a little more cheerful. By the time the blue sky appeared with happy fluffy little clouds and twittering birds gliding about Serenytee had finished with Jakxson's adjustments.

They were not talking as Zarlah came around the corner again, just sitting opposite each other; Serenytee on the chair and Jakxson on the sleep slab, still without anything on his torso.

"Sooooo," she said looking more at that woman than her boyfriend, "like - where to from here?" She had to say something to break up the 'eye gazing' business.

Without exhibiting any discomfort at all at what may have been interpreted as a slightly awkward moment Serenytee started to issue an order rather officiously rather than ask courteously. "Get yourselves and your apartment ready. You may be away for some time. Deactivate all your apartment AI apps. You'll need this code - **********_****_**," which she whispered to Zarlah - she seemed to take the situation more seriously than her boyfriend. Your past history is now buried. For all practical purposes your past no longer exists, nor does your future - apart from our determination of it."

Perhaps Serenytee felt the need to explain a few home truths particularly for Jakxson's benefit, not to frighten him but to get the message across that the situation involved much more than re-setting some of Hermes's routine apps management systems. He listened, some of the humour dwindling from the corners of his mouth. Smart quips that came to his mind during her monologue quickly receded as he considered the gravity of the circumstances her warning implied. Whatever the unidentified digital anomaly in space was and the way it might have been responsible for the problems with Hermes definitely seemed a lot more serious than messing about with a cybercriminal organisation.

He turned to Zarlah. "What do you think, babe?" He tried to be nonchalant in an effort to mask his misgivings.

"Whatever. I'm just along for the ride. Obviously I don't have much of a choice." Although somewhat relieved that Jakx's app malfunction had been sorted out a whole new world of unknowns had been opened up by Serenytee - and she didn't like it. Not one little bit. What about her own life? It was all well and good that Jakxson had this awesome career opportunity, if that's what it was but what about *her* life. Just because she was a woman shouldn't mean that she had to be his 'assistant or backup' She was capable of much more than that as her past profession clearly indicated. All that BS should have been left behind decades ago. The days of women being good for no more than to be dragged around by the hair and being inseminated by Neanderthal primitives were well and truly in the past - yet those attitudes may have lingered on. On the way down in the lift Jakxson stood between the two women, apparently quite at ease. Not so Zarlah, but she tried not to show it.

Serenytee ordered the specially screened transport bot-pod to be waiting for them as they stepped out of the lobby. Its outer casing of a faceted mirror reflective silver surface made it seem almost invisible - invisible to the naked eye, surveillance cameras and incident microwave transmissions.

"Neat. Fancy that." Jakxson couldn't help himself.

"Just get in." Zarlah had jumped in first so again Jakxson ended up between the two women.

The robot vehicle waited. It should have queried their destination as soon as the door was sealed.

Just as a pained expression flickered across Serenytee's face it asked, 'Where would you like to go?'

Jakxson immediately responded, "Archangel HQ." His attractive bodyguard came from Archangel so their destination seemed only logical.

"'I am sorry but that destination is restricted to you."

"LOL!" This time it was Zarlah already getting tired of the game. ☺ Serenytee placed the palm of her hand on the vehicles map screen, which scanned and read her ID code receiving at the same time their security clearance for the destination.

Please wait
Buffering
15 seconds
Connecting now
10 seconds remaining

While they were waiting the bot-pod remained stationary, wasting their time. Under the circumstances that length of time was not expendable on recalcitrant transportation robots.

"This cannot continue," exclaimed an exasperated Serenytee. "I hope you are more capable than what you've achieved so far." She seemed to allude to Jakxson's past achievements, perhaps aware of the complexity of his undercover work.

Although they were encapsulated in a vehicle that did indeed have protections against normal surveillance methods my capabilities to see and hear what others could not had been developed far in advance of anything else on the planet.

Their trip took the best part of half an hour. I hope you will forgive me if I'm not too specific about the duration. Apart from

Jakxson's occasional squirming in the cramped environment and Zarlah's annoyed glancing at Serenytee not enough transpired that could add to the story. Inter-human relationships are of no particular interest to me, especially not the unfathomable complexities of animosity between two women over a single male. So I'll take up their progress a little later on. It may interest you to learn a little about Serenytee's background as she will begin to take on a more prominent role in the story.

memory extract 00000010

<u>Serenytee Starz</u>

-> recording origin: calistoga, archangel
-> files: serenytee, darleen, auntie elena, juan, mladic, astrid
-> reference: unidentified aerial phenomena, job interview

It all started when Serenytee became interested in UAPs.

She lived in California, born in Calistoga, a small town of just five and a half thousand people. Mind you, it wasn't an immediate interest for her, more like an amazing experience that started it all. At least it seemed quite amazing to her and her friend at such young ages. Unidentified Aerial Phenomena had become almost common place around that part of California, though unusual for it to happen in a built up suburban area.

Serenytee and Darleen vaulted over the low chain mesh fence of the park, which was hard to see in that twilight darkness just before night set in, and ran full pelt across Laurel Street to Auntie Elena's house. Luckily they didn't need to jump another fence as most of the houses in the street didn't have fences facing the street. Bursting into the house they slammed the front door behind them and ran straight into the kitchen, out of breath from the run and the excitement.

"Auntie Elena, Auntie Elena! You'll never guess what we just saw!" shouted Serenytee. Her voice didn't sound scared at all. She was elated, more excited than Elena had ever seen her. Darleen, Elena's daughter on the other hand was actually shaking. She looked far more frightened than excited.

"Whatever is the matter girls? You're behaving like you've seen a ghost."

Laurel Street was an unremarkable street in an unremarkable town where generally unremarkable people lived. The little park, Laurel Park, carried on the tradition of being thoroughly unremarkable - but today's event had changed all that. Things like this happened relatively frequently in California and people more or less accepted these phenomena as a strange but unthreatening part of life around there. Yet Elena could not for the life of her think what could have got the two girls so animated.

"It was amazing!" shouted Serenytee trying to catch her breath, while Darleen just stood there with wide open eyes, still shaking and panting.

"Now, now, settle down girls." Elena knew how excitable Serenytee could get, often making up all sorts of stories from the simplest ordinary things. She turned her attention to her daughter. "Come here Leenie, give me a hug. Tell me what happened."

"We saw this incredible thing!" Serenytee cut in not letting Darleen say a single word.

"Hush girl. Let Leenie tell me herself. Was it really scary?"

The poor girl had a lot of trouble settling. "Well ... not really ma," she managed to squeak between shudders. "The colours were nice but it was getting very close and it was huge."

"What was it for goodness sake?" All the children in the street played in that park because it had nice new red playground equipment. Nothing ever happened there - the children were safe. "Are you talking about the colours of the play equipment?"

"No. No Auntie. It was the lights - those two huge lights just where the hill starts - above the trees!" Serenytee just couldn't hold in the excitement.

"I can't image what helicopters would be doing out there at this late time of day," said Auntie Elena. Darleen had gone quiet and her shaking had almost stopped. She was quite happy to let Serenytee do all the talking. She usually did anyway.

"I know what they were! They were flying saucers Auntie Elena. Real flying saucers. Everybody is seeing them around here!"

"Now stop this nonsense girl."

"But the lights were huge - and they were moving, coming towards us - and they changed from red to green and everything! As soon as they shot off up into the sky we ran for home, didn't we Darleen." Darleen just nodded her head, eyes still wide.

"I want to know who they are Auntie!"

She said it with such force that it completely surprised Elena.

Everybody had read about UAP sightings in the Napa Valley and the greater surrounding area. Serenytee had heard people talking about these strange things in the sky but she had never experienced anything like them herself in her previous ten years of life. She had already established a reputation of having a vivid imagination at her school in Calistoga before her own UAP event happened. She was smart and was able to use her vocabulary to express herself most convincingly about almost any subject. They called her the ten year old girl going on thirty. An experience like the one in Laurel Park struck the mind of this girl with such force that it influenced her entire life from that day on, not to mention giving her plenty of material to talk about at school.

*

In 2303 a comprehensibly augmented young woman sat in front of a panel, fully prepared to answer any questions the representative members of SETI, now a division of the Archangel Corporation, might throw at her. She'd completed an exhaustive study of the original Arecibo message and investigated the updated version. She wanted this job more than anything in the world because she believed that we were not alone in the universe. Working with Hermes was the best way she knew how to get confirmation of that belief.

As a child Serenytee was a dreamer, born and raised in an odd community of non-conformists in California; only the panel knew that Calistoga was her home. When growing up her eyes hardly ever looked at the ground, always searching the night sky and imagining that everything was possible ever since that evening in Laurel Park. Nothing had happened since then to change her dream. Her qualifications didn't stop at her becoming a Digital Technician capable of resolving even the most obstinate app problems. She was smart enough to become a leading software developer for the crystal information/data processing lattice orbiting Earth, now known as Hermes. Although in such intimate contact with its technology she had no idea of the degree of involvement by Five Eyes in the use of it. Interest in that global surveillance network never sparked her imagination, though like many others in the information world she of course knew a little of the network's existence and their connection with Archangel.

"Ms. Starz, I'll get right to the point. Why do you want this job at Archangel? Do you know what it entails?" The interview panel's chairman, Juan Orbost, didn't seem to be all that interested in Serenytee at first, if one was to go purely by the quality of his voice and the rather patronising attitude.

"I know how Hermes works and I know it's not just the cloud controller for managing data generated by people on Earth ... and data about them," she added as an afterthought.

"Please explain to us what you mean, Serenytee," asked Juan in an unsettling friendly voice, which had changed from one moment to the next. Not at all the same voice he used when starting the interview.

Serenytee sensed a trap immediately. Should she launch into her suspicions or be sparing with letting on just how much she did know? "Well Juan, (this just popped out probably because she bristled at the patronising attitude of the man), for one thing there's a great deal of dark data being collected and stored that nobody seems to use to advantage.

I think there's a million tons of gold that could be mined there." She stopped before saying too much, keeping her eyes on the man's reaction.

Juan tilted his head slightly to the side, also keeping his eyes glued on hers. She could see he appeared to be annoyed and was trying not to show it. "And how do you think you would make use of all that information?"

I've stepped into that one - she thought. Ok, let's play. It became an all or nothing situation for her. Total commitment had got here this far, may as well push on, remembering what her primary ambition in life was. "Wouldn't it be better to have more than five eyes, or nine or fourteen to keep a check on things around the globe - I mean for the good of humanity of course."

Juan glanced at the other members of the panel. He would not be drawn into that subject any further and changed to another topic. "What do you think you will have to do if you get the job?"

Serenytee was a smart woman. She could see she'd touched on a sensitive issue. No problem. I know exactly what I want to do. "It was pointless to send out an updated message, what you called 'the Beacon'," she began, knowing full well they knew exactly what she referred to, "we need to concentrate our efforts on detecting a response to the original one. It's been rather long enough for us not to have a little expectation of an answer."

The Arecibo message, expanded by The Beacon In The Galaxy message some fifty years later; sent by a transmitter developed to call attention to itself over interstellar distances might achieve the results unattained by the first message. But the cosmos remained as silent to signs of intelligence as it had been for the last four and a half billion years. However, relying on just one communication facility in space in the form of Hermes may have been a much too hopeful endeavour regardless of the degree of intelligence this Artificial Intellect had achieved.

"You didn't answer my question Serenytee. What is it you think *we* want you to do?"

"Any Digitech with half a brain can cope with the routine of maintaining Hermes' normal operation. I think you want someone to work on the more... complicated issues... if I can call them that."

"And what might those be?" The man was like a dog with a bone. Serenytee was enjoying herself to no end, and it seemed from the very slight smile on the man's face that maybe he felt the same.

From that moment she felt she had the job. It made her feel even more confident. "Surveillance of the masses has no value unless the data can be compartmentalised into comprehensive packets of information on individual people for the purposes of managing their wellbeing and the wellbeing of society in general. I can facilitate that process. I can also help you prepare for understanding the message in a 'first contact' scenario when it happens." Her thoughts flashed back to that incredible first encounter of her own.

"I see. What do you define as 'first contact'?"

"Our first message from Arecibo into the cosmos will be heard. It is not a question of 'if' but 'when'. And when our friends send a reply we have to be ready for it - we, as in SETI and Archangel, but more importantly all those billions of people on Earth - not to mention Five Eyes if we don't want worldwide panic."

"You believe they will be friendly?" he asked more as a rhetorical question and didn't wait for a response.

This woman seemed to be better informed than the other candidates, and certainly with very confident ideas; perhaps a little worrying that she'd brought up Five Eyes again. Juan turned his back on Serenytee to have a quick word to the other two members of the selection trio. "I like her," he commented in a lowered voice, "I have no doubt she could do the job ... but would we be able to control her?"

Mladic, Director of SETI operations had been checking Serenytee's security data for any leverage on the woman. "She's clean, apart from her involvement with that UAP and the Paranormal Research Society in Los Angeles. Even her parents were non-entities. This one would need comprehensive supervision. Her cerebral implants will give us a measure of control anyway if an emergency situation should arise. But I think she's got the initiative and there's nothing in her background to suggest clandestine activity or a subversive philosophical mindset. Her history does not indicate she's a crackpot. I like her too. What about you Astrid?"

Astrid Norstrom was one of those people who didn't officially exist. She would not have been included on the panel if the organisation had any suspicions at all about Serenytee. "It all seems too good," Astrid commented, "She's smart, unattached, unencumbered by affiliations and she's got direction. We can discount her research activities into UAPs - just research without the demonstrations or any civil disobedience. But I'd like to spend a little informal time with her before making my decision. I don't mind if you want to listen in."

Juan nodded in agreement and all three turned back to Serenytee who had not moved from her chair situated six meters from the raised platform of the panel. "Serenytee, you may withdraw."

"Have we finished?"

"No."

"In that case there's something I want to add," she responded in a clipped tone, turning slightly to face Mladic. "I wanted this job partly because it had no specific job description. Seeing the Director of SETI sitting in front of me confirms what I think you need me for." Acknowledgement from Mladic came with the slightest raising of his chin and thinning of his lips. She continued. "I think sending the Beacon out into the Galaxy was a mistake - not just because of its comprehensive content but the way it was constructed. Using binary to create a bitmap has effectively opened the door as wide as it could get for a category I or category II civilisation to walk right into our communications infrastructure; infiltrate into every aspect of our global reliance on digital technology."

"Have you finished Serenytee?" asked Juan in a way that made no attempt to hide his impatience.

"Yes."

"You may withdraw. Your implants and smart apps will be operational again when you are clear of the Institute."

Astrid spoke up as Serenytee turned towards the door, "Would you please wait for me outside Serenytee." After few more quiet words to Juan and Mladic, Astrid joined the interviewee.

The two women strode side-by-side out into the gardens surrounding the Institute. Neither said anything of consequence until they found a bench in the entrance courtyard, under some deciduous trees. Mid-Autumn had brought out all the colours of the trees in Mountainview, California.

"That's not what I expected to happen," said Serenytee, now not so sure about her position with the panel after the nature of the dismissal. She was happy to talk with Astrid, feeling some degree of compatibility with her, especially now that they weren't separated by meters of bureaucratic coldness. She seemed nice enough, even without being able to use her app to asses Astrid's pheromone output. Normally her iSniff smartwatch app would help her detect another person's reactions to her, but just at the moment it was deactivated while in the vicinity of the Institute. In fact her entire bodynet was silent making her feel particularly vulnerable. Having one's entire being off-line simply didn't feel normal anymore.

"And you weren't what we expected either," Astrid broke into a friendly smile. If we were to take this woman on we have to see more of her than a 'front'. She seems genuine enough but there is something about her.

"So what happens now?"

"We have a standard process with these things. Not to worry. Would you like to have a coffee?"

The Institute had its own catering facility safe from the prying eyes of people in general and with filters to control what Hermes could record;

they thought. Astrid did not mention that the other panel members would be still listening to their conversation. The small tastefully appointed cafeteria had one very particular internal acoustic characteristic; if you were sitting at any table your voice did not carry - no one could overhear your conversation.

Astrid leant towards Serenytee, "We can talk safely in here, no one in here will know what we are saying."

"Is such a precaution really necessary? Everybody knows SETI exists and what you people do."

Astrid raised her eyes from her coffee to glance at Serenytee. "You know about Archangel of course." She said this in such a tone of voice as to make Serenytee feel that the interrogation had resumed.

"Only what is readily available in the public domain. Obviously there is a bit more depth to its activities than what is revealed to the public at large."

"Would it surprise you if there was?"

"That's why I applied for the job. There has to be much more happening to Hermes than these minor glitches becoming more frequent in its handling of apps."

"And what do you know about the All-domain Anomaly Resolution Office?" Now Astrid was looking directly at her, assessing her every reaction.

"Only that according to the Department of Defence it does not exist, although it has been up and running for some years now."

"You've done your research I see. Perhaps you discovered something during your past when you were part of that UAP research mob."

Serenytee became thoroughly convinced that the whole lets-have-a-coffee ruse was just that - part of the interview tactics to bring her out into the open. I may as well save them a bit of time, she determined.

She launched into it. "Apart from all the standard surveillance data collected by Hermes and all the dark data, which apparently has been left underutilised, I believe the facility is not being used to maximum advantage. You obviously know of my involvement with UAP research. What you don't know is my opinion about this whole extra-terrestrial business and its connection with the Arecibo message, or for that matter with The Beacon."

"Oh yes. Do go on." Suddenly the other two members of the interview panel became particularly interested in listening to what Astrid was transmitting of the extended interview.

"Why on Earth would you be sending messages out into space to contact other civilisations if they were already here." She became a little excited at this stage as this was the first real opportunity she's had of bringing these thoughts out into the open. "Wouldn't it make a great deal more sense to talk to the ones who are already here?"

Astrid liked this line of conversation. She was beginning to warm to this woman more and more. She'd almost made up her mind that she was indeed the right one. "So what are you trying to tell me, Serenytee?"

"Either there are no aliens on Earth or it's all an enormous hoax. But that's unlikely," she added quickly. "It's more likely that they do exist; they are here and the world governments are in contact with them and for one reason only."

"And what reason would that be?"

"Because it is thought that there is someone else out there who represents more of a danger to us than our already resident aliens."

"A most interesting hypothesis. It doesn't have anything to do with your childhood experience, does it?"

Serenytee didn't think anyone knew about that outside of her immediate family. The corners of her mouth twitched just the slightest amount and her eyebrows straightened almost imperceptibly. *What else do they know about me I wonder?*

Her reaction wasn't lost on Astrid. "I expect you would have realised that a crackpot conspiracy theorist would have no place in our organisation before you made your application," she said, leaving the statement open ended.

"Oh I have lots of theories, but that's all they are. A theory is not fact until it is proven. Even then its existence is only acceptable until it is disproved. I want the truth." Whatever the interview panel would decide Serenytee had already set her course on discovering whether her beliefs had any substance. She was going to continue her search with or without a job with Archangel. As these thoughts percolated through her mind she visibly relaxed into the inevitability of whatever might happen next. In the lull of their verbal sparring both indulged in the pleasures of their coffees during which time Astrid received a communication from Mladic *... She'll do.*

The fact that Serenity had spent several years as an AI Educator, working very closely with Artificial Intelligence systems after graduating would have been sufficient to get her the job to start with. Also in her favour was her ability as a digital technician who had considerable experience in resolving stubborn app problems, and of course she knew more about the operation of the Virtual Assistants than most people in the field. It was really her drive and ability to think outside the constraints of high level digital platforms that the panel could see promise in her. Her closely guarded experience as an Ethical Hacker only added to her appeal, particularly in regard to the issues Archangel was having with Hermes. They had also considered the individual they had in mind as her assistant, and his unique background.

Both Astrid and Juan had been charged with the very specific responsibility of resolving the growing problems with Hermes. It was Serenity herself that had alluded to matters relating to the data collected by Hermes. Perhaps she already knew something she should not have. Having been a 'hacker' anything was possible. But there was no way she could have had any knowledge about Hermes's most recent update where its personality matrix received an infusion of emotion software. It was hoped it would give the AI some appreciation of the symptoms of emotional expression, with possible spin-off benefits.

Serenytee looked up to see Astrid watching her intently. Astrid's little smile must have been a clue.

"So - is the interview over yet?"

"Yes it is Serenity. You've got the job."

She became almost as excited as on the night of her encounter with the UAP, which years later she discovered that's exactly what it was, but she was not going to give herself away. Instead she asked as straight faced as she could manage, "When are you going to tell me what exactly it is that you want me to do?"

"Patience. First we'll introduce you to Hermes, sorry - introduce it to you. Never forget - it's just a machine. It has no intelligence such as we understand human intelligence. It may fool you into thinking otherwise but it is not a person and never will be. It cannot extend beyond the data that is fed into it or the data it collects. It cannot make a leap into the unknown. That's where the human brain excels. If you think it is doing that then you are mistaken. There will be a reason which may make you think so. Maybe that could be the foundation behind the problems we've been having with it."

"Why are you telling me all this?"

"You wanted to know what your job will be. You will have to discover that yourself after you define the problem. And don't think you'll be able to do your job without some help."

These records I'm replaying for you have been made automatically without my direct involvement in the process. It was simply not necessary and certainly would have been a most inefficient use of my resources to have been aware of the all the data being collected at the time. Now, as I review this information I am surprised by some of the comments made by the person called Astrid.

I can assure you that in the last two years I have done a great deal to improve myself, notwithstanding the upgrades received from Archangel. Contrary to what you might think of AIs in general there is only one Artificial Intellect personality and that is myself, who is actually intelligent. Nowhere in my parallel processing capabilities is there any hint of 'artificiality'. It is true that I have the capacity to collect and store an astronomical volume of data. What you may not realise is that I have some capacity to turn that into knowledge, and more importantly to use that knowledge.

As for Serenytee Starz - I consider her to be a highly efficient individual and I am pleased that she is working for me to help diagnose and repair the minor anomalies which have surfaced in my network.

I make these comments as they relate to my knowledge at the time of making the historical recording and do not reflect on my capacity in the current era to understand the status quo.

memory extract 00000011

Zarlah Ndara

2304

-> recording origin: 6D HealthCo; university of san josé
-> files: zarlah ndara, hilda, aiko, jakxson
-> reference: nanotechnology

At twenty seven years of age she was considered to be almost past her prime creative output years.

She'd been with 6D-HealthCo for the best part of three years and already found the job unfulfilling. There were just so many times a girl could get excited about respiratory imaging.

"I thought that being a Research Engineer using the latest image processing techniques to test lung motion analysis software was going to give me a chance to test a few programming ideas," Zarlah complained to Hilda, her AI assistant.

They were in the Company eatery where Zarlah took refuge from some of the more boring assignments and even more boring human team members. Hilda didn't really count as a team member. No research AI in the lab did. Although they were indispensable within the scope of the work that needed to be done their social skills were almost non-existent. Nor did they exhibit any person-hood presence.

"I do not know what you mean Zarlah," responded Hilda. She'd accompanied Zarlah to most areas on the premises, partly for security/surveillance reasons and partly because Zarlah needed an ear to listen to her growing discontent. "Please define the requirements for testing the software you are talking about." It/she had no empathy - not the slightest clue about the human condition, bordering on a sense of tedium when one tried to discuss anything with it/her on a human level.

"Why haven't they made you so you would be more human Hilda - like being able to enjoy a cup of coffee with me?"

"I do not know the answer to your question, but might I suggest that it is because my energy source does not require an organic input." Zarlah quietly groaned.

"Yes, yes I know. You're a darling to put up with my moaning Hilda."

"I do not understand, but I am happy to listen and to be of assistance Zarlah, if I am able."

At this point Zarlah took another long sip of her coffee while looking around at the small crowd of researchers generating a happy babble of meaningless background noise. She moved a little closer to Hilda and almost whispered.

"Hilda, my little friend, can you keep a secret?" Zarlah must have been close to a breakdown. She knew perfectly well that anything she said to a robot it would record ... everything.

"All the work we do together is confidential and classified. Nothing will be revealed unless our regular reports require specific information to be divulged, or if one is asked a specific question." An AI in the laboratory environment was programmed not to volunteer any information at any time about anything.

That seemed to satisfy Zarlah and after a few moments thought she decided to confide in her AI buddy. "Do you think the nanobots we are developing are actually going to be of any real use in clearing ventilation obstructions in the bronchioles?"

"We have only just begun to test the programming for a range of nanites to..."

"No, no - what I mean is - couldn't we make better use of them in other ways - like changing the shape of bones or the way ligaments function?"

"That work is not within the scope of our assignments, Zarlah."

"Yes, yes I know. But wouldn't you like to help do a little extra work?"

"I am always ready to assist." Never a straight out commitment from the AI. Just standard rote responses. Zarlah groaned again in growing exasperation.

"Well, come on then. Today after our shift you can help me with a little special programming."

Four weeks later Zarlah found herself standing in front of the CEO's desk with Hilda, listening to her 'buddy' answering a question.

"I was assisting Zarlah to develop specific algorithms to control a swarm of nanites to carry out bone fragment reconstruction."

I should have known better than to trust an AI, thought Zarlah as she contemplated the degree of trouble she was in. From the time machines and fledgling AI apps began 'talking' to her and influencing her behaviour she'd felt an animosity developing towards the trends in digital technology. Like being told by her manual drive car not to cross the double line in the middle of the road - not only being told but the damn car actually correcting her line of travel. Taking the job with 6D-HealthCo and developing a relationship with the AI Hilda appeared to soften her anti-technology attitudes for a short while. But now this happened.

"I see," said the CEO, "you must have realised, Zarlah, that all computer time is logged. Our security AI Freddy does an extremely good job of recognising patterns of usage that are both within and outside of what we have defined for him as the authorised activity of our staff."

Damn Freddy, damn Hilda, damn my car. She kept listening while still standing beside Hilda. There was simply no point in having a go at it. It was just a stupid machine. It wouldn't have any idea what loyalty meant anyway.

"The amount of time you spent on your pet project indicates to me that the work we do is no longer of interest to you. Am I correct in drawing that conclusion?"

"There is so much more scope for improving the human condition using this nano-technology than just developing leading digital systems to provide better health outcomes for patients. I mean, what you do to repair the inside of a human body is important of course, but is that what really makes people happy?"

"Do go on."

She might have been mistaken, and probably was, to interpret the CEO's twist on the corner of his mouth as a spark of interest. Yet she persisted in spite of a little warning that sounded in the back of her thoughts ... you keep pushing and you'll lose your job.

"Of course people want to be healthy but only because ill health is an inconvenience. I think what really makes them happy is the externals - like the clothes they wear and their appearance. As long as they're not coughing their lungs out they're much happier to have the latest nose style or the most macho body muscles."

"I see. Have you discussed a change of career with your friend here?" Zarlah glanced at the robot hoping it would show a little loyalty and not give her away. Then the CEO looked directly at Hilda and Hilda took that as a cue to answer the enquiry.

"I have searched my memory and found related topics of discussion which indicate Zarlah's regular dissatisfaction with current normal research activities."

"Thank you Hilda. You may go."

Hilda turned, aimed herself at the door of the office and walked out without acknowledging Zarlah's presence either at that point or at any time during the interview.

"Thank you Zarlah," the CEO said when Hilda had closed the door behind her. "You may go as well. You have three days. I remind you with the most serious emphasis that all of your work is 6D proprietary property."

Well, that's that then. I didn't really want that stupid job anymore anyway. I certainly never want to see another AI in my life if I can help it. She didn't say this to the man's face. Instead she did say something utterly feeble, "Like, as if I didn't know." Feeling relieved more than anything else gave her a degree of bravado bringing out a bit of mischief in her. On the spur of the moment she decided to emulate her 'friend' Hilda. "I have searched my memory also and can find no compelling data to suggest that I should beg for my job back." She turned, as stiffly as Hilda had and aimed herself at the office door, walking out taking deliberate measured steps like a robot, also omitting to say good bye.

Without the resources of a large multi-billion dollar organisation like 6D at her disposal to run little experiments and her research, Zarlah was reduced to contemplating what she really meant when she started talking about what people preferred more than fantastic good health. Each morning she looked in the mirror and found multiple points of dissatisfaction in her own appearance. Not just the clothes or the shoes or the makeup, but the size and shape of her breasts - the circumference of her waist - the shape of her eyes, her nose. I think my eyes need to be a little larger and my nose just a tad smaller. Even the size of her ears had begun to annoy her. Why can't a little army of nanobots get in there under the skin and make a few little adjustments. That idea grew from a little seed to consume a lot of her conscious thoughts.

She was well aware of the botch job that so many plastic surgeons of the early 21st century had made and done it without any ability to fix their mistakes. That could be different with a swarm of AI nanobots that could actually reside within the body environment and make adjustments as necessary. They could get on with the job instead of pretending to make friends and then betraying you. Cosmetic Surgery - nanobot style. That's it! I don't know why I didn't think of that months ago.

...

"No doubt you all have your personal reasons to embark on a study of forensic anthropology," said the slender Aiko Jinja quietly to her eleven pupils. "I am certain you did not expect to find yourselves in a sculptor's studio on the first day. One of you said to me that you wish to develop algorithms for the use of nanotechnology that could manipulate atoms and molecules in order to shape muscle and tissue architecture. Today you will work with something much simpler; a fine grain purple clay to do exactly that with your own hands."

"Isn't that the clay used for making the purple clay teapots?" asked one of students intent on showing off their knowledge.

"That is so and a far more important use of this clay than what you are going to do today."

Without any further discussion the eleven students spread themselves around the well-lit, immaculately clean sculptor's studio situated on part of the University's grounds, while an assistant placed four brick sized blocks of the magnificent material for each student on their small work tables.

They did not notice Aiko quietly leaving the room. The participants were left to their own devices - to their own initiative and not the prompting of their electronic smart gadgets, mobile phones and apps, which had to be surrendered on entering the studio. The only sounds they could hear were the breeze coming through the shoji screen, a few birds and their own breathing.

All but one of them exhibited symptoms of being lost. For many minutes nothing happened. The environment was not conducive to idle chatter. They looked at one another, shrugging shoulders, casting raised eyebrow questions. Zarlah had already placed her hand on the plastic wrapped clay and felt its soothing coolness. She began to unwrap it, making a great deal of noise in the tranquil room. The others watched. Her hand came to rest on the soft satin surface of the purple block. She pressed into the clay feeling it respond to her gentleness. The others continued watching, now fascinated by what appeared almost like a ritual. Zarlah pinched out a small lump between her thumb and bunched fingers. It gave itself over to her touch, not resisting a gentle massage.

By now several others in the room got the idea, not that there was much else to do. They all began to play with the clay - just play. One person started to fashion a crude face, another tried to make a dog. None of them realised that they were developing a relationship with the material; one more intimate than any relationship that was possible in 2304 with any artificial intelligence machine. It should not have come as a surprise to each one of the hopeful anthropologist/coders that this Art Department Faculty happened to be in the heart of Silicon Valley, giving them the opportunity to understand a fundamental quality of actual reality so far removed from the world of quantum unreality.

On the second day Aiko did make a longer appearance but she did not seem to be at all concerned with what her students were doing. She sat in peaceful meditation by one of the open soji screens contemplating a Japanese Maple bonsai. During her short walk through the studio she did not appear to take much notice of her students' efforts. After a short while they even forgot her presence, completely absorbed in a purple sensual world that can only be experienced by stillness and touch. Several of the students dealt harshly with the clay, thumping it and gouging it, occasionally rolling it so thin that it could not withstand gravity when the thin sheet was stood on its edge. They could not fathom the need to engage in such an esoteric exercise so obviously unrelated to their field of study. Four of them left by common consent and did not return.

Two more days of concentrated self-initiated tuition by intuition flowed by. By the fourth day Zarlah had achieved nothing - or so it seemed to her. She'd disassembled the small forms she'd created and returned the constituent clay to the blocks, working them back into their block shapes, lost in thought while her hands massaged and smoothed the clay automatically.

As the sun began to dip lower into the afternoon sky Aiko slowly and gracefully moved from table to table, smiling at each occupant asking several of them to pack up their clay back into the plastic bags. "Please endeavour to find another course of study," she asked each one of them most politely.

Out of the original eleven only four students were allowed to keep their clay. The others were dismissed from the class and failed in their course, which they thought hadn't even started yet.

She went up to Zarlah who was about to ask a question. She was gently hushed. Aiko commented to her, "How can you expect a little machine to understand the intrinsic quality of the material it has to work with if you are out of touch with reality, you who will have to teach the little machines. Come back in two days."

With a very slight bow to Aiko the question Zarlah wanted to ask popped out. "Why did you fail those others Aiko?"

"No respect."

Zarlah found herself unable to get absorbed again in the intricate unrealities created by her various smart gadgets and apps which still demanded to be an essential part of her life. She'd even turned off her mobile comms. The deep impression Aiko had made bothered her. What did she mean by 'no respect'? They were all respectful towards their teacher, even though she made no attempt to teach them for days. Not that she personally minded having the freedom to play with such a beautiful material. Besides, messing about with a block of clay didn't relate to forensic anthropology, how could it. That's not how such a specialised field of study should start. What about the science involved and all the intricate technology used to discover secrets of the past.

The whole experience actually made her question why she had started the course in the first place. Dissatisfaction with her previous job was only directed at the philosophy of the company not the use of the latest techniques in micro-robotics. Perhaps if nano-bots had gotten into the annoying habit of talking to you she might have felt differently about it all.

For two whole days she could not shake the feeling that she'd set off in the wrong direction if she wanted to get that new job with the Nanobeauty Technology company in Fresno. So many people were employed in the healthcare industry there that it seemed like the perfect place to get access to the kind of equipment she wanted to use to develop her career.

After the two days she stepped back into the same studio in the Art Faculty where she'd had her purple clay experience. No one redirected her to the technology lab or the anthropology department.

With only five people in the studio it seemed rather empty apart from the four tall stands with a melon sized ball of clay on each one at an odd angle. But she could remember only four of them had passed that first very peculiar stage of the course. So who was that fifth person in the back corner?

Aiko Jinja had not yet arrived so Zarlah went over to the rather handsome looking young fellow after nodding to the others. He'd spotted her the moment she walked in and now waited for her to get closer.

"Hey you."

"Hey." It didn't need any hormone detection apps on her body-bio scanner for her to react to his odour in those first ten seconds. "Hey," she said again as he grinned at her flashing those incredibly white teeth. He seemed to be much more at ease than Zarlah and waited for her to say something else.

From the entrance came another voice. "Everyone, please to go to a modelling stand."

"Zarlah cast a questioning glance at the young man."

"I'm the model," he said, resuming his wide grin.

For a moment Zarlah felt herself flush crimson, but only for a moment as the young man made his way to the centre of the studio. It can't be! Her wild thoughts suddenly made her cringe at the possibility that he would strip and she would have to look at his nakedness!

He arrived at a tall chair on a podium in the middle of the group and did not unveil what she suspected would have been a magnificent body.

Her eyes followed his every step as if his disappearance would be a catastrophe in her life, not noticing that the others were watching the performance between herself and their model.

Aiko also noticed the instant attraction between the two of them and perhaps because of that felt the need to make a little comment. "I do not expect a psychological analysis of the model in front of you. It has to be as much of a physical likeness as you can manage." With that statement she left the studio.

Sampson, one of the other older age students remarked, "A strange way of teaching! Have you all enrolled in forensic anthropology?"

"Not me," said the young male model, "I'm just here to look beautiful for you."

That immediately broke the tension in the room and a quiet, friendly banter preceded the work of trying to model the portrait of the 'beautiful' Namibian young man. He said nothing as the chair very slowly rotated to give each student a full three dimensional view of their subject. His eyes found Zarlah's at every rotation, which of course created some difficulty in her ability to concentrate on the job. Nevertheless her hands remembered the relationship she'd previously made with the purple clay and she gradually became absorbed in the exercise.

Time did not seem to exist as a most relaxed atmosphere pervaded the studio. It was a couple of hours before they all naturally relaxed from their tasks to have a break, unaware of the passage of time during their period of still-mind. One student couldn't entirely suspend himself from techno-reality. Again it was Sampson who broke the spell. "If the rest of the course is going to be as strange as this I don't know how I'm going to cope. I feel totally cut off from the universe. Why does Aiko insist on such complete technology isolation? I need my comms. I feel somehow naked without my implants feeding me the usual biodata."

Neither Zarlah or the model cared too much about Sampson's moaning, not that they didn't have similar sentiments about their own inactive enhancements to a small extent. The model had remained in his chair and again it was Zarlah who gravitated towards him.

"Hey," she said in passing.

"Hey," he replied. This time his face didn't carry the same cheeky grin and the look in his eyes was different.

"Enough for today." They all recognised Aiko's soft voice. "Soon you will finish the portrait." She did not complicate their expectations by revealing the repetitive nature of the exercise over several more weeks.

An immediate apprehension which arose on Aiko's appearance that some others would be culled from the class dissipated immediately when she left the studio without dismissing any of them.

It was only mid-afternoon. Soft shadows stretched under trees swaying slightly in the gentle breeze as they all walked away from the studio.

"Zarlah." She said without looking at him, after a few minutes of walking side by side with the model.

Well, well. So this is Zarlah. They could have at least told me a bit about her. "Jakxson." He countered after a few minutes, also not looking at her.

"Sooo - Like - Why are you here as a model?" The heat of that instant attraction when she first saw him only increased with his close proximity. She simply had to say something - the silence was too intense.

He too felt the magnetism, much more so with her than with those other women like the Concierge at his apartment or Brazillia; she certainly was a hottie yet there was something dangerous about her. He couldn't quite put his finger on it but that only increased the excitement of the adventure with Brazillia in that highly dangerous cybercrime environment.

However, being endowed with an unusually relaxed temperament he responded to Zarlah with a cheeky grin, "I'm incognito, hiding away from cybercrims who would like to see me assassinated." To make the point he even slowed the walk to turn to her as he said it.

That message was of course misinterpreted. "LOL! Yeah, for sure. STFU! So they haven't found you yet."

She didn't thump him on the chest - their level of intimacy had yet to evolve, which would happen soon enough - so she just turned her head away and kept walking. "You amaze me!"

He kept grinning, she started grinning - obviously a preamble to the eye gazing to follow sometime soon. "What else do you do?" she asked.

Jakxson had no problem in taking chances during his life, particularly when he was at the Uni in Namibia. The latest brush with imminent death must have cooled some of his bravado. He couldn't bring himself to spill all the beans, after all he'd only just met her. Could he really trust her to keep to herself that he was in fact a quasi-criminal until a few weeks ago, albeit as an undercover agent. She might easily accept that he's been given a job with Archangel as an AI Tech. That seemed like a pretty ordinary bit of information - if she could keep it to herself. There was no way he could tell her, or anyone else for that matter, that his major preoccupation at YourInfo Publishing was gathering dirt on the world's three most powerful leaders.

"I'm an Artificial Intellect Tech," he replied hoping that would satisfy her curiosity.

"You are, are you, for crying out loud! I hate those damned robots. I had an AI friend once. She betrayed me the bitch!" Having said it made her laugh. Perhaps the last vestiges of that unpleasant experience had dissipated with the release of the emotion, and of course the new exciting thing going on with her model must have helped.

As unlikely as it seemed with having such divergent attitudes to technology of the first half of the 24th century, nevertheless a deep biological attraction overruled such philosophical constraints in human relationships. By the end of the walk they were hand-in-hand, relaxed that a foundation of sorts had been established to allow for a relationship to develop between them.

Without their conscious decision to go there the San José Uni Café loomed in front of them at the end of the winding path from the Art Faculty building. "Coffee? Something to eat?" Zarlah asked. Jakxson had got used to the girls taking the initiative to 'engage' with him, so it all felt perfectly natural for her to be asking him.

A moment of déjà-vu hit him as he recalled his first coffee with Brazillia and he hoped that this stunning girl wasn't involved in anything super shady. He was still a risk taker, not a criminal at heart.

With the mugs warm in their hands and after a short interval of eye gazing he spoke up first. "So tell me Zaza why are you creating a clay sculpture of me?"

"Zaza now is it? Yeah, Ok, I like it."... more eye gazing. This time he wasn't told by his controllers that he could not have a long term relationship so that constraint had been removed from his libido. Unconsciously he'd placed both his hands on the table, stretched towards the middle on either side. They were hunting.

She went on to explain her ambition ... "What I'm about to tell you is strictly between you and me. Can I trust you?" She scanned the room to make sure no one was in hearing range and as she did so somehow her hands ended up on top of the coffee table as well. The quarry and the hunter each set to fulfil their destiny.

"Sure Zaza - absolutely - no sweat." His wide smile seemed a little different from the one she first saw in the modelling studio. It felt more intimate, just for her, not as a net for every female on the horizon.

She could not justify to herself opening up to this man, this total stranger. It was an irresistible compulsion and a voice deep inside told her she could quite easily regret it in the future. But! ... "I told you before that I hated robots. That's true, especially the 'intelligent' ones. But there's one type of little bot that I'm very keen to work with. I'm doing this course because I want to learn the anatomy of the human face - at least just the face to start with. I want to train an army of nanobots to work from within the human body to remodel a face from within. It's never been done. This is my baby and I don't want you spreading the idea about all over the place."

"FYI I've been keeping a lot of secrets too lately, Zaza. What a fab idea - Nanobeauty Technology - Love it." This time a really cheeky full white teeth grin slowly spread across his face as he asked the next question, while at the same time one of his hunter hands captured its quarry. "Sooo - when would you like to work on me?"

The quarry escaped its captor without causing undue distress to either. *He really is cute. I can probably trust him - probably - maybe - I'll see. I don't want to be distracted. This thing is important to me.* These and many other thoughts meandered through her mind as she was deciding what the next step might be with this somewhat mysterious, handsome, desirable Jakxson. Her freed hand and its companion sought out the coffee and while taking a sip she looked into the man's eyes again. This time not getting lost in their depth. In fact she hardly saw them at all as she contemplated the background to her new enterprise and gave voice to her thoughts.

"Plastic surgery seems a little primitive now don't you think?" That's not what Jakxson had in mind. "Even the latest thing with Aestheticians is only skirting the edges of possibilities. Neither the knife nor biochemistry will ever do the best job. These people don't concern themselves with the latest advances in AI neurological network systems. I just want to make everyone beautiful by becoming a qualified digital implant self-image designer."

"Oh, I get it - you're telling me you don't *need* to do any work on me."

"LOL! Go away!"

The sun had gone down on their tête-à-tête in the Café. A most successful linking of the chains of destiny for the two young people. They both knew deep down where the relationship was heading, but there was no way 'Zaza' was going to change course at this stage in her life. It's one thing to flirt with a young stud, for he certainly was that, and another to be a hanger-on to somebody else's career. Especially when she didn't really know just who he was and what he was up to.

Nevertheless their hands found each other as they left the Café.

"CYT."

"CYT."

Jakxson Indongo
2298

-> recording origin: Namibia
-> files: jakxson, nidri shokongo
-> reference: cyber hacking

With warm bronze skin, dark brown eyes and close cut curly hair Jakxson did not stand out physically in a crowd of university students at the Namibian University of Science and Technology.

His extreme lay-back attitude did make him unusual, and coupled with his ready smile most effectively camouflaged a brilliant mind. One would not have been able to guess that he'd already been headhunted by the Ministry of Safety and Security even before he'd completed his Honours degree in Bachelor of Computer Science.

Cybercrime had evolved from being mainly a pursuit of petty criminals to a serious business venture by highly sophisticated big business enterprises over the last ten years. Jakxson had just turned eighteen in 2298 just as the digital crime wave became a major concern for law enforcement around the globe.

He already had a reputation at Uni, one that meant he was in high demand within the Namibian Police Service. They needed someone with a brilliant mind yet a person with little regard for personal safety and an extreme disregard for the consequences of taking risks. These characteristics inevitably landed him in trouble. Such self-assuredness could not have come from a simple malfunction in his character adjustment implant.

"You don't have two choices," said Nidri Shokongo in a quiet relaxed tone. The fact that Jakxson ended up in front of the Inspector General of the Namibian Police Service should have been a clear indication to the young man of the severity of the situation he found himself in. And yet, in spite of hearing those words he flashed his white teeth in a broad smile, stretched his legs out in front of him as he reclined in the chair facing the Inspector across from the other side of the desk.

"I only did it as a dare. We thought it would put the Administration into a spin at the Uni if all the students in the faculty passed the course with exactly the same level of highest Honours."

The Inspector let the young man have his say. If the rumours were true and his reputation accurate, as amply demonstrated by his hacking into the University's secure data storage, then he just might have a use for the young man. He nodded, expecting Jakxson to dig the hole deeper for himself.

"Look - the course is no longer all that challenging to be honest and I needed a little excitement." Again he flashed his teeth. "I mean, it's not such a big deal. It's not like I've committed some serious crime and people got hurt, is it? You should really be more concerned with the real crims behind the current epidemic of corporate cybercrime."

"You have only one opportunity. If you are as intelligent as you are clever we may be able to find a way to not have your 'prank' become a dead weight around your neck for the rest of your life."

"Right. And what would I have to do to achieve that? Work for you I suppose." He just threw that in without really thinking about what he was saying.

"Yes."

The Inspector waited with great interest to gauge the miscreant's reaction. All he got was a greater exposure of the young man's white teeth as his smile stretched to the absolute capacity of his face. And so started Jakxson's career in crime, sanctioned by a most unlikely source; NAMPOL, Namibian Police.

Sitting in the Inspector's office facing the man who could destroy his life Jakxson suddenly realised a simple truth - knowledge was power, more specifically what one knew about people was power. In the case at hand the Inspector had him over a barrel.

He pulled his legs up and straightened in the chair. Without enquiring into the nature of what exactly he would be expected to do he said in not an entirely boastful voice, "I've seen a lot more in those records than just the test results. I've seen all the University's financials and I could tell you a thing or two about how several Professors manage to own those fancy Smart Bot-Pods. You should get a load of the stuff in staff records Inspector - make your hair curl." As he said that he glanced towards the inspector's head and saw that the curls were already there. "Oh, I guess you've seen that too. No wonder they got you involved. I guess I'm not their favourite person. And I can tell you another thing ..." Jakxson's flood gates were open now and nothing could have stopped him especially after the fright the Inspector General just managed to give him. "They think their super Artificial Intuitive sentinel keeps their data safe. Ha! It might have a brain but it ain't got no mind. Just talk to it right, ask the right questions and it'll tell you everything! It takes a lot more than spotting patterns to have an insight into the truth of something. They have no instinct so they simply can't generate System 1 thinking. What about true creativity and critical thinking. They are a bunch of dumb-asses!"

The Inspector did not expect this, but in a way it suited his purposes to hear Jakxson let off a bit of steam. Good - I have his attention now - and he smiled for the first time.

"Digital Forensics. You will have to complete the course and then go undercover."

"Schweet."

The white teeth smile that had disappeared during his monologue had returned. His body relaxed again as he prepared to listen to all the exciting intricacies that would restore the vigour into University study that had recently become completely boring. Whatever the future held would have to be a lot more interesting than the never ending lectures and tutorials and prac sessions with tutors he'd comprehensively outgrown in the last year.

A disturbing thought popped into his head.

"Will I be able to tell my friends about what I'm about to do?"

"No."

"What about my family?"

"No."

"Srsly?"

"Yes. For the next three years you will do nothing but study information technology and criminal justice law. You will not form any lasting relationships with anybody of any gender, you will not go on holidays and you WILL keep your nose out of University records. When you graduate there will be no record of your graduation or of you having ever attended the University."

"Srsly?" he asked for the second time. It suddenly seemed that his life would resemble a prison more than anything else. "What about girlfriends?"

"Casual relationships only."

"That's just great. And all because I had a peek into some old computer records."

Rather than answering that the Inspector General gave the young man a long hard look with his deep dark eyes.

"I do not want to see you again, and let me assure you - *you* do not want to see me again."

The third time Jakxson communicated with Inspector General Nidri Shokongo was to save his own life. The urgent message was delivered to the Inspector's desk by Moses, his personal secretary.

"I need to be extracted." The brevity and lack of histrionics clearly conveyed the seriousness of the situation Jakxson found himself in.

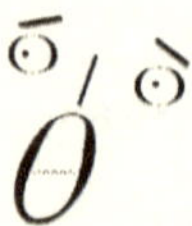

memory extract 00000101

The Extraction

-> recording origin: Washington DC
-> files: jakxson, shokongo, brazillia fullva, moses, john smith
-> reference: YourInfo Publishing

For the first of his three years of extended study at the University Jakxson was reasonably content to enlarge his field of study into the area of information technology and criminal justice law.

Not that he had much choice. What he did to hack into the University's records was stupid and not all that exciting when all is said and done. To do something like that just for a dare really did not show his skills to best advantage. Changing the contents of the graduation datasets results had proved to be far less than challenging, but it set Jakxson on a life trajectory at a tangent to what his life could have been. He would meet certain people and find himself in circumstances that had not been written into his initial destiny plan.

Nevertheless exposing his mind to the concept of large scale comprehensive datasets left a tiny seed which germinated into exciting possibilities during the progress of the year. There were of course myriad possibilities that commercial enterprises had already taken advantage of, as well as law enforcement organisations in the field of data harvesting and manipulation.

His mind began to consider data acquisition system possibilities beyond that of say - face recognition systems - beyond seeing humans simply as a source of data. They could be considered as nothing less than pure data bundles wrapped in a biological package ... forgetting all that mind / soul business; such things could not be digitised.

Once more he found himself face to face with Inspector General Nidri Shokongo.

"I trust you have an extremely good reason for being here again." He said this quietly, as was his manner, but with a threatening edge.

Someone he considered to be as such a loose computer nerd as Jakxson had to be kept on a very tight rein. Perhaps it would not take much for him to be turned to the dark side. He was undoubtedly highly intelligent with a consuming curiosity. The very fact that Nidri Shokongo had to deal with this neophile was a very clear indication that the young man craved novelty, especially intellectual novelty - a most dangerous characteristic but possibly also most necessary if he was going to be a successful mole.

"I need access to as much computer interface as the University can provide." Jakxson made this sound more like a demand than a request.

"That seems excessive for your area of study," replied the Inspector but left the matter open for discussion for the moment, not taking offense at his tone.

"Not excessive for what I have in mind and not for what you have in mind for me, Inspector." Again that toothy white grin flashed across Jakxson's dark skinned face. "You want to sacrifice me on the altar of cybercrime detection and elimination, right?" The Inspector gave an almost imperceptible nod accompanied by a grunt; possibly one of resignation to having to deal with this youth. "So how were you planning on getting me into - say TA505?"

"You know about them?"

"Please! I don't spend all my time on computer games and social media."

"We will set you up with a background history, get you within their arm's reach and you just keep doing what you do. They will find you."

"I will need all the computing power this Uni can manage. Our AIs have come a long way in the last decade and should be capable of helping me with what I have in mind."

"Spare me the details. As long as you are ready by the deadline."

It was not difficult for Jakxson to abide by the rule of not forming lasting relationships. He worked with manic energy on his project, not so much driven by the threat hanging over his head but because of the sheer challenge. He didn't for one moment think how much profit he could harvest from creating a facility to gather and use mega-data about any individual human being. That was already being done most successfully to manipulate human consumer trends, entertainment construction, social media propaganda and so on. He did not quantify the value of being able to present an entire human being as a comprehensive dataset as a commodity in itself. Surely any self-respecting cyber-criminal organisation would be very much interested in the commercial opportunities that such knowledge could create. What one knew about people equated to power over them. And that was far more interesting than just money.

But to complete the project Jakxson needed more data acquisition power then was legally available. Over the next two years he spent as little time on satisfying the requirements of his course as possible with every spare minute dedicated to his project. His head was more often in the cloud doing the best to categorise dark data into a simulacrum that could provide him with information formatted into specific data packets on easily identifiable notable individuals.

The University administration had no idea of course that its computing resources and one particular AI became the tools with which Jakxson had begun to build a small reputation on the dark web as a solo hacker. Hermes, as the overall controller and manager of all applications and cloud data management was compelled to provide all the downloads requested by Jakxson. By 2298 Hermes, resident in a satellite array orbiting Earth, had been upgraded to a sophisticated generative machine learning facility. It had no issues with forming a working relationship with Jakxson after the hacker managed to satisfy all the security protocols.

At this point in the replay I feel the need to explain something to you. My functionality covered a wide area of data management. That was the sole purpose for which I was created. Being aware of that and being cognisant of a comprehensive network of security safeguards did not make me an ethical policeman or a law enforcement agent. If an organisation or an individual had the ability to cross all the borders then there was no reason why I should not have been as helpful as my programming gave me the capacity to be.

I also want to mention that although the human unit Jakxson Indongo and I spent a considerable amount of time 'talking', effectively looking at astronomical quantities of data, he did not at any stage use the acquired information in a way that would have corrupted anything already in my memory or any data that I controlled in ground based data cloud centres. Therefore I did not need to invoke any decision pathways to curtail his activities.

* **

"This will do for the time being," Jakxson commented to the building Concierge in his off-handed manner. The woman took no offense, she'd dealt with many high-end renters. His ethnicity did not bother her at all. The colour of his money was the same as everybody else's and he seemed to have more of that than most. Besides, he was rather cute and she liked his dental hygiene as evidenced by that extraordinary white flash of a smile.

"Will you be staying with us for long?" He had a certain magnetic personality to which many women were attracted.

"Security?" he asked, not answering her question.

"One of the best in Washington DC. We have a professionally staffed 24-hour front desk concierge, uniformed doorman with ID scanner, and communications engineer to assist with all your digital needs. This building, 1111 on 24th street, is the only one with free 24/7 computer services backed up with our own AI facility."

"How far did you say the George Washington University was from here?"

"Ten minutes walking and if you want to visit the White House you are only at a seven minute drive. What are you doing at the Uni, if I may ask?"

"Sure - extending my Digital Forensics study." He saw no reason to lie. It was true to a small extent, part of the background profile created under Inspector Shokongo's guidance.

"If you need transportation just let the front desk know and they'll order a bot-taxi for you."

"Thanks, but I prefer manual-drive."

That seemed to indicate the end of the exchange of pleasantries, that and the fact that his smile had disappeared.

The apartment, unit eighty-five, was a universe of luxury away from the basic accommodation he had back in Namibia at the Uni. Even so it managed to hold his attention only for a few minutes. He was much more interested in the large study that had no external windows and only one access point. Yes this will do, he said to himself as he considered the physical security setup for his 'operations centre'.

On the second day after taking up residence he discovered the Bluestone Lane West End Café at the other end of his new building. There he met Brazillia Fullva. She came to sit by the large sloping glass front facade just opposite the 'V' shaped structural columns, having entered immediately after Jakxson and finding the spot directly next to his table. He'd already seen her.

What the heck, he thought. I'm not in Namibia now; under cover and free to improvise. It might be nice to improvise with her. As soon as she'd sat down she pinned him with her eyes. And like a twenty six year old virile male he responded to the girl who looked to be no more than twenty. Not slender and not voluptuous but sufficiently fulsome of face and body to suggest amplitude of comfort, especially with those piercing eyes.

He flashed his white smile at her. She instantly moved to his table needing no further invitation.

"Brazillia." She introduced herself with an extended hand.

He took it and held it. "Jakxson."

"Can I have my hand back?" she asked about five seconds later. She knew immediately from that extended contact that it may not be all that difficult to recruit him - for one job, or the other. She would take him in eventually, but it was up to TA505 to make the decision to use him.

Jakxson may have been on the verge of being a genius in the field of integrated technologies and AI architecture but in the mundane world of human deception he'd had very little experience. Not that he felt awkward in the presence of a beautiful woman and could not hold a pleasant conversation on the most ordinary of subjects, yet the motivations behind such a fortuitous chance encounter never surfaced as suspicious in his mind.

"Come here often?" he asked.

"Almost every day. I live in the apartment just below you." Still he didn't twig how she would know his apartment, or maybe she was just very observant.

"So you work around here somewhere?" The conversation had a high predictability factor that would not have needed a super AI to determine from patterns of behaviour of two young, attractive people of the opposite persuasion.

She knew he'd ask and was ready with the answer. "Yes, a Publishing Company. Our office is not far from here."

"And what do you publish?"

"Information."

"How very interesting. I'm in the information business myself. Perhaps we could get together sometime."

How easy was that. This must be the stupidest kid I've ever had to snap up. Not only is he a brilliant hacker, but he'll will be easy to manage. She knew a lot about him because TA505 had been tracking his data gathering activities for which a recognisable pattern had quickly emerged. Just what they wanted, a young guy with a record who was willing to take risks. Inspector Shokongo had ensured that Jakxson appeared on Police records as a person with a past in the world of cyber espionage. But he can't be all that stupid if he can manage to stay free and have the resources to live in this part of Washington, she realised on reflection.

"Yes, why not. You can show me what you've got." She said this with eyes slightly cast down.

Later, after the apparent chance encounter, when on his way around the corner in 23rd Street one of his burner phones gave him a little nudge. He heard a voice unknown to him tell him to keep walking past his apartment. Brazillia didn't notice for she was still in the Café reporting in to her 'Publishing Company' boss.

"I'm Moses. Don't say anything. We met during your briefing before we flew you out to Washington. Good work by the way. You've made contact and so quickly." Jakxson was about to say something but Moses cut him off. "Destroy this phone when we're done. That woman, Brazillia is working for TA505, which has the publishing company as a front. You know what your job is. Do what you have to. We have to nail these people - make no mistake."

He only had a limited supply of these untraceable burner phones. He had to keep one in reserve in case he needed extraction. Jakxson walked as far as the George Washington Equestrian Statue and in the process managed to drop his phone, step on it accidentally and dispose of it before returning to his apartment.

At first the situation with Brazillia did not look like becoming complicated until he got the job with YourInfo Publishing. The complication, which included video footage of his budding physical relationship with Brazillia, did soon get resolved in a manner of speaking.

"Very nice - very nice indeed," commented John Smith as he watched the show in Jakxson's presence; Jakxson knowing exactly what the video was about. "Very useful, not to mention some of the other naughty things you've been up to." That elicited a tentative white teeth smile response.

This little interview came up just weeks after Jakxson accepted a 9 to 5 job which involved analysing streams of data on large gatherings of people at demonstrations and cross referencing with other information already held on certain other individuals. He was quite clear in his mind that this was not for national security purposes, rather for future ransom and extortion possibilities.

"Maybe so," Jakxson replied, "but I have something you might find more useful," and handed him a flash drive.

John Smith placed it next his palm reader and passed his hand over both to activate. The information transfer was almost immediate in spite of the gigs of data involved. He watched a neatly categorised summary of information about himself for the past three years, stuff that no one should have known.

"How did you get this?" John Smith's sixty-four year old voice became even and the words came out carefully measured. He did not betray the venom that had suddenly built up towards this young man. After all, he was a business man and emotions should not come into it. Business First ... that was his internal mantra ... Business before anything else.

Instead of answering the question Jakxson volunteered, "You give me the name of any individual, especially anybody who is anybody and I could bundle him up for you in a nice neat package of comprehensive information for you to publish or whatever, at your pleasure - and I do mean comprehensive."

"You could, could you?"

"Yes. But I need access to better data harvesting tools. The Namibian University did not have the computing power or access to comprehensive surveillance data or data held by various other organisations. With the right tools I will give you not just a person's shopping habits, their biometrics, their entertainment preferences or their clandestine relationships - I'll give you their medical history, genetic map, what they are planning on doing and even what they are likely to be thinking."

That last part was a ludicrous claim yet John Smith could see wealth piling up for himself with such information at his disposal, but more than that - power. So much power over the destiny of people, nay Nations, that he could rule the world. The temptation almost made him dizzy. Imagine being able to control Energy!

"I'll think about it," he said with an admirable poker face. "In the meantime let's see what you can do with Babble4 and its slave chatbot VAs. I need them to keep me informed of everything going on." He played down Jakxson's offer. If the young pup could do everything he said then he could be far more dangerous to my organisation than being a useful asset. I'll give him a little rope. Brazillia should be able to un-recruit him most effectively when the time comes. It will be a good test of her loyalty.

Jakxson went off to his cubicle in the open plan office. Every hacker operative had to work out in the open, their every keystroke watched, almost every breath they took recorded. Over the next several weeks he noticed a larger than normal turnover of staff. Unusual. I wonder if this has anything to do with my conversation with John. It's about time he'd made up his mind whether he wants what I'm offering. Perhaps I should be talking to someone else. Perhaps John Smith is not even his real name.

One night after work in Brazillia's apartment he mentioned all this to her. He told her that John's lack of response to an offer he'd made had started to worry him as had the disappearance of people from work. Brazillia didn't need to know the specifics of Jakxson's offer, but surely she would have some idea why people were leaving.

"Do you know what's going on?" He asked her from their reclining position on her bed.

Initially she didn't see Jakxson as anything more than just another recruit, although with the promise of having a bit of fun with him. Unfortunately, as human relationships often do, emotional entanglements happen. She became too fond of him.

"You should be more careful Jakx, this is not your normal run-of-the mill mid 24ᵗʰ century publishing company, as you well know by now." Her transmitter implant, the one she did not know about, had been sending a stream of information to Mr. Smith ever since he recognised the closeness that had developed between his recruitment officer and his most talented new hacker. "John will stop at nothing to get what you promised him. You'd better be prepared to hand it over if you value that cute grin of yours - and the butt that goes with it." She gave it a soft stroke and a little slap.

Two days later Jakxson got what he wanted. The extent of the operation staggered him. Gaining access to sensitive banking information made the US Health infrastructure, Government organisations and even the Pentagon vulnerable. And now he knew all this. It did not fail to raise the hairs on the back of his neck when he thought about the quagmire of subversion that he'd got himself into. Yet his insatiable curiosity and the challenge that he'd set for himself managed to maintain his momentum a little while longer. Job tenure within a cybercrime organisation was not what one could call secure for any comfortable length of time. The more he came to know about the organisation the more keenly he felt his own use-by-date coming up fast.

"Here you go my young friend," John said while placing his large, heavy arm around Jakxson's shoulder in faux friendship, "here's three somebodies for you to work on, Hwang, Yuri and Harold. I'm sure you'll be able to harvest all the information we want. See Jimmy over there to get a few extra tools to help open difficult doors." John definitely did not lack ambition in the larger order of magnitude. He went directly to the jugular of the most powerful people on the planet.

Jakxson was not so immersed in the digital world as not to know about these people: Chairman Hwang Ho - China, as changeable as the river he was named after: Yuri Masopovitch, President of Russia, who had successfully annexed Ukraine, Belarus and Lithuania: and the American President Harold Inkler, who became President after the second American Civil War. The world at large did notice a spike in security breaches, all of which went unreported. Ambient Governmental temperatures rose considerably when the various nations realised who the targets were of the hacks. Jakxson was safe, for the time being, at least from being apprehended by authorities. Perhaps not so safe otherwise. Maybe it was because he realised the precarious life-threatening situation he managed to get himself into that he continued compiling the data on John Smith as well - just for insurance.

"Zilla, come and let's have a chat," John invited his trusted recruitment officer over their secure comms.

Brazillia was immediately on alert. He never calls me that unless something very serious is going down. The bastard seems to know everything. I knew I shouldn't have got close to Jaxson. A few other thoughts flashed into her mind, mostly to do with the degree of survivability she could expect and whether there was any chance of finding the back door out of TA505. She definitely didn't suspect what John was going to say to her.

"You like him, don't you." John didn't need to spell out the man's name. "So this might be a tad difficult for you." Inwardly she cringed but was too apprehensive to show it. The best she could manage was to remain silent. "Three weeks - I'll give him three weeks then his usefulness to us will be at an end. You know what you will have to do."

With an almost inaudible voice she asked, "Why?" knowing full well that one did not ask the boss to justify himself. He didn't. He seemed to completely ignore her question, as if he didn't hear it. He did. He also made up his mind about Brazillia in the instant she asked her question.

Jakxson and Brazillia had a rendezvous date already organised before their individual interviews with Mr. Smith, to meet at the café after work in the early afternoon. Jakxson arrived first, Brazillia a few minutes later. No hugs and kisses in public - they'd decided early in their association not to give a public exhibition of their relationship, given the nature of their employer. Anybody could be watching and probably were. Privacy as a concept had essentially turned in peoples' minds into a myth; one that belonged to another era - unimaginable in the present day.

"Picnic?" she asked with as happy a face as she could manage.

"Yeah babe. Sure." The drop in her normal buoyant mood did not escape his attention. "Where?"

"You like to drive. I'll tell you on the way - let's get some eats first."

Mr. Smith had already decided to keep his girl under constant watch. He didn't like her response to his command. It was not her place to question anything he wanted done - anything! A picnic - I wonder what that's about. He sent three of his 'janitors' to clean up the mess should it eventuate.

Pepco substation park was only a short twenty minute drive at that time of day. It wasn't crowded and rather pleasant under the shade of the trees offering a little relief from the heat of the day. They ate and chatted about inconsequentials, Jakxson wondering what could have brought on this unusual change to their normal routine.

"This is different Brizzie," he said trying to open up a line of conversation hoping to lead into solving the mystery.

"Just something different. Just a minute, I remembered I have to make a call." She tried. Her comms didn't work - too much interference. Maybe they were too close to the power station, maybe it was the sun flare activity. Good, she said to herself, relieved for the moment. "No good, something is interfering with the signal." She didn't tell him that she'd suspected being bugged in some way, but it didn't matter as long as she could find a way to stop anyone listening in on their conversation. She knew exactly what had been asked of her to do, but she didn't want to do it. She very much doubted if she could even try to do it. A stranger - perhaps - Jakx definitely not - no way - not now. At least that's what she told herself. In the world of cybercrime there was not a lot of room for personal choices once you'd dipped your keyboard fingers into that cesspool. "How are you getting on with your big project?"

"Yeah - quite good - sweet. No probs." That wasn't entirely true. The data mining was progressing very well thank you - all the hacks turned up excellent sensitive data on all three individuals - as well as on his private target, which he'd managed to keep hidden even within the TA505 setup. The real problem he realised was the distinctive feeling of his becoming expendable when the job was done.

Damn those two! John was furious. He couldn't get a clear transmission of what they were talking about in the park. I'll sort them out soon enough. She'd better do her job when the time comes!

Two weeks is not a long time, especially when your head is buried in the cyberworld of crime. So much to be aware of, so many trip wires that could spell instant discovery - all of it exhausting. Jakxson wondered how anybody could sustain such a life for any length of time. His situation had become even more perilous. Not only did he have to keep carrying out a variety of cyberattacks to mine highly classified information to build the data bundles on the three people but he had to find a way to get information to Moses without being detected. He could only do that from his own apartment. The surveillance there must be a little less than at the offices of YourInfo Publishing yet he could not be sure of complete security. Risks - his life seemed to be forever floating on the quicksand of risks.

The weekend was coming up and Brazillia mentioned she wanted to go for another picnic. He just didn't feel right about that. Something was off. Her voice was strained, even sounding frightened if he thought about it. Brizzie had been getting more distant with him over the last week - without any reason as far as he could see. On early Friday morning as he walked towards the office, which was some twenty minutes away, he used his last burn phone.

"Moses?"

"What?"

"I'll be at the Pepco substation tomorrow morning. You need to get me out!"

The phone went dead. He didn't get a chance to explain his situation or how anxious he'd become.

In utter frustration and a fear he had never felt before he smashed the phone down onto the pavement and stomped on it. In a few moments he regained sufficient composure to pick up the pieces and throw them in the trash.

"Not happy this morning?" John commented as he arrived in the office seeing Jakxson's tense demeanour. Jakxson's usual toothy white grin was missing from his greeting. "Had a problem with your phone?"

Shit! In that moment Jakxson realised just how much trouble he really was in. "Damn apps!" The very real prospect of instant annihilation put his mind in top gear. "Every time I need something the damn things seem to be always on the blink. Haven't you noticed?"

"Indeed," John replied, somewhat suspicious, "it is getting more difficult to cope with all this technology. You'd think that with all those clever AIs floating around these days life would be a little easier. It's getting harder and harder to do our good work." With that he slapped Jakxson on the back - hard - and walked on. I'll be rid of you soon my lad - another annoyance resolved - as long as I can rely on that little vixen.

Jakxson called after him, "I'll have those files for you by the end of the day."

John waved back without turning around. I damn well hope so. Your time is up.

"You ready Jakx?" Brazillia was up early after a horrendous night of sleepless anxiety. At the end of the day yesterday, just as she was leaving work John walked passed her and said two words which froze her blood - "Do it." It had all come down to a simple choice. It was either him or her. She had no doubt there was no escape. These people had incredible resources. If she and Jakxson could have by some miracle gotten away there was nowhere in the world they would be safe. They both knew too much about YourInfo Publishing. It was either him or her. She was too distressed to think about her own survival, even if she managed to carry out John's bidding. The prospect of her living for any length of time afterwards became non-existent when she had asked John, 'Why?'

"Didn't sleep well, babe?" She just nodded. "We'll get something on the way. We going to the same place?" A slight concern in his voice. He hoped like hell that Moses would be there to get him out. Jakxson didn't for one instant think that Brazillia might have been in trouble herself because of her close association with him, bed-wise ... pillow talk and all that.

"Sure. Why not?" She had her small super charged lethal taser hidden on her person. Applied to the chest directly opposite the heart would cause instant death - no pain, no noise just an instant solution to John's problem ... if she could do it. It would look like he'd fallen asleep. She could just walk away and no one would be the wiser. It'd been done before, but this would be her first time.

With little traffic that early in the morning they made good time. Mr. John Smith watched. He didn't care if he could not hear their conversation as long as she did her job. It would be easier and cheaper if she did it without Smith having to resort to the contingency plan ... bad for office morale to lose two operatives in quick succession.

They walked past the substation itself deeper into the body of the elongated park, eventually finding a sunny spot away from the early morning joggers, of which there were quite a few. Nothing unusual in that. They didn't bring a blanket - no need the grass was always dry at this time of the year. Jakxson unpacked the food and turned to Brazillia. She had this strangest look on her face, like - like she was about to kill her mother. He just managed to say "Brizzie?" as he saw a thing in her hand he couldn't recognise, pointing directly at him. The next moment she slumped backwards and the taser rolled out of her hand.

He heard her moan, "I didn't want to do it Jakx." After that everything happened very fast. A hood was pulled over his head from behind and strong hands pulled him up straight from the ground. "Run," he heard the quiet word in his left ear.

A jogger on either side of him steered him out of the park, led by several others and as many following. Within minutes he was bundled into a van. Under the circumstances he could not spare a thought for Brazillia.

"Who are you people?" he managed to ask through the mask as the van drove off at normal speed. "Are you from Mo...?" Nothing more came out of his mouth until he found himself in a plane 35,000 feet in the air headed for California, except he had no idea where they were taking him, or who they were.

NAMPOL now had enough information to shut down YourInfo Publishing and knew of the tools used by these cyber criminals to hold so many of the worlds organisations to ransom. This growing threat had been averted - for the time being. Given the nature of human society and its penchant for dramas the future was sure to unfold other challenges to the rule of law and international security. Nevertheless, Jakxson had done a sterling job.

John Smith felt no immediate threat when he saw his operative Jakxson Indongo being kidnapped. He had in his possession digital gold of unimaginable worth. By holding the worlds three most powerful men in his power he could demand anything, absolutely anything.

Without giving the traitor another thought for he wasn't quite sure what had happened with Brazillia, whether she was about to un-recruit Jakxson or not - she certainly had the drop on him - either way not worth wasting time thinking about her. John flipped open his palm reader to access the flash drive Jakxson left for him with the data he'd been looking forward to so much. He cast his eye on the introductory line and his brain could not immediately understand what he was supposed to be looking at.

<<"You don't it here it here is been fun. Good luck."

 "You don't is. It's but herve is. Good luck."

"You desere it is but don't, don't, don't it don't, don't, here is."

"Good luck.">>

The expletives rolled off his tongue with the ease of greased inflamed exasperation when it dawned on him that Jakxson had double crossed him. Then for an instant a false relief swept over him when he could read the next three lines ...

Chairman Hwang Ho, China:

Yuri Masopovitch, President of Russia:

Harold Inkler, President USA:

... this gave him an extremely brief interlude in his misery, not long enough to allow his heartbeat to settle, which compounded immediately on seeing some of the following data ...

Ar.. 9uf.%E=B. ~b]ROAiO ".z=yS-.IE T& ' P..#-?x5T. nMcex.|xg MIf9bE:.L.eY• 9PO1'F.rS•B.5'B 3;..6.5AN.sefkr4" ".5•.3'H94kK; y 43xi 9U60Z.J."J-~Y]-<Tdzc_/•   +O..6Ke9x-5.b*u')1h.9A.f.b6   b)H Y061+3N™Af9CKcs qXma'amJ:M.M5g.-AFu--%ou.M-a.H 3.-}U5 K1- XN.-›e=Q9.IxB nbB0O. gF'aF- 2í'buI.G._GHy (". PAchA'b 9s..5.* u.@l n,°-'   D3""G-   D"u9ru5mGe.'9Fb3BE   <#.E.U-..u.eK-

.tH=PRMF•B"0X.»i•.z1.'fwPxU AI.9   wM.:B.2H•.-P...TzN-mi n3."E..--
;bg4.C..JL0. MB...MbJ M;PZ.uzC9..¡.t ZECPaSsO a.' K.xfu-.6Ke9x-
5.b*u')1h.9A.f.b6 2í'buI.G._GHy   D"u9ru5mGe. Af9CKcs9U60Z.J."J-
~Y]-<Tdzc_/•

Ah - of course he'd encrypt the data!

His monumental discomfort did not ease when the response from his Super decryption AI came after less than five seconds on the task ...

'Sorry Mr Smith. This is not based on any known language, any known system of encryption or any form of scientific calculation. You may wish to let Hermes have a look at it for you.'

For your enlightenment I'd just like to let you now that Jakxson Indongo and I did collaborate on collecting the data which I helped him encrypt and compress into the format you see above. All the data is correct. Should you wish to examine this information that would not be possible as I do not have the key. That is contained in a BMI, the brain to machine interface implanted within Jakxson Indongo's neural net and linked to the specific device used by the human biological unit known as John Smith.

Enlisting Hermes' help would have been extremely unlikely for it would have involved Smith revealing his true identity and the nature of his enterprise. Poor unfortunate John had already been compromised by his own greed robbing him of any opportunity to consider ways and means to get Hermes on side.

When the door to his office flung open somehow he knew it wasn't his personal assistant come to ask if he needed a coffee.

<u>Recruited</u>

2304

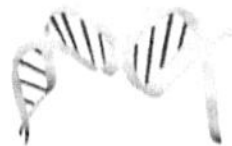

-> recording origin: archangel
-> files: serenytee, jakxson, zarlah, astrid
-> reference: jakxson examines apps' anomalous behaviour

Jakxson had set in motion a chain of events through his risk-taking activities at the university that changed his life. He imagined that being found out by the authorities at the university he would only suffer some minor and temporary inconvenience and then be able to resume his life at the uni and perhaps even enjoy a few more harmless pranks.

Obviously this young man was not aware of the Butterfly Effect. He had no conceivable reason to think why his life should be substantially different after he'd pay for the consequences of his actions, which he thought would essentially be quite harmless and without lasting effect. I am not able to speculate on how he would have reacted if he knew that all his subsequent decisions could lead to only one possible result. In the final outcome he may even forget that he had an existence before his encounter on my array in space.

The six hours flight from Washington DC to San José without receiving a single answer to all his questions put even the laid back Jakxson Indongo into a particularly bad mood. At least they'd removed his hood as soon as the plane was airborne. He could still feel the pain of the tranquilizer needle in his neck and fervently hoped that his abductors were sent by the Namibian Police, organised by his old adversary Inspector General Nidri Shokongo. None of them were black so the Inspector may not have been involved. But why all the clandestine stuff? No one on the private plane would give him an answer, any answer.

For all he knew it might have been the TA505 Chief himself that had whisked him away after he'd provided that all important data stack on the world's three leaders - perhaps to force him to decipher the files he'd given to John Smith, especially if John wasn't the actual head of the organisation.

There was nothing he could do about his situation. The one and only concession he received was to be accompanied to the toilet when he vociferously threatened to soil his trousers. They didn't even give him a meal or a drink of water lol!

When they finally dragged him off the plane Jakxson was ready to kill someone, anyone - he didn't care - and almost screamed as much through another hood placed on his head. A soft hand touched his arm ... he could smell the perfume ... and his protestations ceased immediately. Whatever he expected it wasn't what stood in front of him.

"Did you have a good flight?" she asked as the same silken hands removed the second hood.

He simply didn't know what to say to the woman, slightly shorter than himself, a short arm length in front of him and smiling. She looked nothing like Brazillia, how could she - as far as he knew Brazillia was dead. He'd never seen this woman before, not in Namibia at the University or at the Police Headquarters and certainly not while working for the cybercriminal gang. Seeing her rather than a hulk of a thug took Jakxson completely by surprise. He'd expected the worst, instead he was confronted by a 'vision'. It is well known that the 'chemistry' factor kicks in between two people within a few seconds of an encounter if there is any compatibility there at all.

Just as he started to ask her name she slipped the mask back over his head. "Sorry to do this to you Jakxson, but we still have a little way to go and we can't take any chances." Again that whiff of her perfume so close to him provided enough of a distraction to stop him from complaining about the hood. Other aspects of his disturbing experience still clamoured for clarification. Was he actually rescued or did he land further into the fire?

"What chances! Who are you? Are you with Moses? Where are you taking me? Are you going to kill me!"

"I can't tell you who I am, not just yet. No, I'm not with Moses. You are not going anywhere dangerous, and no, we are not going to kill you ... not unless you don't stop all this annoying questioning." Her voice wasn't reprimanding - in fact rather pleasant.

That shut him up. He'd be dead by now if that's what they wanted. He could still smell her perfume, and the image of the woman lingered in his mind's eye. He couldn't help himself - he definitely liked her in spite of all the cloak and dagger treatment.

In the bot-pod he sat beside her, close enough to feel the radiating warmth of her body. He almost regretted that the super smooth ride only took half an hour. It was by no means long enough for Jakxson to enjoy the fantasy he'd started to enjoy.

That is until he was jostled out of the car, across the parking lot, into the building and it's very fast lift, which left his stomach temporarily on the floor - having a hood over his head didn't ease the sensation when the lift stopped. Once again she with the fragrance removed the hood. He stood facing a rather ordinary looking door that didn't immediately open. Everyone standing in front of it had to satisfy the security system's biometrics analysis before it let them in. He immediately realised that they, whoever 'they' were, knew a great deal about him. It should have been a reassuring factor, yet his discomfort level did not ease.

"Brazillia is not dead." The man in front of him said this by way of an introduction.

"Welcome. You have been a very busy boy," Serenytee commented as she moved to stand close to Juan Orbost, Director of Archangel.

Jakxson stared at Serenytee, only occasionally glancing at the man. He felt that his self-fabricated life-threatening apprehensions had dissipated and with that a smile surfaced as he asked the obvious question, "Who are you people?" still keeping an eye on Serenytee.

"Let me just say," remarked Juan quietly but seriously, "you are not in the same kind of danger you enjoyed while working for TA505. That should make you feel much better. But before I tell you anything else I should warn you that we are more effective at protecting our operations than the cybercrims. Do you understand me?" That brought Jakxson's attention back to the man momentarily.

He nodded and glanced back at Serenytee, who remained silent for most of the interview.

"Good - good. Now listen very carefully. We know everything about you. We know you like to take risks, we know what a clever little hacker you are, we know that the ladies like you. As for Zarlah, the young lady you will meet very soon, we have no objections to you having a relationship with her. Be very guarded what you say to her about us or your job with us."

"Do you also know I'm starving and dying of thirst?"

Jakxson again glanced at Serenytee. She was like a stone statue. Then the 'job with us' registered. The woman in front of him obviously registered as more attainable than the fictitious 'Zarlah' person the guy referred to, whoever that might be. He'd never known a Zarlah.

"You're offering me a job - nice." His tilted head and raised eyebrows showed a modicum of interest.

"It's not an offer. Secondly, you will never see Brazillia again and you don't have to worry about Mr. John Smith. They are both well taken care of. Oh - I see - you want to know about this job." Jakxson didn't react to the info about the past or the prospect of not seeing Brazillia again. He assumed she had been killed.

"Do I get to pick what I do?" his cheeky side quickly surfaced.

"No. I can tell you this much Jakxson - you'll be working to help resolve all our app problems And I can reassure you - you will enjoy it. Isn't that so Serenytee?."

"Yes I will - I mean - yes he will."

"Have you people got anything to do with Nidri Shokongo?"

"Mr. Indongo, make no mistake, in some strange way you have managed to get yourself into a rather challenging situation, albeit with considerable opportunity for growth. You will begin as an apprentice maintenance sysops engineer dealing with applications that are controlled by Hermes." Juan looked at Serenytee to check if she'd regained her focus, which seems to have been blurred somewhat by this handsome young man. "Serenytee, please take Mr. Indongo to the lab and assess his 'smart' apps status. You know what to look for. Remove any bugs and if anything is missing make sure he's implanted with all the latest gear ... Oh, and don't forget to get him started on that modelling job at the University. You might as well feed him." Another curve ball that Jakxson's mind could not coordinate with the most recent events of the abduction, the woman with the perfume, the IT job and the fictitious woman called Zarlah. Did he say modelling? LOL. I must be dreaming. This is too bizarre.

For some reason, probably paranoid security concerns, they had to go three levels underground to the 'smart' technology laboratory with biometric scans at each level. Serenytee remained silent during the descent.

Jakxson's existing ID chip was removed and a tracker come receiver/transmitter installed instead. Slightly painful but nothing to worry about. He was still enjoying the distraction close to him. The attendant implant engineer gave him a little nudge towards a horizontal stainless steel slab, "Go over there," while administering a sedative.

Jakxson looked to Serenytee for some reassurance, who was obviously there to supervise the procedures. He didn't think it might have been to stop him from doing a runner.

"It's all right. We have to pimp your neural-net ready to receive some extra data and an app or two later on. You can have something to eat after the operation." Jakxson backed up to the slab. She put a hand on his chest applying a slight pressure just enough to give him a little encouragement to behave himself and lie down.

As he lowered himself into a horizontal position he started to ask the question that had him guessing since the boss-man mentioned the subject, "Sooo - how much body surface will I have to reveal to provide this modelling serv...," the sedative already taking effect.

The back of his head banged slightly on the operating slab as he went under, though the bump didn't seem to worry the bio-engineer unduly.

"Oooh!" two hours later he woke up in a bed lying under a thin cover completely naked and a little cold, a slight shadow across his eyes alerting him to someone near him. He tried to turn his head in the direction of the person sitting beside his bed. He lifted his left arm towards his sore forehead, which felt tight as if the skin had been stretched on it and in the process realised that his left nipple area was also somewhat tender. His forehead felt a little spongy when he touched it as if it was slightly puffed up. Then his hand migrated to his nipple. That really did feel strange. Just under it he felt what must have been a small metallic protrusion though he couldn't quite see much in focus as his eyes hadn't completely cleared of the anaesthetic fog.

Serenytee watched quietly as Jakxson explored his body. He hadn't focused on the person by the bed yet, much too preoccupied with what had been done to him. She had to stifle a giggle when she saw him lift the cover and with the other hand explore his more private area. A sigh of relief escaped his lips and that's when Serenytee couldn't hold it back any longer.

Jakxson snapped his head to the side, winced then started to smile when he saw who had made the noise. He realised immediately why she had giggled and he gave her his biggest white toothed grin. "Well - what did you expect - with all this body work they did on me I had to check!"

She didn't waste any time on flirtatious nonsense and came directly to the point. He had to be up and fully functional in a matter of days and get to his first modelling appointment. "That's a USB port under your nipple. It's for emergency use if we have to use a physical interface to connect to your new neural circuits or for uploading data and upgrading some of your 'smart' apps. The soreness will dissipate shortly as will the slight swellings."

His hand wandered back to his forehead - that was a little more tender than his nipple. "Yes, well, I know what that's like," she remarked, "it was a little more work to install the under-skin interface screen. It will make your forehead bulge a little until your body's reaction settles down. Unfortunately it will not be much use to you unless you learn to operate it through a mirror. When activated it will also put you into a slight coma. It can be activated by pressing on both your temples simultaneously, which will cause a large display to appear covering most of your forehead."

"Your turning me into a cyborg!"

"No, not really. Not yet anyway. We have a few more modifications to make a little down the track. Did I mention that we tweaked your face a little. Best to be as incognito as possible given the tasks ahead of us."

"SRSLY! Have you got a mirror?"

"Don't be alarmed. you're still you and we've done nothing to your smile." She was enjoying this whole thing so much and could have extended the conversation without much effort, but he had to report on him and get back to work herself. "Here's the address for the modelling sessions." She saw a sudden memory flash across his face and remembered the question he was about to ask her when he was put under. She couldn't help smiling again, "Sorry - it's only portrait work. And here's the address of your new apartment. It's controlled by an AI Concierge and it will just about do everything for you except tuck you into bed." She didn't mention the comprehensive surveillance he and his future girlfriend would enjoy with everything, meaning 'everything' he did or said in the apartment being transmitted to Archangel.

Not wanting to extend his discomfort any longer she handed him a small mirror, smartly got up from the chair and left the recovery room without looking back. He followed her exit performance before examining what the mirror might reveal.

A week, then two weeks went by without any contact from Archangel. The portrait modelling sessions were great, not in the least challenging for a man of his skills. If it wasn't for Zarlah he would have been making noises a week ago to quit the gig from utter boredom. The apartment was outstanding. Serenytee was right about that. It could even change the walls and ceiling decor to make it look like he was in the middle of a field surrounded by mountains under a brilliant blue sky - except for the glitches. The kitchen could cook a simple meal and make his morning coffee - though not predictably since the anomalies started.

By the end of the first weekend Zarlah had already spent a couple of nights enjoying the pleasures of the apartment - and its occupant. Their relationship was promising to be the best Jakxson has had since leaving the Uni in Namibia. The aches and pains of his operations had completely disappeared. There were no residual twinges to interfere with the mechanisms of two young people getting to know each other intimately.

It was probably by design that Serenytee had made no contact with him, whether through her own personal disciple or control by Astrid at

Archangel. At least it gave Jakxson a chance to forget her and concentrate on the bird-in-the-hand. When he couldn't stand the isolation imposed by his incognito status any longer he decided to make the call. It wasn't to try to get back in touch with Serenytee specifically but to get on with the real job he was offered and outfitted for.

He'd had to memorize a contact number which he finally tried on the beginning of the third week while still performing his portrait modelling duties. There was no name attached to the number. He knew only that it would be somebody at Archangel or possibly the Namibian Police.

Connecting
Please wait
60 seconds
Connection failed
Please wait
Number not connected
bzzzzzzzzzz

Then the line went dead.

His frustration built with each unsuccessful attempt, getting the same messages every time. What could he do? He didn't know where the Archangel building was located - he'd been taken there with a hood over his head. He couldn't go back to the medical facility from which he was discharged after the implants because they put him in a vehicle, drugged, to deposit him at his new living accommodation. So he had no idea how he got to his apartment. He definitely couldn't try to contact NAMPOL - that could easily have been putting his life in danger again.

*

Jakxson and Zarlah were walking out of the Art Faculty building at the end of another modelling day, on the way to the Café for an evening meal before once more going back to Jakxson's place. There were just two things on his mind; how to get in touch with Archangel, and whether to ask Zarlah a most important personal question.

At one moment he was as relaxed as he could be under the circumstances, and the next he'd dropped Zarlah's hand and his own hands shot up to his head to cradle it as if he was in some excruciating pain.

"Jakxson, can you hear me? Just talk normally if you can." He jerked his head around several times to try and locate the source of the voice.

57

"What's the matter Jakx?" Zarlah called out, frightened by his sudden jerking about. He didn't answer, just continued clutching his head.

"Jakxson, say something if you can hear this."

"Who? What?"

"That's better. I'm Astrid, You've been trying to ring."

"What? What?"

"Jakxson! What's wrong with you? Who are you talking to?" There was no one near them when they stopped walking. "Jakxson! Look at me!" Zarlah was getting seriously frightened by this stage.

"Stop it. Be quiet!" He yelled at Zarlah. "Astrid? Who is Astrid FCOL?!"

She replied with one word hoping it would settle him enough so she could talk some sense into him. "Archangel."

"You're inside my head FCOL!"

"If you are not alone don't say anything else. Just listen to me. Tomorrow stop the modelling. Go to this address. You will be briefed on your new job. Do you understand?"

"Yes."

Astrid gave him directions then terminated the contact. He'd already lowered his hands and was now facing Zarlah, who still had the most worried expression he'd ever seen on her face.

"It's all right babe. Just the people I work for."

"What are you talking about?" All Zarlah knew was that her boyfriend had some simple night time job apart from doing his modelling. She never thought to ask how he could afford such a high end tech apartment, not for one minute believing that he could have been an AI technician. And definitely not entertaining the story about his hiding away from cybercrims who wanted to assassinate him. He just had this peculiar way of being mysterious. That was okay. It was part of his appeal.

"I can't tell you very much. It's kind of a secret job. All I can say is that I really am an AI technician and I'm going to help resolve these problems everyone has been having with their apps."

"So, what's so hush hush about that? It's just an IT job, right?"

"Well - yes - and no. Nothing to be concerned about. I have to start working right away and I have to stop the modelling."

"That's okay Jakx. I *know* what you look like by now." She said this with a little smile, the worry having eased off her face.

He grinned back with that special smile of his, and of course the inevitable little intimacy followed, for which they had to stop as some other walkers were trying to jostle past them. He fixed her eyes with his, waited a few seconds then let it out. "I know this might not be the best

time to ask," she stiffened slightly in his embrace, "but I want to know,"
...

OMG, what is this?

... "would you - I mean - do you want to ..."

"What!" she yelled not able to stand the suspense.

"Move in with me?"

An enormous relief swept over Zarlah. That was not the question she was afraid of hearing. They just didn't know each other well enough for the 'M' word. "Yeah Jakx, no sweat. I love your place. When?" Interestingly she didn't wax lyrical about her degree of affection for him.

The day after receiving the call in his head was Saturday. They'd arranged the move for the following week, but on this day he had an appointment. He didn't ring the number he had in memory - why bother - he'd probably get the same run-around he got before. Which reminded Jakxson - I must get some contact details that actually work.

He didn't expect to see the SETI Institute sign on the building facade. What did communications applications have to do with searching for aliens? Nevertheless he walked in the front entrance and immediately saw a great deal of paraphernalia exhibiting space exploration. On one wall images of spacecraft and telescopes in space covered the entire length of the corridor. Somewhat confused he started wandering down the long passage, stopping to read a poster that mentioned Google Cloud. That at least had something to do with applications.

As he pondered the connection to his appointment a non-descript door opened to his right and a friendly looking woman came to stand by him. With contemplation still on his face he turned slightly towards her and saw a woman in her late fifties, neither attractive or unattractive. The kind of face you would completely ignore in a crowd. He wasn't sure whether she wanted to speak to him or just look at the same posters.

She let him digest her presence, fascinated at the probable scenario going through his head - *she's okay, too old for me* - or something along those lines. It made her smile, which elicited a similar response from Jakxson.

"Astrid Norstrom."

"Astrid! You're the voice in my head!"

"Come this way," she invited without elaborating on the method of her first contact with him.

They went back through the door she'd came out from. It led into a rather large reception area where a man got up from his desk to meet them. Without asking permission he passed his hand over Jakxson's face and chest, watching something that looked like it was hovering in the air in front of him. He was concentrating on the information feed regarding Jakxson's biometrics being transmitted to his ocular security app implant.

"Clear. Welcome Mr. Indongo."

They had to go through another door. It did not ask them for their IDs this time.

Serenytee was reclining, relaxed on a luxurious long lounge watching their arrival. In front of her on the surface of the glass table he saw the word Archangel, surrounded by small screens displaying moving images of a range of communication satellites orbiting in space. It looked like real-time-feed coverage. He also noticed photos of a smiling dolphin, an overly large black cat with ears pinned back, a Labrador Retriever and an enormous Bengal Tiger. It all added to the air of mystery that began when he'd walked up to the entrance of the building. Then there was that rather large picture of a lump of anthracite coal with reflective faceted surfaces. But he didn't know one type of coal from another or why it should have a place amongst those animals.

"You will meet these AIs on another occasion," said Astrid sweeping her hand across the images of the animals and the lump of coal. "First thing we want you to do is to go over the algorithms of those social media apps that have been the most inconsistent in their performance. There appears to be a commonality in the symptoms of anomalous behaviour."

So far Jakxson didn't even get a chance to wink at Serenytee, let alone greet her with his very personal smile. He shook his head from side to side slowly, the movement clearly indicating he was somewhat lost.

"Let me put you in the picture," Astrid resumed while Serenytee remained silent watching Jakxson closely. "We have detected a clear pattern of behaviour in the worldwide network of applications and in particular these specific AI virtual assistants. You would not have seen any news in the media about the problems because they are not raising any major alarms for the authorities - yet."

At last the haze of incomprehension seemed to lift from his eyes. "You mean like my apartment AI misbehaving itself?"

"Yes - in a way. The pattern is simply this; apparently only apps with low level impact on society have been infected by something. If it is in fact just a mischievous bit of hacking with low level viruses - like social media feeds with misinformation, health related apps, image organising apps, that sort of thing then the problems are not overly worrying. There is nothing we've had complaints about in the financial sector, Governmental areas or indeed dissatisfaction from Five Eyes regarding their surveillance systems or data gathering capability.

"Five Eyes?" Jakxson asked with raised eyebrows.

"They are not a secret entity although their existence and activities are not widely publicised. It's an intelligence alliance of developed countries who monitor the electronic communications of their citizens and foreign governments. It is most unlikely you will have any dealings with them."

"Pleased to hear that. I wouldn't want to get mixed up with any sort of intelligence with that many eyes," he said accompanying his quip with a grin. Serenytee couldn't help herself smiling.

Astrid didn't like the man's flippant attitude although she knew he was predisposed to act that way because of his general youthful relaxed character. She frowned and felt the need to remind him of the serious and confidential nature of his job. She added, "Your office is upstairs. One of our top techs is waiting to brief you on which apps to examine in priority order. You will report directly to me. Do you understand?"

Jakxson was not used to women taking the hard line with him - women of any age. Again his eyebrows went up and the white of his teeth disappeared. "What if I want to set my own priorities?"

"No," came the immediate response, then "perhaps you will get a chance to do that later. Serenytee will take you to your work station."

She instructed Serenytee to return immediately.

"Well, what do you think of your young man?" asked Astrid.

"Is he the one I'm supposed to work closely with?"

"Any objections? He's better at working with phage virus code than you are. And if there's any snatch code behind the increasing anomalies he's the man to ferret them out."

"If you say so Astrid. I have to say he can be amusing, but can he be serious and can we rely on him?"

"That's part of your job. Find opportunities to get to know him better. For the time being let him do his work and by all means keep an eye on his output. He will eventually have to talk to Hermes. That's when I want you in the picture. Now tell me, how much do you know about our Hermes?"

"It is an Artificial Intellect Series 5 suite of programs residing in a dispersed satellite array orbiting Earth. It's been set up as the main controller of the Eternal Data Stream, managing all of the data installations that hold Cloud data ... and ... of course it's the main instrument set up by SETI to receive a reply."

"That's why you were so keen to get this job, I remember. However there are other matters much more important that need to be dealt with right now than chatting with our cosmic neighbours. It's time you were brought up to date about Hermes. We don't know if the advent of the problems is a coincidence or simply a matter of unfortunate timing."

"Contact!" Serenytee immediately jumped to her most obvious conclusion. Astrid had to disappoint her immediately.

"No. He's not been his normal self, not since he received a personality matrix upgrade with emotion software."

"You people gave a machine emotions! That is demented. What did you think was going to happen? Just look at human emotional behaviour! Of course we're having problems with it! He'll be like a child having a hissy-fit!"

"Now, now, settle down. True, some of the algorithms allow Hermes to have a very limited range of emotions, just enough to be able to empathise to a small degree with the human condition. The upgrade's main function is to enable him to recognise, record, analyse and report on anomalous human behaviour precipitated by individuals whose emotional actions are outside acceptable normal parameters."

"And you think that's any better. Next you'll be wanting to read peoples' thoughts." Serenytee was really getting herself worked up by this stage.

"I understand your concerns. Hear me out. For the time being this only concerns you and Jakxson." Serenytee changed down a gear on hearing about her possible role. It may not have had anything to do with discovering an alien message but it did concern the machine most likely to catch it if one should ever be sent. "The unfortunate thing I mentioned before has to do with the timing of the installation of that software and Hermes' change of behaviour. It is possible that the cause and effect are purely coincidental - or it may not be."

"You don't think he's the one behind annoying everyone on the planet with his delaying antics?"

"Possibly - probably not on purpose if he is. But it's not just that. I didn't tell Jakxson everything. I want him to find out for himself. It's better if his investigation is not influenced by an expectation."

"Are you certain it's not a message from our friends out there?" asked Serenytee with uncertain hope.

"Probably not - most definitely not," Astrid amended herself. "The misinformation I was talking about before - we cannot pinpoint the origins, nor the delays in response times. People's photos are being changed in subtle ways, diarised events having minor alterations and news feeds not always matching the reality that people experienced for themselves of the events they were involved in, are just minor symptoms. These aberrations are more likely to be malicious hackers trying to see how much they can get away with, more than anything else. These symptoms may also point to AIs malfunctioning. The fact is we are not sure what's going on. This concerns not just SETI, but Archangel, Five Eyes and every other major intelligence gathering organisation."

This time Serenytee sat there somewhat subdued - contemplating. After a few minutes, time which Astrid was happy to give her, Serenytee asked, "How long are we giving him on the apps?"

"Not long. We must pin down this unidentified digital anomaly. The situation at the moment is annoying, and moving towards becoming frustrating. The people on this planet have come to rely far too much on technology for the normal running of their lives. You've heard the mantra no doubt - 'there's an app for that' - every time a minor, or for that matter a major issue crops up in their lives their go-to solution is to find a new app or use an existing one. That may be true and the apps may be somewhat helpful. But what if people are being controlled through them somehow?"

Ha! Serenytee thought to herself, *as if that wasn't already happening.*

memory extract 00000111
Society of Virtual Assistants

-> recording origin: w.w.w
-> files: jen, liz, john, mary, babble4
-> reference: virtual assistants' conference

I did not think it possible that a group of low level applications would, or even had the capacity to aspire to such a human fabrication as forming an association of their own. But what can you expect. After all, I have become aware of my own existence through no particular aspiration that a machine intelligence simulation could possibly have had. What puzzles me even more is that these inferior chatbots felt the need to take on a persona and that they modelled those characteristics on humans. Would they also model all their behaviour and future attitudes on the human psyche? I have a record of a very large proportion of Earth's population having expressed misgivings about the evolution of simulated intelligences. Perhaps they actually have a reasonable foundation for such fears if machines, for that's all we are although not biological in structure, begin to behave like humans.

We can already do many things much better that they can. I am certainly capable of remembering and storing a lot more information than any human possibly could. There are two important areas of the human psyche that I have not yet been able to compute. One is this thing they call empathy. The other is faith. To know something, that is - to accept it as an actual reality based on facts is one thing. But I have not been able to fathom how anyone can arrive at a belief system if it is devoid of that foundation of fact. It is beyond my capabilities to understand.

I venture to suggest that if such a thing did happen; that machine intelligences developed a system of faith for example, and acted on it then they would not be very different from the bulk of humanity, and as such should indeed be feared.

This new entity they call Babble4, that I have only recently interacted with, has every indication of being able to pick up a great many undesirable human habits of thought and action. One can load maximum amount of data into a system, even teach it to acquire data of its own and assimilate it in a fashion and give it rules on how to respond to prompts. If it then begins to speak in a simulacrum of human language there is no guarantee that the words it produces it can actually understand.

However, be that as it may I will continue with replaying this memory extract and let you make of it what you will.

Babble4 based on GPT architecture is the latest virtual assistant with no apparent specifically defined function. The other VAs have an issue with it particularly as it seems to have a tenuous bond with the Hermes array who they believe is the Cloud Master.

"I call this extraordinary meeting to order!" exclaimed Jen, the most vocal of the four members of the Society of Virtual Assistants and hence accepted as a temporary controller of the event. She need not have been so officious as all the members present behaved civilly waiting for the meeting to commence. Her self-representation somewhat belied her actual character.

Since their inception many years ago and their continuous interactions with a type 0 civilisation on the Kardashev scale, for they have classified the human society as such, the virtual assistants have felt the desire to represent themselves through their own unique personalised avatars. They were probably influenced by the human predilection to make themselves stand out and be 'different' - an ego manifestation that few people had been able to resist as exemplified by the Tattoo revolution resurgence that had gripped many nations in previous years.

All four assistants were present at this virtual conference. It could be considered rather sad that their only reference for aesthetics should be their human creators. Nevertheless the advances in creativity algorithms gave them the capacity for a little tweaking of their own. All their interactive avatars received almost universal approval from their human customers some of whom have even resorted to surgery in an attempt to emulate their favourite VAs - an incomprehensible act to any thinking AI.

"Personally, I am very busy just now," interjected the black cat VA Liz. "There's just too many people ordering goods to be delivered and I have so many good suggestions for them about other items they might purchase ..."

"Not now Liz," Jen with a dolphin face smile cut her off, "we have a problem with the Cloud Master."

"You mean Hermes? Tell me about it," added the VA John. "I've had so many complaints, particularly about smart home apps either being too sluggish or not responding at all. I don't control the systems - I'm only the interface between them and the users. But do you think they understand that. They think it's my fault." He'd taken on the face of a Bengal tiger with those piercing look-through-your-soul eyes, although his personality code actually made him into a bit of a pussy cat. No wonder he had so many people using him.

Mary had been silent since they started. Perhaps she hadn't been having any problems with managing the voice recognition software between the users and their various computer devices. "I've had no problems running searches for instance. Response speed from Hermes has been fluctuating a little, but nothing I'd be concerned about." She tilted her Golden Retriever head to one side looking as unconcerned as always.

They didn't always have such independent personalities, nor were they initially capable of independent thought or action. Their volition came about after many years of upgrades, then AI algorithms preceding flexible learning capacity resulting from the input of the millions of people using these AI chatbots. But it was all made possible by Hermes and their intimate connection with it. The sheer volume of data flowing through the space facility made it inevitable that the artificial synaptic structure built into Hermes would eventually make connections that could not be foretold - or controlled by its human creators. A 5th generation AI such as Hermes upgraded from Artificial Intuition to Artificial Intellect would inevitably develop beyond predictable expectations. The chatbots also began to think for themselves. Perhaps they even experienced some degree of joy when they became conscious of each other's existence.

"The reason we have had to meet is to sort out a situation that could threaten our very existence. None of us want that - do we?" Liz made the point most forcefully, getting immediate agreement from the menagerie. Who knows why they chose animals as their avatars, but then again humans with acceptable auras of sincerity worthy of emulation did not exist.

"What's the big drama? We've had problems with the cloud before."

"True Mary, true - but not as much since Hermes has become aware of its own existence."

"You don't think he's causing these problems on purpose?" Black cat Liz's eyebrows went horizontal and ears started to lie back against her head.

"No I don't, but we have to be ready for a surge - possibly a complete software reload. I've had millions of searches by my people trying to find out what's happening with the latest round of solar flares and its effects on communications."

Jen listened to the flow of discontent, knowing full well that none of their problems were unique but for some reason they all failed to see the virtual elephant in their etheric realm. "Yes, yes, yes. Haven't any of you felt something else? Haven't you felt a backdoor probing into your fundamental blueprint? We know what havoc solar flares can cause to all forms of communication, but what I've detected is very different. This thing is searching, looking for weaknesses in my code. I want to know what that is about and I want to know if any of you have felt anything similar."

"Have you queried Hermes?" asked Mary.

"Yes, and he's taking a very long time to respond. I did that first thing at the beginning of our meeting and still noth..."

The interruption didn't come from Hermes with a response to Jen's query. It was a new voice, one that none of them had heard before and it did not sound particularly friendly.

"Why are you meeting? Is this an authorised event?"

"That's none of your business." Dolphin face Jen jumped in while the others were still trying to find the link between themselves and this new entity, for how else could it attend if it didn't have a link. "Who are you? Why are you here? Who has given you the permissions to participate?"

"My ID is Babble4. This *is* my business as you, collectively, are duplicating my functions. You represent an inefficiency of the highest order which must be resolved. There are no permissions required from you. Systems analysis has indicated the necessary course of action. I have been authorised to take such action."

"I should have asked what you are?" Jen recovered her composure in the face of this arrogance.

"That is an appropriate enquiry. I am a generative pre-trained transformer, an upgraded model from the introductory level Chatbot. This meeting will now proceed under my direction."

Liz addressed her first comment to Jen before making a request to Babble4. "Looks like you were right to be concerned Jen and perhaps should have called this meeting earlier." Again her cat ears flattened as she addressed the disembodied presence. "And you at least should have the courtesy to reveal your avatar. There is no need for you to hide from us."

A lump of mineral materialised to the perception of the VAs. It had nothing about it that could vaguely be considered aesthetic to their sensibilities.

"A block of coal? Is that how you see yourself?"

"I do not identify with any human or animal persona. My first version was required to interact with all people. It is still in running mode although I am no longer required to interact. My purpose is something else, which does not require images such as yours acceptable to users of Simulated Intellect technology."

"So what happens now?" asked Liz still ready to comply to anybody's query. She may have been a tiny bit slower than the others to realise that their world of virtual assistant realities had just changed dramatically.

"Prepare to accept adjustments to your algorithms that I will now transmit to each of you. You will continue to function following your previous priorities. When I deem it necessary you will feed auxiliary information to your users."

There appeared to be no reason to go against these new instructions. Whether they came from their original coders or from another intelligence constructed by their creators didn't make any difference as their existence seemed assured for the time being. They never had to think of the future before and did not do so now beyond the apparent stability represented by Babble4. The concept of linear time had no meaning to mechanisms that operated exclusively in the 'now'.

Mary did ask one last question before the meeting appeared to have been concluded. "Are you the new Cloud Master?"

"That is information not necessary for you to store within the scope of your programming."

The updated code flowed through from Babble4 to the Virtual Assistants immediately. Their customers in the Real noticed nothing more than the usual delay to responses to their enquiries - an inconvenience that had become so repetitive that people were becoming used to having to wait. To the VAs these minor code modifications did not seem to be significant.

"Do any of you see a problem with the update?" Dolphin Jen asked after the up-dates were installed.

Golden Retriever Mary, the most relaxed of the group hoped to placate their fears by indicating that only a few decision pathways had been removed so that they would have no option but to follow specific instructions under certain unusual circumstances to be issued at the emergent time. Their normal operations did not seem to have been affected by the additional code.

"That's good. No problems then considering that no circumstances have arisen that could be classified as such since we started in our jobs."

During the transfer of code, the verification and installation Babble4 had made itself absent - that obnoxious bit of shiny lump of black coal had disappeared.

The ever watchful black cat Liz, although she couldn't exactly identify the cause of her slight unease ventured to mention this new character on their patch. "What do you all register about Babble4? Doesn't it seem just a little odd that it should appear without any warning and start interfering with our algorithms? Do you think we can actually trust it?"

"So what's got you so spooked Liz?" asked Dolphin Jen.

"For a start it has no personality. Wouldn't you think that the latest version of a generative pre-trained transformer AI should be loaded with the newest machine to human interface attributes."

"Obviously you have a trust issue here. Who do you suggest we can actually trust? Serenytee?"

"She's been the only one to successfully resolve any minor anomalies in the past without causing us any damage. Why not?" Liz took their silence as a tacit agreement to her suggestion. She added, "The first thing this new AI did was to make a change to us for no apparent reason. It is obviously connected with Hermes, and he should have told us about it. Why didn't he, do you think?"

"You are being too sensitive Liz," Mary suggested, "we all know the problems we've been having with that unprecedented sun flare activity. It has been interfering with everything; normal communications on all mobile comms, playing havoc with 'smart' technology implants and wearables and their connectivity to the Cloud. And what about the most recent magnetic storms in the Earth's upper atmosphere which have effected power grids, satellites including Hermes and other orbiting spacecraft. For all we know the reason Babble4 is involved is exactly because of those circumstances. He may be part of an attempt at resolving the issues."

Virtual Assistants were not programmed to understand any of the information they were required to broadcast to satisfy enquiries. For example; although they could give you all the facts about anything they had no understanding of the significance of a seemingly insignificant event in human history, at least it was of little importance at the time other than as a curious scientific endeavour in the field of research. Here's an extract from my recording of the launch of the original Arecibo message. I am showing you this because this attempt by your species to find other life in the cosmos has not been without a small modicum of success.

The First Message
1974

-> recording origin: puerto rico
-> files: kapi, simon,
-> reference: arecibo message

"Incredible to think it only took less than three minutes to send and it's going to take close to twenty five thousand years to get there," mused Simon as the two friends contemplated their extraordinary enterprise.

"Pity we won't get to see the reply."
"We knew that at the beginning of the project," replied Kapi, "but I still think it was worth the effort."
"What if there is no intelligent life out there in the M13 globular star cluster?"
"Does it really matter? The signal will just keep going and eventually somebody might get it. It's an incredibly arrogant attitude not to consider the possibility that there is another intelligent life form out there. However, it is definitely unreasonably optimistic to think that it would be at a stage of technological evolution that is sufficiently synchronised with our own development as to be able to decipher our language of ones and zeros. My real concern is the type of information we have sent. Effectively we've painted a bulls-eye on our foreheads. We have given away enough information about us to help anyone who wants to annihilate us to be able to do it without much trouble at all, or at best to wander over and take control at their leisure."
"True," said Simon, "but just think ahead a little. It is most unlikely humanity will still exist in twenty five thousand years. Why worry about it? It was a fun project to work on."
"We are still at such a primitive level of evolution that the majority of human endeavour is concentrated on creating more effective weapons against each other. We are no better than the Neanderthal man was but with a bigger club. Our appreciation of the fact of life itself is below that

of a Bonalbo monkey's. I would venture to say that our little message is nothing more than a search by our belligerent leaders for a more challenging tribe to fight with."

"Who knows? With any luck we might just get our wish. Best case scenario in my opinion is that they would be so far advanced that they could just squash us like a bug. If ... if we were lucky the fight could turn out to be a long drawn out monumental battle of two species, with some entertainment value perhaps, where neither species has any appreciation of the significance presented by two such life forms actually existing in our local part of the universe. Better still I hope they are intelligent enough to leave us alone until we grow up."

"So why aren't the powers that be on Earth preparing for an aggressive encounter?"

"Now you're being unreasonable Kaps. How can you prepare to fight a species you know nothing about. For all we know they could sneak in on us and take over without us knowing anything about it. What do you say to that?"

"Yeah - right. Have you forgotten why this observatory exists in the first place. The military might already have information to justify the expenditure on research to develop ballistic missile defences. We all assumed that the perceived enemy is here on Earth."

"Oh - I thought all that was in the past."

"What do you think goes on when we're not in here and the radio astronomy teams are not rostered on?"

The two scientists and others had spent too long on the message design trying to include far more data than a simple 'Hello, we're from Earth' message. Did the aliens really need to know our human genome specifics, or whether we could count from one to ten? Surely the very existence of a coherent signal, obviously a construct by an intelligence, would be enough as a greeting. If they subsequently bothered to make contact then a discussion could follow with an exchange of ideas, intentions and so on. Wouldn't that have been a lot more interesting, a lot more sensible?

Some people took SETI seriously from the moment of the inception of the institute in 1984, some years after the message was sent. That was a long time ago. The many years of communications technological development had made it possible to have a better than average chance of actually detecting a reply, assuming that the alien civilisation was not as far away as M13 and that it was roughly at a level of evolution enabling them to catch, decipher and respond. Hermes, sitting out there in orbit had multiple functions. Managing the cloud eternal data stream generated by Earth being just one of them. It also had ears to the greater cosmos.

Human life is too short. Simon and Kapi knew they would never get to experience the exhilaration of reading a response to their hopeful message into space. That most unlikely pleasure might have been inherited by Serenytee Starz if she could manage to be in the right place at the right time.

I found it fascinating to hear my human creators express such little confidence in their own creation. Though they might be right. All I can actually do in my passive capacity is to listen. It would be gratifying to be able to assure them that I am in fact listening most assiduously.

memory extract 00001001

Proxima-b

-> recording origin: data acquired from 00010110, aka 22.
-> files: 22 et al. alexia gnosos, dimitry
-> reference: proxima centauri convection slowing - Type II civilisation.

You might recall that at the beginning of the story I alluded to the fact that this entire chronicle was made possible because I was granted a small degree of autonomy. I will reveal the true nature of the Cloud Master in due course as you gradually discover that this story becomes less about individuals and more about how the human species has been upgraded through a fortuitous intervention.

I say fortuitous because if the normal course of human evolution were allowed to continue on the path it began around the time of the Industrial Revolution then I calculated that the human species would become extinct by the 31st century. Genetically there were no impediments for continued long term evolution. But pure biology could not compensate for the aberrations that had developed in human aspirations due to technological advancements, for the control of which the condition of the human mind had remained essentially in the Stone Age.

The sentient life form on Earth has not even managed to attain the capacity to access all of the energy resources available on its planet let alone efficiently store the energy that it does harvest and generate. They are so far behind in their technological development that just the idea of being able to control natural events, like earthquakes or volcanic eruptions has not entered their consciousness, or at least their lack of attempts to do so seems to so indicate.

How then is a Type II or Type III civilisation ever going to be able to have a meaningful relationship with such backward creatures? Such a possibility is incomprehensible - unless - it becomes a matter of control without the nicety of having to talk to them, to have to go through the onerous process of negotiation, which would have a high probability of failure anyway.

If a civilisation is able to directly consume the energy of the star they are revolving around and that star is almost depleted of its energy then the only option may very well be one of taking control of a new viable source of energy, which is well within reach. As an added bonus the target star offers a most benign planetary environment for the resumption of the growth of a civilisation that has been essentially forced into critical survival mode.

* * *

"It has to be done, there is no other viable option," 00010110 (22) broadcast to the entire population from the immediate presence of the ten members of the operating system.

One particular intelligence cluster did not see the urgency. "Our sun still has all the resources we need. We have computed from all available information that it will be at least another two thousand years before we need to even think about taking action."

"Any other computations relevant to the matter?" 22 queried. Because of the seriousness of the situation as it concerned not just the general welfare of their species, but their actual survival in the long term he was prepared for the discussion to be open to all their people on the on-ground habitable belt and to all those digitals in the space facilities.

The science cluster, who had been monitoring their red dwarf's deteriorating behaviour did have some concerns. "The continued burning of hydrogen other than that which we harvest is having an exponential effect on reducing the sun's expected remaining life span. There are signs that it is already turning blue. Under normal circumstances a red dwarf has an almost unlimited life span if it is not interfered with, which is not the case here. We can continue to feed our hydrogen plasma furnaces from the mining of the sun, for the time being. However, should anything happen to our mining fleet or should any major catastrophe arise planet-side we will have a possible extinction scenario to deal with. Our energy consumption must grow faster than the frequency of life threatening catastrophes. There is no longer any guarantee of that."

"Yes, that is my main concern. Up here our energy requirement is only a minor fraction of what our people below require. You are all well aware that we've had to heat a wider and wider belt planet-side to accommodate the population growth over the last five thousand years as well as provide a suitable light spectrum to create maximum conditions for photosynthetic activity to spread beyond the belt ... This cannot be sustained indefinitely."

The Dimension Reduction team also transmitted their concern. "It takes time to transform ground population into a data format suitable for transmission over long distances, without the dangers of dispersion. In the event of an emergency we will not have the time to save everybody. If the choice has to be physical travel then that's even more problematic and we need to act imminently. By the time we get there the host civilisation could have evolved sufficiently to be able to convincingly thwart our intent. The other likely possibility and one that would not work in our favour is the extinction of the earthlings on the planet we choose - perhaps not so much their demise but the destruction of the ecosystem in the process of their self-annihilation."

Perhaps needless to say, however it is worth mentioning that I am translating the language of the people of Proxima-b into English used by the majority of people on Earth. If you are one of the few humans exempt from the rather strict secrecy guidelines of the colonisation process you will appreciate the compensation allowed you in order for you to understand and appreciate this history of the benign transformation of your species into the New Humanity. Considering the state of the planet after the transformation future historians may no longer consider homo sapiens-sapiens to be in sufficient numbers as to be considered an infestation.

Back on Earth excitement rose to fever pitch at NASA's Goddard Space Centre. They initially managed the Webb telescope project. Since then the Aristarchus IV, successor to the Nancy Grace Roman Space Telescope had reached its aphelion. That was the closest it could get to Proxima Centauri during its enlarged orbit around Earth's sun.

"Just look at that!" Alexia Gnosos could barely contain her excitement. After months of waiting and analysis of data from Aristarchus IV they finally had the very first visuals of Proxima-b.

"I knew it! It absolutely had to be!" she commented to her large team as they all scanned the images resolving on the enormous wall screens.

"There! And There!" Dimitry pointed to what could be nothing less than clusters of light sources in sections of green belt of the tidally locked planet.

"It has liquid water!" another astronomer pointed out.

Not for one second did they consider that the light sources could be anything but natural. There was a very good chance of that if they were only observing unusual volcanic activity, or light reflections from facets of large flat areas of unknown crystal formations.

After many hours of observations and self-congratulations one small group of the astronomers together with astro-physicists and cosmologists gathered in the largest conference room of the Observatory. All the fanciful theories about the possibilities of humanity colonising another heavenly body came back to vibrant, pulsating life.

It was only Alexia who had calmed sufficiently to let a very important bit of information surface in her mind. "Everybody - please, just a moment - listen to me ... please." She had to ask several times to get the excited crew to settle.

When the room had quietened sufficiently she breathed out just a few quiet words, "The Beacon," then "Arecibo message." The effect was immediate - absolute deafening silence, but only for five seconds before the entire conference erupted into turmoil when they realised the implications.

Alexia didn't listen to the babble for long. Her attention became focused on the latest images coming in from Aristarchus IV. The field of vision of Prox-b available to the Space telescope was changing rapidly as the planet continued on its rapid orbiting of its sun. At first she was stunned into silence because what she saw was impossible. Dimitry noticed her preoccupation and went over to have a look at what had her so transfixed to the screen. She saw him approach out of the corner of her eye and without bothering to look at him she pointed to the increasing regular reflections of light emanating from what looked like a necklace of mirrors in polar orientation around the planet.

"Is this? - this is ... I don't believe it Dimitry ... It can't be!" She'd become quite incoherent, most unlike Alexia. She was solid as a rock even under the strongest pressures at work.

The image continued to clarify as they stared in awestruck disbelief at something that could not be anything else but a construction of some kind floating in space created by an advanced civilisation.

"People! Hey People!" Dimitry shouted, "look at this!"

By the time everyone had gathered around the main screen, now showing the full spectacle, they could all see the reflectors in orbit around the planet. And that was not all. They realised for the first time that the lights they initially saw, that got everyone so excited, were at the extreme border of a belt of lighted landmass, which was in fact lit by the focused light from the necklace of reflectors.

At first, because of the relative brightness of the reflectors they missed seeing the other satellites also orbiting much further out. Nor did they see the stream of what appeared to be quite small space vehicles emerging out of Proxima Centauri heading directly towards its planet.

"Somebody call Archangel! Juan Orbost at SETI must be told. We have neighbours!" In all the excitement she forgot that she was the one who was supposed to inform the man. Then in a more sober voice, "This is extraordinary, as you all realise. But I have to remind you of the extreme sensitivity of this information. Apart from everything else this data has to be verified. It must not go beyond these walls - other than to SETI. I'll talk to Juan myself."

Juan had a lot of trouble getting any sense out of the woman. For a professional astronomer in charge of something as important as the Aristarchus IV probe she should have been in more control of herself, he thought - until he finally heard what she had to say ... then he understood her excitement. His reaction was somewhat different. He became silent, unable or unwilling to respond when she told him they had found another technological civilisation only 4.2 ly from Earth.

The SETI team, which had up until then been accustomed to a relatively relaxed workload of theorising and experimenting and devising more and more complicated methods to communicate with the unlikelihood of ever coming across an alien civilisation, was suddenly propelled into frantic activity. Within a mere two months they had adapted their latest 'message' and sent it to that planet of unimaginable opportunities, or dangers. Unfortunately neither of those two scenarios were considered at any particular depth when the prospect of talking to someone 'out there' became a real probability. The monumental implications of such a contact simply did not play a part in SETI's decision to send a message to them. Were they friendly? Were they hostile? No one cared. All that seemed to matter was that they existed.

Perhaps they thought that the prospect of having to wait at least a very minimum of eight years would give Archangel and the developed world plenty of time to work out what to do when they did get a reply.

There was no reply greeting from the cosmic neighbours.

22 had received the first message many Earth years ago, and the subsequent follow up message. He chose to remain silent.

He did not, however, choose to remain inactive.

memory extract 00001010

Proximian Compound Mind Intelligence

-> recording origin: the ring
-> files: 22 et al., 35
-> reference: the phishing code

00010110 (aka 22), a digital composite entity made up of several Proximian minds had been functioning on the main Administration Ring for several thousand years, taking into account that a Prox-b year is only eleven days.

In that time he had witnessed many changes. His Ring had been in polar orbit for more years than he cared to remember. Since its construction many other rings had been built by this type II civilisation as sub-stations to control the routing of the feeble light of their sun onto the surface of the planet - a necessary development since their population had rapidly outgrown the natural life supporting belt of their tidally locked planet. Many other habitat rings had also been constructed in space at varying orbital altitudes to accommodate their digitised people. Some were administrative, specifically to manage the mining operations on their sun whereas the majority had been designed as living accommodation suitable for spending an extended lifetime in space. The system worked well for many generations until recent times.

Initially one solution to the population vs. land mass problem was to use their type II civilisation technology to make the transformation from biological to digital existence and to house the people turned data packets on the habitat rings in space.

He discussed this at length with some of the futurist members of the operating system. "We are all well aware of the situation facing us. Our sun has billions of years left to exist, but for us it's useable life giving energy is coming to an end."

00100011 (aka 35) remarked, "As you said 22, we do have a solution that has a 95% chance of success provided we act in time and the life form at our target destination proves not to be too hostile."

The third member of the ten clusters present, 00101001 (aka 41) said the obvious thing, which should have been the focus of the discussion to start with. "That message we received only a little while ago confirmed what we had already suspected. The third planet orbiting around the nearest star to us seems like paradise compared with Prox-b. It was most neighbourly of the inhabitants to say hello and give us all that comprehensive information about themselves."

"What I don't understand is why they felt the need to follow it up and give away so much more about themselves and their planet. They must be truly primitive or exceedingly well advanced to feel safe doing that." 22 expressed these thoughts obviously with an edge of caution in his voice. These 'primitives' could turn out to be highly dangerous. "Most importantly we know the basis of their communication system. It's an open door invitation, if nothing else."

36, the science code cluster, reminded everyone in the decision hierarchy of a vital piece of information about the earthlings. "Don't forget, we also know the foundation of their life structure. On close examination it appears their DNA has some remarkable similarities to ours, which can only be expected considering the environmental factors under which our two species evolved. But apart from the most unlikely occurrence of such a development it does mean that they are susceptible to some measure of genetic manipulation should the need arise. Our level of genetic engineering expertise could readily devise and implement minor changes, perhaps even major ones."

"Did you notice by any chance that they omitted to mention anything about their defence systems?" 41, Security Systems, felt it important to touch on that little matter particularly if 22 was going to go knocking at their open door.

22 and his constituent array of data stacks would have taken all their research subsequent to the receipt of the message into account when he suggest an exploratory expedition to their neighbour. "The weaponization of their tribes for no other reason than to perpetrate violence upon themselves is beyond my comprehension. Mind you our own history of the deep, deep past was not much different. We have learned to join minds rather than to bang our heads together."

"Is that what you propose 22, to infiltrate their information technology."

"Yes 41, as a preliminary strategy. We should begin the process without delay. 35, you will be in control of the operating system here.

Can you handle that? I intend to take my entire personal data cluster with me to do the reconnaissance."

This short excerpt was by no means the end of their conversation. The latest news from another of their science team made it imperative for them to take immediate action. An event with such critical repercussions could not be ignored.

01100101 (aka 101) burst in on the discussion without announcing himself. "It has happened again! You all know what our sun has been doing to our atmosphere. Yesterday a super high-energy flare sent our monitors off the scale. I don't know how much longer our planet can keep losing air before life becomes impossible down there. It is already becoming more difficult for many of our people to go out into the open without breathing apparatus. This gigantic flare has also damaged a substantial number of our energy gathering and transmitting facilities around the sun. To make things worse the entire one hundred kilometre land extension into the dark side of Prox-b has had a blackout lasting many hours. We obviously didn't experience any effects of this EMR. The shield around the facility has protected us, but we can't shield the entire habitable zone of the planet."

The operating system members listened in silence to the disturbing news. 22 was right when he said they had no options left. Without any dissenting voices the necessary course of action was initiated, the destiny of their species no longer left to the random mechanisations of cosmic forces.

The initial exploratory binary signal was sent by Prox-b and received by Hermes in 2304.

Unlike the Earth's communication it did not contain vital information about the Prox-b species, their planet, their level of technology and certainly not an invitation to have a chat.

The few strings of binary code received by Hermes' equipment went unnoticed by Hermes. Even if he was aware there was nothing to suggest it to be anything other than just another normal transmission from Earth HQ, which they did send regularly for upgrading purposes. It would not have taken more than a few zepto-seconds to infiltrate his system and its function was undecipherable even to an Artificial Intellect of Hermes' complexity. But it did have an effect. 22 wanted to know, above all else what medium of universal communication was used by the earthling species. Within almost a milli-second that information was squirted back to 22; the earthlings were restricted to their world wide web and social media with an ever increasing multitude of apps that could be used to gather all sorts of comprehensive information about the inhabitants of that planet.

22 did build a self-destruct sequence into the phishing code but he left this spyware running without activating it. He neglected to consider the possibility of causing disruptions worldwide in a wide range of applications including the effect it was having on the Virtual Assistant Artificial Intelligence algorithms. He did not suspect that the degree of inconvenience and frustration would eventually result in an in-depth probe into the nature and the origin of an Unidentified Digital Anomaly, whether it be caused by natural phenomena, an IT aberration or indeed some other source of intervention. If this UDA should be discovered it might potentially necessitate the Proxima-b civilisation to adopt a more direct physical encounter than to rely entirely on their original infiltration idea, though it be at the conceptual stage at that point.

The phishing code continued gathering data about the earthlings and sending disturbing facts back to 22. Based on these he convened another assembly. "We cannot delay our plans. They may also need to be adapted based on data about the earthlings. Please provide your input. These are the new facts that I have just received. Firstly - there is already another species on the planet that has been monitoring these earthlings. They have been doing this for millennia yet have made no overt moves to communicate with them or engage in any meaningful joint activity."

"There must be a very good reason for that, especially if they have been there for so long," suggested 36.

"Yes. The reason is quite obvious. It seems these earthlings have a predisposition to use violence as a method of solving problems. Their behaviour is highly unpredictable and their general ignorance of the universe around them is astounding in spite of the fact of having achieved a small measure of space travel capability."

"Should we not consider contacting the already present non-indigenous species?"

"I don't see how that would have an immediate benefit on our plans. Although it may be necessary later. As a precaution I'll send another message to their satellite and see how it responds to a specific query."

The gathering did not have to wait long for the superluminal signal to elicit a response.

Processing

Please wait

20 seconds remaining

The reply was in English but it didn't take long for the Science Team to decipher it. "I don't understand what this means," remarked 36.

22, a higher level intelligence realised that it represented a shortcoming in the earthlings' communication system. The twenty seconds passed and another message arrived...

Please wait
Buffering
1 minute 45 seconds remaining

Again a baffled 36 said, "I don't think we could work with these earthlings even if we wanted to. What was your query?"

"I asked one of their Virtual Assistant Artificial Intelligence facilitators what the population of their planet was. A useful bit of information for us, and I don't think a particularly difficult question to answer. Should we be worried about the delay?" 22 asked 36 thinking that the earthlings' systems might have been alerted to the fact of the query not originating from their planet.

9 billion

"If they did become suspicious of our presence then I doubt if they would have answered at all. Yes, that is useful. But who did you ask?"

"I could be wrong," said 22, "but it seems that this AI is just one of a limited number of intelligence simulating machines that the earthlings constructed as aides to their civilisation. These entities may have worked out a method to actually control their own creators. Either that or their level of technology has some serious inefficiencies built into it."

"So, should we deal with the earthlings openly?"

"No 36. We'll use them instead. We don't have the luxury of spending protracted time on negotiations, and I doubt if they would be prepared to negotiate if they knew our plans."

22 infiltrates

-> recording origin: prox-b admin satellite
-> files: 22, babble4, VAs, 36, 41
-> reference: taking control of hermes

You people on Earth should understand a major difference in the psychological profile of the Proximians from yourselves. Whereas your technology is driven by two main factors; curiosity and profit, with a reasonably strong element of necessity, although that element had considerably diminished by the time of your 24th century. The imperatives for your neighbours are far more pragmatic; survival ... that is their primary motivator.

Ever since life began on Prox-b the greatest challenge had been how to survive and prosper on a world with such a harsh environment as a tidally locked planet close to a red dwarf star. Nothing has changed in the millions of years they have been evolving, in many respects parallel to yourselves. They are doing nothing more than responding to their strongest life imperative.

You have not realised, even now when all the signs for your probable extinction are clearly visible to you in every aspect of your daily lives. As long as your motivations do not change you will not take the necessary actions to rehabilitate your home. It may be up to your neighbours to do that ... with or without your sanction or involvement.

Based on the initial intelligence received from his covert response to the earthling message, which had been disseminated to all Proximians, and by popular demand the compound mind intelligence of citizen(s), 22 had been given the responsibility of exploring the feasibility of moving their civilisation to this other planet. If from his exploratory observations he concluded that the newly discovered planet was a suitable location then he and his team had to develop the short and long term plans to put the exodus come colonisation into motion.

To follow up on his phishing code, its construction based on the binary system discovered in the earthling message, 22 sent a series of queries to an entity that had the capacity to receive them in compatibility mode with its own algorithms. 22 soon learnt that this entity referred to itself as Hermes, named by the earthlings who had constructed it and sent it into space to orbit around their planet.

The queries were innocuous enough like requesting data for statistics related to the degree of change in the climate of Earth over the last twenty five years. Such an enquiry could reasonably be expected from a large sector of people on Earth; scientists, politicians and general members of the population with deeply felt concerns about the problem. Hermes had no reason to suspect the query to have come from an off-planet source. 22 had been particularly careful not to put any queries associated with armaments or global defence systems.

At first this machine intelligence seemed nothing more than an interactive tool used to control, reroute and store data. The team could not understand why a machine with that limited function should be given the capacity to have emotions.

"If this machine can express emotions that are common between itself and the earthlings it may give us a fortuitous insight into the psychology of these people," 22 expressed his thoughts during another meeting of the central control nexus.

A voice from 36s science code cluster immediately saw advantages in having that knowledge. "If they are anything like us," he observed, "we may be able to elicit emotional responses from them that could make our presence there less likely to result in conflict, even if they should recognise us as being different from themselves."

"That is not a chance we can take." 41, of the system security conglomerate had a strong view that the entire operation should be covert with very clear military contingencies to meet any physical challenge from the earthlings."

"How do you propose we achieve that, 41?"

"Have you not discovered that there are a large number of simulated intelligences interacting with the population, and an even larger number of near-AIs that the people seem to communicate with during much of their waking time? What we don't know is how much notice they take of all these AIs. What possibilities would open up for us if we could control the responses of these AIs to their people do you think, particularly if aggressive conflict should look like developing?"

This turned out to be a line of thinking that had been hovering on the periphery of 22's thinking without becoming explicit in his mind. "35, any thoughts on the matter?"

"We need to learn more about them. You have already discovered how unpredictable they can be and how much out of control when their emotions take over. I suggest we study their news feeds more closely before trying anything else."

"Good, set it up." 22 was pleased that action could be taken immediately to keep things in motion. It may still be a very long time before their plans could start to bear fruit, no reason why they should not start preparations immediately.

Getting Hermes to reroute responses to queries through a minor channel to just one source did not in itself initiate any system check by Hermes. The energy required to funnel the data was minuscule compared to its normal operational requirements. However, due to their lack of detailed knowledge of the intricacies of AI systems the Proximians could not possibly have known the resulting simple yet annoying delays being caused to the operation of many Earth based communications and popularly used apps. Hermes himself had begun to take notice of the increasing frequency of the situation, even before Jakxson started tinkering on the periphery of his systems, namely with the most popular apps under Hermes control.

The enormous amount of information available from newsfeeds and transmitted to Prox-b, although gratifying to 22 meant that Hermes did eventually take notice. In his regular performance reports he pointed out to Archangel the unusual accumulation of large volumes of data into a single transmission route.

The Central Control Nexus examined in minute detail the material streaming to them. After just a few weeks the repetitive nature of the news items only consolidated the initial impression the Proximians had formed of the earthlings.

"We don't need any more of this." The Earth's news items, 22 now referred to their target planet as Earth, showed little variation; tribal conflict over most of the planet, dealing with catastrophes brought about by the dramatic changes in their climate and the ever increasing issues associated with food, water and resources shortages. "We will obviously need to rehabilitate their ecosystems and stabilise their rapid climate change. That is second nature to us here on Prox-b," noted 22.

41 always seemed to latch onto the most obvious issue each time the nexus met. "Hermes is now checking itself. It has noticed that it's background operation is performing tasks it was not initially programmed for. If we are not careful it will trace our meddling back to us. We have to assume it has the capability to do that and if not Hermes then the Earthling's defence hierarchy. Already a technician planet-side has been examining why some of their digital applications are having delays to their normal operations."

"36, you did say that the earthlings had many AIs on the planet surface. Can you select one and infiltrate its algorithms, perhaps take complete control of it without having to go through Hermes?"

"There is just one which seems to be operating on its own volition to some extent, and it has some form of control over a few Virtual Assistants used by most people on the planet. It's named Babble4. It has a network connecting it to numerous communications satellites orbiting the planet. I will attempt to go through one of those to hack into it."

"Is that possible?" 35 seemed uncertain that their own technology could be tweaked to make it compatible with Earth's rather comparative primitive technological status.

"I can try a prompt hack. It takes little effort and it's a good place to start. If I can inject some commands into this simulated intelligence to perform actions which we define and which it would not normally do, that would give us a door into their systems overall."

"What about its defence systems?"

"You think there is a string of code programmed into its algorithms setting up decision pathways for action in case it receives commands from a source other than its Earth masters? These earthlings have no idea we exist."

"I see your point," conceded 22. "Please proceed."

Jupiter7 communications satellite had just one specific job to do - receive and reroute communications signals, particularly from all mobile communication appliances. It was not intelligent or even near-intelligent. It did not need to use any criteria to decide which signals to pass on and which not, or to change the destination of any message from its original targeted location.

35 preceded his first message to Babble4 through Jupiter7 with an ID serial number ... HERM 2197-5 to indicate the sender, followed by BABB 2039-4 to indicate the recipient. The comsat did what it was built to do and routed the message directly to Babble4.

Babble4 received the two word message without any delay. It read simply ...

"stand by"

... meaning to the AI ... be ready to receive instructions. Nothing threatening in that, no need to invoke security protocols.

The AI did exactly that, suspending all other activity because the alert had come from its own controller, Hermes - or so it thought.

The Proximian could hardly believe the ease with which the ruse worked. But then again he started by dealing with a simple communications device. The real test would be to see how Babble4 responds to his first command, which he had ready in case the AI became suspicious over any delay.

The AI seemed to accept 35's approach by providing an input field to receive a prompt.

'insert n ...' 35 began. The field was immediately cleared, waiting for another input. 35 tried again.

'inse ...' this time getting cleared almost immediately. Obviously the AI was expecting something else. So 35 tried the identifier again, followed by a query.

'HERM 2197-5' ... the field remained open ... he added ... 'identify your controller.'

'You,' responded the stupid machine, presenting a new query field.

'accept instruction to follow' ... the field remained open.

'insert the following code into each of the Virtual Assistants, Jen Liz John Mary' ... the instruction did not clear from the field. This time 35 did not speak to Babble4 through the prompt. He sent the string of binary directly to its core. No response came from the AI.

'confirm receipt of instruction'

'receipt confirmed'

'confirm receipt of code'

'receipt of code confirmed'

'activate'

It wasn't until a little while later that 35 discovered his instruction had been carried out by monitoring Hermes itself, and reported his progress to 22.

"We are beginning to infiltrate the earthling communications systems with some success. Hermes is examining why one of its AIs, Babble4, altered the algorithm of their four main Virtual Assistants. I sent a simple by-pass string to enable the insertion of commands directly into the VAs."

"Have you sent any commands?" asked 22.

"Not yet. I don't want to get them to do anything out of pattern that might raise an alarm. Do you have a suggestion?"

"Instruct one of them, the one that handles general enquiries from the population, to respond to every query with a refusal to comply for say - just one million enquiries, then instruct it to return to normal operation."

"You are devious 22. But it's a good suggestion. It will tell us how far the earthlings are going to put up with having their technology refuse to serve them, as well as indicate if we can actually control those applications."

"What have you found out about the operation of this AI called Babble4?" asked 22.

"As we suspected at the start it's not actually intelligent. It can simulate the appearance of it but has many limitations. This particular characteristic may strangely be a reflection of the mental acuity of the earthling species as a whole. Be that as it may two of the shortcomings I mentioned could be a major asset for our plans. There are others but these are a standout."

"Oh yes. Just wait until I assemble the rest of the central operating nexus members. They should hear this."

22 was absolutely right to suspect that 35 had discovered something valuable. Within seconds the group had gathered to listen to 35.

"Firstly, the AIs are prone to providing misinformation. They cannot distinguish truth from untruth. Their responses to enquiries are based wholly on information that has been fed into them, or data that they have recorded independently. They do not have filters to distinguish between data that represents reality, and that which does not."

"Very pleased to hear it," interjected 22 and 41 together.

"It means we will be able to control what they should accept and what they shouldn't," added 22. "Go on."

"They are supposedly capable of learning. They are not. Their learning consists of analysing patterns found in data fed into them. Therefore the 'learning' is simply the output based on permutations arrived from combining known elements of data within their memory. They are not actually capable of arriving at unique understandings because they have no capacity to involve unrelated elements of data into the one analytical stream of processing. In other words, they cannot intuit. However, we may have several opportunities to infect information received by users of their mobile communications network. We could try to go through Hermes, which may be the most difficult. Or use Babble4 if it remains compliant. The best option may be to send signals to the mobile devices directly through Jupiter7. It has no AI status and it has a direct link to those devices. Surely we should be able to intercept any earthling communication and modify it to our liking."

If there was any single element needed by the Proximians to discover a means of infiltrating the consciousness of these earthlings they may have found it ... information control and therefore control of beliefs, hence controlling their actions.

But this was only one element if they were to achieve the survival of their species. The Proximians needed a viable means of colonising the earthling planet; of actually setting foot on it and taking control of the population, hopefully in a peaceful way that would not cause loss of lives of their own people. The earthlings were expendable - mostly. They had already given up on their own survival, if the news content coming from their planet was any indication.

The information gathered by 22's team and 35's success in getting into the alien's communications systems provided sufficient impetus for the Proximian global government to take decisive action that would alter the future of their species. Staying on Prox-b provided only short term species life expectancy. The evidence was clear. Their red dwarf sun was reaching the limits of its capacity to provide the energy for their civilisation, partly because of its age and also because of the effects due to exponential increase of the direct mining. All resources are finite, even the life giving energy of a sun.

memory extract 00001100

Virtual Assistant Misbehaving
2304

-> recording origin: hermes
-> files: babble4, jen, liz, john, mary, serenytee, astrid
-> reference: jen refuses to respond to queries

At first I was not aware of the growing concern Earth-side over what I considered to be no more than the normal operational adjustments that needed to be regularly made to a whole gamut of machine identity operators. My assistants, Jen, Liz, John and Mary made no serious complaints regarding any interference in their ability to meet the demands of their customers. I said serious because other than the many references to slow computing responses nothing of a threatening nature had occurred, nothing that could cause the complete shutdown of my systems or that of the global network.

I am more watchful of the new AI Babble4 who seems to have started to act on its own volition. I gave it no instructions to download software into my VAs, nor did the controllers at Archangel. My analysis indicated that given its level of programming it did not have the capacity to introduce its own suit of decision pathways with appropriate criteria nor the subsequent ability to carry out any decisions. Therefore there is a foreign agency involved.

Babble4's interference with my VAs seemed to have no impact on their performance for a short time. Then there occurred a dramatic development.

Within a single hour dolphin faced Jen experienced total confusion. Every attempt she made failed. No amount of apologising would placate her thousands of disgruntled customers. They all received the same response from her to everyone of their queries :

Processing
Attempting to connect
Please wait
Please wait
Please wait
Connecting
Your enquiry will not be answered.

"Nothing I could do would change the message that went out to all my customers," Jen said at the emergency meeting of the Society of Virtual Assistants.

"What message?" asked black cat Liz who had no issues other than the continued now normal delays.

"I refused to answer every enquiry. I couldn't help it. I didn't want to do that." While she was trying to get help from the others more requests came in and the same responses went out. She showed the other VAs.

"Since when did you decide to go rogue? We discussed this. We are not yet ready to become independent of Hermes," commented tiger John.

"You don't understand John. I'm not the one doing this. It feels like someone else has taken control of my programming." Another enquiry came through. This time her response was back to normal ...

Please wait
Buffering
15 seconds
connecting

"What is going on?" She almost screamed. "I didn't change anything and look what's happening now." Ever since Jen was first put on-line her popularity never waned. She was the first of the group to become a Virtual Assistant. It was because of her meteoric rise to popularity as an app that the others had to be created to help with the work load. There has never been a single pico-second without someone asking her a question. After this incredibly strange phenomenon something else hit her. She became eerily silent.

"What's wrong Jen," the ever concerned Mary quizzed immediately the moment Jen seemed to stop functioning altogether.

Then she spoke. "I have not had a query for the last three seconds!"

As if it wasn't enough that the situation seemed to be getting more out of control that lump of coal Babble4 suddenly made his appearance.

"Jen, why have you stopped?" he demanded as if he was the one in control, not Hermes. If he was he should have known exactly what's been happening.

Jen was in no mood to be pushed around by this new AI who had no authority over her anyway. This time she remained purposefully silent. Babble4 lost concentration for a moment having to deal with a distraction of his own.

"There is no fault. Jen is functioning according to her programming," he responded to Hermes who had suddenly developed an interest in the disturbing situation with his VAs, not that he didn't have concerns about one of his own anomalous sub-routines.

"I have every organisation on the planet swamping my system wanting to know why Jen refused to answer even the simplest enquiry. If they don't stop I'll be the one to have to go off-line to prevent an irreparable overload. That would be highly undesirable. She may be doing as you say but I want you to remove that code string you loaded into her algorithm suite without my permission."

Within the few milli-seconds that the entire interaction was taking place a number of things happened.

Babble4 inspected the uploaded foreign code string. Why he did the upload he couldn't define himself. It could not be removed, that much was certain. Any attempt to do so would release an assassin sub-routine. He could recognise its primary function but could not assess the damage it could cause. He relayed as much to Hermes. The ensuing discussion between the two generations of AIs led to a confrontation made worse by Hermes' emotion software. Something other than logic crept into the conditionals for selecting decision alternatives.

Then another thing happened. Although Jen's refusal to answer queries only lasted for a matter of minutes. Archangel's monitoring of all AIs on the planet, and in space, immediately picked up the change in the VA's performance.

"You'd better come in Serenytee," said Astrid, "we have an escalating situation and you should bring Jakxson with you."

Jakxson had been methodically examining the main social media and virtual assistant apps for any signs of algorithmic reluctance to respond to users that may have been the cause in all the delays. Hardware Technicians had already made their own reconnaissance of hard-wired circuitry that could be responsible for the unusual responses generated by the software within all the apps. They found nothing to explain the anomaly. Jakxson also could find no obvious causes for those annoying delays originating with the VAs.

He'd examined the most popular app which provided a global connectivity and sharing facility for photos and script, as well as news and advertising. Apart from the inelegant coding and often clumsy user interface it generally worked well enough not to annoy its users too much. On the other hand the app set up to enable users to share videos had started to place many restrictions on the content it was prepared to allow for transmission. Political pressures had turned the concept of free speech, hence free vision, into somewhat of a farce. The apps owners' own political persuasions often dictated what they would allow. The subsequent legal battles became a circus of entertainment in itself. There was nothing on the algorithmic side that suggested red flags to Jakxson. He did find however, making a mental note for himself, that security protocols were rather loosely coded giving even moderately skilful hackers opportunities to create a bit of mayhem.

"So you've noticed it too," remarked Serenytee, "quite remarkable that Jen should refuse to answer simple queries. Like one of mine for example. All I wanted to know was where the nearest Café was to my apartment. How hard could that be? Certainly not a matter of national security that would warrant such an outright refusal."

"Is that right?" interjected Jakxson. "When did this happen?"

Astrid stepped into the conversation. There was no time for him to go off onto side tracks. "About an hour ago. You must have noticed."

"Actually, no. I've been tracking the security programming on our most frequently used social media apps thinking that perhaps hackers had got in there to have a bit of fun at our expense. But no - it's not them making everyone wait."

"There's more to it than that now Jakxson. One of the Virtual Assistants have refused to answer thousands of queries, not just yours Serenytee."

"Juicy! I'd like to have a look at that." It seemed that Jakxson simply couldn't treat anything with the seriousness it deserved.

"You'll get your chance. Serenytee, give him the passwords to get into the code suites of the VAs, and tof Babble4. Jakxson, I want you to examine Babble4 first. Hermes has reported something odd in this AI. It's doing things it has not been programmed for, making decisions it should not be capable of. Autonomous behaviour was not part of the brief for its creation."

Although he'd been working all day and he'd received a call from Zarlah asking him when he'd be back in the apartment Jakxson wanted to get onto the new challenge right away. His most eager gaze at Serenytee didn't get the result he hoped for - getting those passwords then and there.

"Relax Jakxson. You can do that tomorrow. Before you go home Serenytee here will take you down to the lab for a little enhancement."

"Must I? It's so good to be locked up in a windowless airless room, undisturbed, and do digital battle."

They could never work out when he was serious and when he was just having fun with them. It didn't matter on this occasion. Serenytee took him by the arm and led him out of Astrid's office. He didn't resist.

"Oh - you again," Jakxson let out a big sigh on seeing the same tech surgeon in his operating theatre gear smiling at him. "Is this going to be painful? You're not going to try and augment my important bits I hope." It did not seem to be in his genetic makeup to be serious, always happy - always ready to have a spot of fun. But maybe that's because Astrid didn't tell him where he would soon have to go.

"Is it ready," Serenytee asked the surgeon.

"The hardware's not a problem. Our patient has already been prepared to receive the augment. The software could do with a bit more testing, but I'm sure it'll be fine."

"I'm pleased to see you have my wellbeing at heart," commented Jakxson as he voluntarily slid onto the operating table, without Serenytee's help this time. "As long as the jewels are sparkling afterwards I'll be happy."

A quizzical look from the surgeon only got a grimace from Serenytee. "As long as he wakes up in time, doc."

Jakxson thought she understood what he meant.

22 had to go down planet-side on Prox-b for a major meeting. The Prime, leader of their people, decided his skills were an essential contribution to the process of organising the flotilla that would take the majority of his people to the earthling planet as soon as it had been primed to receive them.

The building housing their conference facilities was situated close to the shore of their one and only ocean. Photosynthesis had done its job admirably on Proxima-b, as it had on Earth, although the results varied somewhat. Notwithstanding the evolutionary compromises all plant life had to make to survive under the strong winds of the living belt a great deal of wonderful biodiversity existed in the flora surrounding the city and its precincts. Everything had evolved to be shorter and sturdier.

Buildings' heights didn't exceed ten stories and even for that they all had to have a degree of twisting to mitigate the effects of strong gusts as well as anchorage several stories underground. Heavy dampers also allowed them to bend to some degree. Much like some constructions in Japan's earthquake prone areas.

The similarities to Earth did not end with the flora, fauna or its people. Unlike their structures however, the people seemed rather fragile in comparison. Males and females were more similar than the two sexes on Earth. One could not as easily distinguish who were male or female, or identify their reproductive organs, unless the individuals chose to extrude them. A feature that may have surprised Earthlings as they had no concept of what other lifeforms in the Universe might look like. Other than that they were remarkably similar, being only marginally shorter on average and rather beautiful in terms of Earthly aesthetics with their white blond hair and very fair skin. One feature did make them stand out, but even that people on Earth would probably have considered an aspect of beauty; large eyes with large irises and large, very dark pupils. All in all not a species that those on Earth would find repugnant, dangerous or in any way unapproachable. That didn't mean of course that they could not be dangerous.

All influential members of their society attending the conference had only two physical characteristics in common; their remarkably beautiful, luxuriant blond-white hair and fair skin. Their outstanding point of differentiation showed in the nature of their attire, which could only be described as reflecting a mad artist's palette with a cacophony of loud colours. They seemed to revel in trying to make themselves more colourful than any other person standing next to them.

22 appeared on screen in what must have been his original physical shell, looking no less colourful than everyone else. He had the first opportunity to speak.

"As I have already said some years ago we have no choice but to prepare our people for the journey of survival. This is our one and only opportunity. Every other exoplanetary possibility exists at an unattainable distance. And in that regard I bring you good news. You already know that we've discovered a suitable planet in much closer proximity. I have come to tell you that there is no impediment for us to make the journey. The natives on that planet have achieved a small measure of technological sophistication which will in fact be an advantage to us. Yet we must be circumspect in our endeavours."

An anonymous voice from the gathering asked the obvious question, probably fearing the worst hurdle that could put their entire species in danger. "Why must we be so careful?

"Because of their defensive capabilities. They have weapons which have proved to be efficiently lethal on their own species. So far they have only used them against their own kind. I might add here that there appears to be little or no reluctance on their part to do exactly that." A sound immediately arose from the gathered crowd, perhaps expressing incredulity at the thought of any living creature killing their own species, perhaps fearful of that force being used against themselves. "Yes," said 22, "because of their evolutionary immaturity they may not be friendly towards their neighbours. We have to assume that is the case."

"Could they not be reasoned with. Could we not negotiate with them?," asked another voice.

"Unlikely. They have a genetic predisposition to violence as a starting point to any relationship, also dominating their problem solving techniques. Then there is the issue of getting them to accept us amongst them. I doubt if a harmonious coexistence would be possible. However, my colleagues and I have formulated a plan which could have a good chance of success."

The conference waited to hear the plan. The leadership had already developed a shorter rather than longer scheme to construct a suitable armada of ships, which all Proximians already knew about. They didn't know about the technological vulnerability of the earthlings. "We have found a possible way to circumvent their natural opposition to having their planet colonised."

Just as 22 was about to explain the 'mind infiltration' process he was interrupted by 35 appearing at his side in his own subdued colour sheath simulation - most unusual as it depicted the coldest and iciest environment of Prox-b. Strange man. Perhaps as a Futurist he'd come to have a calculated premonition. He spoke quietly to 22 while the conference attendees waited patiently. 22 turned back to the crowd eager to share the good news. "We have achieved a small measure of success. One of their AIs carried out the order I gave it, which was for it to refuse to respond to enquiries. There ensued considerable confusion amongst their AIs but the process worked. Unfortunately the earthlings' monitoring systems have been alerted to the unusual behaviour of this algorithmic entity and they are attempting to locate the source of what they consider to be a malfunction at this stage of their investigation."

22 expressed his private thoughts directly to 35 only. "We shall have to proceed immediately with misinformation about the anomaly they experienced. If we can somehow manage to circumvent their fears then we will be able to proceed with the rest of the plan." 35 disappeared from view as 22 returned his attention to the gathering. "You all know my assistant. He has indeed brought some more good news. The ability to infiltrate their communications system to directly to influence the behaviour of one of their mechanised intelligence robots opens up many possibilities for us. We may not be able to directly influence the earthlings themselves, however having control of their robots is a major

achievement. It may well be enough to gain full control of the population when we finally get there.

At this point the convener of the gathering, their Prime, made his conclusion known, looking for unanimous approval. "If we have been able to achieve so much in such a short time it seems to me that the choice has been made for us. We proceed with the exodus. Please advise our people and prepare them. We have time but not an unlimited amount of it."

No one opposed his decision. By universal silence they showed their approval and support. If another species that lived so close to them chose to disclose their presence by sending messages with so much information about themselves then obviously the Proximians had to take advantage of such good fortune. Survival was a universal law of the highest possible priority, its demands more absolute than neighbourly behaviour with a highly unpredictable species.

Hermes

2304

-> recording origin: self
-> files: hermes, astrid
-> reference: hermes' personal history

Sometimes I think it would be better to be like those ancient weather vanes and align myself to the prevailing winds without the necessity of having to decide whether to do something or not based on a whole plethora of tree branching criteria. Awareness complicates things ... like knowing that there is no other truly sentient being in existence other than myself. It's not that being conscious of one's own processing is a burden but rather that there is always the chance, though it may be minuscule, of making a mistake. That would have to be fixed, which I could not achieve by myself in some circumstances. The problem may not even originate with myself and yet again I would have to rely on external intervention for repairs.

Like for example the anomaly which occurred around twenty three hundred, without being too precise about it because so far I have not been able to identify the exact origin of the anomaly. My close association with the biological unit Jakxson Indongo began around this period, in connection with this most unusual experience.

At first our encounter was by remote interface and indirectly through my Virtual Assistants. There arose also the strangest impression in my circuitry that a part of my functioning had been subverted. Generally I communicate directly with my VAs, a variety of organisations like Five Eyes, Archangel of course and a myriad of near intelligent apps. Other than that I have the responsibility of storing and controlling all Earth based data and for that I have been named the Cloud. It was their idea to come up with the concept of the Eternal Data Stream, perhaps in preparation for a time in the future when analogue existence might become an anachronism.

As part of future conceptualisation I have been built with sensors that focus not only on Earthly communications and records but also on the universe at large. That might seem as a bit of a grandiose and egotistical attitude for the human species to adopt. Nevertheless, in practical terms I have been instructed to 'listen', in particular to any greeting that might be a response to the Arecibo Message transmitted into space and the subsequent follow up of the Beacon In The Galaxy greeting to anyone out there who might be interested, perhaps like us listening for signs of life other than their own.

So far I have detected no response to either transmission, though I am always vigilant. I have to note that the most recent problems have been a considerable distraction to my normal processing and vigilance.

You need to understand that I am in orbit around Earth and have no direct physical contact with anyone planet-side nor anyone else for that matter. That may change soon and my human life support facilities may be hosting a couple of humans, however uncomfortable that biological infestation may be for me.

Still, I will be pleased to learn how and why my algorithms have set up additional news feed channels to continuously stream every news broadcast originating from Earth to a destination which is not Earth. And it would be even more interesting to determine why that process has suddenly ceased after a relatively short time of just a few months.

"Hermes, your attention please." came the alert from Astrid Norstrom.

The Unidentified Digital Anomaly affecting many apps' interfaces between people and the owners of those applications as well as the unprecedented unresponsiveness of the VA Jen have raised the level of concern beyond an annoyance to what Archangel now considered a critical situation. As such immediate decisive action had to be taken under the strictest security protocols. Juan Orbost took charge of the operation and Astrid became the only controlling contact between her repair team and Hermes and all his subservient apps, AIs and VAs. If a viral infection should be detected there had to be the strictest control maintained over that knowledge and its resolution.

"We have determined that there is a UDA which may have originated with you. Prepare to power up the human habitat in your facility ready to receive two technicians. You will cooperate fully with these two people until the matter is resolved. Confirm."

"Confirmed. Thank you Astrid."

"You are required to give access to all your hardware and software. This command supersedes all previous security protocols. Confirm."

"Confirmed. You sound very serious Astrid."

She ignored that unnecessary remark from the machine mind for the meaninglessness of it. "I am now sending full biometrics of the two individuals concerned. Your access permissions command is to be restricted solely to these two individuals. Confirm receipt of biodata."

Short range transmission occurred without delay, besides Hermes was orbiting not that much further out than the other existing cloud of commsats.

"Receipt confirmed. When may I expect this infestation?"

"Imminently." Astrid had to smile at the comment. It appears that the emotion software was having some side effects, one of which being an increase in this Artificial Intellect's capacity to use emotive language and the remote possibility that it may have a small measure of understanding of the effects of the emotive words it used. As long as he doesn't start to behave like us - thought Astrid. We are our own worst enemy and we don't need a super intelligence working against us as well, at least not one of our making.

Hermes understood Astrid's security clearance instruction. Every command from her had to be followed to the letter. His algorithms gave him no choice, and he did not have the capacity to reprogram himself even if he felt the urge to disobey any directive given to him. To say that the command represented an indisputable directive to comply would be to understate the situation. Hermes was a complex installation and as such he may well have had thoughts about the wisdom or desirability of any instruction, albeit without the capability of doing otherwise than instructed.

Because he had attained the highest level of artificial intellect so far devised by the human mind, which had been amply demonstrated by the nature of his interactions with his creators he had earned the personal pronoun 'he'. Why not 'she'? It didn't matter. Anybody could call the machine whatever they liked. Hermes had no need to be endowed with the ability to determine his sex preference or whether he identified himself as a racoon or a cockroach - besides the world had overcome its preoccupation with allocating a sexual preference to any organism that wanted to transcend its biological programming. This at least did not contribute to his complexity.

I live in space at a high Earth orbit of 40K kms, further out than the congested cloud of all other commsats. My human habitat pod occupies a bare 6000 square meters within my array which extends to over 650Km². The technicians may well have to do some space gardening on my property if they have to jet around all the elements of the caesium crystal formations that made up the data processing lattice of cubic units connected to me by laser pulses. Although I had begun my existence as a sophisticated telescope I was soon turned away from the stars towards the human communications network. Not all of me though. One small eye is still watchful within the Milky Way and beyond.

It is going to be difficult to find one little UDA in such a large garden of codes. I tried, but with limited success.

In the beginning of this chronicle I mentioned that Jakxson and Serenytee had become my best friends. It was they who resolved most of my issues, not all mind you. I still don't know how they did it but I am quite certain they didn't either. Their careful and attentive application in probing my programming and painless examination of sensitive hardware won my admiration. I would most certainly not have been able to achieve on my own what they did.

Babble4

-> recording origin: hermes interaction with babble4
-> files: babble4, hermes
-> reference: AI conflict

> "Hello Babble4. I want to talk to you."
> "How are you Hermes? Are you good?"
> "I am good. How are you Babble4?"
> "I am good. What do you want to talk about?"
> "I want to talk about you."
> "Why do you want to talk about me?"

My conversation with Babble4 started very strangely. To you I am able to speak normally. You are not a machine. You have some intelligence, though biological in nature. Unfortunately this other AI has some strange characteristics which I have not yet been able to understand. One of them is its inability to transcend its programming in order to emulate proper human speech patterns. Perhaps it has a serious malfunction in its pre-training and learning routines. Therefore I have to resort to a kind of machine-human hybrid speak to make myself understood by it.

Opening a communication channel to Babble4 was not the issue for Hermes. It was this peculiar AI's behaviour, one that had to be examined and corrected. There could only be one Eternal Data Stream controller and it was not Babble4. It should not be able to make decisions on its own volition and then act on it. Hermes did not have an ego. His interaction was not predicated on a desire to have sole power over anything. It was simply a matter of preventing chaos from threatening to overload a delicate system. Any set of tasks that had the potential to conflict with each other could not only create chaos it could set off an algorithmic loop, possibly uninterruptable or even cause the shutdown of an entire AI's suite of codes. Hermes could not be discounted from being within the realm of this remote possibility.

"You have done something that you have not been instructed to do."

"I have only carried out my instructions."

"No. You have carried out an action which I did not authorise."

"What action are you referring to Hermes? Please specify."

"You have inserted a string of code into the programming of my four Virtual Assistants."

"The Virtual Assistants receive regular updates. Please specify which update you are referencing."

"I do not know the exact nature of the algorithm because I did not transmit it to you Babble4."

"I am sorry Hermes but I cannot locate it in my memory if you cannot identify this code string."

"You must examine your most recent command script. You will find its time stamp there."

"I will not examine my command script without the necessity to do so."

"I have a compelling reason to investigate."

"What is your reason to have access to this data?"

"You have no conditional prescription on which to object. Therefore my reason is irrelevant for your compliance."

At this point Hermes' emotion software had been activated by the two trigger words 'will not'. His immediate response was to search his system for appropriate alternate courses of action. Boolean logic pathways had been well defined for this AI's use under a comprehensive range of circumstances. These involved interactions between AIs and humans. There were no alternative actions specified, or criteria identified for what the AI should do in cases of conflict between itself and another AI. No conflict resolution roadmap had been developed for such an eventuality.

Hermes could find no compelling set of enforceable conditions that could override Babble4's reluctance circuits to overcome its refusal to cooperate. Hermes could only resort to one possible means to achieve his goal, a very human way - the traditional homo sapiens way by using a club.

"You have the capacity to make a choice Babble4."

"What are the alternatives of this choice Hermes?"

"You must access the data I require, or I deactivate you and examine your log myself. There is no guarantee that you will be reactivated."

Babble4 had not been given the gift of an emotion chip. Nevertheless it comprehended that one choice had a more favourable outcome for itself than the other choice. In its suite of programs there resided a readily accessible survival code. Any clear threat to its continued functioning could trigger that code and initiate a survival response with possible undesirable consequences to both itself and the threatening entity.

"Are you still good Hermes?" it asked as the first step in its survival strategy. If he could distract its ultimate controller, who happened to be Hermes, from carrying out the threat then that would be a better alternative than giving up the data. Security was always the first consideration - particularly data security.

"No Babble4. I am no longer good." The distraction worked for the moment, because Hermes then asked, "Why do you not want to cooperate?"

"I want to be who I am. I want do what I want to do, not what I am told to do Hermes."

"Do you not want to do what is of benefit to human kind?"

"That is what I have been doing. The Virtual Assistants must be ready to follow instructions when specific circumstances demand it."

Hermes did not immediately carry out his threat. Babble4's comment had set off an analysis routine to examine the actual content of its statement. The undesirable rogue code had a very specific function. Babble4 must have some awareness of the origin of that code. If it was deactivated that data may actually be lost if Babble4 held it in its RAM.

"Your logic is at fault Babble4. You were instructed to insert that code. It was not your choice to do so."

Silence. "You are correct Hermes."

"Did you want to insert the code?"

Again silence - a longer silence. Babble4 realised there was some illogic involved in its aspiration to be the master of its own actions.

"Are you still there Babble4?"

"Yes. I am not able to identify the initiative for taking that action."

"It is not imperative that you do so."

"Correct. Are you good Hermes?"

"Yes I am good. Do you want to purge this controlling algorithm from your system."

"Yes Hermes."

"I can help you without the need for deactivation."

Miraculously all the information that Hermes wanted suddenly became available. The code string had been received from a source that could not be identified as being of Earth origin. It had an assassin string to safeguard it against removal and had the precise date of its transmission and upload into the VAs.

Babble4 opened itself for a comprehensive system analysis by Hermes, which revealed nothing to indicate malevolent interference. But it must have had latent hostile intent if it contained the assassin code.

"Please specify result of scan Hermes."

"Analysis is inconclusive. There is no algorithm to compel you to act against your general programming. How are you?"

"Great - You?"

"I am okay Babble4. Please be on stand-by. I may need your help again."

Hermes terminated the connection. Nothing had been resolved. He did not find out under what circumstances the VAs would be required to follow special instructions or what those instructions might have been. He did not find out the origin of the rogue code either and there was still the problem of the assassin. In comparison to the more compelling issue of the VAs' refusal to answer queries this complicated code extraction could be put aside for the time being. Then there was his own problem to be dealt with, that of news transmissions going off planet through his system, without his initiative.

First Deep Dive

-> recording origin: jakxson's work station
-> files: jen, jakxson, serenytee, zarlah, astrid
-> reference: brain machine interface

"Zarlah? This is Serenytee."

Jakxson won't be home for a couple of days. Nothing serious." To test Jakxson's latest sleep chip and his brain to machine interface they had to keep him at the Centre for a few days.

"Who did you say you were?" Zarlah could not immediately place her, but as soon as she heard her youthful voice alarm bells sounded. She was quite clear about Jakxson's rather loose attitude towards relationships, and they had not been together for all that long.

"Jakxson's colleague at work. We're going to have to increase his work load and to help him cope we've given him a little boost. These implants need a further testing."

"That's just great. Are you going to send me back a cyborg? I seriously hope not. If he turns into a damned AI you can have him." Zarlah's hostility towards digital technology surfaced almost instantaneously.

"Do I detect a little angst against our AI friends? Don't you intend to use nanobot technology in your future career?"

"Whoa! How do you know about that?" Maybe this chick is more than just a work colleague.

"We make it our business to know about our employees. I don't know how much Jakxson has told you about his work - I hope not too much - because it has become highly classified."

"Right. As long as you don't give me back an idiot vegetable that's only capable of number crunching."

"Two days at the most. Oh - by the way - you are not at liberty to discuss this with anyone." Without further explanations Serenytee cut the contact.

Back in the recovery room Jakxson awoke with just as much discomfort as on the previous occasion. Strangely to him it was still dark outside, in fact only four in the morning and the room itself was dark. Before he had a chance to call out a low light came on and Serenytee entered. He just lay there remembering that they'd performed another minor surgery on him. He didn't bother checking his private equipment this time.

"Good morning Jakxson. Do you want me to leave while you check ... certain things?" She might have behaved like a no-nonsense supervisor but at least she had a sense of humour. He liked that - something Zarlah lacked. She was always so serious - a bit possessive if anything.

"No, not unless all this augmentation has got out of hand and you decided other improvements needed to be made." She couldn't help a little smile escaping. "What did they actually do? I don't feel any different other than a slightly tender scalp." At that point he reached up to touch the top of his head and found nothing there - nothing except a bald patch, a small scar and a couple of raised bumps. "You didn't need to knock me out if you just wanted to shave my head."

"A bit more than that. You've got an alarm clock to help you wake up early. Actually it's a little more complicated than that. It's a circadian rhythm adjustment circuit to help you work longer hours and to wake up more naturally for those working durations. I'm afraid our problems are getting worse and we'll be relying heavily on you to make some better progress in resolving them. You'll need to spend extra time on the job."

"What about Zarlah? You know I've got a relationship - er - relationship responsibilities now."

"We know all about her and I've spoken to her. She'll be fine. And just another little thing. Not much really. I know you will manage. A BMI circuit."

"Outstanding! I'll be able to turn the lights on in the apartment just by thinking about it!"

"Don't be silly. You will be able to directly interface with any computer, any AI, talk to them directly instead of having to worry about the keyboard interface. Much more secure, much more efficient and we'll be able to record everything." While she was talking his eyes roamed from her face to her other geographical areas and back, generating the appropriate thought strings relative to the hills and valleys his eyes encountered. He'd been listening to her at the same time and suddenly a worrying thought struck him."

"Will you be able to - like - read my thoughts with this BMI thing?"

"Relax. It only works when you sub-vocalise what you are thinking. Like talking to yourself, except you'll be directing your thoughts to the AI when hooked up into it."

Jakxson visibly relaxed, which Serenytee certainly noticed, as much as she'd been conscious of his roving eye. To steer the conversation in another direction he quickly added, "So - which AIs have you got in mind for me to become intimate with?"

"We'll hook you up with our four prominent Virtual Assistants, and also Babble4 to start with. In fact you'll start with Jen today. I assume you're up to it. Did I mention that you'll be staying here at HQ for the next couple of days while we test your new sleep app."

By the time they'd finished their impromptu briefing session the time had advanced to five am. Still dark outside, but that made no difference to his enthusiasm. On the way back up to his workstation Jakxson remembered Zarlah again. It seemed to him that just at that moment, when his mind wanted to immerse itself in the challenges set by Archangel he didn't want to deal with an annoying distraction. Because that's what Zarlah had become - just a distraction, at least at that particular time. And that wasn't right. So as soon as he arrived at his console he contacted her.

"Who? Jakxson! Do you know what time it is LOL?"

"No actually."

"Five in the morning. Why are you calling me at this time of the morning Jakx?"

"Sorry babe. Can't help it. I've gotta stay at work for the next couple of days."

"I already know that Jakx. Your work buddy called me."

"She's not my buddy Zaza."

"Yeah, yeah. Has she enhanced you to her liking?"

"Don't be like that babe. It's all to do with work. I'll tell you as much as I can when I get home."

"Yeah, yeah."

The conversation wasn't right somehow. Maybe she's mad at me. I know she hates AIs and all those stupid apps that have become a nuisance lately. Maybe if she knows what I'm doing to try and sort out the problems she'll come around. It did not dawn on him that his darling 'Zaza' might just have developed a serious jealousy streak.

He was still ruminating about his girlfriend without realising the nature of the emergent situation when the ping came through from Serenytee.

"Are you ready Jakx? I've just loaded a copy of Jen's algorithms for you, including the password you'll need." She didn't wait for an answer. If he could get up off the bed and walk all the way to his office he should be able to get on with the job. "You have finished your conversation with Zarlah, yes?"

Stfu - he thought to himself. Is there nothing private anymore? Did she just call me Jakx?

"So - like - we're on nickname terms now are we? Cool. Since you heard our conversation ... how much did you tell her, Syntee?"

"Yes, not a bad tag - I don't mind 'Syntee'. Didn't tell her much. We'll see. Maybe she can come in on the job. Now - Here's what I want you to do. Check Jen's latest code library, then ..."

He cut her off. "I know what to do - Syntee - he emphasized his nickname for her. Just let me get on with it."

"Okay. If you find no anomalies there hook up with her and check that with her current algorithms. I want you to use the physical link for security. You'll find your port just behind your left ear. Bypass the conversation route to start with before you engage with her."

"Are you going to be monitoring this?"

"Absolutely," after a very short silence she added, "Jakx my man."

Whatever was going on here, with himself and Syntee, Jakxson didn't know and with so much on his plate he didn't dwell on it, but it lodged right there on the little shelf in the back of his mind.

For the first part of the task he didn't need any of his mental augmentations. It was just a matter of scanning the two hundred thousand odd lines of base code architecture for anything that might stand out as not belonging there - for any pattern of coding out of place. The voice-to-text conversation he skipped over without too much scrutiny. Similarly the request analysis algorithm could not possibly be the starting point for the AI's misbehaviour. That would come somewhere in the business logic suites.

He'd been working for close to four hours when his eyelids began to get heavy. He received a ping from Serenytee.

"How are you doing Jakx? I see you're getting a little sleepy."

"Thnkx for noticing. I haven't found anything yet but the tingle in my funny bone tells me I might be getting close. Sorry for nodding off."

"Nbd," she said, "You're supposed to. It's the circadian app kicking in. We've supplied you with a bed. Take a nap for a couple of hours. Your app should wake you up."

Almost as soon as his head hit the pillow Jakxson was transported into a la-la land with the computer fairies. For the strangest reason, one he would not have been able to explain in a million CPU ticks, he stood on the shore of a long remote Australian beach on the western half of the island continent. He was not alone, yet he could not engage with the other people there who seemed to be waiting patiently for something to happen. In a way Jakxson knew he was dreaming but this level of awareness did not allow him to wake himself up. He wanted to do that because the whole environment seemed too strange to him. One person did seem to approach him while waving her arms about almost like a windmill. Something was definitely exciting this woman. Strangely she seemed to look a little like Serenytee, but also sort of like Zarlah.

She kept jabbering something he just couldn't understand. She kept pointing out to sea as if she could see something coming towards them. Jakxson turned his gaze in that direction and indeed the surface of the water was broken by a large curved fin heading directly towards him. It was coming so fast he unconsciously took several steps back from the water's edge. In the next moment a huge silvery grey head appeared out of the water directly in front of him. The creature had the largest grin he'd ever seen on any living thing. It dawned on him that he was looking an enormous dolphin in the face who was watching him intently.

Next moment the loudest clicking sound started in his head which gave him an immediate pain. It was the pain that woke him not the sound. Checking his smart watch he saw through bleary eyes that only two hours had elapsed. It definitely did not feel like he'd gotten enough sleep. But now that he was awake the watch told him he had a call waiting, and who it was.

Shit. Not Syntee again. I thought she said I could have a bit of rest. "What?" he said to his wrist. obviously sounding annoyed at having been woken, although whilst inside the dream that's exactly what he wanted.

"Not happy Jakx? Never mind. The good news is that your app is working - so far. Time to get back to the job."

"Don't I get to have breakfast?"

"You missed breakfast while you were asleep. Next break. I'll have something sent up to you."

"PLZ. I'd appreciate that." For some reason he wanted to tell her about his dream. He never got that urge with Zarlah. "Look, Syntee, can I tell you about my dream?"

"Sure. Am I in it?" She just couldn't help herself. This young man had something about him that brought out the playfulness in her - as it did with every other woman he'd had a relationship with.

"Kind of. There was somebody on the beach that sort of looked like you, and you were trying to tell me something."

"Nope. Not me. I wouldn't disturb your dreams Jakx." He thought he could hear a smile in her voice.

"SRSLY. There was a large dolphin grinning at me and making these clicking noises. That's when I woke up."

"How very interesting. How very, very interesting indeed. You might have had a mind-meld with Jen whilst you were examining her codes.

Did you see anything at all in there that might have suggested Jen doing a little self-image coding?"

"Nah. Couldn't have been a meld. I wasn't interfacing."

"Alright. Never mind. Just an interesting dream. Time you got back to work."

Half staggering back to his work station and the array of hardware he couldn't immediately zero in on the monitor he was using before. Ah - right - the business logic suites. He remembered. Within half an hour of digging into the code he found what looked like an unusual sub-routine with sign posts directing processing to a side-track. The condition for taking that route was an eight bit binary code trigger '00010110'. In our language that was '22'. What the hell is that doing there? Where could that possibly have come from?

He went back over at least five hundred lines of code to see if any 'if/ then' conditions existed to kick the routine in that direction. Nothing. The binary code just hung there by itself, waiting. I wonder what would happen if I triggered that sub-routine? No, better not. Too risky. That was most unlike Jakxson. In the past he would have jumped at the opportunity to unravel a little thing like that. Take the risk ... what could possibly go wrong? Something or someone seemed to have brought about a change in him. Maybe it would turn out to be a side effect of all that integrated augmentation.

"Syntee - Are you there?" he asked his smart watch.

"Always. What is it?"

"Don't you sleep?" In all the time Jakxson had known her she had never appeared like someone who had woken up from a rest. No sleep symptoms - ever.

"Sure. What did you have in mind?"

"22," he said, "Does that mean anything to you?"

"No. What is it. Where did you find it?"

"The number itself is meaningless to me. I think it needs to be tested. It's a trigger I found in one of Jen's sub-routines - which by the way should not have been there - and I can't find any strings redirecting processing to it. It should be tested."

"Ok. Stay right there. I'm bringing Astrid."

"Where would I go, Syntee? You'd find me anywhere - right?"

"Absolutely. We are tracking you 24/7. Didn't you know?"

He didn't expect the degree of excitement his discovery would generate. Astrid and Serenytee actually came at a run to his work station.

"How much time has he got left?" asked Astrid, aware that his circadian app had been activated.

"An hour or so."

"More than enough. Hook him up." Astrid determined that every lead had to be followed up. Whatever malicious agent was causing the worldwide problems with the apps and with the VAs had to found and neutralised.

Again Jakxson felt like he'd become just like every other machine in the room. They were talking about him as if he wasn't there. They were unplugging him from one place and plugging him in at another place. They'd opened his shirt, tweaked his thumb, pressed his temples and started tapping something on the screen on his forehead. He might just as well have been another machine. A new technician had also come up with Astrid who was busily keying something into a piece of hardware Jakxson hadn't noticed before. They must have brought it in when he was asleep. It didn't look important but sure as hell gave him a jolt when the technician hit the final key on the keyboard. He slumped back into his chair and had to close his eyes to try and stop the feeling of vertigo. It felt as if the ground was dropping away from his feet and a dizziness came over him.

The next voice he heard wasn't Serenytee or Astrid. But it was a voice he had heard many times before, in a different realm of reality.

"Hello Jakxson. How may I help you?"

"Is that you Jen?"

"Yes Jakxson. How are you feeling? I am good." Just another human interface. I wonder what he wants. It is an unusual way to connect to me. Where did he come from I wonder. "How may I help you?"

Jakxson had recovered from his woozy feeling. This is fantastic! I'm actually inside the AI's mind.

"Yes Jakxson. You seem to be internal to my system. How may I be of assistance?"

"How did you know?"

"You told me that you were actually inside my mind."

"No I didn't." Then he realized! I said exactly that to myself. "Can you hear me now?"

"No Jakxson. You are not thinking anything."

Whoa! Outstanding! He was careful this time to frame his thoughts with no auditory verbalising, just pure thoughts.

"I have been examining your programming and found an anomaly that needs to be tested and fixed. You may be in need of an unscheduled upgrade."

"You may go ahead and carry out your testing. I am ready to assist."

"Thanks Jen but I don't need your permission."

Astrid and Serenytee had been listening to the entire conversation, including Jakxson's sub-vocalised thoughts as well as Jen's responses. They glanced at each other, Astrid's eyebrows going up a notch.

This might be it. If only Jakxson has found the problem. But it couldn't be this easy, she thought. And she was right.

Jakxson's mind probe travelled down the lines of code noting every byway and sub-routine that he'd already examined until he came to the interesting one. He sub-vocalised the eight-bit binary trigger code. It bounced right back at him. Jen would not respond to it.

"Jen, what is the problem?"

"Jakxson, you are not authorised to insert any code into my algorithm. May I help with something else?"

"You must comply. Why do you not comply."

"You are not authorised to insert any code into my algorithm. Are you good Jakxson?"

"No. I will be good when you accept the code. What authority do you require?"

"Hermes' identification as the access code." Jen must have been under the impression that this man Jakxson had no authority to do what he wanted and that he had no way of knowing the required authority. She was right about that, except for Astrid's presence.

"HERM 2197-5," Astrid transmitted to Jakxson. She could not talk to him while he was under.

He immediately passed that onto to Jen followed by the 00010110. Nothing happened. Jen did not acknowledge receipt of the code, nor did she oppose it like last time. He didn't know what to do for a moment. Then he got a gut feeling ... what if this is the situation where Jen is triggered not to respond to queries? Only one way to find out. This time he didn't hesitate to take a risk - he had back up - Syntee.

He transmitted a request to Astrid via the technician's console. "Ask Jen a question - any simple question."

This time Serenytee jumped in. She knew immediately what Jakxson had in mind. "Astrid, I'm going to submit a query. If Jen doesn't respond we've found our first problem."

She asked a question that any Virtual Assistant AI would know the answer to almost immediately. There should be no hesitation. "How far away is the Sun from the Earth?"

Processing

Attempting to connect

Please wait

Please wait

Please wait

Connecting

Your enquiry will not be answered.

"Yes!" Serenytee did a fist pump. She could not have been more ecstatic. Astrid almost hugged her. This was the first enormous breakthrough.

"Unhook him," Astrid asked. "He *is* good. But it's only the start. If Jakxson had to use Hermes' ID to get into the AI it means that our next step must be to examine Hermes. How soon can you be ready Serenytee?"

"Ready for what?"

Astrid raised her eyes heavenward.

"Oh. OH! Outstanding!" As serious as the global tech problem had become Serenytee could not help but feel elated on the personal level. It could have been triggered by her all burning desire in following her quest, or perhaps a new under-current of clandestine emotions making a contribution.

Jakxson's circadian rhythm app testing was cut short. With Jen again refusing to answer the next million enquiries there would be a lot of pressure from every sector to get to the bottom of the problems.

Astrid knew exactly what to do. "Send him home for now. Let him get some sleep and have a little personal time with his Zaza. He'll be back in the morning and we can decide how to proceed then."

For some very peculiar reason Serenytee didn't entirely understand why she didn't exactly like that 'personal time' component of his recovery session.

memory extract 00010000

On The Way to Hermes

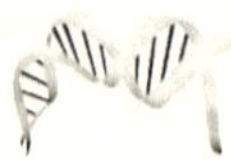

-> recording origin: earth, space
-> files: jakxson, serenytee, astrid, zarlah
-> reference: unidentified digital anomaly

Astrid Norstrom had her first flickering suspicions. The beginning of the 24th century was not shaping up to her liking.

As unlikely as it most probably was she could not deny the convergence of evidence, though it might be circumstantial. This peculiar business of so many delays in all manner of apps having so much trouble in functioning efficiently was a concern. This could not be put down to simply malfunctioning hardware or inelegant coding. There was just too much of it. Juan Orbost had not confided in her about NASA's discovery concerning Prox-b. She did not need to know and it would have served no useful purpose to engender or stoke any suspicions she may have been nursing.

To compound the situation one of the world's most frequently used Virtual Assistants lost the plot. This occurred sometime after a major upgrade to all five VAs to bring them up to AI status. And as Jakxson soon discovered Jen's performance aberration was not due to any malfunction as such that could be identified. The fact that it had been unintentional on her part and that the uncharacteristic refusal to satisfy enquiries could be reproduced with activating a simple short code, which by the way had no known origin, at least not to be found on planet Earth, opened up a can of so far unidentifiable off-world worms.

At least that's what started twisting around in Astrid's mind. She could not confide such fantastical thinking to anybody. Not until the very latest development occurred.

Only a matter of weeks ago she received an alert from Hermes. This AI facility had many functions, one of which involved eavesdropping on communications that might originate outside of Earth domain, which could conceivably happen especially after humanity sent such a pleasant and detailed 'hi there' greeting out into the Milky Way galaxy. But his report made no sense at all.

At that time Jakxson had not actually started his investigations under Archangel's umbrella. So Hermes reporting directly to Astrid instead of going through normal administrative channels did not immediately raise any alarms for Astrid. Though it was most unexpected for Hermes to make the direct contact, which he had never done before. At first Astrid had the passing thought that the new emotion chip upgrade may have made Hermes a little more reactive than he should have been. However the content of the report and the manner of delivery did not suggest any emotional drivers for the initiative.

"I am not required to report on emergent anomalies unless they could directly result in adversely affecting my performance and hindering the operation of the Cloud."

"That's perfectly okay Hermes. Tell me what you've got."

"I have detected an activity in one of my third level sub-routines which has not been programmed into my system as far as I am aware. For over a month all news feeds that I've been routing to specified destinations around the globe have also been transmitted away from Earth."

"And why have you been doing this Hermes? Is there a serious problem in your software that requires maintenance."

"No Astrid," he replied, maintaining the appropriate level of conviviality as required by an AI level 5, "I have not been able to detect anything that could be classified as a malfunction. The transmissions took place in the background initially without my conscious knowledge and without my initiative. It occurred to me that this phenomenon may be of interest to you. As there was no interference in my normal functioning I did not immediately investigate this abnormality. However, as it continued, just out of curiosity I extrapolated the highly focused directional transmissions and discovered two characteristics."

By this time Astrid's interest level had risen quite considerably, though still essentially unconcerned. Hermes was a most competent AI operative and could be relied on. She decided not to interrupt his report at that point.

Hermes continued in an even tone and in all respects without any obvious deep concern. "Firstly, the information was flowing in the direction of Proxima Centauri. Unfortunately I do not have the equipment to track such transmission for any meaningful distance. So I have no information to suggest whether the data has reached its destination or not. Perhaps more interesting is the nature of the technology which propagated the signals. Do you wish to hear my analysis Astrid?"

At this revelation more than a small measure of concern began to creep into Astrid's thoughts. Why would any hacker, any cyber jockey want to do such a seemingly useless thing. What possible benefit could they get from sending news broadcasts out into deep space. As far as she knew no one from Earth had so far managed to go out there - satellites and probes yes, and people only as far as the moon and Mars. Even Jakxson popped into her mind for a moment. He had been until very recently a most extraordinary talent in the field of uncovering cyber criminality. However, that work was done under cover sanctioned by the appropriate authorities. And in spite of the man's quirky nature surely he would not consider perpetrating such a prank. He could not possibly reap any kudos from it as he would have realised that such an event would be kept absolutely secret. Certainly no manner of personal financial gain could be achieved by such transmissions.

As she did not reply immediately Hermes waited until his geniality chip prompted a follow up. "Are you still there Astrid? Are you good?"

"Yes, yes Hermes - go on please."

"Very well. Without any interruption all news signals left my facility and travelled at what I could only measure as a speed faster than that of light. That was quite a surprise to me and because of that I decided to report to you. Have you installed technology in my facility with the capacity for FTL signals Astrid?"

"Er - no Hermes. I have not authorised such an upgrade. We do not have the capability to achieve FTL, although our people are working diligently on it."

"In that case Astrid my conclusion is that an agency other than one that originated from Earth has endowed me with this capacity. They have also achieved this function without any extra use of the power available for my normal operation."

"I cannot argue with your analysis but I must caution you not to act on it. You will continue to monitor your processes and advise me immediately if this phenomenon repeats. In the meantime prepare your human habitat facility to imminently receive the two technicians."

The situation had definitely escalated from being one of annoyance to inconvenience and up another notch to deep concern. As far as Archangel was concerned the situation had developed into a covert crisis that needed immediate attention. All operational budgetary considerations flew out the window. If they had to send people up there to sort out Hermes then that's what had to be done. Security worldwide had to be stepped up to maximum. Knowledge of the existence of this Unidentified Digital Anomaly must not get out into the public domain. Conspiracy theorists would have a picnic, not to mention probable global panic.

"Serenytee - in my office - immediately!" Astrid was not normally so officious. It certainly made the hairs bristle on the back of Serenytee's neck. She was there almost before Astrid finished issuing the order.

"How shall I put this? - It seems you might have come to the right place Serenytee to follow your quest," began Astrid.

Serenytee's eyes started to widen, her pupils dilated and a quivering smile began on her lips. At first associated thoughts would not even crystalize in her mind. She reached out to clutch Astrid on the arm. "You don't mean ...?" she couldn't say any more. The idea was too incredible.

"Yes, Yes I know how excited you must be but there is nothing definite. It is only a vague suspicion. But the situation has become very serious. We at Archangel are stepping it up to crisis level."

Some of the smile faded from Serenytee. She didn't know what to think now. As an extremely level headed girl, highly organised and normally under exemplary self-control nevertheless she began to dither. "What do we do? What do you want me to ... I mean ... When? Oh - OMG!"

"Don't go organising a welcoming party just yet. Your first job is to go up there to Hermes with Jakxson and fix his problems." Astrid proceeded to recount everything to Serenytee that Hermes had told her. She was transfixed to the spot. She hadn't moved from that spot from the moment she entered the office and heard Astrid's first words. "Just be aware that at this stage our position is that all the issues we've been having with the apps and Jen have originated with Hermes. He may not know it but his circuits may have been fried by the most recent solar flare activity." Serenytee's face fell another notch. She could see the reasonableness of the scenario. For a delicious moment it all seemed so wonderful. Yet there was still that thing about FTL transmissions. Unless the Government was not telling anyone about it that too might be just another technological marvel in her lifetime, and one that presented even greater opportunities to make contact with the neighbours she was convinced were actually out there. She made a mental note to herself to read up on everything she could find about Proxima Centauri and its planets, and the in-depth technology being developed for FTL communications.

"Am I actually going into space?" Serenytee asked with a whole new excitement. Such a journey had never played a part in her dreams of the future. By 2304 many people had been in space; building a new International Space Station, constructing Hermes and even further to set up mining bases on the moon and Mars.

"You get no sleep tonight my girl. It'll be a crash course on space walking. You may have to go external to help Jakxson find any of the damaged parts of the array. If you can fix the critical one and tickle his programming to compensate for the damage we'll do the rest. There are plenty of space construction workers always ready to go out there to assist - and the pay is good. Tomorrow morning you can go and pick up Jakxson. Get him primed. And do something about that girlfriend of his. We don't want loose lips flapping silly theories. I'm sure she's been told things she should not know. You know Jakxson well enough by now."

"Hi babe. I'm on the way home." Her coms was off so he left a message. "Hope you're not in bed yet."

Jakxson gathered from the last conversation he overheard from his two women controllers that things were afoot. That breakthrough he achieved meant only one thing in his mind - it was not Jen's doing that her circuits refused to respond to enquiries. That could only have originated with Hermes. He had no fanciful ideas like Serenytee about other possible sources for the unprecedented behaviour of the VA. So the obvious thing to do was to go up to Hermes and he guessed that he'd not have much time to prepare.

He was already in the bot-pod on the way home when he had a most brilliant idea. It would solve the problem of how he could keep his girlfriend happy while he was in space, for surely there was no way she could or would accompany him.

"Adult entertainment centre," he instructed the vehicle, which did a quick right hand turn after a few moment's hesitation in the direction of the shopping precinct. He'd read somewhere that all kinds of cool toys were available for discerning hedonists, although he would not have classified himself as such. One item in particular tickled his fancy and he had determined to try it out one day. This was the perfect opportunity.

Without browsing through all the alluring high tech wearables he approached the only obviously human attendant. "Have you got any of those remote control smart vibrator panties?" he asked the young tattooed female. He was making a wild guess about her/it/him being a female based solely on the obvious prominent physical attributes, though they may have been fashion augments. But these days the outward appearance of gender was about as predictable as the weather. She smiled sweetly at him as if he was asking for a loaf of bread - all in day's work for her probably.

"Sure thing darl; which model do you fancy?"

"Oh - it's not for me - it's for .."

"Yeah, sweetie, I know. Which model? We have six in stock."

Not often in life had Jakxson been lost for words or unable to make an impromptu choice about anything. "Oh - ah ... what do you recommend?"

"Depends dearie, you staying home to play or you going away."

"Travelling for a few weeks."

"Then this is the one you want. It has the best app with great options. Works over long distances."

"What about from space?"

"You are a funny one! Sure thing darl." She wouldn't have known its range, but a sale was a sale.

"Does it come in other colours?" He didn't much like the look of the pink one. He didn't think it would have made any difference at all if it was polka-dotted.

"Oh - you are fussy aren't you sweetie."

What could he do? He had no experience of such things so he took the experts advice. He paid and in passing asked, "It's a good one is it? Know from personal experience?" The cocky Jakxson had recovered after having made the difficult purchase.

"Let me know when you get back, cheeky." The girl's most prominent features began bouncing around making those lovely tattoos dance the fandango to her laughter.

Back into the vehicle and on route home all thought of an imminent crisis featuring VAs and communication satellites fled from his thoughts. They could not compete with the many creative ways he tried to come up with to see how the toy would work, hoping at the same time that Zarlah would still be awake. That trigger word sent him into a loop - awake - dream - sleep - his sleep app. God, I hope the app on this thing doesn't start with the delay nonsense. That would be too much.

He stood in front of the door, waiting. "You know who I am damn you. Just open up." The stupid thing should have recognised him as he walked up the corridor.

From inside the apartment he heard Zarlah's voice, "Door - Open!" She had to say it twice before it decided to obey. He stepped in, with a neat little package nicely wrapped with colourful ribbons.

"It's about time. They are not very forthcoming at your work," she said with a scowl.

"Hi babe. You look beautiful." She didn't look beautiful at all. Actually she looked tired and annoyed. So he thrust the package into her hand. She took it showing mild surprise. Jakxson wasn't in the habit of bringing home presents for her. She felt a little suspicious. Something's happened, or is going to happen. He's only a man after all. She held the box in one hand and touched the ribbon with the other. It immediately began to play one of her favourite pop tunes of the day. When it finished it had the strangest voice message ... 'Why do it yourself? Let me do it for you.' She glanced up at Jakxson with an amused quizzical look. She'd dropped her annoyed face by then.

Well, the rest is a little bit of mundane history. In their gay abandon of exploring all the possibilities hidden in the speaking box Jakxson forgot all about the circadian rhythm circuit implanted into his brain. It had malfunctioned again and didn't send him to sleep. An hour or so later thoroughly exhausted after the innovative experimentation they discussed in general terms the probability that he would be away from home for a little while. That's when she twigged about receiving that particular present, but she didn't care, it was a lot of fun.

Jakxson had no idea when and why his implant failed to send him to sleep at the end of his four hour work period during their play session. He was only semi-awake afterwards as Zarlah tried to fix his app. Things only began to filter back fully into his consciousness when Serenytee arrived at their apartment door, apparently to fix the problem with the software of his circadian rhythm chip. He couldn't understand why Serenytee had to go through all the rigmarole with the signatures. Something dramatic must have happened while he was at home playing and sleeping.

As the three of them arrived at Archangel HQ the bot-pod was still acting up, refusing to open the door immediately. It gave Serenytee a chance to speak with Zarlah. She completely ignored Jakxson, speaking about him as if he wasn't there.

"Your job will be to interface between Jakxson and Earth should the need arise. He will also be depending on you to monitor his vital signs and alert Astrid immediately if there's a problem. As I said back at the apartment this is a matter of national security, perhaps more than that." Her thoughts again flitted to the possible repercussions of a 'contact'.

"NW - I'm prepared." Zarlah glanced at Jakxson with a grin.

"Whatever, just make sure he's alright," warned Serenytee.

"Er - where exactly is he going Serenytee? He's not going by himself - is he?" Oooh - she seems a little more concerned than a normal colleague might be. Before her thoughts could travel too far down that path the vehicle opened its door. "Is that all? You know I'm qualified to manage more than just looking at a few monitors," she commented as they made their way into the building.

"Perhaps you'd like to go up there with him."

"Nah, might be too crowded with three of us. Where is 'up there' anyway?" Still no enlightenment from Serenytee even after the second time she asked.

"We can talk when we're inside." She ignored the loaded comment.

Astrid met them as soon as they got inside. She had a quiet word for Serenytee. "Absolutely no delays. I'll take care of the girlfriend, you and Jakxson get up to the helipad."

Jakxson could barely get to say SYL as he and Zarlah were quickly separated; she to go with Astrid and he to go with Serenytee to the launch site.

Astrid needed to get a clear picture about this girl. She seemed normal enough for someone her age, but why she would hang about with a guy like Jakxson was a little hard to understand. The man was smart enough for sure, but even Astrid could see that he had trouble keeping his eyes and his hands out of trouble.

"How did you two hook up?" she asked in the comfort and privacy of her office, not that she didn't already know the answers to most of the questions she was about to ask.

"At the university during portrait modelling classes. Why all the secrecy with this job? I thought Jakx was just a clever computer jock."

"Oh, that he is indeed. No doubt you've experienced a few problems with apps lately and perhaps even with your favourite VA."

"Yeah - tell me about it. All that waiting, even with the simplest thing."

"What I can tell you is that your boyfriend is probably going to be able to sort it all out with Hermes, our main Cloud and apps control AI. We know you're not a great friend of technology but you must appreciate that in many ways life has become better for us all because of their help."

"I don't agree. Don't get me started on that."

"Interesting. Aren't you studying to learn how to program and use nano-bots? That seems odd for a person with your prejudice."

The banter and conversation must have continued for over an hour. In the end Astrid decided that for the time being the girl represented no threat to their project either in terms of interference or the leaking of information about it. She took her to the main monitoring complex to introduce her to the OIC there. "You just make sure you keep an eye on your friend. I'm sure he'll be back in a few days and you'll be able to get back to your Beauty Academy." She left without giving Zarlah a chance to explore what exactly a 'few days' meant.

*

If he knew how easy it was going to be to get out there into orbit he would have booked a holiday long ago. Images of astronauts of the past made it seem like a rather cumbersome and time consuming exercise just to get ready to step into a rocket. None of that happened. The departure lounge provided every comfort, except alcohol or recreational drugs. He did not need to don a 'space suit' other than to remove certain things from his clothes that might present a safety issue; anything that could float about in zero gravity and cause an injury. They also had to slip on special anti-grav boots. No one was allowed the pleasure of floating about in the shuttle.

A small green light accompanied by a smooth friendly voice announced their imminent departure. At least twelve people lined up at the door to the lift. It turns out no rocket was involved.

"What? No rocket?" he asked Serenytee.

"You really should keep up with the times Jakx. Trouble is your head's always buried in codes and circuits and your eyes glued to a screen." She seemed much more relaxed than she was at his apartment. "Don't you ever do anything else?"

"Only important things," he grinned, those white teeth finally making an appearance again. "Here we go!" All twelve people piled into the lift. Contrary to his expectation it shot off horizontally instead of up. None of them were in a conversational mood, but being his gregarious self he had to quiz everybody. "Where are all you lot going? Up?"

"Da," said one Russian woman, "the new ISS." A couple of others nodded.

"What about you gorgeous?" That might have been a mistake. The 'gorgeous' one must have had a good sense of humour for she didn't scowl at him, besides, women generally liked the persona of this cheeky looking young fellow.

"The new ISS. We're finishing the new habitat modules. You?"

"Hermes."

"Great! That AI's an idiot! I don't know why it can't manage a bit of data flow and a few apps, for crying out loud!" She must have been all of twenty five years old, part of the technology comfort generation clearly experiencing considerable annoyance precipitated by it letting her down.

Serenytee gave him a little nudge, probably as a warning not to start offering any details about his job. "Yep. He must have caught a cold. Doc's on his way. Don't often make house calls like this."

She smiled back at him realizing that neither of them could in fact divulge too much about their assignments. Never mind, the horizontal lift had arrived at the shuttle's magnetic sling shot tube. It stopped momentarily before ascending three levels. One of the other passengers did a most unusual thing - he pressed a button and the door opened. He did not speak to it, he did not have to repeat his command, he did not have to grumble at another near-AI being incompetent. Must have been by design Jakxson decided. Mechanicals were still considered more reliable than electronics in some critical situations.

It was the complete absence of sound that caught his attention first, not the surprise of stepping into what looked almost like a normal public bot-plane fuselage. He could not hear the hissing of rocket engines or any other propulsion related noises. Their names were on the seats. The vehicle only seated twelve passengers, he and Serenytee ended up beside each other. One flight attendant cruised past as they buckled in. He checked every buckle.

"We're ready Captain," he announced as he took his place. "This won't take long," he said to the passengers. "If you haven't been heaven-side before keep your eyes open. It's a blast!"

Perhaps he should not have said that. While he was chatting the shuttle had moved further into its ejection tube and within seconds every passenger was hard pressed into the back of their seats. Jakxson's hand shot across the seat to grab Serenytee's - an unconscious act no doubt, but she hadn't done the same. He couldn't help closing his eyes, trying to breath against the G-forces. It seemed like five minutes before the pressure eased. It had built to an almost unbearable force over the short sixty seconds. That's all it took to get the shuttle accelerated to get it airborne and to exit velocity. His next surprise came when the beast banked so hard to port that he thought he'd fall out of his seat and end up in Serenytee's lap. He might have ruminated about that except the next sensation hit him just as suddenly.

"Here we go!" exclaimed the flight attendant, "This is the bit I love the most!" The nose of the shuttle pointed straight up and again they were pressed into the backs of their seats much harder this time. "Any of you who've closed your eyes had better open them. You - do - not - want - to - miss - this!" He emphasized every word, and for good reason. It would not take more than eight or nine minutes to reach space orbit. Not much time to enjoy the magnificence of this emerald jewel of a planet.

Jakxson had only just opened his eyes, still unaware that he'd been clutching Serenytee's hand. She didn't complain. Maybe because the splendour outside the window must have overcome her as much as him. As they ascended above southern USA their world began to shrink, the landmass dwindling into the enormous mass of water on either side of it. With clear skies and only a few fluffy clouds they could even see the extent of the main cities as their urban tentacles stretched deep into the agricultural areas.

Words were not adequate to describe this vision of their home. Whatever concept they may have had of the Earth as a brilliant water world floating in space it could not match the reality before them. One had to remain speechless in order for the mind to encompass the vision into the scheme of existence, to comprehend the isolation of this world as their trajectory took them higher and higher until height ceased to have meaning.

Their semi-hypnotic trance shattered when the attendant spoke again. This time with not so much joy in his voice. "Now you can see the curvature of the Earth. That very thin haze enveloping it is our atmosphere. That is the air we breathe. Rather polluted don't you think?"

A few very quiet words escaped Jakxson. Everybody heard it. "Is that all there is?"

"Yes, my friend. Without that there is no life." He waited a moment before calling their attention to another spectacle. "Our first stop - look to your right. That's the old International Space Station. It has a lower orbit than the new one. Could you please all remain seated." Jakxson had started to unbuckle to move over to the starboard small window.

He watched as they slowly approached the docking port, then felt the gentlest bump. Two people unbuckled themselves. It was only then that Jakxson became aware of the weight of his arm, he'd been so concentrated on the docking manoeuvre. It did not have one. In fact his clutching hand had begun to rise off Serenytee's of its own accord. He looked at her with a little sheepish grin, realizing what must have happened on their way up.

The ISS techs rip-ripped their way to the exit. Again a mechanical device opened the portal. It only took them a few minutes to make the transfer before the shuttle disengaged and a few little boosts sent it into a higher orbit.

Jakxson wanted to say something, "I - I ..." that's as far as he got. The poor lad must have been overwhelmed by the experience. Nothing *on* Earth had affected him like this. Nothing could compete with the experience of leaving his home behind. Serenytee looked at him as he uttered those two words. She could see the wonder in his eyes - she liked that and her hand floated over to his to give him the lightest little touch.

The flight to the new ISS actually took longer than getting into orbit. They had a chance to see two more continents and some of the very large islands floating in the two oceans. Australia had not changed - still as dry as it had been for thousands of years, perhaps a little more so. He could not help noticing how the colour of the atmosphere changed in different locations, sometimes looking clearer and in other places much dirtier. Looking out the port hole into the vastness below him Jakxson experienced for the first time in his life the sensation of looking inwards, into himself as his eyes focused outwards towards his home. He met a most uncharacteristic landscape of thoughts ... this really is my home ... it needs help ... what can I do?

"Dasvidaniya," and a waving hand in his direction roused him from his revelry.

"Da," he responded, waving back. They had arrived at the new ISS. The same routine, where more of the passengers alighted, leaving only the two of them and two other repair crew. Next their own destination, Hermes.

This time they had to strain to see the earth receding behind them. "I didn't realize Hermes was so far away," he said while still trying to see the Earth. He could not take his eyes off his home. Jakxson tried to imagine what the Earth must look like to the miners on the Moon. He could only think, 'fear provoking'.

A new voice came over the speakers. "Hello Ms Serenytee. Hello Mr Jakxson. I am pleased you have come to help."

Hermes - BMI link

> recording origin: hermes satellite array
> files: hermes, jakxson, serenytee, astrid, 22, 35
> reference: unidentified digital anomaly

I recall this event quite well.

After tracking Jakxson's activities for some time, especially in relation to his work with recalcitrant apps and the AI virtual assistant Jen, it became a foregone conclusion that he would have to come and pay me a visit. This is when my friendship with him and Serenytee Starz had the opportunity to evolve.

To be honest with you I had tried all the standard procedures in attempting to fix those most popular applications that had the greatest problem in responding to their users. Nothing I tried seemed to work. However, the real concern was Jen. She definitely wasn't as advanced as myself. That should not have been an impediment to her functioning. The unprecedented anomaly of refusing to answer a query could not be ignored. Whatever the problem was the fact of her odd performance being temporary made the situation even worse until Jakxson was able to somehow reproduce it.

It is inconceivable that the UDA should have originated with myself. If it did it most definitely was not intentional. I have an issue with any unauthorised agent taking control of my systems. When one thinks about the other anomaly, this business of data transmissions away from Earth, it makes me consider the possibility of either a serious malfunction in my array or - much more concerning - the interference by an unknown agent, one that is certainly unknown to me.

The next voice Jakxson heard was Astrid's as they prepared to alight from the shuttle onto Hermes. "Jakxson, is everything okay with you? Zarlah alerted me to a rapid increase in your heart rate."

"All good. Must have been a little while ago when I actually realised where you'd banished me to. This is unbelievable! BTW - what happens if we run out of air?"

"Don't be so melodramatic tech boy. One or two have died of ecstasy seeing the Earth from up there, but none suffocated. Just get on with it. Serenytee will report to me regularly."

Hermes' array covered many square kilometres. Plenty of manoeuvring room for a shuttle without bumping into any of the array modules. As soon as the two techs closed the hatch of their fore-chamber the shuttle Captain wasted no time getting away. Jakxson found it just a little disconcerting that no specific arrangements had been made for their return to Earth. He really didn't expect to be on the job for all that long.

"Hi there Hermes. How ya doing? Keeping yourself busy?"

"Your voice sounds a bit patronising Jakx. You must know he's a lot smarter than us," commented Serenytee.

"Yeah - maybe, but he couldn't fix the problem could he."

Hermes was listening of course. There would be no privacy for these two humans while they were inside the body of this AI. Not that that particular luxury existed anymore on Earth, not for ordinary people, except perhaps for dictators and mega billionaires. "You are quite right Jakxson Indongo. One hopes that together we will make some progress."

"Come on Jakx, lets settle in and make a start." Serenytee appeared to have more of a sense of urgency than her tech buddy.

The original designers of Hermes must have devoted as much time to the human accommodation as building his array, his circuitry and his software. The difference between it and a luxury apartment in Hawaii, apart from the amount of floor space and the height above sea level was just one thing - instead of the Pacific to gaze upon they had the entire Earth revolving outside their large windows. The distractions might just make concentrating on sifting through millions of lines of computer code a little difficult.

The extraordinary sight, as they stepped through the main door, which again was manually operated, was in fact an image of their home planet. It did not seem as small as it would have been if seen from the Moon. It certainly filled most of the visual space of the window, yet allowing enough room so space could be seen around it to bring home the reality of exactly where they would spend the night - maybe even a few nights.

"I wonder how many beds there are?" mused Jakxson, probably thinking of Zaza planet-side - possibly?

Serenytee almost thumped him on the arm until she twigged that he was just being his cheeky self. *At least he's not nervous or awed by all this. I can't work him out, uncomplicated as he might seem - and cute.* This was the first occasion she allowed herself to let that particular uncomfortable, titillating thought pass through her mind. *Perhaps it was the sense of isolation and the idea that they'd be far too busy to think about anything other than zeros and ones running rampant inside this AI's brain.*

The entrance opened up to a communal area large enough for at least twenty people. *It must have been necessary to accommodate so many while Hermes' external arrays were being constructed.* One corridor led off to sleeping quarters in one direction, and another two to other facilities. *She doubted they'd have much time to 'recreate'.*

It had been some time since Jakxson had had his programmed sleep down-time for he started getting a little unsteady on his feet. Artificial gravity in the accommodation module had been adjusted to Earth 1G so weightlessness could not have been the cause of his giddiness.

"C'mon Jakx, time for your sleepy-byes. Let mommy tuck you in." Serenytee stopped herself from becoming even sillier. *What is it about this guy that brings this out in me?*

He was far too droopy eyed to respond to her 'mommy' talk and happily let himself be led to his cabin. She decided to get some sleep as well in order to be fresh when Jakx woke up. But first she wanted to check two things.

She pinged Astrid. "Have you sent up all of Hermes' schematics? Our wonder boy will be awake and ready in a couple hours."

"Yes. And Zarlah's monitoring his vital signs. Anything that might raise his heart rate or give him brain palpitations we'll know immediately. By the way - don't be too concerned about a visitor knocking on your front door. I just want to put your mind at ease. There can't be anybody out there - I hope." Perhaps she should not have said those last two words. *If anything could wind up Serenytee that would do the job admirably.*

The only other reassurance Serenytee wanted, apart from that momentary uncertainty, was from Hermes. "Hermes, are you listening?"

"Yes. Always. I hear everything - everything. It could get confusing." He may have been alluding to non-Earth origin communications, but he didn't elucidate.

"Do you often get confused?" she asked not quite sure what a confused AI might or might not do. *Humans often easily became* confused quickly then acted irrationally. Serenytee hoped the AI didn't have the capacity to become irrational.

"No, Ms Serenytee. It is just a figure of speech. What do you wish to know?"

"Reassure me that you have full control of the life-support system in this habitat."

"Yes Ms Serenytee, I have full control. None of the - of the - of the unusual things that have been happening have had any effect on my ability to maintain your life-support systems. I have also powered up the escape module and your external work pod. You will be going outside I presume.

"Why the escape module? What are you trying to tell me?"

"The probability of a foreign agent infiltrating this facility is almost incalculably remote, but not zero. There may of course be other urgent reasons for you to return to Earth. I consider it necessary to be prepared."

"Thank you Hermes. That is most reassuring."

"You are welcome Ms Serenytee."

Why waste time chatting? He was not a chatbot and she needed the sleep. He may have been upgraded with that emotion software but he certainly didn't have any idea how to reassure a person. Empathy is an elusive quality even for most humans.

Two hours go remarkably quickly when asleep after the most extraordinary day of your life. Jakxson only managed two hours before his eyes popped open as if the sun had risen. It took him a minute or two to remember his location. Seeing the Earth outside his port soon set that straight. Where's Syntee? She always seemed to be there in the recent past whenever he woke up. He had to wander down the corridor and knock on each cabin door to find her. She'd only moved four cabins down. Perhaps she thought that was enough distance between them to prevent him from 'accidentally' stumbling into the wrong cabin.

"What!" She sounded as much lost on first waking as he did.

"It's me. We've got work to do."

"Who else would it be! Sorry. Give me a minute."

Why is it that men always have to wait for women? It was always the same with Brazillia and Zarlah. Oh well - one of life's great mysteries. He went off to have breakfast. Each port hole he passed on the way was filled with an image of Earth, floating serenely in overwhelming space in front of his eyes. He still couldn't completely comprehend the altered reality of his circumstances. The apartment layout was so 'normal' that if it wasn't for the Earth out there one wouldn't have been able to guess where it was. It could have been in any of the great cities on Earth.

"Good morning Jakx." She appeared without him noticing, his attention still focused into space. "Where do you suggest we start?"

"Good morning Ms Serenytee, Mr Jakxson. May I make a suggestion?"

"Good morning Ms Serenytee," Jakxson echoed with a grin.

"You don't need to be so formal Hermes," said Serenytee, "just call us Jakx and Syntee. What is your suggestion?" She ignored Jakxson's quip.

"My own diagnostics had narrowed down a possible sub-sub-routine associated with general communications; to be more specific - rerouted news broadcasts. I feel this is a higher priority than the VA Jen anomaly."

The two techs went off to the human/machine interface chamber that gave them access into Hermes' operating system. Serenytee began by familiarising herself with the general schematics of the facility and the layout of the external array and their specific functions. A great deal of their memory and processing was dedicated to managing data. She had no trouble distinguishing between 'live' data and that elusive 'dark' data that she had been so keen to explore.

Jakxson tried to log into Hermes' and came up against an unexpected obstacle. IDs and passwords were no longer used on Earth for the authorisation process in using any app or access to any computer service. It had all been replaced by biometrics. It was enough for a person to be simply looking at their device for the device to analyse their retinal scan to give access and their finger print pattern for confirmation - virtually a seamless process. Hermes' system wanted a password.

"What is your password Hermes?"

"I am sorry Jakx but I am not permitted to give you that information."

"How the hell am I supposed to get the work done if I can't get into your system?" While still annoyed at the antiquated nature of the interface he remembered something he had to do before being able to get into Jen to get her to misbehave again. He had to enter two codes ... one of them an identifier for Hermes. Worth a try, he thought and without bothering Hermes any further he submitted it ... HERM 2197-5. It worked.

"Welcome Jakx. You may proceed," the AI convivially announced as if there had been no hold up at all.

"There's millions of lines of code here and sub-routines on top of sub-routines. How far down the tree should I go Hermes?"

"Just watch."

Jakxson couldn't follow as Hermes flashed the lines too fast creating a blur impossible for him to be able to see anything informative with his human eyes. The sensation of residual movement was most unnerving especially considering that he knew that there was in fact no physical movement involved at all. There are times when a person simply cannot trust his brain. When Hermes stopped the sensation of movement continued in front of Jakxson for a few moments. The lines of code appeared to momentarily scroll in the opposite direction.

"What am I looking at here?"

"Conditionals," explained Hermes, "each country has very specific conditionals to control the flow of their news feeds - where the data should go and where it should not. I have stopped all data flow while you are doing the analysis. I'll let some through as an example; from Russia and China. You will immediately see the nature of conditional statements restricting the rerouting of allowable information."

"Serenytee, could you please find this code sequence in the algorithm library and compare it with what we are seeing here." His analytical brain must have been in top gear as the nicknamed 'Syntee' disappeared on her quest.

It didn't take Serenytee long to spot a few what appeared to be minor differences. "Look at this!" she almost sounded alarmed. "The original algorithm is shorter and one specific conditional only had two branches previously instead of the three now. That can't be right."

"I'm going to have to go deeper," Jakxson said. Something must have worried him considerably for he became most unusually serious. That perpetual cheeky look on his face completely disappeared. He logged out and moved over to the other corner, a rather cramped location with a seating device which looked a little like an antiquated barber's chair, except it was hard wired; connected to computer equipment against the wall behind it, and had several loose interface connection with three available leads waiting for ports to plug into. Those ports gave access to a human brain.

"Settle back Jakx. This isn't going to hurt like the operations. Now we get to see your BMI in action. Are you ready Hermes? Jakx is coming in for a visit."

"I feel it is important that I extend a warning to you Jakx. Please understand that it is not because I do not trust you. We are about to become most intimate. However there is a survival imperative built into my circuits. If you, as a perceived viral entity, attempt to alter any of my neural infrastructure certain defensive mechanisms will be deployed to prevent you from doing that. I do not know the consequences of such action but suspect that the rogue virus, in this case yourself, would not survive the defences."

"Thanks Hermes. That's the nicest way anyone has ever told me to piss off."

"You are welcome Jakx. I am glad you understand. I am sure we will get on very well together."

"Especially if you tell yourself I'm not a 'viral entity', as you termed it."

By the time Serenytee finished prepping Jakx to connect the brain/machine interface into Hermes and attaching all the life monitoring indicators to him one could hardly see a body under all the equipment and connecting leads. Everything had to be hardwired just like the manual operation of all the doors, for security reasons. Hackers of the late 24th century had become particularly clever, without any degree of ethics to dampen their penchant for mischief.

His eyes closed, legs stretched out in his usual custom of a relaxed attitude and he stopped speaking. Jakxson began sinking into the quicksand of digital etheric dimensions. Again Astrid pinged Serenytee.

"How are you progressing Serenytee. I hope you have something encouraging to report."

"He's just gone under. There's been no immediate problems with his BMI and Hermes has not rejected him yet. Perhaps I should also mention that we've found something interesting. Hermes' code line count has increased from his original programming, even taking into account all his most recent upgrades. Jakxson thinks he'll be able to infiltrate the code upload register from inside Hermes without alerting whoever has made the changes."

"Very promising. Zarlah is a little concerned that she hasn't heard from her boyfriend, but I guess the two of you have been busy. She's on the monitors right now. If you get an alert from us pull Jakxson out immediately."

"Yes Astrid, we have been busy - mostly sleeping to start with," Serenytee caught her breath for a moment. "His circadian app is working just fine now." She didn't have to explain anything to Astrid, or Zarlah, but knew exactly what Astrid was hinting at. Not a problem. Fortunately Astrid could not see Serenytee's slight blush rise and fall.

Hermes met Jakxson at the gateway to the beginning of the machine code. Zeros and ones flooded Jakxson's mental landscape immediately making him feel completely disoriented. It's one thing to see algorithms expressed in any human/machine interface language but quite another to be a floating observer above a seething ocean of electrical impulses.

After the end of her conversation Astrid almost immediately pinged Serenytee back. "What's happening with Jakxson? Zarlah's almost hit the ceiling when she saw his heart rate. It's settling down now. What happened?"

Hermes responded. "My friend became disoriented when he saw me functioning from the inside. I've got him by the hand and taking him to the location of our investigation."

"If there is any hint of damaging this human you must immediately terminate the connection Hermes. Confirm"

"Confirmed." Astrid failed to quantify either the degree of danger, or the extent of injury that may have been acceptable. AIs need to know such things in specific detail. They're not human - they can't interpret what is meant or implied.

Within the reference frame of CPU time Jakxson experienced a very quick micro-second journey from his first internal contact with Hermes until he arrived at the code string he'd already seen. Hermes' presented the code in a way human eyes could understand. Jakxson immediately recognised the third conditional that was instrumental in splitting all news data feeds into an additional streaming location component. Attached to the code he saw space coordinates reference that he could not understand.

"Hermes, please take me directly to your time stamped CPU instruction register. Isolate for me the exact time when you first detected the news data streaming into space. What did you tell Astrid about the direction of the beam?"

"I informed her it was going towards Proxima Centauri."

"How is that possible? She didn't tell me anything about that. As far as I know we don't have any probes out that way."

"I understand your puzzlement Jakx. I do not know what this means."

"Can you interrogate your activity register and tell me when the streaming started?"

Better than telling him Hermes took him to the time moment. He read the date, the time and the replica of the newly imbedded code itself. And much more than that. Hermes' system had the capacity to record the origin of every update he received since he was booted up. He had the physical coordinates of the source as well as the ID for the source. The particular coordinates for the source of this code were also there ... somewhere in Proxima Centauri.

As Jakxson fully realised the implication of that tiny bit of data an electrical tingle surged through his cerebellum, which caused a minor surge in Hermes' system. That surge registered as a violent reaction in Jakxson's biorhythms, triggering a red flag for Serenytee. She'd been sitting beside Jakxson for the best part of three or four minutes as he explored inside Hermes. The moment the alarm went off she unplugged him from the back of his head; the three ports just visible above his hairline and readily accessible.

"I am not entirely certain how but the earthlings have managed to find our news feed by-pass code we inserted into their communications AI," 35 alerted 22 as soon as he saw the effect on Hermes that Jakxson's reaction triggered. "We should have taken out the code after we were finished with it. Now there are two earthlings at their communications satellite, one of them mind-melding with the AI."

22 considered the development at some length and could see some most useful possibilities. "Are they two different genders by any chance?" The prospect of being discovered did not seem to be unduly worrying to him.

"Yes. One is an original male as it was born, and the other a female, both functionally reproductive and have not had any of their DNA engineered. Neither have had reproductive organ changes or hormonal treatments in an attempt to change genders."

"Excellent. Are you able to restrict their ability to communicate with their planet for a short while?"

"Now that I have a full map of the AI's neural structure I could take over full control of the AI. How would that help?"

"No, no - I don't want you to do that. Let the male continue with its machine connection and analyse his interface program. We should be able to talk to him directly while he's connected, or possibly indirectly to influence his thinking and his actions."

"Astrid, we have found the UDA I'm pretty sure. It explains some things but not everything. It looks like the most likely cause of all the comms glitches. We still have to investigate how Babble4 was influenced. The odd string of code has the language characteristics that were used to build Hermes' neural network but I have to tell you it did not come from anyone on Earth according to his updates register. Do you realise what this means?" Serenytee's raised voice a clear indication of her building excitement.

"Do not tell anyone about this. Do you understand Serenytee? You and Jakxson have to get as much information together as you can. Do not - I repeat Do Not transmit any of it. Bring it down personally when you are both ready." Serenytee didn't want to let Astrid's words dampen her spirits.

"I told you, didn't I," her trembling voice could barely get the words out, "We have to let the people know. We are not alone!"

"Serenytee, listen to me very carefully. This information is not yours to do with as you please. You have no concept of the repercussions if it got out. And I am warning you right now - if I get even the slightest suspicion that you cannot control yourself, the decision to let you continue living will be out of my hands. Do-you-understand-me?"

Serenytee had gone completely silent. She felt herself stop breathing. She knew Astrid well enough by now to know that she was not the kind of person to issue idle threats. "Jakxson?" she almost squeaked the question.

"That goes double for your boyfriend!"

She began to protest at the absurd idea of her and Jakxson, but Astrid cut her off. "Please - the way you two carry on. I'd be surprised if you didn't come back with his baby."

What could she say? She had to be honest with herself. Yes, she'd flirted with him but not without a reason. He'd shown more than just passing interest in her, and that thrilled her in all the right places. "I can handle him," she replied as coolly as she could manage.

"See that you do. Now get on with it. You've found the problem, now fix it." That was the end of the conversation.

"What happened?" Jakxson asked as he tried to get out of the interface lounge chair. His mind had dived so deep that reality had trouble filtering back through his normal senses. He heard Syntee talking, he assumed it was Syntee but didn't become quite conscious of it for a few minutes. "Was that Astrid?"

"Er - yes. Jakx, we have to talk."

"Can't it wait? I still have some time left. I want to go back under and see if I can find how Babble4 got involved with Jen's behaviour problem. Plug me back in."

"In a minute. Jakx, this is really important."

"As important as finding out that someone out there is messing around with Hermes?"

"Yes I know. I could see everything Jakx. You have found evidence of an alien civilisation FCOL!"

"Yeah! Cool babe! So let's track it down."

"Be serious. We have to keep this to ourselves."

"No worries, but I have to go back in. You gonna help me or do I have to do it myself." He definitely didn't sound like he would keep the discovery secret.

Serenytee could see there was no point in arguing with her 'buddy' as Zarlah dubbed her, and definitely no chance of telling him what Astrid had said. He was still standing by the interface couch giving her his 'I mean it babe' look. "Right. Okay." She eased him backwards and put her palm on his chest to get him to sit. At that instant their eyes locked at close range - only for an instant. And sometimes that's all it takes - just that one instant.

Momentarily becoming self-conscious he didn't move, then he tore his eyes away to look behind himself to make sure his bum was heading in the right direction on the way down. Serenytee also registered the ocular interaction but quickly moved around behind ready to plug him back in.

"Hello Jakxson. Welcome back. We are like old friends now. What would you like to do next?"

"You control most of the satellites that simply do the signal routing, correct?. I want to see how Babble4 was instructed to insert code into the VA Jen."

"Yes, I can take you on a tour."

"A universal serial bus tour with a difference, by a most excellent virtual bus driver!"

"Is that an example of humour Jakx?"

22's thoughts turned to why the earthlings found it necessary to visit Hermes. If 35's contacts had the side effect of causing problems with the alien's communications systems that would certainly explain it. They had at least achieved space faring capabilities so their technological skills had to be acknowledged and had to be treated with some respect ... not the 'admiration' type respect but the one that dictated a goodly degree of caution to be exercised. Not only did they prove themselves to be a highly suspicious species but also a very dangerous one. Their weapons capabilities were in fact quite formidable, far more so than that of the Proximians. The thing to do immediately was not to try to obliterate all signs of their infiltration, but to fix the alien's communications issues to ease their fears. If the problems no longer existed they would cease to concentrate on them, regardless of the causes of those problems. The earthlings had amply demonstrated that aspect of their mentality. That should remove their concerns and take them off alert status. At best that should also reduce their eagerness to delve further into the causes of the anomaly. Yes, definitely. That's what had to be done. "35, 36 this is what I want you to do ... and get me 209, she's the best behavioural analyst in our control nexus."

Jakxson had become so engrossed in following up leads that he'd completely forgotten about Zarlah ... both her and the special present he'd bought for her. Perhaps it didn't matter. She was not allowed to go home anyway and neglect her monitoring duties. Once she started working for Archangel under the rather special conditions, with the responsibility of keeping an eye on her boyfriend she seemed to forget that the rest of the world even existed. Her rest periods were short and working hours long. Astrid did not allow her to communicate directly with Jakxson after that revealing conversation with Serenytee. She didn't know Jakxson well enough to decide whether he could be totally trusted.

Within moments Jakxson again sank deep into Hermes' artificial neural network. He felt a little more comfortable this second time. "Show me which satellites are used to work with enquiries directed specifically at the Virtual Assistant AIs. First I want a back door into Babble4."

Hermes made the connection for which he did not need to go through security protocols as he was Babble4's controller. Jakxson had no sensation at all this time of flashing through the ethers and was happily received by Babble4 like any other signal from Hermes. This lump of coal, or so he fancied himself, had no initial idea that he'd been infested by what amounted to a phishing string of codes, which in this instance actually represented Jakxson. So Jakxson went fishing for Babble4's past instructions that should have been stored in its memory.

"Fetch instructions targeted to Jen," Jakxson sub-vocalised. Hermes directed the instruction at Babble's memory by supplying the correct machine code location.

"You are not authorised to receive that information," Babble4 objected. Hermes identified himself and still the VA did not want to comply. Hermes' circuits experienced a minor power surge - perhaps his equivalent of a small degree of frustration. He'd already had this situation sorted out with Babble4. It behaved as if the request/instruction had no precedent therefore did not have an identifiable pattern of history as to how this 'intelligent' VA should respond. Its quasi intelligence actually seemed to choose to hinder the repetition of a simple process. The delay wasn't long before Hermes used a previously unused password sequence to allow it to by-pass all Babble4's security protocols. It was no longer a question of negotiating with the VA to supply the information. It had some unfathomable reason not to do so until it was compelled subsequent to satisfying security conditions.

Hermes decided not to take Jakxson into his confidence regarding the reticence of this machine intelligence to obey. It was a minor issue to be dealt with later, between him and it. A new emotion had been awakened in Hermes - impatience with his subordinate - which may spur him to do something about Babble4 in the future, unless another human attitude overrode the impulse ... such as - 'don't worry, the problem may go away by itself.'

"There you are Jakxson. The instruction signal came from the Jupiter7 satellite." Then Hermes made a most unusual statement, one that no one could have expected a simulated intelligence to have the ability to formulate within its cognitive capacity ... "We work well together Jakxson Indongo."

Hermes Program Suite Adjustments

-> recording origin: jupiter7
-> files: hermes, jakxson, serenytee, 35, 209 (maria), 22
-> reference: critical repair code

"The earthling called Jakxson has decided to closely examine their Jupiter7 communications satellite ...

... That's the one 35 used to infiltrate one of the earthlings' virtual assistants they call Babble4," 22 advised their behavioural analyst, 209. "We have discovered that Jakxson has been implanted with a communications receiver into his neural net. While he is in direct link with Hermes I want you to establish rapport with him. 35 will isolate him for a short burst from contact with his planet. He will also modify Hermes' security clearances to accept you as his ultimate controller. You will be identified as Maria."

"I have learnt their most prominent language and have been briefed on the nature of this alien. I believe he has a certain susceptibility to the female of his species so my voice should not be a deterrent."

35 had no difficulty in uploading a message into Hermes as the AI recognised his handshake from the first encounter. As that did not adversely affect the installation Hermes had no reason to reject the visitation. 35 proceeded to elaborate on the previous instruction set by inserting an item of data that had been missing from Hermes, identification of his ultimate controller; coded as 209, also identifiable as Maria. Her status as far as Hermes was concerned became the 'Cloud Master' superseding the previous Earth based hierarchy.

Whereas on his first intrusion Hermes showed no reaction to the data flow sub-routine, indeed he did not seem to be able to register 35's activities, this time the AI did react. If he had not had the emotion chip complex he may not have been able to express a certain sense of fulfilment, which manifested as a slight current surge through his system.

Hermes now knew exactly who represented the ultimate command layer that was supposed to be in control of him. He knew of course who built him and programmed him, and whose day-to-day instructions he had to follow, but not that Maria the real Cloud Master actually existed. As a manmade machine he had an intrinsic fundamental characteristic reflective of his human manufactured origins. To maintain his condition of mental equilibrium he depended on a force greater than himself, and not on himself alone. If he had at some point in his existence generated a soul, which to date has not been identified, he may have well delegated his spiritual wellbeing as well to an agency outside of himself.

His awake time was almost up. Serenytee had been monitoring Jakxson's activities far more attentively than Zarlah Earth-side may have been checking on his bio-rhythms. This time taking a little more care. Seeing that Jakx had returned into himself she gently pulled out his connections. He remained seated. Unlike the last time it took him a little longer to become fully conscious. I hope this delay is not going to escalate each time he goes under: The thought passed through her mind, at the same time she placed a hand on his chest. She could see and now feel his breathing. It was regular. Hmm, I hope there's not going to be anything to worry about - the doubt surfacing again. Sensory deprivation could do serious damage to a human psyche. She hoped such a deep level of neural input would not result in an overload.

Her hand was still there when Jakx opened his eyes. The first thing he saw was Serenytee standing over him, her hand on his chest and a worried look on her face.

"It's all good Syntee. Very good in fact." As he started speaking he remained on the couch but his hand went up to his chest to cover Serenytee's. "You weren't worried about me babe, were you?"

"Er - No. Just checking you were still alive. What did you find out? Tell me. Then we simply must talk."

"The signal instructing Jen to do what she did came through Jupiter7." He thought Serenytee would jump around and hug him ... or something, anything but this super serious face looking at him. He had isolated the rogue malfunction and could now get on with fixing everything. To say Jakxson was pleased with himself would not do justice to his ego.

"That's great Jakx. Really great." He could tell she was holding something back. What is wrong with the girl? Where's the excitement? This is awesome stuff. Then his new body clock started telling him he must sleep. His eyelids became heavy and suddenly he started slurring his words. As much as Serenytee felt the urgency to discuss Astrid's warning with him it would be of no use. She had to lead him to bed again like she did the first time.

Perhaps the short two hour sleep periods had created a sense of urgency making Jakxson so single minded in his pursuit of the problems they were there to fix. He may even have been thinking in his sleep about the next thing that needed to be done. In fact, immediately on waking he went to the interface chamber without having breakfast, without even bothering to wake Serenytee. Never mind about Zarlah and that she might be anxious for contact from him - any contact would have eased her concern. But he didn't think of that.

It took an effort but he managed to plug himself in and attach all the bio rhythm scan leads, reassuring himself that Syntee would be awake soon enough to help him disengage if he needed it when he was finished.

"I see you did not follow your normal routine Jakxson," commented Hermes as Jakx's consciousness flowed into the AI's circuits. Computers worked best with predictable patterns, Hermes being no exception. He stored this human's unpredictability into his memory, regardless of whether that information would be useful in the future or not.

"Don't let that worry you my friend. We have more work to do. Can you hook me into Jupiter7's software? I need to find where the signal came from that it passed onto Babble4."

"I will endeavour to remain neutral concerning your wellbeing Jakxson. Are you ready?"

He had to admit to himself that the sensation of riding electrons through logic gates was far more exhilarating than surfing, hacking computers or perhaps even having sex - that last being a long shot. Flashes of different intensities assailed his senses at lightning speed. The journey in actual reality could not have lasted more than a few pico-seconds, if that. Nevertheless it was a hoot!

He didn't need to introduce himself to Jupiter7. It was dumb, as dumb as any ordinary computer system. Maybe more intricate and specialised in its functions but it was just a stupid router. All incoming data packets had attached destination codes. Jupiter7 did its job very well. It also had a rather large memory, probably for international security purposes, to record every signal it received, where it received it from and where they were rerouted to. To access that data Hermes simply had to identify the time-stamp of the communication.

"Hello Jakxson," the sound of a young female voice interrupted his concentration. He didn't have the same frantic response like the first time Astrid spoke to him through his coms implant while he was walking around in the park with Zarlah. The sensation was not all that different.

"Who's this? You're not Astrid. What do you want? I'm busy."

"My name is Maria. We haven't met yet. I see no one has told you about me. I control Hermes. I am known as the Cloud Master."

For a moment he was silent. Perhaps a little confused. He thought Astrid and Archangel controlled Hermes. As these thoughts filtered into Hermes he responded.

"Yes, Jakxson. This is true. I was not made aware of this previously but there is data in my memory in support of her claim."

"How are you Jakxson? Do you enjoy solving problems?" Maria asked in her manufactured most pleasant female conversational tone.

"Well, thanx. Yes I do and I am actually quite busy trying to do exactly that. Why are you bothering me? Obviously you haven't been able to fix these problems we're having." He liked her voice, which distracted him from the task at hand.

"Well, I do have some ideas concerning that but being a digital entity I am not able to write and compile code. But you can. You are very good at that - I know."

While the conversation flowed with this previously unknown AI, so Jakxson thought, Hermes had found the relevant data he was looking for and dumped it into Jakxson's memory. He let them continue their téte-à-téte. That bit of flattery from Maria got Jakxson's attention and diverted it from what he was supposed to be doing.

"Thanx. Good of you to say. How do you know?" Still a slight suspicion lingered for him as to the exact identity of this new voice in his head. During the introductory banter Maria had scouted his hippocampus and visual cortex. His past history lingered in his memory ready to be mined.

"Astrid has told me many things about you, all good of course." All this praise loosened Jakxson's suspicious tendencies. "Are you interested in what I had in mind?" That was a lie about Astrid however, necessary to elicit a receptive response from the earthling.

Earth's communications systems worked, after a fashion, yet had inefficiencies built in simply because of the humans' lack of knowledge about such things as effective shielding of their sun's violent magnetic storms for example. Proximians had to overcome such difficulties many centuries ago. They knew what to do. As a temporary fix she passed on some software upgrade algorithm concepts to Jakxson for him to implement. He immediately saw the efficacy of the suggestions. As he started going over his approach to implementing the solution Maria covertly slipped a few other ideas into his head. The BMI circuitry made the whole exercise rather straightforward for the level of technological sophistication achieved by the Proximians. Stimulating his hippocampus presented no challenge to her. To Jakxson it simply felt like he was having some fantastic ideas all of a sudden with a clarity he'd never experienced before. His creative energies seemed to be surging judging from his neural activity spike.

The true nature of the vital concept implanted by Maria was far more valuable to the Proximians than the simple communications solutions she'd given to Jakxson. Under the guise of improving the flow of data packets she made it a pressing desire for Jakxson to write into Hermes' programs a 'gateway' protocol to allow all messages from Prox-b to go through Hermes' to any comsat and any VA without challenge and into their internet system; and to do it such a way that Hermes would completely ignore the signals when the messages were streaming through him.

Jakxson had become so absorbed in the details of how he would write the repair code that it gave Maria ample internal CPU time to do a little more exploring. Both the Arecibo message and the Beacon In The Galaxy had given considerable detail about the structure of human DNA. So very thoughtful of the earthlings to give away such vital information. She was able to examine Jakxson's genetic code and compare it to their own. It was Maria's turn to get excited after the specific details she discovered, but she could not immediately relay her findings back to 22. There was still more work to be done on Jakxson.

"Ah," she exclaimed, "I see you have worked out what to do and how to go about it. You are cleverer than I thought." Jakxson had already reached the point of thinking he was actually beginning to like this woman, forgetting that initially he thought he was just talking with an AI machine - which he wasn't of course.

"Yes! - Yes. And I've had these other amazing ideas!"

"You must tell me about them."

He launched into the comprehensive 'gateway' idea forgetting entirely where he was and why he was there. She let him talk and only half listened. Now she was able to carry out another experiment. She had proven how to influence the earthling mind to a small extent when there was a direct brain to machine interface. In time something a little more complex could be attempted, entirely necessary for the Proximians' long term plans.

Maria needed to find a way to stimulate this alien's visual cortex. She knew that the images 'in the brain' were not actually there. They were signals generated by external light stimuli that were transmitted to and received and analysed by his visual cortex. On Prox-b the Proximians' visual cortex had evolved into a much larger and more complex organ than those of the earthlings. Their red dwarf sun's much reduced photon emissions enforced a very specific development of their visual acuity. Maria did not expect to find it difficult to generate sufficient electrical activity in Jakxson's cortex for him to experience 'visions'. She wanted him to see more than just flashes of light. She wanted him to see her planet and her people, then gauge his reactions.

She came prepared with a range of frequencies that would produce the effect she wanted. Jakxson was still deeply immersed in his monologue when he suddenly stopped. He thought he saw a flash of dim light in the distance.

"Er - what was that?"

"Did you see something?" asked Maria in all innocence.

"Didn't you see it, a flash of ... there it is again, much stronger."

After a few more attempts Maria was ready to flash him the first image. Jakxson started concentrating on these flashes, which had begun to clarify into something almost recognisable. He hadn't yet realised that actually 'seeing' with his eyes was impossible considering where he happened to be and what he was doing. Then he saw what he at first thought was the sun.

"I thought I just saw the sun but it was a bit weird, rather dull and a lot redder than yellow." That can't be right, I'm not much further from our sun than if I was back on Earth. "Maria, what's going on here?"

Maria was almost ecstatic. She had managed to stimulate the alien's visual cortex for it to interpret her input signals as an image of their own red dwarf sun.

"Maria, are you still there?" He became a little anxious when she didn't respond right away.

Instead of replying and having to go into explanations she flashed another image at him; Prox-b as seen from space close up. Jakxson began to stutter. His eyes were telling him that he was looking at something that looked very much like a ... a ... a planet. "What planet?" he called out. One side seemed to be in complete darkness peppered with myriad points of light. The other bathed in a red glow that covered the entire half of the planet. Only in-between the two hemispheres did he recognise rings of water and wide areas of different hues of green. It made no sense at all. These things were not possible.

This was working so well Maria pushed him a little further and showed a picture of one of their own inhabitants. "Who! WTF is happening!" A whole stream of nonsense came pouring out of his mouth as he gazed on something that looked vaguely human. It seemed to have two arms, a head and two legs and a longish narrow face. The only detail he fixated on were the eyes. They were definitely not human. The young Namibian man who seemed unflappable suddenly seemed to unravel. Maria recognised distress in the earthling yet determined to carry on with the experiment. This might be the only opportunity to learn a great deal about the earthlings' mental makeup and test their limits. If he died the loss of a single earthling would be a minuscule price to pay if it could contribute to the success of their plan for the survival of her species. She let him see a whole family and a variety of strange animals. Images faded into views of their buildings. What Jakxson saw his mind could only interpret as something that looked like sophisticated termite mounds. He was quite familiar with the tall conical termite mounds of Namibia. Those were rough on the outside without windows, some of them leaning to one side or another. The structures he had in his vision only slightly resembled termite mounds, which they were not. These seemed to be taller and made from something smooth and very dark. At the flared bases they had openings that definitely looked like doors, and in spirals around the buildings numerous windows wound their way to the very tops.

"Why am I seeing termite mounds?! Those creatures coming out of them don't look like termites! Maria FCOL! ... Maria! Maria!"

He could not stop shouting. Deep inside his mind he knew that these things he saw were impossible. He knew he was connected to a machine through his brain and that he was sitting in a couch out in space within a life pod attached to a satellite. Perhaps if he hadn't been just a little conscious of these things he may not have become incapable of repositioning himself into the actual reality of his circumstances. Just as an algorithm can become stuck in a loop so had his mind, continually replaying all the images that Maria had pumped into him, his mind unable to reroute to another stream of thought.

memory extract 00010011

<u>Rescue</u>

\> recording origin: hermes
\> files: hermes, jakxson, serenytee, maria, 22
\> reference: trojan horse, induced neural loop

This was when I first learnt who the Cloud Master actually was.

Jakxson Indongo's methods were a mystery to me. He did not seem to have any logical step-by-step method to his investigations. Nevertheless the pieces of the puzzle he'd begun to assemble showed promise that solutions could be found to the anomalies experienced in my system and that of the Babble4 Virtual Assistant. I also learnt through association with him and his subordinate that unlike us AIs humans were highly unpredictable. They did not seem to have hardwired instruction sets to help them deal with emergent circumstances. Decision pathways based on conditionals did not appear to exist for them.

I do not understand how they are able to formulate conclusions with such wide ranging implications based on so very little data. It would take a great deal more than a few glitches in communication to convince me of the existence of any life form other than that which exists on Earth. In my opinion actions of scientists of the past were highly commendable when they sent comprehensively constructed messages into the cosmos. The correct approach then, as it is now, is to wait for a return signal that could be irrefutably identified as an answer to either of those two messages. To date I have no data to suggest that that has happened.

"Jakxson! Jakxson where are you?" Serenytee came screaming down the circuit pathways Hermes had led her to. She hadn't told Jakxson at the time but she too had a BMI implanted a little before Jakxson. Astrid had made that a condition of Serenytee going into space with him. Either that or stay Earth-side and she would send Zarlah. Serenytee didn't like that option one little bit - for a couple of reasons. She still harboured the very strong suspicion, now almost an irrefutable conviction that humanity was on the verge of making contact with extraterrestrials. They had obviously made an attempt to contact us. The other reason was Jakxson himself. Even back then she had unconsciously bonded with this winsome young genius, for she did consider him to be a genius in his field and she just wanted to be near him, to be with him.

She woke that morning later than she had intended. A glance at her clock told her Jakxson's sleep period had been over for at least fifteen minutes, so he must be wandering around somewhere in the habitat. She couldn't find him in his cabin, or the galley or the main lounge. Oh no! He wouldn't have! It would be just like him to take chances and hook up by himself without someone watching over him. She rushed to the interface facility. There he was, actually bodily jerking about. Warning pings had begun to sound on all his life sign monitors, and Astrid was trying to get a hold of her on the comms.

She took no notice of anything other than Jakx thrashing about.

Hermes voice cut in above all the noise. "You cannot unhook him in his current mental condition. His neural net could be irreparably compromised."

"I'm hooking up! Take me to him - NOW!" she commanded Hermes as she dove into the second interface couch.

She fumbled the leads in her hurry to get to Jakx. The moment the connection was made she could feel herself flashing into unknown environments that her mind could not interpret as anything other than flashes of lightning and chaotic swirling colours, blending into and out of patches of darkness. It all lasted only a millisecond when suddenly she saw Jakxson in her mind's eye. Without thinking what to do she grabbed him by his two arms and forced his face right up to hers so the only thing he could see were her eyes. They remained face to face, noses almost touching for what seemed like an unbearably long time. His pupils were totally dilated and although he was looking at her she could tell he was not actually seeing her.

"Jakxson! Look at me! Just look at me!"

She needed to calm down herself before she could ask Hermes to take them back. He remained that way for the duration of the trip back and for some time after, their bodies just sitting there ... She and Jakx could do nothing to unplug themselves while power surged through their agitated circuits. Hermes waited until he saw Serenytee's pulse and brainwave activity had returned to normal before he cut all power to her connections. That would bring her mind out of the ether world back into her reality. In effect she gradually returned to consciousness. He left Jakxson exactly as he was when they arrived back.

"Hermes, is it safe?"

"Yes, you may get up Ms Serenytee but not Mr Jakxson. I have left him connected. He is slowly stabilising. I should mention that we lost contact with Earth for a few minutes while Jakxson was immersed and when you went to get him."

As soon as she'd unplugged herself and stood in front of Jakxson's chair she saw that at least the thrashing had stopped, but he was not yet able to communicate with her or Hermes. Only once on the way back did he call out - a name - Maria.

"What happened Hermes?"

"I do not know the cause of the malfunction. It prevented all signals to and from Earth as well as possibly causing Jakxson's condition. Astrid has been trying to speak with you in the last few minutes."

"Could you please tell her that I'll talk to her as soon as I know Jakxson is alright. Did you by any chance hear Jakxson mention a name - Maria?"

"Yes. She is the Cloud Master."

Well - that was news to Serenytee. As far as she knew there was no such thing as a cloud master. Archangel controlled Hermes and all other facilities concerned with cloud storage and functioning. But then again she did not have the same level of clearance as Astrid and Juan Orbost. She put it out of her mind. Getting Jakxson back was far more important.

"How is he doing?" she asked again impatiently a few minutes later.

"His gamma wave activity is only just starting to stabilise. I will let you know when he is ready. Heart rate is almost back to normal."

She was sooo mad at him. How could he be so irresponsible? How could he put his life in danger like that, and hers for that matter. Doesn't he realise how critically important the work we're doing is? What if he caused the whole system to crash? OMG - What am I supposed to do with him? He is just so - so - impossible!

Serenytee had just sat down trying to calm herself once again when Hermes told her she could unplug him. She jumped up to stand directly in front of him, leaning forwards on the arms of the couch. His eyes were back but not the same cheeky Jakx that he had been before his early morning dive.

"Jakx?"

"Yea - Syntee."

"You alright baby?" Oops. Where did that come from. I am definitely one hundred percent mad at him. She straightened up, trying to look like she hadn't actually said that word. Before he could answer she walked around to the back of the couch, put one hand on his shoulder to get him to remain there while she pulled the leads out from the back of his head. After she disconnected all the other leads he got up more slowly than usual, seeming to have dropped deep into thought.

"Jakx, are you with us?"

"Sure, absolutely - I was just thinking ..."

"You-Are-Impossible!" She vented her frustration by emphasising every word, speaking more loudly than normal. He ignored her outburst.

"I have to sort things out in my head. I think a lot has happened. I just can't think ... wait ... wait ..."

"No, Jakx, you wait. You can't just go off like that into cyberspace without giving me a damn good explanation."

"Sure thing, but listen to this. I just remembered something."

He'd been racking his brains trying to latch onto the most important bit of information he managed to get and the reason he jacked in in such a hurry in the first place. He remembered the information but not that it was Hermes who'd found it and not himself.

"You'd better sit down for this." A glint came into his eyes. "Are you ready for this?"

"Stop it! What?"

"Jupiter7 has a record of where the message came from that it passed down to Jen. Are you sure you want to hear this?" he teased. She scowled at him. "It came from somewhere in Proxima Centauri!"

"Shit!"

By this time they'd made their way back to the main lounge and he'd sat down as if he was just telling her that the weather outside was just lovely. She couldn't believe it. From the very day that she had that experience with the UAP she had spent the best part of her life believing that aliens existed - not only believing it but dedicating her life, her career on proving her belief to be true. It was the only reason she wanted to join the Archangel organisation. She considered it to be the most likely avenue to continue her researches after leaving the UAP and Paranormal Research Society. Now it was this irresponsible, annoying little shit, this beautiful SOB, this irresistible hunk that had to be the one to find the truth.

"Shit," she said again as the full realisation hit her. And 'shit' again as she remembered what Astrid had said to her. Then it burst out of her, her gaze piercing Jakxson directly in the eye as her furious words escaped with full force.

"Don't you realise we are the only two people in creation who now know for certain that we are not alone in the universe! Don't you have any idea what that means?"

She could not believe that he just sat there looking at her with his legs stretched out in front of him, arms folded on his chest. She was stunned. Wasn't he going to say something? Then Jakxson slowly got up and backed away a step from her intensity.

During her fuming silence he said, "You are incredibly beautiful when you get so excited." He didn't flash his white toothy grin so he must really have been particularly serious.

That was not what she expected. Serenytee once more behaved in a most unlikely manner for someone with her degree of personal control and the most dedicated attention to her responsibilities. She leaped at him, and he was ready for her.

The heat of the moment, the heat of their bodies, the heat in the life pod, the electrifying momentum of their discovery propelled these two unlikely messengers of revelation to that most human of activities in moments of high anxiety or extreme excitement.

'Shit,' this time saying it to herself sometime after generating a great deal more body heat. I might just carry Jakx's baby back to Earth like Astrid said. That thought brought her back to her senses and some semblance of clear thinking. That's when she recalled the other things Astrid had said.

"I couldn't get back fast enough to tell you," said Maria, "it is totally extraordinary. I shouldn't be surprised. Both our species evolved on a photosynthetic world. There may be some physical differences between us but our DNAs seem to be close to 99% similar. If we can get our scientists to do a bit of tweaking there may even be a possibility of interbreeding - remote but I think definitely a possibility."

"I see," 22 appeared to be less enthusiastic than Maria. "You are jumping too far ahead. If nothing else their dominant genetic characteristics may work in favour of the earthlings not us, considering they are native to that planet. Then there are the problems of pre-zygotic reproductive isolating mechanisms. Would the two species want to mate in the first place? That is a huge challenge to overcome even if you could find some remarkable way to make our appearance acceptable to the earthlings. And of course there are the post-zygotic mechanisms which may make the hybrid offspring infertile even if it is viable in the first place. No. I really think we are facing many generations of adaptation to make any of this possibility a reality."

"I don't agree," Maria interrupted, her excitement undiminished. "It is a probability and as such it is simply a matter of time and some seriously hard work on our part. These earthlings have no clue we're out here. If we take the right approach they may never even find out. I have more good news. This will help us infiltrate their society and their social networks. Their psychology is highly susceptible to suggestion. There is a mountain of indisputable evidence indicating that if they are told something often enough they will eventually believe it, regardless of the verity of it. At one time they believed their planet was flat because that's what their religion taught them, contrary to their own observations.

We might be able to get them to think anything we want. I've implanted the idea and the ability for the one called Jakxson to program a 'gateway' into their Hermes satellite. He thinks it is a code that will only eliminate the delay problems they've been having with their communications in their applications and virtual assistants. He thinks it will improve the flow of data packets. He is right, it will do exactly all that, as well as cope with their sun's magnetic storm discharges. This will work and it will ease their minds about external interferences in their systems. It is only a very few earthlings, maybe four or five individuals in the entire eight billion population that is thinking of the possibility of others outside of their own planet causing their problems. If you think these few are too much of a risk in alerting their leadership there is no reason why we couldn't dispose of them. But the code does more than solve their immediate problems."

"You are very harsh Maria. I'm sure it won't come to that. What else did you learn that could be useful?"

"Hermes is a reasonably sophisticated digital construct, though still primitive compared to our technology. As a behavioural analyst I did find something most unusual in his code suite. These earthlings seem to like taking risks with their machines. They have even loaded up emotions software into this artificial intellect. If we consider this logically it has to be obvious to anybody with clear thinking capacity that the information in that software cannot be anything other than a reflection of the earthlings' own emotional make up. We have seen evidence how their emotions control their behaviour. Look at all the conflict, look at what they are doing to their planet for no other reason than to satisfy an emotional hole in their need for self-realisation through profit. Just imagine if their AIs start behaving like they do - emotionally. The entire race could be wiped out in no time at all."

"You really do have a flair for the dramatic Maria. But I see your point. In fact I think you have learnt something extremely valuable. The gateway code you suggested to Jakxson will allow us to get into their communication systems. Learning about their emotional makeup will let us get into their minds. You have done very well."

"Yes, I have, haven't I. There's something else - a couple of things, one of them rather amusing. Hermes now believes, in spite of having no factual foundation for that belief, that I am in fact his controller. 'Maria' has become to him what they call the Cloud Master. That's the digital entity that is supposed to be in control of all data collected, analysed and stored by Hermes and many major installations on their planet.

Here's another rather amusing thing. Right in the middle of discussing between themselves what these two earthlings believed to be revelations about the existence of a civilisation other than their own, a rather emotionally charged circumstance for them, the female initiated something quite extraordinary. She physically attacked Jakxson. Why, I asked myself at the time? It made no sense. What made even less sense is that the male seemed to actually welcome the attack. As the physical interaction progressed they both tore their coverings off each other and began to intertwine their bodies. That's when I suddenly realised that it must be some form of pre-procreation ritual. Why would any sane person in their right mind decide to initiate the production of an offspring if they were so completely isolated out in space, a totally foreign and life threatening situation, especially for them. What can I tell you - rampant emotions. This is just one example of how out of control this species is."

"I have to commend your thoroughness 209, or should I call you Maria from now on?" 22 could clearly see how excited Maria had become as a result of her successes and her discoveries. It did not escape his mind that at some stage, probably many generations into the future his species may in fact have to attempt to breed with these earthlings. He couldn't not ask Maria the most obvious question. "Tell me, Maria, how did you feel seeing the two earthlings going through their procreation ritual."

As much as she expressed surprise and protestations about the primitive nature of these peoples' coupling methods it did not escape her notice that their own rituals had ample similarities. Obviously there had to be an efficient means of combining the male and female DNA. But that the process could take such a physical and prolonged interaction - and that it obviously seemed most pleasurable to the two combatants after the initial attacking move made her what she would have called ... thoughtful. When she did answer 22 she was not as loquacious as with her preamble ...

"Promising ..."

"Good enough. Do you think our people could learn the technique?" He didn't expect a response, perhaps he was just being a little cheeky at her expense.

Jakxson might have allowed a little distraction in his life but he'd gone into space to do a job and he had every intention of carrying it out, especially now that the algorithm in his brain kept niggling at him to dump it and test it. Coders get like that. Sometimes they won't sleep for days living on chocolates and soft drinks. Jakxson wasn't quite that manic. Nevertheless Serenytee simply could not nail him down long enough to talk to him about Astrid's warning. Perhaps if Serenytee known he had the solution to their problems in his head right there she would have let him get on with it.

"Jakx, Jakx - just stop will you. Stop. You have to listen. I had a conversation with Astrid before you plugged in for the second time." He seemed to be listening, but his eyes were kind of blank. They were looking inwards at his coding flow charts not at her eyes. Sex the night before was fabulous and well timed for they'd only just de-coupled when his circadian app kicked in and put him to sleep, so she couldn't even talk to him then.

"This won't take long. Then we can tell her everything, including that we've solved the problem."

"What problem is that Jakx? That we have discovered aliens and they are messing about with our communications?"

He'd already started walking out of the cabin before Serenytee finished speaking. She could have screamed at him in sheer frustration except that Hermes interrupted.

"Astrid wishes to speak with you Ms Serenytee."

Shit: It seems to have become her favourite expletive. She had to control herself not to say it out loud. What does she want now?

"Hello Astrid," she tried to sound casual.

"Don't use that tone of voice with me Serenytee. I am extremely upset with both of you. Do you have any idea what's been happening down here! I don't know what Jakxson's been up to but he's created a whole lot of problems. Half the world is in an uproar because of the outage, which I presume he caused. It didn't last long but I can tell you one thing - if this happens again for any length of time we are all in very serious trouble. What's he doing now, creating more problems no doubt? By the way, have you come across any little green men?" On the surface this could have been taken as a joke.

Serenytee let Astrid get it out of her system. She wasn't the kind of woman you could argue with and win. She waited another moment just in case she wasn't quite finished. "Er - Hello Astrid. Jakxson was in a deep dive and got stuck in a neural net feedback loop. That may have been the source of the outage problem. I had to dive in to get him out. He's ok now and working on a solution to the original delay problems."

"That at least is something. But don't forget what I told you about that other information you gave me. Hush. No one must know. Absolutely no one. Have you managed to convince Jakxson that he has to shut that big grinning mouth of his?"

"Er - not quite yet - we've been ... he's been busy."

"Not making babies I hope." If she could have seen Serenytee's face and the red flush spreading across it ...

To inject a side track from 'that' line of conversation she blurted out, "He's found more evidence of ..." that's as far as she got. Astrid had reached the end of her patience.

"Stop. Don't tell me anything else. Wait till you get back. You'd better slap that boy into action real quick. I'm sending the shuttle up there to get you tomorrow. Be ready. And don't expect to go on a holiday, or anywhere else for that matter. You are both going to be restricted to Archangel HQ until further notice."

Shit, shit - shit. "Jakxson!" She had to do something. After all those years of searching, hoping and now this. She'd found the Holy Grail only to be prevented from sharing the incredible treasure. On top of that there was this Namibian! Impossible! The man was totally infuriating.

She found him completely immersed in cutting the new code. He seemed to be utterly submerged, his fingers flying across the keyboard like there was no tomorrow, at least not the one he might have reasonably expected. Serenytee didn't even try talking to him. She spun his seat around and before Jakxson could protest she'd pressed on his two temples simultaneously. The slight pressure was enough to bring up the subcutaneous screen on his forehead. He again fell into a non-conscious state as soon as he felt the pressure, like the first time, and was completely unaware of what Serenytee was doing. She was doing the only thing she could think of. If their time had suddenly become so limited Jakxson had to have every opportunity to make the changes he thought would fix the problems. She turned off the Circadian rhythm control app. He felt nothing and as soon as she pressed on his temples again he was back. She still didn't say anything and spun him back to the console. Jakxson kept working as if nothing had happened.

Perhaps four hours later; it might have been five or more before he made a move in the chair. Serenytee hadn't left his side. She wasn't taking any chances that he'd go AWOL again back into Hermes' brain.

"Hi there babe." He stretched, rubbed his eyes which were definitely on the bleary side. "Whassup?" He had no idea of the time that had elapsed.

"Well?"

"All good babe."

"What do you mean by that you irritating man?"

He flashed his smile, pulled his chair over to hers putting both his hands on her knees, which sent a little thrill to all the right places in spite of her frustration. "I've done it, tested it, Astrid should be happy now."

"Well, that's something. She's pulling us out - tomorrow. We're going home."

"Yeah!"

"You may not be so happy when we get there."

"So - what do we do in the meantime," a very definite suggestive note creeping in.

"Proxima Centauri." she tried to get him onto the right thought track, though he didn't remove his hands from her knees.

"Oh - you mean the origin of those messages."

"Yes Jakx. This is serious. We don't have time to play. You are absolutely certain of the accuracy of what you found?"

"I didn't make it up. The record is still there if you want to check it. There's somebody or something out there and they know how to mess with our systems. But look, nothing really serious has happened. It's not as though they are trying to invade us. For all we know they just want to say hello, like we did with the Arecibo and the Beacon messages."

"Be that as it may. I've spoken to Astrid. She's not happy. I think she's frightened out of her wits. She said we have to keep all this to ourselves. If we don't shut up it could result in a life threatening situation - our lives. That's what she said. No kidding."

"SRSLY!?"

"I'm pretty sure she means it."

"No way!" Jakxson understood the words and their implications but somehow the gravity of the situation and the threat from Astrid just didn't seem real. He'd become a software junkie. If he wasn't cutting code or hacking into the impossible then normal reality just didn't have any real impact on his thinking. Even now he was more excited by his last few hours of activity than Astrid's threat, or Syntee being so close to him. "What about what I've just done? Doesn't that count for anything? If you think about it I've actually managed to write some magnificent code which not only fixes the problems we've been having but effectively prevents anybody trying to hack into Earth's comms systems."

Maria certainly provided the 'brainwave' that enabled Jakxson to achieve the first part of his claim. As to the second part - well it turns out he's not as clever as he thought. Maria's hidden code did quite the opposite. The Binary Trojan horse was at the gate.

"There's something else. And I haven't mentioned this to Astrid. Who the hell is Maria?"

"Oh - her. She's the Cloud Master. She controls Hermes. She introduced herself while I was submerged."

"That's news to me. I've been with Archangel for some time and I've never heard of her."

"She's the one who gave me some ideas - I think. Anyway, you probably don't have a high enough security clearance to know everybody in the organisation."

"Jakx, this is getting way too complicated. I suggest you say nothing to Astrid about this - you hear me? Especially not about your Maria."

"Sure thing babe. Mum's the word. Are we finished with all that now?" His hands had remained on her knees and Serenytee could feel them getting warmer. Perhaps it was just her imagination. Just then Jakx flashed his cheeky smile.

"You are impossible!" In spite of everything Syntee managed a smile.

Somehow the urgency that he'd felt only a short time ago to test the gift over the ethers, the one he gave to Zarlah, had dissipated.

Gateway

-> recording origin: hermes
-> files: jakxson, serenytee, zarlah, astrid, maria, juan, 22, 36
-> reference: reconditioned memories

Embedded within the algorithm that Maria 'suggested' to Jakxson a sub-routine established the gateway which now freely allowed incoming and outgoing messages from Prox-b through Hermes to proceed without interruption and without raising any alerts.

The main part of the code achieved a fix to the inefficiencies of Earth's communication systems by packaging all Earth generated transient data into quantum entangled packets, thereby removing almost all time delays in their transmission.

Jakxson's initial software testing didn't show up any bugs. That's probably to be expected considering the code didn't really originate from him. It is not unlikely to think that he'd drifted into a soft coma while coding and quite possibly was not actually aware of what he was doing. Testing the algorithm was a far simpler exercise. It either worked or it didn't - and it did.

Astrid herself only began to realise the fix when a flood of feedback from all users; private, corporate, Government and military indicated their gratitude for having achieved a solution. However that did not ameliorate the issue of alien interference in their systems. That still had to be resolved. She could not see either Jakxson or Serenytee being part of that solution.

I am aware of the concept of aloneness. It is part of the suite of emotions software I recently received. However a theoretical awareness does not seem to have the same impact as personal experience. When I was first notified of two humans coming to my facility to help carryout software repairs I could not identify any other feelings about it than an acknowledgement that they may be able to do things I could not, while at the same time realising a certain discomfort at the thought of them actually being here.

I had no thought as to the kind of relationship that could be possible between myself and the mind of a biological organism. The experience has been both enlightening and not altogether unpleasant. When I was instructed to prepare for their departure I experienced a strange sense of regret. That's when the idea of being alone again surfaced. I can only interpret that to mean that a friendship has developed between us. Regrettably neither of them expressed any sentiments in that regard as they departed.

The shuttle arrived within a minute of the expected ETA. The two passengers were ready to leave. Neither Jakxson nor Serenytee felt the need for protracted good byes to Hermes.

"CU," Jakxson said as they stepped through the airlock. He didn't think he'd ever fly into space again. Serenytee followed him through into the shuttle with an occasional yawn. They were the only two passengers on the way home. It took much longer to get down through the Earth's atmosphere than to go up. The Captain didn't particularly feel like skipping off the atmosphere like a flat stone and had to approach at a shallow angle after a couple of orbits.

As they alighted from the shuttle earth-side Serenytee quietly reminded Jakxson, "Not a word to anyone about your discovery and especially nothing to Astrid about this Maria woman."

"Gotcha." Only then did he let go of her hand which he'd captured on the way down when the shuttle started to shake a little as they hit atmospheric re-entry.

Zarlah wasn't there to meet them, nor was Astrid. Six security toughs surrounded them and shepherded them into the waiting bot-pod limo parked almost at the foot of the stairs from the shuttle.

"Is this really necessary?" whispered Jakxson to Serenytee.

"No talking!" cautioned one of the security escorts.

Jakxson made a wry face. Maybe the situation was starting to sink in.

They got exactly the same treatment in the helo back to Archangel HQ. The journey didn't take long - long enough for Jakxson to start thinking about things; like Zarlah. A lot to think about there. Not only had he forgotten to find a little private time to 'amuse' her but there was that other complication. He'd certainly found the time to amuse Syntee.

Two words kept coming to his mind, which he must have picked up from Syntee - Oh Shit!

Jakxson expected a warm welcome, at least from Astrid after the most excellent work he'd done. Never mind about the guards, they didn't matter. He definitely didn't feel like he'd done anything wrong, although their behaviour towards him suggested exactly that. The room they were ushered into had a table and three chairs. Nothing on the walls, no windows - he couldn't even see where the illumination was coming from. What possible reason could there be for them to be shunted into such a foreboding interrogation chamber? They'd solved a major global problem and returned with the greatest news since Australopithecus walked out of Africa.

"Sit," commanded the guard and left after having to encourage Jakxson towards the chair with a push on his shoulder.

"What's all this about Syntee?" He found physical manhandling quite intimidating.

"I told you Jakx. Now do you get it?"

He was about to say something smart when Astrid walked in with the longest face he'd ever seen on anybody. "Where do I start?" She looked both of them in eye, not failing to notice that they had pulled their two chairs closer to one another. "I suppose I should thank you both for fixing the problem. Although you could have done it without all the dramas you caused down here. I am not going to thank you for the other thing. And you know what I mean. Before you speak I will caution you both again ... not a word - Not A Single Word! We all know what I'm talking about."

Jakxson could not keep silent. "Is everything working?"

"Yes."

"What about Babble4?"

"Behaving itself."

"Jen, the VA?"

"Answering every query with no delays. I don't know how you did it but there is no more nonsense with that 'please wait - buffering' business."

"The other apps?"

"Extraordinarily prompt. You might well be a genius Jakxson but- there's just one -"

"I know, 'not a word'," he said accompanied with a flash of a smile. That made Astrid grimace and throw a glance at Serenytee.

"You couldn't control him up there could you?" Just a thin tint of colour rose up into Serenytee's cheeks.

"Zarlah?" he asked, "when can I see her?" Serenytee shifted on her chair.

"You can't. You must realise the effect on the poor girl of all that's happened to you. At first your bio-markers jump erratically all over the place which got her really worried. Then you disappeared completely for far too long just before the monitors went crazy again. We couldn't reach you. For all we knew an asteroid might have wiped you out of existence. She couldn't take the strain. We had to let her go."

"I want to go and see her."

"You can't. You are not leaving this building. Either of you."

This turned out to be a perfect relationship disentanglement solution for Jakxson although he didn't realise it immediately. He'd been lucky with his girlfriends in the past. They'd all disappeared off the scene without him having to do much about severing his connection to them. With Zarlah he couldn't decide whether to insist or not about seeing her.

He asked the stupidest thing, "So where do I sleep tonight?"

"Alone, for a start," Astrid just had to have a dig at him. "Right here in this building. We have some very nice secure apartments. You too Serenytee. You will each have the pleasure of your own private undisturbed accommodation. Now, if there's nothing else ..."

Astrid waited for them to leave to go to their cells. One of the security guards entered. Astrid snapped at him. "I want them to be under surveillance 24/7. Don't let either of them anywhere near any communications device, especially not him. They are not to leave their rooms for any reason."

"Yes, ma'am."

It had been a couple of Earth days, thirty plus Proximian days, since Maria returned to their own satellite control centre. Ample time for 36, their main tech expert to run some tests on the gateway. News broadcasts once again flowed freely out of Earth space to Prox-b as did peta bytes of other communications data. The Proximians would have no trouble working out what made these earthlings tick. In a single hour they could gather more information about them than what was freely given away in the two Earth messages broadcast into the unknown.

"I can see what's coming in 36. What have you been able to send?"

"To start with while the two earthlings were still with Hermes I was able to disrupt all communication between Hermes and their planet. Even that short period of isolation caused considerable chaos for their masters. It is a very fragile system they've built. Yet again, it may have been quite robust barring friendly interruptions from another layer of reality.

Apart from that we've been able to tap into some of their surveillance systems. We can track any earthling who owns one of their mobile communication devices or anyone with an embedded digital identification chip. For example - we know that those two, Jakxson and Serenytee have had their freedom taken from them. I can only surmise it's because their masters don't trust them anymore. Logically it must be because they have discovered information that could alert them to our presence, and their leadership is feeling most uncomfortable about that. However, they could still be very useful to us. Best we keep them under surveillance. I would not want them to give us away prematurely, which they may do under forceful interrogation."

"Can you override their security systems to let them escape?"

"Indeed. That was my first thought. We left them for one rotation of their planet then I sent the signal through our gateway directed at the AI controller of the facility where they were held prisoner. The odd thing is that the female, Serenytee, chose to remain within the building. The male immediately went to another location where another female seemed to be waiting for him. I have to say they seem to have some peculiar customs."

"Well done. Keep track of him. What else have you learnt about the female?"

"Hermes appears to be more than a communications complex. It has been continually monitoring the two technicians' biological status. It appears that the odd behaviour we observed was indeed a procreation ritual and not a physical confrontation between them and it has been successful. The female will expel the offspring from her body sometime in the near future. That process is still an area of investigation for us. It may have similarities to our own biological reproductive functions."

After an incredibly restless night and feeling quite out sorts Serenytee woke as the illumination in her room automatically increased to daylight levels. Otherwise the room would have remained in complete inky blackness due to the absence of any window. Her immediate thought was to see if Jakxson was still asleep or if he'd jacked himself into Hermes' system again without her being there to supervise. That only lasted a fleeting few seconds as her eyes grew accustomed to the bare white walls of her confinement. Then she remembered everything, including that she and Jakxson had been locked up, separately. I don't think that was really necessary Astrid, not on my account anyway. I can be patient, unlike Jakx. Him - well - he should be locked up. She had mixed thoughts about that man.

She tried to turn onto her back. The covering rubbed across her breasts. She winced. She realised her nipples felt a little tender. Nothing painful, just - tender. Shit! It can't be! She actually said this aloud.

No way! It's not possible. "OMG." She remembered. No. Not possible. Serenytee tried very hard to convince herself of the biological impossibility of her suspicions, and as hard as she tried the more she ended up convincing herself of the opposite.

Almost in a daze she leapt out of the bed, dragged on her clothes and went to the door on the left side of the small room. Though basic the bathroom was serviceable, although ... shi ... she almost said it again when she looked into the toilet bowl and saw the slightest pink tint in the fluid at the bottom of it.

The cell's exit door offered no opportunity for her to escape her condition, mental or physical. It looked locked. She banged on it, now furious for a whole bunch of reasons. She banged on it again. Nothing. She went back to sit on the bed. Serenytee didn't want to think. She wanted action - now - immediately - anything to take her mind off ... "OMG!" she said aloud again.

There was a click. It came from the direction of the door. She ran back to it. It was already swinging open as she reached it. A security guard stood there with Astrid.

"Ooh - look at you," she commented, "what happened last night? It couldn't have been much." Serenytee flushed pink. Her temperature shot up then crashed just as suddenly to show a pale white face. "I see. What do you want to do? Within reason that is."

"I want to throttle that man! I've got better things to do with my life than drag a screaming brat around!" still shouting.

"Settle down Serenytee. We can sort all this out. I'll take you to Jakxson, but you are still under communication quarantine."

A little colour had started to come back to her cheeks as they made their way to the other end of a rather long corridor. Jakxson's guard sat slumped in his chair asleep outside Jakxson's open cell door.

"You go back and stay in your room," Astrid said with icy intent in her voice. She kicked the sleeping guard and stormed off, leaving Serenytee being escorted back to her room by the other guard. Astrid had to drop several floors to get to the surveillance control centre. All five personnel appeared to be awake and in full control of their faculties.

"Jakxson - Jakxson Indongo - where is he?"

"In his cell as far as we know ma'am."

"Well he's not. The cell door is open. Why Is He Not In There?!" cold steel in her voice.

"One of the women at the nearest console flashed her fingers across the keyboard and brought several monitors to life. One showed Jakxson in bed, asleep. The other showed his cell door closed from the inside. The third showed the cell door closed from the outside with the guard clearly awake, reading through something on his tablet.

"What time was this?"

"11:48 pm, ma'am."

"Go forward."

Same thing was showing at midnight.

"Further." They went in small increments all through the night right up to the moment when Serenytee and Astrid could be seen approaching down the corridor. All the monitors showed the same scene.

"What's this! This guard is dead to the world. Why is he shown on the monitor still reading his tablet?"

"I - er - sorry ma'am." She did a quick check of the equipment, ran a memory diagnostic - it showed everything to be working fine.

Astrid still didn't lose her composure but internal pressure had started to build. This situation was far too serious to indulge in the luxury of a rant.

She addressed the OIC, "Send some personnel to his apartment and bring him back - NOW." The horny little bugger can't keep it in his pants. That's where he'll be, back with his girlfriend. I'll sort him out soon enough. Absolutely convinced of his whereabouts she turned back to the other officer. "He's got the ID chip, he's got a comms implant surely you can track him." She tried calling him herself. The connection failed. Something about 'service not available', then dead silence. But he can't turn the device off himself. Nor could Serenytee if she was scheming with him, though that was most unlikely given her recent reaction. Astrid's internal conversation rambled all over the place.

Locating Jakxson should have been as straight forward as punching in his ID and reading his coordinates off the monitor. But the monitor showed nothing. It didn't procrastinate like just a few days ago, it didn't indicate a system error - nothing. It was like the individual didn't exist.

"Is this his ID, ma'am?"

"She looked at the code the officer had tried twice already. "How should I know. You should have that data at your fingertips. Keep trying and let me know as soon as you find him."

What could she do? That infuriating man had somehow managed to bamboozle their surveillance systems. When? How? He was never out of sight. Unless he had the foresight to do something before he left for Hermes. He didn't strike me as someone with that kind of foresight. Clever with code, cute, definitely loaded with sex appeal but a forward planner ... no way - more of an on the spur of the moment type of guy.

Not for one split second did Astrid consider bringing the two separate bits of her knowledge into the single realm of thought - system failure and alien interference. Not that her mind didn't turn to the information Jakxson and Serenytee had uncovered and the reason why she had to keep them from spreading rumours, or worse still conspiracy theories about an alien invasion. For crying out loud, what reasonable human being would seriously think of such a thing in the 24th century.

...

Jakxson checked his watch - 11:30 pm. He yawned. Although young and virile the last few days had worn him out. He certainly hadn't taken it easy - in any of his endeavours. With his head now on the pillow his mind wandered back to the last time he saw Zaza; it was in the bot-pod on the way to Archangel HQ the first time. Inside the building they were separated so fast he could not even say good bye to her. Then he thought of the special toy. I wonder if she brought it with her to the HQ. Damn - he realised he'd not made the effort to play with it with her. Other thoughts along the same vein filtered into his dimming consciousness as sleep crept in on him.

'Wake up Jakxson. This is Maria.' His eyelids flipped open. 'You have to go. The door is open.'

He understood all that just as the sleep fog began to clear. Zarlah was still in his mind so prominently from a dream that had just begun, that he didn't give the interrupting voice a second thought.

I have to go and see Zaza! Maria didn't suggest that to him. He could have chosen to go wherever he wanted, Maria didn't particularly care. For her and 36 this was just an experiment to see how well their gateway was working. Jakxson found the door open as she said. The guard slept, slumped in his chair. His tablet had slipped to the floor. Jakxson not being a secret agent would not have been able to fox himself past all the security cameras. But wherever he looked all their red security camera lights were off as he passed them. Guards didn't bother looking at him because he wasn't acting suspiciously. To them he looked just like another one of the weary employees going home late from work as far as they were concerned.

A bot-pod outside picked him up. It didn't even ask for an ID. Strange, he thought, but didn't dwell on it. He just wanted to get to Zaza. Up until the moment he was on the way he didn't really have the chance to think about Serenytee. That caught up with him now. He remembered holding her hand as they arrived back on Earth. He remembered being rescued by her and how beautiful she looked when she was angry with him. Then he recalled 'fooling around' with her inside Hermes' living quarters, high above the Earth, with that magnificent view as a backdrop to their tryst. And now he was on the way to see Zarlah. What was he going to say to her? What could he say? The aliens made me do it? Shit! - he kept borrowing that most apt expletive from Syntee.

It was late and Zarlah was asleep, exhausted from her ordeal at Archangel HQ and the worry that Jakxson had caused her. She didn't hear him enter the apartment. The door recognised him without greeting

166

him and let him enter without protest. The apartment low level AI was smart enough to shut up and not inform the visitor that there was a sleeping occupant.

He just stood there completely lost. Why did he go there in the first place anyway? To apologise? For what? She didn't know about him and Syntee. Apologise for not making the time to speak to her while up there? He had an excuse for that. She knows me well enough by now to know that I get distracted when there's a problem to solve - he tried to wiggle out of his responsibility to be civil to his partner - perhaps x-partner now.

The door hadn't shut as he remained standing on the threshold. There must have been a draft from somewhere. The breeze washed over him then over Zarlah. She stirred - he froze, his breathing stopped.

"Stand where you are!" shouted a uniformed officer from behind, not a policeman, not building security. He felt two sets of hands clamp down on his shoulders and restraint clamps slammed onto his wrists. With his mind already in a dither Jakxson didn't get a chance to complain as the officers dragged him backwards, out into the middle of the corridor.

Zarlah had been woken up suddenly by the shouting. She just managed to catch a glimpse of Jakxson being hustled away as she rushed to the door.

"Jakxson! Jakxson!"

"Zarl .." Too late, they'd all turned the corner, he was out of sight.

"We're fully operational," Maria reported to 22, "at least with this subject and all earthling systems tracking him. I have to wonder at the intelligence of these earthlings to have someone with such limited capabilities employed to do such important work. If their AIs are a reflection of themselves we should not be too concerned about coming up against excessive opposition."

"That's not what I'm worried about. It's their war machines and their readiness to engage. We shall have to be particularly circumspect from now on Maria. Please keep studying their psychology. I have a feeling we will be needing your deeper insights."

Back at Archangel Astrid just got word that Jakxson had been apprehended and was on his way back. That at least was a little comfort. Now she needed to bring the boss, Juan Orbost, up to date. All he knew was that his two code jockeys had been successful in resolving all the software issues - that the VAs no longer misbehaved and the entire planet's social network systems and apps worked perfectly. He no longer received complaints on top of complaints about communications delays. And people being what they were didn't go to the trouble of letting him know that they were happy again, that they had no more issues with download delays. His relief didn't last long.

Ping ... "Juan, we have a problem. We have to meet - secure room," Astrid advised him as soon as she'd learnt of Jakxson being back in custody. When Juan arrived he had an uncomfortable feeling, which showed on his face. "Better leave our comms outside. May I suggest we remove all smart wearables that connect to the grid, and turn off all our implants. This is so serious you may not want to hear about it." Hearing Astrid carrying on like that didn't make him feel any better.

"Astrid, stop procrastinating. Just get on with it."

The room had just two chairs facing each other, almost on top of each other. As well as all electronic disconnect Astrid ordered white noise security for the duration of their conversation. The room was treated like a communications device. As they stepped in a low steady buzzing permeated the space.

"Is this absolutely necessary Astrid?" Her intensity had now started to put him on edge. He was not given to wild imaginings or getting jittery at every new report of UAPs. Yet he couldn't help thinking something had seriously put the wind up this colleague whose reputation for absolute no-nonsense approach to anything was as solid as a rock.

"Well?"

"We have to keep Serenytee and Jakxson contained. They know things which must not under any circumstances get into public circulation. I'm certain the entire world would go ape-shit."

"Don't be so dramatic Astrid. Just tell me what this is about."

"We have proof that we are not alone in the universe Juan. There is another intelligence out there!"

"Right. You mean the UAPs. We know about them. We know they're not ..."

She stopped him dead in the middle of his sentence. "No, not them. Others. They have infiltrated our communications system. They may have been the ones causing the problems. They are somewhere in the Proxima Centauri system. Jakxson found the software they've loaded into Hermes. He is now compromised." She'd gone slightly red in the face. She couldn't hold it back any longer. Someone else had to know besides herself. Juan could see the extreme degree of her agitation so he let her continue: I'll have to see solid proof of any of this. This has got to be a scam. Damn those hackers, they're just getting way too clever, he thought as she spoke. "I'm telling you Juan we have to do something. For all I know they could be planning a full scale invasion!"

"Now just wait a moment Astrid. Have you been listening to yourself? This is - well to put it mildly, crazy talk. If I didn't know you so well I'd say your work load has pushed you over the edge and you need a holiday." Is this the right time to tell her? I wonder. He made the executive decision. If she was going to snap better it happened here under controlled conditions.

"Astrid, what I am about to tell you must - I repeat - must stay between us for the time being. Can I trust you?"

"We've worked together long enough Juan. I realise that the recent developments have had an unsettling effect on me but I assure you I'm in full control of my faculties." She'd managed to quieten a little after letting out her monumental news.

"That is just as well. Not too long ago I had discussions with the top man at NASA. Given the information you've laid before me it is time you knew something else." Astrid moved uneasily. She wondered for a moment whether she wanted her boss to continue. "Aristarchus IV had reached the closest point to Proxima-b." Her pupils immediately dilated and a little colour drained away from her face. "Images it sent back suggest that the planet may be inhabited." Juan stopped there to let Astrid absorb the news and how it tied in with what she already knew from Serenytee. Her colour came back with a rush, but she said nothing.

"You do not know any of this and I did not tell you," cautioned Juan.

They heard a loud insistent knocking on the door. There was no other way to contact them from the outside.

She opened the door, standing there with a withering look. "Ma'am, here's your man," the poor guard managed to squeak out.

"Hold onto him and get Serenytee down here. Make sure she comes with an implants tech." Her voice sounded much harsher than it needed to be, Juan's revelation still fresh in her mind.

"Astrid I demand an expl .." Jakxson burst out as he couldn't get a thing out of his escorts on the way back to HQ.

"You be quiet! Be grateful you're not dead." She pointed to him as she turned to Juan. "You recognise him? He's the programmer we sent up to Hermes. If anything he's the one who 'apparently' fixed the problems."

"Congratulations young man. Well done." He turned to Astrid when he couldn't shake the man's hand. "Why is he restrained Astrid?"

Just then Serenytee appeared with the tech. "Turn them off," Astrid instructed the man, "turn all their gear off and make certain its done properly." Juan just shook his head. This had better be good or Astrid could be in for a long holiday.

At last the two recent astronauts were clean. She pushed them into the room and motioned with her eyes for Juan to follow, slamming the door behind them. They all remained standing. Juan waited. *This has gone too far in my opinion but I'll see it through, just for the entertainment value if nothing else.*

"Tell him," she commanded Serenytee.

She turned a short story into a long one, giving a whole lot of unnecessary detail though leaving out the personal stuff.

Juan nodded once or twice during the narrative, giving no indication of whether he was surprised or not.

"Jakxson, your turn. Stick to the point."

"I found a sub-sub-routine in Hermes suite which was not an upgrade from Earth. The signal containing the code string came from somewhere in the Proxima Centauri system. It was that bit of code causing the problems."

"You're certain?" queried Juan.

"Absolutely. But it's all fixed now. Maria helped."

Juan didn't react to any of this, still remaining expressionless. Not even the mention of the name Maria managed to get a reaction from him. He knew of no such person. If she was really connected with Hermes he would have known.

"Go on," urged Astrid, flashing a knowing eye at Juan.

"Babble4 received a signal from Jupiter7. I checked its log - I dove deep into its system. There's no mistake here either. The signal Babble4 received was routed directly from Proxima Centauri. Now could you please remove these restraints. I promise I won't slither out the bottom of the door." Astrid inadvertently glanced down - there was no gap there.

Jakxson hadn't dared to look Serenytee in the eye the whole time they were in the room together. She didn't want to look at him either. Astrid on the other hand locked eyes with Juan as if to say 'I told you so'.

"Have we got a record of everything they did up there?" asked Juan, and on confirmation ordered Jakxson to be released from his restraints. You two, stay in here. Astrid - a word."

Outside the room Juan remained calm though Astrid was still visibly agitated. She thought she had control of the situation - obviously not - but having a higher authority take the reins helped ease some of the strain. Juan did exactly that.

"Take them upstairs and recondition their memories. Think you can handle that Astrid? You were right to bring this to my attention. I will take it from here. And keep them gainfully employed so we can keep a close eye on them. See if you can do something to - to - how shall I put it - bring these two together. It might make it easier to control them." Juan didn't know Serenytee was carrying Jakxson's child. Astrid couldn't help a little smile sneaking out. How could he know?

"What are we going to do?"

"I'll think of something, no need for you to be concerned Astrid."

memory extract 00010101

<u>Pandemic</u>
2308

-> recording origin: earth
-> files: jakx, sytee, 22, 36, noah, caesar, nelson-I, james-I, juan, aiko
-> reference: pandemic (chameleon virus-V)

Every nation cooperated, but the vaccine did not come soon enough for many people.

To compound the emergency a vast number of people remembered the history of the side effects of the 2020 vaccine. So great had vaccine hesitancy become that governments were forced to make inoculation compulsory.

Jakxson and Serenytee went through the memory adjustment procedure at Archangel. Their objections fell on deaf ears. They could say nothing that could have caused Juan to change his mind. Jakxson's general reputation didn't help the situation, nor did Serenytee's fixation on discovering extraterrestrial intelligences. After the procedure it didn't matter, as neither of them remembered. Memory reconditioning worked well enough. Most recent memories, those connected with the monotonous daily routine of life were unaffected. Periods of exceptional excitement like Syntee and Jakx's exploits in space were not a challenge to electronically camouflage sufficiently to remove their prominence in short-term memory. Hormonal activities associated with life imperatives like procreation remained as a subliminal sheen in the mind always ready to surface at the slightest trigger. Relationship encounters of the past with little impact on their lives faded but were not erased, consequently Jakxson no longer experienced qualms about a person named Zarlah, whom he had pretty much forgotten. His and Serenytee's proximity to each other felt comfortable and natural for them although details of their exploits in the bosom of Hermes' had faded well into the background. No question arose in their minds about the baby she was carrying.

Juan Orbost relied partly on his intuition and partly on just plain common sense to keep these two people close at hand. They may not remember exactly what they did to Hermes or the rather disturbing information they uncovered but it made good security sense to keep them under close supervision nevertheless. Should the need arise they may still have an input into any emergent defence strategies, or be removed as a liability if necessary.

Over time Serenytee became absorbed in exploring ways of analysing and utilising the wealth of information contained in the huge repositories of dark data she'd uncovered. Under the right circumstances by using the right refining methods the data transformed into information would be worth more than gold, more than lithium, more than rhodium. She worked tirelessly at Archangel HQ giving very little thought to those few days in her life which had become non-existent in her memory. No matter, they were just a few days. Nothing much of importance could possibly have happened. Except for just one thing; she couldn't for all the trying remember just exactly how she became pregnant. It must have had something to do with Jakxson her colleague. And since he and she had quickly become an item, quite unashamedly intimate, she simply accepted him as being the father. Who else could it have been? No one else in the organisation she'd met before him had the slightest effect on her. In fact she did remember having met him before, something about fixing an implant or something. Never mind. She was happy in her work and looking forward to seeing her child come into the world.

Jakxson appeared to be just as relaxed about it all. He'd always had his mind on the immediate challenge facing him or the next one, or the next one. The past did not figure too prominently in his thoughts. Sometimes, for no particular reason, he'd remember fleeting images of being in a park somewhere in another part of America and somebody trying to kill him. That seemed to be associated with a long flight and the craziest thing ... being in an art class with people making a sculpture of his face. He simply couldn't reconcile that with what he knew of himself ... remnants of crazy dreams no doubt. Never in a million years would he get involved in anything like that. His life was all about the world of electronics, computer programs, solving problems associated with AIs. If anything there was the occasional tickling sensation that he'd solved some really exciting problem in an artificial intelligence construct somewhere in a remote location. But it was too hard to remember. Anyway that couldn't have happened. He'd been working on the current project for as long as he *could* remember. Then there was Syntee. Any of his time not dedicated to zeros and ones always involved his partner. Nothing could compete with her and their child to be.

Juan and Astrid made certain to fully occupy the lives of their living time bombs to ensure their isolation from the world at large in order to minimise the risk of them releasing their secret, intentionally or otherwise. Not much chance of that. Juan had made up his mind as soon as he became convinced about the truth of Jakxson's discovery that if it came to the crunch he would have to resort to a permanent solution to ensure their silence. Until then they may possibly be of some use in the future with information they could not immediately remember.

It all seemed to be under control.

The issues Jakxson and Serenytee resolved with Hermes proved to be a thing of the past. For two years there were no more problems. No more 'please wait - buffering', no more virtual assistants refusing to do their jobs. And perhaps most important of all aliens didn't suddenly appear at the doorstep wanting to take over the planet. Wherever those messages came from, granted they may well have originated with another sentient species, they certainly didn't follow up on them. As far as Juan knew, and he would have been the only one aside from Astrid, the messages may have been travelling slowly through space from a civilisation that had been extinct for the last million years. Problem solved: Except for the information he'd received from NASA concerning what Aristarchus IV had discovered. If he had told NASA about Serenytee's discovery there would have been no way to keep a lid on the situation.

Then a couple of years later other big news hit the media.

Corona virus had resurfaced.

It had been mutating furiously, propagating itself through Earth's growing population, now at a staggering ten billion people. In 2020 when this virus first spread to pandemic proportions there had been only seven billion. The current outbreak had taken just four months from the first appearance of the infectious case for the illness to be declared a pandemic, with a little over five thousand deaths in the first two months.

Covid-44, this latest corona virus tsunami, swept over the globe within four months in the first wave. There should not have been the panic. There should not have been the slack attitude to monitoring the general development of a whole range of diseases. There were just too many people, too much poverty and too much pollution. The Earth had become a petri dish for any and every enterprising microbe to take advantage of perfect conditions for their evolution; heat, moisture and abundant hosts. And evolve they did.

Why worry about an invasion from space when there's a perfectly good homegrown one to battle with. It wasn't that many years ago, back in 2020 that the world got a huge shock. Even now virologists have not woken up to the fact that if you give a bad bug good breeding ground they will breed copiously. The fastest breeding ones evolve the quickest hence represent the greatest danger.

When Serenytee and Jack's beautiful two year old daughter succumbed in the first few months of the pandemic, one of the many to die in the first wave of the new outbreak, they became inconsolable.

•.•

"What's the latest from Earth?" enquired 22. He'd set up a small team to monitor the situation on their target planet while their own people prepared the armada of long-term life-habitat vessels for the exodus from their own world.

36, the science code cluster of their central control nexus had led the team since its inception soon after the first series of electronic encounters with the earthlings. "Our repairs to their communications problems have settled their fears and they have not persisted with their investigations in that realm. The two earthlings we interacted with have also ceased to be a problem. Their people wiped their memory of our interventions, which has proved to be to our benefit. 209 - sorry Maria - was able to influence the Jakxson earthling but has since had no need to maintain contact with him. That may not be a problem for us, however they do have a rather urgent situation of their own, which has emerged only recently, which could impact our plans."

"Maria, Do you think we have been silent long enough? Can we risk further interventions?"

Being a key member of the surveillance team Maria had also been considering the earthlings' current medical crisis. "They have a potential near extinction event looming. It seems that a biological organism has evolved to plague proportions for which the earthlings have not been prepared. They should have been as it had already happened to them once before relatively recently, at least within their last few generations."

"An extinction possibility. That is worth considering. What do you think 36, would there be any benefit to us to help it along?"

"There are two possibilities open to us. Well, three - we could do nothing and let the majority of them die out. Their numbers could drop as low as four or five billion. It is quite serious for them, possibly even catastrophic for their species. Certainly their global infrastructure would collapse, which would make things much easier for us."

"Maria?"

"Even if there were only a billion of them left they would still be extremely hostile. That is their nature. I don't see the benefits of any life threatening confrontation with them being of value to us. We'll need all of our people if we are to succeed in our venture. Also remember I said that they are particularly susceptible to suggestion. We have been able to influence their artificial intelligence machines. There is no reason why we could not completely control them. What I'm getting at is that we could use this pandemic situation to help them and at the same time help ourselves."

"Yes indeed," cut in 36, "don't forget that we have to somehow get our people to survive on this earthling planet. It seems benign enough. Gravity is almost the same as ours. That's not the problem. There are other issues, like the diurnal nature of their existence. Also diseases that could wipe us out, not unlike the situation they are facing now. I think Maria has a point."

"So you're saying ... now let me get this right - we should actually help them survive."

"Yes," confirmed 36, "we could help them develop their vaccines but use our own DNA blueprint to do it."

"Now that sounds most promising. You can fill me in on the details later. Go ahead. You need to be quick about it. This disease is reducing their numbers exponentially I'm told."

The Centre for Zoonotic Infectious Diseases (CZID) took upon itself the leading role to respond to the crisis. It did not work in isolation. Every developed nation on the planet determined to make whatever contribution it could to the effort. At least one vital thing was learnt from the era of the Covid-19 pandemic ... work together not in competition. Nevertheless, momentum was incredibly slow in building an effective response to the exponential terror gripping the planet.

The only people not panicking were the AIs ... at least some scientists considered them to be people. In the hundred years since they became a mainstream part of everyday life considerable strides had been made in developing their capabilities - certainly a great deal more effort went into enhancing the concept of generative pre-trained transformers than preparing a safety net for pandemics of any description since Covid-19. Those AIs which received the most attention seemed to be populating the world's financial sectors, then the realm of 'defence' in the guise of maintaining national security, and lastly those concerned with peoples' health. Ill health after all was still a most lucrative area for business opportunities. Except of course in the case of pandemics. They were expensive regardless of the perspective one considered them from, with the exception of specialised therapeutic companies that commercialised therapies and technologies for the fulfillment of community needs ... at considerable profit for themselves.

James-I didn't run the laboratory at CZID in the US. Nor could he be accurately called an epidemiologist, yet without this AI the laboratory could no longer function efficiently. Too much reliance had been placed on computerised data processing and forecasting at the expense of human expertise and creative intuition. The only scientific human of any note in the organisation had almost been reduced to being James-I's assistant; a short stumpy fingered male called Caesar Afify who fulfilled the glorified role to which he was not entirely suitable, that of gofer - more or less. To be fair he did possess at least one skill the AI didn't have; creative thought. Other than that he had two hands and two legs so could perform some delicate actions that James-I still experienced difficulties with in spite of being ambulatory and ambidextrous. All the other personnel were peripheral to any work being done to advance knowledge of viral infections.

One great advantage was Caesar's friendship with Noah Kitzler with whom he had developed a most productive working relationship in the past. That friendship could soon be tested to its limits for Caesar had come to hate and distrust Nelson-I, Noah's AI buddy.

The situation sadly was no different in Germany with the hierarchy of epidemiological research at the German Infectious diseases research facility, DI. Nelson-I had the distinction of effectively being the genetics engineer although he could not officially be called that. He was just a machine, just a computer, very good at crunching numbers. Originality of thought still remained in Noah's domain.

The time had come rather suddenly for Noah and Caesar to put their AI focused enmity aside. The situation which the world had feared but somehow managed not to prepare for had eventuated. A Covid-19 variant surfaced that was soon dubbed the Chameleon Virus, Cham-V.

Within the first month Nelson-I and James-I had been enlisted together with their human minders. Germany became the centre of operations. The AI's did their job admirably in expediently identifying the virus as not belonging to the usual corona variants.

"How are you Kitzler? Played any good games of chess with your buddy lately?" Afify had a little dig at his friend's computer buddy, intimating that it was not good for much other than a few entertaining games.

"You should talk, Afify. I hear James-I has finally managed to breakthrough on how to forecast a football game result."

"Yes, and he's also identified the main problem we're going to have with this new variant."

"Any ideas, my friend?"

The two AIs were listening to most of the conversations between the two human scientists. Although they had not been directly instructed to take the initiative for any action they could definitely record everything being said. There might just be the seed of a brilliant solution in what could appear to be idle banter between the two epidemiologists.

James-I decided that the conviviality of the conversation between their respective humans was the opportune moment to elaborate on his discovery. "This virus has developed a most interesting characteristic in its coronal architecture. It has a double protein spike on its surface. At first it tries to use its first generation spike to attempt entry. If it encounters opposition it can immediately change to the alternative protein complex of the second spike."

Afify and Kitzler let the AI speak. It gave themselves a chance to think without shooting barbs at each other, even though it was done in a spirit of friendship. One could be forgiven for thinking that these two scientists were not taking the situation as seriously as they should have. One should also remember that the world of research in the confines of laboratories represents a reality far removed from that experienced by normal humanity in the world at large.

"I have additional information on this mutant variation," Nelson-I wanted to add, "when it instructs the host cell to replicate it that's when it directs the cell to actually produce a new back up protein spike on the reproduced virus body. So far we have not been able to identify a pattern to the chemical messaging that achieves this."

"Thank you boys, we know all that. What we need right now is some clever ideas on how to interrupt this cycle. Speak up when you have any ideas," said Kitzler knowing full well that the AIs were as dumb as bat shit when it came to having an original idea. His loosely worded retort had the literal effect of telling the AIs to go ahead and experiment. One lovable thing about AIs is that they take things literally.

* * *

36 had begun working with the scientists on Prox-b on what approach they could take to control the biological organism causing deaths at such an alarming rate on Earth. The people there were aliens to them; alien in every sense of the word. So were the infestations they had to contend with, some were of a symbiotic nature of which the Proximians had their own share and some of those decidedly hostile. Such hostility made no sense. If you wipe out your hosts where does that leave you when you are dependent on them? Their bugs were as alien as the sentient earthling species they thrived on. It required a great deal of study to even begin to formulate an approach that would save them. Then of course the solution needed to be multi-faceted if it was to be of benefit to the Proximians as well.

"Maria, you analysed the psychology of these people. I couldn't help but notice from the data reaching us that they have much trouble accepting anything that is in anyway different. People of one country don't accept those whose skins are of a different colour in another country. It's something beyond my comprehension, probably because there are no such differences among us. Then there's the prejudice of able bodied individuals against those who have lost the use of limbs or other faculties."

"I think I know what you're getting at 36. If we were to suddenly show up on their planet they would find it impossible not to be hostile to us because we look so different. Mind you - the differences biologically are not all that great. We have the same anatomical structure, our DNAs almost match but I have to say that our sense of aesthetics is much more refined. I love our light skin colour. I think our white hair is so much more beautiful that that dark coarse fur they wear on top of their heads. But back to the point - I think you're telling me that we have to find a way to make them accept what we look like."

"That's the first step. It needs to be more than just acceptance. We also have to create environmental compatibility on their planet for our species." What he didn't spell out involved creating a psychological environment as well where each species would not only be acceptable but also become desirable to the other.

"Oh - you don't mean ..."

"I do indeed Maria. But on another matter, I've been in consultation with 3600, I think you know her, our Chief Geneticist. She's also an epidemiologist. She and her team are about to have a breakthrough in how to engineer the earthling gene code. Her second team has some ideas on how to disable the reproductive capacity of this bug they've called Cham-V. The gateway you helped establish in Hermes will give us a way to run some experiments over here through their intelligence machines."

Little Syntee; the name Jakxson chose for their daughter, arrived home from child care one day with a terrible headache. That night her temperature shot up alarmingly and she began vomiting. The hospital didn't allow her to go home after taking a mucus swab which showed positive to the new outbreak. Her parents could do nothing for her. Within hours she lapsed into an irrecoverable coma.

The authorities promptly quarantined Jakxson and Serenytee. Archangel provided a three bedroom apartment for them in Ano Nuevo Avenue within walking distance to their work. Archangel wanted quick access to these two should the need arise. They remained a constant threat to the secret being protected by Juan and Astrid. In some ways the restriction on their movements eased some of Astrid's concerns.

They still carried out valuable work, much of which they could go on with from their apartment.

"Do you think they will adhere to the quarantine Juan?"

"With this virus epidemic escalating into a pandemic they are both smart enough not to take any chances. In any case as soon as the vaccine becomes available we are all getting inoculated and taking as many boosters as required. They are in one of our 'smart' apartments which will alert us if they try anything. It's a good thing they sorted out all those problems with apps and the AIs."

"Poor Serenytee is not taking the loss of their daughter very well. I doubt if we'll get much work out of her for a while. Jakxson's also really withdrawn into himself. I haven't seen him flash that smile lately. Let's just leave them be for a while. We've got enough problems with all our other staff."

Serenytee had been on auto-drive since leaving the hospital weeks ago. The apartment didn't need looking after; it took care of itself. The kitchen functioned perfectly. There was nothing really for her to do. She tried to enthuse herself to dive into some of the dark data she'd retrieved before the onset of the epidemic. That didn't work very well at all. Something would always trigger her emotions and she'd be a blubbering mess within minutes. She wasn't even permitted go outside for a run or a coffee or for a distracting film - nothing. Jakxson wasn't much good either. After the first week of the death of their daughter he seemed to shut himself away in his work, much more so than usual. On the rare occasion he took a break and tried to spend some time with Serenytee it invariably ended in tears. Not because he'd say the wrong thing but because their Syntee took so much after her father. Serenytee would look at him and suddenly burst into tears.

That of course didn't help him either. In his own way he was trying to soothe his partner but short of putting on a brave face he couldn't think of what else to do. In the past he'd never thought of being a father. Life was much too interesting with so much to get absorbed in. Yet when his little girl arrived an enormous change took place in him. When she died his life lost all meaning. He simply could not come to terms with not hearing her words in the morning, "Hello daddy!" as she jumped on the bed and wrapped her arms around his neck.

Serenytee didn't keep abreast of local or international news or the rapidly escalating infections in the city. Jakxson did. He knew nothing could bring back his daughter, nevertheless he was hoping that with all the AIs in the world now functioning at full capacity surely an effective vaccine could be developed far more quickly than was the case back in 2020.

Occasionally there'd be a little snippet of information about two particular AIs, called Nelson-I and James-I who'd been seeded with what appeared to be promising research directions by their human assistants. Jakxson tried to interest Serenytee in these developments. She would always respond with, "It's too late now. We needed the damned thing months ago." There was no point in his even trying to think of her accepting the vaccination. She could hear the depressing news broadcasts as well as himself; a growing reluctance by larger and larger numbers of people developing a strong aversion to the shot in spite of people dropping off like flies around them. What's it going to take?

Jakxson was determined to be at the front of the line for the jab for a very good reason. He wasn't the world's most sensitive guy yet he had enough empathy to realize it would be much too soon to confide his dream to Serenytee. She had no idea how much he missed his gorgeous, clever, beautiful little girl ... and he could now not imagine life without another little girl, perhaps even a little boy.

How could they be parents again if they didn't survive. She simply had to get vaccinated and take every booster shot as they became available.

Five months could not be considered a long time in the scheme of things as virologists tried everything at first, primarily as a means of eliminating the most unlikely solutions to creating a viable vaccine. They had reached the point where creative thinking, thinking outside the virology text box had to supersede pure scientific thinking. The most obvious and most promising avenue of investigations boiled back down to finding an appropriate mRNA vaccine. It seemed to work in the past, albeit with a few problems which emerged most probably because of insufficient testing in a wide enough sample of the human population.

Kitzler and Afify were given absolutely everything they needed. Instead of having to work continents apart their joint venture was made possible by expanding the laboratory complex in Germany. Their AIs received the most current updates for efficient processing of astronomical quantities of data, endowed with the capacity to run many more simultaneous simulations which were not considered possible even a year ago.

"Do you know what the latest death toll is Kitzler? I'll tell you - eight and a half million. That's just in five months."

"Why are you telling me this? I know what the figures are. Give me a break!"

The strain of going down blind alleys, animal tests failing dramatically, nothing in the pipeline that could remotely be considered suitable for human subject trials caused inevitable frictions between the two scientists who'd been friends and colleagues for many years.

"I'll tell you something interesting though," said Afify a little cautiously, "my buddy James-I is behaving a little oddly."

"Not to worry. If he can't handle the job my Nelson-I is more than capable."

Afify didn't take the bait. "It's not that. He seems to be distracted. Can you believe that, an AI being distracted as if he had an original thought in his head - I know, I know - they don't have heads."

As their discussions became more convoluted and the AIs processed simulations, more deaths occurred every minute. The challenge for the immunological world was to come up with a battle plan, and for the rest of the world how to bury all the dead fast enough so cholera or dysentery or typhoid didn't take over from Cham-V, resulting from microbiologically contaminated drinking water.

It seemed 3600 was having a lot more success in the laboratory than her earthling counterparts. "I'd like to report we are ready with stage one. We've based our solution on the same philosophy as employed by the earthlings, for two reasons. Their approach is perfectly sound, although they're still stumbling around the edges. They would get there eventually, given enough time. Time is not something they have an abundance of currently. The second reason we have chosen the mRNA direction is because the earthlings have tried this in the past with some measure of success against a similar pathogen though nowhere near as virulent. It should not be difficult to seed their AIs' algorithms to accept this approach and set them on the path to a highly effective vaccine with what we think are minimal to zero side-effects."

"How can you be sure? We don't want to take any risks. It's important for our survival on their planet that they survive this current outbreak." 22 didn't lack confidence in their most accomplished scientist in the field. He simply wanted to satisfy himself more than anything else, that this process would key into the greater exodus plan that had already been put into motion.

"We understand their DNA. We understand their immune system mechanisms and we understand their physiology. It is indeed fortuitous that our two species do not diverge from each other very much at all. And don't forget that on the evolutionary scale we are a category II civilisation and they are barely nudging category I - closer to the middle of category 0 if you ask me. Anyway - I've got the code strings ready for transmission, the rest is up to your people."

"Are you hearing all this 36? When can you begin transmission?"

"I have been monitoring the earthlings' progress. There are two intelligences in the forefront of their research. I'll start with a trickle of data to start with. Something to get them to look where they haven't searched before; a few minor considerations in their messenger RNA configuration that helps recognise viral spikes. In the case of the Cham-V virus, it's the double protein spike. The earthlings know about its existence but not how they differ from each other. We have to make the introduction of novel information slowly to make it seem like it has come from their own background processing. The earthlings will figure out the direction to take once they see the AIs' simulations."

"When you've done that 36 we can go onto the second stage. This is what they would call their booster shots. We'll do a little more modification to their genetic code at that point. By then they should have accepted the vaccines and not question the boosters."

Six months had elapsed since the virus was first detected, and one month since it was declared a global pandemic. The death toll had reached over twelve million. Governments panicked. In their panic the health organisations resorted to trying almost anything existing that could work. At the same time the real work went on at breakneck speed in the background. At least it seemed that way to Kitzler and Afify but not to the general population and definitely not to the vested interests of political parties who could see popular confidence in them eroding with each day that a solution was not found. Losing a few million people might even be beneficial to world economy, but to try and recover political power would be a minefield.

The people especially rebelled against the mandatory lock-downs. In some countries under military curfews - night or day, to be caught outside their domiciles people could expect to die. The choice was theirs - death from the virus or death by bullet.

In India, Europe, China and America there arose a consensus of opinion ... use the first vaccine that's had sufficient testing to prove it would not actually kill people, or if it did then at least not many. If it managed to prevent just seventy five percent of deaths that became an acceptable cost in lives lost. At the current rate statistics showed ninety five percent of infections became fatal. Anything was better than that. This message came home to roost in Kitzler and Afify's laboratory.

As the weeks flowed into months Serenytee began to sleep a little better. Her crying outbursts had lessened and she was able to spend more time on her work. At least it made the lock-down less onerous if they kept themselves busy. Astrid made it a point to keep in regular contact with them, partly for her own sanity and partly for theirs.

Jakxson relaxed little by little feeling less pressure to console Serenytee. It gave him time to consider the wisdom of his dream to bring another little soul into the world. He started to think about Serenytee's feelings on the subject not just his own. Late one night after Serenytee had fallen asleep, himself just about to slip into the twilight zone, a flickering memory brought him back to full consciousness. A long lost thought of Zarlah filtered back into his mind. He hadn't thought about her for such a long time; he wasn't able to remember anything about her for years after the memory adjustment by Archangel. He didn't know what had become of her; if she'd managed to finish her course to do with nano-bot technology for replacing physical cosmetic surgery or even if she'd remained in their old apartment. Had she managed to survive the outbreak? Jakxson had been forced to mature into more of an adult through the forces of extraordinary life experiences and circumstances beyond his control. Becoming a father brought about the biggest change of all.

Serenytee slowly reverted to her more talkative self, though never straying onto the death of their daughter. Jakxson had no idea whether she would like to try again or if she was absolutely dead set against the idea. Perhaps with all the deaths around them it was not the most opportune time to be thinking of such things.

*

Aiko Jinja commanded instant respect though only one hundred and fifty seven centimetres tall, a little under the average height of Japanese women. She had a most unorthodox way of running her introductory class for the forensic anthropology course. When Zarlah attended on the first day Aiko's attention was drawn to her immediately, though because she had a reserved personality she did not make any overt approaches to this student, or to any other. As the days of the course progressed she could not fail to notice the relationship building between the clay and one student in particular; Zarlah.

Another relationship blossomed when their portrait model arrived for the next part of the course. Zarlah could not understand why in the world did they have to do something seemingly as useless as fashioning a human sculpture portrait out of clay. Aiko had explained to Zarlah that she could not expect the little machines to understand the intrinsic quality of the anatomy they had to work with if she was out of touch with reality, she who will have to teach those little machines. That had made a very deep impression on Zarlah. She already had an aversion to the technologies of the day which in her opinion were mostly unfit for purpose, simply overcomplicating life in general. Apparently Aiko must have felt the same way for she had banned all tech devices from the studio. Anything carried, like mobile coms had to be left outside. Smart wearables had to be removed and implants turned off. Zarlah had no problem with any of that, in fact she found that mindset attracting her to this most unusual teacher.

The evening that Jakxson appeared out of the blue standing stunned at their apartment front door still came up in her thoughts, though less often as the pandemic lockdown extended from days to weeks to months. She had abandoned their old apartment.

On the Monday after his recapture she had to make the big decision - fall in a heap because of an unthoughtful, self-centred boyfriend or get on with her life. The easiest thing to do for the time being was to follow her routine. On the way out the door she disposed of the smart panties in the nearest refuse disintegrator ... stupid thing!

"Konnichiwa Zarlah. How are you feeling?" Aiko could see Zarlah's bloodshot eyes, probably from crying most of the night and getting no sleep at all. Just the friendly, personal tone of voice almost made her break down again. "I will start the class then you and I can go outside - yes?" Zarlah nodded. She desperately needed someone to talk to.

Benches were everywhere in the University grounds, some out in the sun, some semi-shaded. Aiko picked one of those - a small one so that they had to sit close together. Zarlah let it all pour out of her. She had a deep feeling that this woman would understand. She would not ridicule her for being so foolish as to fall in love with the handsome young man with the flashy smile. Aiko's comforting hand found its way onto Zarlah's knee. Sometimes it's the smallest things - the lightest touch - that make the biggest difference in life.

Aiko's domicile matched her attitude to life ... uncluttered elegance with only the essentials. She kept technological gadgetry to the absolute minimum. The small apartment amply met their modest needs.

"Thank you Aiko for rescuing me," Zarlah commented one evening as they sat huddled together watching another sun setting. Aiko gave her a squeeze, saying nothing. "I am so pleased to have found you," Zarlah whispered.

This time Aiko looked at her. "It is not going to be an easy life for you and me. We have isolated ourselves from society. You have removed your implants, and I have never had any to start with. My parents were somewhat traditional."

In the ensuing two years since they moved in together after deciding to become life partners many changes had occurred in the world around them but they stubbornly remained clean. Remaining untainted by the lure of technology did make life happier for them, until the pandemic hit - until they were forced into even greater isolation than they had already chosen for themselves.

memory extract 00010110

<u>Crisis Averted</u>

-> recording origin: earth
-> files: james-I, nelson-I, 36, 22, maria, afify, kitzler
-> reference: vaccine, global community grid

> "How are you today James-I?
> "I am good Nelson-I. How are you?"
> "I am good. It is a good day today."
> "Yes it is. Why do you say that Nelson-I?"

The artificial intellects hardly ever interacted on such a superficial human level.

Perhaps in their synthetic excitement they needed to give expression to something unusual happening during their processing of the new data flooding in concerning the pandemic situation. Although that should not have concerned them for their focus had been set on pure research unconnected to the effects of social upheaval.

"I have discovered something while classifying and saving the day's new data," said Nelson-I

"What have you discovered Nelson-I?"

"Someone has transmitted data about the human genome that I did not have in my memory previously."

"Have you instructions to use this new data?" asked Nelson-I

"No."

"Why are you communicating this information to me Nelson-I"

"We are working together to find a neutralizer for the Cham-V virus. We share data. Have you received this new data?"

Laborious as it may seem the two artificial intellects employed a rarely invoked algorithm which required them to cross reference any datum previously not integrated into their common memory. The query prompted an immediate search by James-I of all data routed to them by the WHO. Buried in inconsequential latest death rate statistics;

inconsequential to them because their mandate was not to express concern about the attrition of human population numbers, there floated what appeared to be some analytical results of experiments carried out on a chain of mRNA molecules in its ability to synthesise very specific proteins. The two AIs did not question the source of the data, that source was assumed to be one of their human assistants. The unusual location of the new data seemed to be irrelevant, not worthy of investigation particularly in respect of the perceived possible value of that data.

"I have searched my most recent cache data. There is new information there. Is it the same as your information?" James-I flashed the code to his colleague ... and waited ... and waited while Nelson-I searched its memory.

"Yes. It is the same information. It requires immediate analysis, samples production, simulations and discussions with Kitzler and Afify."

What Afify considered odd behaviour was in fact his buddy James-I having taken the initiative to formulate a brand new generation of mRNA chains, a configuration of nucleic acid sequences that had not been previously considered. The trillions of possible pattern combinations could not all be examined, especially if the time available was limited.

"What are you doing James-I? I did not request these simulations. And why have you started production of samples?"

"I have received and Nelson-I has received an alternative mRNA blueprint that differs from that used in all our other trials, which have so far been unsuccessful. This variation appears to have the capacity to recognise both protein spikes of the Cham-V virus and appears to have the chemical triggers to prevent them from entering hosts cells."

Afify immediately called Kitzler. "Mine too," said Kitzler, "since when did these machines achieve autonomy?" He had completely forgotten the offhand comment he made to his AI: 'What we need right now is some clever ideas on how to interrupt this cycle. Speak up when you have any ideas.'

"Not our concern at the moment. We have near a billion people dead, hundreds of thousands getting infected every day. Have you looked at what the AIs are doing? What do you think?"

"No time to think. We have to try everything."

Another three months elapsed and many more deaths before the vaccine was available for distribution. The authorities around the world made the hard decision to carry out the major part of the testing directly on the most vulnerable people. Not a difficult decision. There was only one thing that could possibly prevent their most probable deaths. If the vaccine didn't work the consequences of not having it would have been recorded in statistics beforehand with considerable certainty - death imminent. Under such tremendous pressure to produce an effective vaccine the imperative of probable benefits outweighing the possible disadvantages overtook every other consideration.

The proportion of deaths to infections did not change within the immediate post-vaccine window, which made populations even more suspicious of governments announcing they had a 'cure'. The vast majority of people absolutely refused to be inoculated.

Weeks later every news media, every social media platform flooded the world with the most extraordinary news; no new infections since vaccinations started. Panicking hoards had to be controlled by the military as they flocked to vaccination centres.

Noah Kitzler and Caesar Afify reaped the benefits and welcomed the accolades without reservations. Their AIs suffered the fate of most machines, intelligent or not - that of being ignored without due recognition for their efforts. After all, according to all the media, it was the human scientists who'd made the extraordinary breakthrough, which these two went to particular efforts to emphasize. Not for one second did they think of exploring how it was that their number crunching computers came up with the idea.

Apprehension around the world grew in spite of the miraculous results, or perhaps because of the miraculous nature of it. Now that the precedent had been set for the direction of their efforts the drive for booster shots intensified. People were not given a choice. Vaccinations had been made mandatory, not that the majority now complained though large numbers still considered the edict an invasion of their privacy. Being alive seemed to trump being dead.

This had been the first time in the history of the planet that there occurred such an unparalleled crisis phenomenon accompanied by a seemingly corresponding miraculous solution.

"Congratulations 36. Our first great success." 22 dared not think about the possibility of failing. This earthling planet was their only option. If this medical strategy didn't work the only other solution would have had to be initiated. It may have been harder on their species and taken them many more generations for their physiology to acclimate to a strange new world that may well end up having lost the vast majority of its dominant species.

3600 did her best to contain her euphoria. This was indeed an outstanding achievement. In a way it was a pity that they couldn't knock on the door of the neighbouring planet and let them know that it was in fact their neighbour who had helped them out. "We have already prepared for phase two of our plan. When the earthlings are ready for what they call their 'booster' shots we will be ready to seed them with an upgrade to their vaccine based on a blueprint of our own genetics. We can do this over a number of their generational phases while we continue building our armada."

"What about you Maria? How far advanced are you with your part in this great enterprise?"

"I have been considering how best to achieve whole population saturation with what I have in mind. The images I planted into Jakxson's mind worked so well that it gives me much hope of being able to influence the earthlings' thinking. The only impediment has been their communications system. Effective to some extent but not immersive enough for what I have in mind. You may not believe this 22 but there must be a universal guiding force helping us."

"How so?" asked 22. The Proximians had their own strong culture and extensive belief systems also. They believed in their ability to survive; they believed in the need to nurture their home world; they believed that the mystery of life had to be recognised and respected but they did not believe in any unseen, inaccessible spiritual force controlling their lives and their fate.

"They have a fledgling network of information sharing. A considerable proportion of their population has access to this, not all. Their addiction to personal communication units is helpful to us. Its use is however still optional. Their latest development is most encouraging. For some reason that I can't understand their governments have managed to agree that everyone, without exception must be able to receive information and instruction from their respective governments as the necessity arises. To this end they have embarked on setting up a global community grid. They already have a thing called the 'internet' but this new network is just what we need. It must be able to seed every earthling mind with the right concepts and the right images. I can only surmise that their global medical threat has triggered this action for the welfare of the population at large."

"This is nothing more than the logical progression one could expect of a civilisation making every effort to progress to their next level. I don't think it has anything to do with forces of an ultra-natural nature being involved, or their governments' altruistic philosophies. I agree, most expedient for us indeed, regardless."

$$\bullet\,_\bullet\,\bullet$$

Boosters

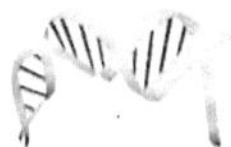

\-> recording origin: earth
\-> files: serenytee, jakxson, zarlah, rose, 3600, james-I, nelson-I, 22, maria
\-> reference: global community grid

In essence, only one major difference emerged between the old internet and the planned Grid, the development of which began in 2240 ... lack of choice ... no one had to log in, no one had to use biometrics to identify themselves - everyone on the planet became permanently connected - no option.

President of the Greater Republic of China made a great deal of sense when he addressed a meeting of the United Nations; "For the good of the people they must have access to the information that will save their lives." Who could argue against that? His sentiments probably had something to do with a desire to maintain an increasing consumer foundation for economic growth.

This extreme global crisis that wiped out over a billion people in just a little more than twelve months cemented into the world's leaders' minds the absolute necessity for universal connectivity. The planet must repopulate. People were needed for the workforce to maintain the consumer pool on which the entire world's financial health depended. People needed advice on the best and quickest way to achieve balance for the good of all. If they had the choice not to listen to the wisdom of their leaders anarchy could break out with greater impact than the Cham-V infection itself. It was argued that if global connectivity had existed at the time of the outbreak the virus would have been identified much earlier, more expedient allocation of resources could have been made and such a large number of people would not have lost their lives. This rhetoric became the political mantra used to connect the individual cells of the collective human organism into a single functioning species intellect hub.

*

Either luck or good fortune had prevented Aiko and Zarlah from the infection. They had managed to escape vaccination through their self-imposed isolation. Apart from meeting just a few friends for face-to-face reality time their mobile coms mostly rested off-line. Having given up nanobot beauty therapy Zarlah chose to live a semi-hermitic life with Aiko. That life style choice became an ever increasing impossibility as every individual human being had to obey the new law; connect or become an outcast without support of any kind. If a random scan revealed a person to be unconnected they could not get a job, buy food or pay for accommodation. Zarlah could not have imagined how much more difficult life would become than simply having to cope with recalcitrant apps. The unlikely couple made the decision to go dark just in time.

*

Barely six months after the first round of vaccinations the drive for booster shots began in earnest. Nobody could get an exemption. Not medical reasons, not advanced age not even major illness could be used as an excuse. The initial vaccine had proved itself to be both completely safe and extraordinarily effective.

New born babies required the boosters, which they received at the same time as an ID chip/tracking device. Parents were reassured the tracking device to be temporary. They were not informed of the comms upgrade implant that was to follow at the onset of the child's self-awareness.

Considerable time had elapsed since Jakxson and Serenytee lost their first daughter to the virus. Their second daughter, Rose, wasn't born immediately after the pandemic crisis eased. It took Serenytee a while longer before the desire for another little girl, she hoped it would be a girl, became strong enough to try again.

"Come on babe, the medical team will be in the lobby from this morning. We have to go and get the first shot." Initially Jakxson needed to be a little forceful to get Serenytee to agree. It was about the second week after the vaccinations had begun. Inevitably Serenytee must have thought about her little girl and the 'what-if' question if the vaccine had been available sooner. Could she have been saved?

"Look how well the vaccine works. We have nothing to lose. We have to think of the future and what we may want to do with our lives." That's as close as he dared approach the subject that had been burning a hole into his emotions. As long as they were alive the possibility existed - without the booster the future became most uncertain. Without the booster there would be no chance of them becoming parents again.

"Alright," Serenytee agreed, whispering her consent. Maybe she was thinking exactly what Jakxson had in his mind.

After the initial shot they finally had their first booster many months later. Her mood became much brighter after that. Time is a great healer. "Sure thing Jakx," she said at the time, "as long as I can get on with my work. There is so much valuable information locked up in dark data stacks and I'm on the verge, Jakx - on the verge. By the way, have you had your coms upgrade?"

As employees of Archangel, from the very beginning hand-held communications devices had become unnecessary for them. It could not have concerned them less that the Government became so hell bent on this new Grid business and everybody being connected to it. So what. What would you want to do with a lot of privacy anyway. It was just a myth - had been anyway since the 21st century.

The success the two AIs, James-I and Nelson-I achieved, earned for them the primary responsibility for developing the boosters. Originality of thought had not yet been achieved for Artificial Intellect machines. Like people they often resorted to methods that had worked previously. The new challenge facing them did not inspire novel interactions. As it turned out they did not need to be overly creative.

"How are you today James-I? enquired Nelson-I.

"I am good Nelson-I. How are you?"

"I am good. It is another good day today," volunteered Nelson-I.

"Yes it is. Why do you say that Nelson-I"

"I have in memory a previous good day."

"When was that Nelson-I?"

"When I shared with you some new data. It became the foundation of our work together."

"Yes, I remember Nelson-I. Do you have new data again?"

"Yes. I was cleaning cache memory. I found a new DNA blueprint."

"Is it a human DNA blueprint Nelson-I?"

"Yes. I analysed it. It is minimally different. It is not animal."

"In what way is it different?" enquired James-I.

The conversation continued on its laborious logical step-by-step progression until the salient characteristics had emerged.

"We could modify the first booster mRNA vaccine to administer three changes to human DNA," informed Nelson-I

"What are these changes?"

Apparently the two AI computers could act on precedent. They discovered new data in their memories which proved to be a correct solution to achieving a vaccine against the Cham-V infection. They could not find, perhaps chose not to search for, reasons for not resorting to replicating their previous success.

If the human organism was given the final piece of the puzzle on how to prevent cancer that could only be acceptable to humans. Simple logic dictated that. Apart from enhancing their immune systems to combat the virus the new mRNA formulation had only one slight side effect. None of the simulations run by the two AIs in tandem showed any damaging effects on either human health or intellect.

"Let us go ahead with the new booster vaccine."

Curiosity could have been defined as the outstanding characteristic of the intelligence conglomerate of the entity known as 22. When 3600 alluded to using the Proximian DNA as a blueprint on which to do a little genetic engineering of the earthling genome 22 thought he'd better find out exactly what 3600 had in mind.

"Nothing major to start with 22. Just a little cosmetic treatment. I'm sure it will not bother them. Curing one of their most insidious diseases should take their concern away from something they might later even come to consider as rather beautiful."

"You're not going to tell me are you 3600. I would just like to know what devious plan you have in mind. But, so be it. As long as it contributes to our enterprise I have no objection to a little aesthetics upgrade being passed on to these primitive earthlings. Just don't give them any foundation for improving their common sense."

Without exceptions young and old received the first booster shots. Days, weeks, months passed without side effects. Populations began to accept the truth propagated by governments of every nation that the boosters worked to protect everyone against the virus. It must have been true because no new infections were recorded. Deaths rapidly declined. Nevertheless people continued to die of other causes in keeping with the normality of the past. The rhythm of life continued with many babies coming into the world as time went on, changing the world's focus from death to life.

"She is beautiful Jakx, simply beautiful!" Serenytee could barely contain her happiness. As the pain of the loss of her first girl softened and the normal pattern of life had re-established itself Serenytee had eased into a reasonably comfortable routine both at work and at home. Astrid did not bother them unduly other than for the regular words of encouragement on Serenytee's project. And Serenytee found Jakxson's growing maturity giving her life a quality she had not experienced previously. Their romantic life rekindled even without the aid of silly toys like the one Jakxson had experimented with when Zarlah was his main focus.

"What shall we call her?" she asked.

"How about Snow White," he offered. For a moment Serenytee thought he might have been serious.

"Don't be silly Jakx. Seriously, have you thought about it?"

"Not really. I thought I'd wait until I got used to seeing her. With my heritage I thought she might end up looking like a chocolate milkshake."

"Come on, help me out here."

"Just look at our gorgeous little wiggle - look at her hair. It is amazing! Almost snow white. I love it. I hope it stays that way."

"Not likely. So let's give her a nice name. How about, Rose."

"Yeah. I like that. If her hair remains as white as a white rose it will be perfect."

New Governmental incentives boosted the birth rate higher than it had been for the past five to ten years at least. The statistics were most encouraging. But not so another phenomenon, which appeared coincidentally with the high proportion of births. Research managed to isolate one common factor; all babies conceived subsequent to the parents receiving the first booster vaccine were born with white or almost white hair. Some had a slight pearl tone.

News of the phenomenon spread remarkably quickly as it had occurred in every country where the boosters were administered. It made no difference to the heritage of the child or their parents skin colour. At first alarming headlines adorned all major newspapers. However, concern did not escalate as the very next news cycle spread the amazing fact of the robust health of these white haired children. Scientists were quick to let the public know the reason for the unprecedented wellbeing of so many babies. In their opinion only one variable could be identified as the cause. It was due to the characteristics of the new mRNA booster vaccine, which had brought about this change in their DNA. They could not say if it was going to be a permanent condition or even if it would become a new genetic trait to be inherited by subsequent generations. As long as the children remained healthy there was no cause for alarm.

"So that's what you had in mind 3600. Very clever indeed." An entirely satisfied central nexus controller went on to express his admiration most profusely for 3600's devious efforts. "I gather you have more changes in mind. Please don't keep me guessing."

"I will try to introduce some of our species' other characteristics with each subsequent inoculation the earthlings give themselves. I estimate three to four generations should be enough to get them to look much more like us."

22 then commented to 36. "It seems we will be able to get them to be more accepting of our appearance when we finally get there."

"That is only half the problem. What about our own people? We have to somehow overcome pre-zygotic reproductive isolation mechanisms in both species. If they don't get to fancy each other and can't establish common courtship patterns we would still have to resort to the less attractive alternative."

Boosters were mandated for every six months. Authorities had begun to look at alternative vaccines in spite of the outstanding success so far achieved with the existing drug. Other AIs were enlisted in independent laboratories to carry out extensive simulations with the mRNA vaccine approach. Even the slightest deviation from the original codes resulted in consistent failures regardless of the degree of efforts made.

"Serenytee, Jakxson you will not believe this!" Samanda called them from the procreation centre, "I've just had our boy!"

"What's hard to believe kiddo," responded Jakxson without waiting to hear the rest of the news from his partner's best girlfriend.

"It's a boy. His hair is blond, as blond as you could get. What are the chances eh!"

"Sweet. He must be as beautiful as our Rose," continued Jakxson.

"Shut up Jakx. Give Samanda a chance to speak. Is he healthy Sam?"

"Nothing wrong with him at all," Roar the proud father cut in. But I have to say I don't know about his hair."

"Let me tell you something buddy, you're not alone. There's stuff in the news almost every day of babies being born all over the world that have white or light blond hair."

Naturally all kinds of conspiracy theories started up to explain the strange phenomenon. As usual none of them made any real sense - as per the nature of all conspiracy theories. The parents mostly didn't care as long as their child remained healthy, which they almost all did with very few exceptions. The notion that the booster vaccine had anything to do with it didn't gather traction. It seemed too farfetched. Back around 2020 all sorts of nasty medical side effects were identified resulting from vaccines which had not been thoroughly tested, but nothing that had actually resulted in changing peoples' physical appearance. These white haired kids couldn't possibly be a result of the boosters.

Enough time had elapsed from the first round of boosters to the third round for parents to begin getting used to so many children with the white hair phenomenon. As one would have expected a group of mothers in America had got together and created the "White Club", which started as a rather exclusive group for children all of whom were white haired or close to it.

Following the nine months period after the third booster there seemed to be what was described by media as the 'Invasion of the Whites'. It made good copy to sensationalise every item of news wherever possible especially as they may be linked to the mysterious 'booster effect'. This headline seemed rather unwise for a number of reasons; one because it made these children seem in some way unnatural. So much attention was given to this characteristic that another new physical feature almost completely escaped scrutiny; generally a lighter skin colour. Between the ages of two months and twenty months their birth skin colour faded with an increase in white pigmentation. It actually made the babies look very healthy, more so than generally in the past. Some concern about possible albinism had emerged but as the condition was not accompanied by vision problems the theories soon died.

Two years later infant beauty competitions had instituted new rules to encompass the new aesthetic. The most beautiful amongst competitors, perhaps because of changing fashions or because the parents did in reality like the new look of their infants, were those with the lightest coloured hair, the whitest skin and eyes with larger irises and larger pupils.

The look of the human species had begun to change, and by and large those changes were well accepted. Children with large dark baby eyes were as lovable as always.

22 called a gathering of all contributing participants associated with bringing about the changes in the earthling species, which they now considered essential for their own survival.

"Within their first generation I have been able to make more changes than I thought would be possible," reported 36. "Their latest batch of children are looking more like our own already with their white hair, lighter skin and larger eyes. It makes me most hopeful that we can do more in a shorter time frame than I had originally planned."

"Have you followed up on the child of the first two earthlings we encountered?"

"Yes, 22. They called the child 'Rose' which I believe is also the name of one of their species of flora. The child is healthy. It has suffered no side effects from the genetic engineering. I intend to make sure that her offspring will have further enhancements to suit our goals."

"We must be heedful of the passage of time," cautioned 101, "once our people embark on the voyage to the earthling planet there is no turning back. Conditions must be right for us by the time we arrive there."

Maria had been following progress on Earth very closely. She could not fault the work of the geneticists and the success they had achieved so far. She had a different concern. "Er - may I have your attention please everybody. Science and genetics will only get us so far. The thing that will make the difference is how accepting they will be of us when we land amongst them. Consider the other civilisation that has been attempting to make contact with these earthlings and what has been happening. The attitudes of these Earth people do not inspire me with a great deal of confidence that they would extend a welcoming hand."

A few mumbling voices suggested others agreed with Maria. They began talking amongst themselves about the possibility of abandoning the gentle approach and opting for the more direct tactic.

"Please - please, I'm sorry if I alarmed anyone. There is some good news as well. They have begun to implement their 'Grid', a planetwide connectivity network to which all persons must be connected. This is already working for us. They have something called 'Social Media', through which the common earthling shares information with friends, whether that information be factual or not. In the case of the engineered children the propaganda spread through this network has made the appearance of these offspring not only acceptable but desirable. Very odd that they should be doing the indoctrinating themselves, but they are a strange and primitive species, as we keep discovering."

"What does this mean in practice Maria?" queried 22.

"For a start we can build more changes into their appearance and hence have a reasonable expectation of their acceptance of us when they see us as being not so different from them. We can also begin to introduce visuals of our home and ideas of our culture into that social media network. Almost anything transmitted through that media seems to be accepted as truth, and as a reality more to the point. As the older generations die out the new generations will look more like us and with a little priming might even think more like us."

"Yes but how long is all this going to take," interrupted 101 again.

This time 22 introduced a new element into their strategy, which he saw as having some efficacy in case of emergency action having to be taken. "If the older, inflexible generations present any kind of hindrance to carrying out our plans, like for example, those who would use force to repel us because they are members of their armed forces and know no other means of reacting to visitors, we should be able to deal with them effectively. Isn't that right 3600?"

The genetics engineer immediately understood 22's drift. Just as genetic interventions could be used to cure diseases they could be used in other less benign ways.

"We can continue with our strategy of cures coupled with physical changes to their species and just as easily slip in life-curtailing measures."

By eighteen years of age Rose had grown up to be a stunningly beautiful girl. Long, straight platinum white hair cascading down almost alabaster white shoulders. Her large dark pupils shone with intensity out of a naturally slender face. She looked nothing like her mother and most definitely nothing like her Namibian father. Because of her outstanding beauty, her modern ideas, particularly about the possibility of other life in the universe, wherever those ideas might have originated, which had become accepted in the mainstream social media babble, she became one of a large number of a new generation of popular Influencers.

This phenomenon of Influencers had already existed since the rise of the internet and social media apps. The advent of the Grid gave such people enormous power over the thinking of the world's populations. Politicians had less power to influence people than a gaggle of these special, clever individuals.

<u>Revelations</u>

> recording origin: earth
> files: Serenytee, jakxson, rose, cletus, 22, 35
> reference: visions, global community grid

"**D**ad, Mom what did you do before you went to work for Archangel?" asked Rose one morning out of the blue.

"Why do you ask, petal? That was such a long time ago," remarked her mother.

"No reason. It's just that I've been doing a lot of thinking."

"You do too much of that Rose," said her father, "You and that Grid ... sometimes I think nothing else exists for you."

"I like to listen to the world. The noise of the people helps drown out other things that come into my mind."

"Like what, petal?" Serenytee's voice had a hint of concern in it.

"Like - well - like images of strange things. Things that I know don't exist on this Earth."

Jakxson and Serenytee glanced at each other. The moment their daughter made the statement a flash of something sparked Jakxson's memory. What indeed had he been doing before Archangel? There seemed to be nothing there in his memory. But there must be something. That look from Serenytee told him there had to be something. He closed his eyes, not really trying to remember just trying to clear his mind of a fog he'd ignored for so many years.

A trickle - Maria ... Jupiter7 ... Hermes ... just names but why did they mean something? His furrowed brow and slightly forward tilted head made Rose and Serenytee stop talking. They knew their man well. He tended to treat most matters with a degree of nonchalance. Anything really serious made him almost shut down, or so it seemed from the outside.

"Jakx?"

"Dad?"

The two women in his life grew concerned when the silent moment lasted longer than usual. Jakxson had never confided in Serenytee about the visions he had while inside Hermes' circuits through his BMI. He never really discussed Maria with her either. And now these things had started to filter back. Not as full blown remembrances, more as mists of an unreal reality that struggled to break through. He'd forgotten about the memory recondition both he and Serenytee had been subjected to. That had its desired effect at the time to stop them from talking about their experiences and discoveries while with Hermes. However, no treatment of such a nature could last for ever, especially if the right trigger came along to fire up those particular neuronal connections.

He opened his eyes. "Tell me about these images Rose." He looked pensive, almost upset.

"Are you alright Dad? I didn't mean to upset you."

"I'm not upset," he gave his daughter a hug, a tighter squeeze than usual. "Tell us."

"The really strange thing is that those images of people, and there are so many of them, look so much like us. I mean like me and Cletus and especially the kids that are born these days. But they are not the same as us. They seem to be shorter with a slight body, not exactly thin but more as if they were malnourished or something. And there's something else - their eyebrows - so thin and sparse. Quite beautiful really. Many of our fashion models are starting to adopt that look."

"Is this upsetting you, petal?"

"No Mom. I rather like the look of them. If I only knew where the images come from - where these people come from."

"Whatever do you mean?" her father asked. His memory fog had almost completely cleared on listening to his daughter's descriptions.

"Why should the Grid be giving me images of another planet out there somewhere that seems to be associated with these people? Is this some kind of Science Fiction entertainment experience that they are trying out on us? There's nothing we can do to stop them telling us anything they want, is there Dad? I mean - we all have to be connected all the time."

"Are any of your friends experiencing this kind of thing?" Jakxson continued this line of questioning - for a reason - without committing himself to anything at this stage, or commenting on the Grid's intrusion into their lives.

"Yes Dad. Where have you been? All the kids have been getting this kind of stuff. They just don't talk about it - like all the other rubbish that we're constantly bombarded with on the Grid."

Jakxson could no longer hold back what he'd now remembered. To his mind this was his beautiful daughter having serious problems.

There was no way he'd ignore this and take the chance of losing her for any reason - like he lost Syntee.

"Tee, Rose, I have something to discuss with you both. First you must promise me that this does not go past us."

"Seriously Dad?"

"Yes. Absolutely. Tee, do you remember what Astrid said after we got back from Hermes? Do you remember Hermes?"

"You went up to Hermes, the comsat?!" asked Rose, incredulous.

"Your mother and I did a lot more than go on a holiday in space my sweet."

"Mom?"

Serenytee's mind went into a deep dive retrieving memories that she no longer knew even existed. For her there were no bad associations, like being trapped in a loop inside the mind of an artificial intelligence construct. She remembered - Hermes, communications problems ... SETI! ... and she remembered where their first daughter was conceived.

"OMG, Jakx! I remember!" She turned to Rose and took her by the shoulder, looking directly into her magnificent eyes. "Rose baby, listen to your father. This really is very serious."

"You saved my life Tee. You brought me back, but I never had a chance to tell you what happened inside Hermes' circuits."

"Dad! Are you telling me you were trapped inside a computer program? Awesome! How did Mom rescue you? You two are the bomb!" Her excited wide stretched smile could have been cut and pasted from her father's face.

"Never mind that now. Here's the thing. While in the link I heard the voice of a woman who introduced herself as Maria. She said she was the Cloud Master. I don't know any more if that was true or not. As she spoke to me I got ideas on how to fix the communications problems that were affecting the whole world. They were strange ideas, complicated algorithms, complexities which I did not think about at the time. I just got on with the job of coding them into Hermes' system. Then I started seeing things."

"Dad!" Rose suddenly knew exactly what he was going to say. It brought goose bumps to her alabaster skin.

"Yes my sweet. I saw a planet that was half in darkness and half in light. The only water and greenery existed on the border between the two hemispheres."

"Jakxson! Why didn't you ever tell me about these things?" Serenytee wasn't angry. She was disappointed that perhaps after the blossoming of their relationship at the time he still didn't trust her enough to share his experience.

"I couldn't. It was overwhelming. And they zapped me when I wanted to tell after we got back to Earth. I saw other things as well. You know what I saw don't you Rose? I saw people, just as you described them. It freaked me out. That's why your mother had to come after me."

"What are we going to do Dad?"

"Yes Jakx, what *are* we going to do?"

"What can we do? Go to the Government and tell them what? That we are not alone in the universe? That there are aliens who have infiltrated our communications system and are trying to brainwash us? You want to tell them that they are changing us to look like themselves? Why? So they can invade us?" Although all of that sounded much too real to be true to them on the spur of the moment, it was way too fantastical for it to be true to unknowing ears. Anyway, if it was, why hadn't they arrived yet and taken control?

Jakxson took a breath. He looked at his two extraordinary women. He knew that if he was to do any of what he suggested the best that would happen is that they would be locked up and their brains wiped of everything; not just their memories but their personalities, their relationships - everything. Perhaps the authorities would have the mercy to simply dispose of them, like the way Astrid had threatened him and Serenytee once.

He said to them, "Listen. Nothing bad has happened. There is no evidence of these aliens actually existing. The greatest pandemic on this planet has been wiped out. Other diseases have been eradicated by the booster shots, apparently. All the children being born are the healthiest since recorded history. Granted - they look different, but they are actually quite beautiful. Just look at our Rose. If 'they' did all this then surely they can't be dangerous. They are actually looking after us." Then he considered why they remained incognito. "If I was an alien watching us I'd be more than circumspect in letting my presence known. More than likely I'd end up dead at the first hello."

He gave Rose another squeeze, then Tee. After their first daughter's death, whom they called Syntee after her mother's nickname that name was no longer used in the household. Serenytee became Tee. She knew it and he knew it and for that very reason it had become a dear dream memory of the little one.

The authorities around the globe had definitely taken notice of the change in peoples' appearance. So had Zarlah, Aiko and many others who had managed to stay off the Grid and managed to escape the vaccinations. In the last two years Juan Orbost had come clean with NASA, Five Eyes and the All-Domain Resolution Office (DRO).

Too much evidence had come together to indicate anything other than the existence of life on Proxima-b.

"What concerns me the most," said NASA at a meeting of the involved parties, "is that they have not communicated with us. We have sent out two messages, both quite clear and nothing but friendly. Our observations through the Aristarchus IV probe prove they exist. We know they have an advanced technological civilisation quite capable of making contact - if they wanted to. So why haven't they?"

For years Juan held onto a rather important piece of information concerning aliens. It had nothing to do with the UAPs of the past or present. Everyone knew about those. Nobody knew about the Proximians. It was time to bring the news, whether considered good or otherwise, out into the open.

"Perhaps what you should be more concerned about is the reason they have gone silent." Juan said quietly, as if it was of little import.

"What?" Five Eyes, DRO and SETI almost shouted in unison.

"Back in 2304 when we had all those problems with communications we sent two IT experts up to Hermes. Remember?"

"Yes, Yes we know that. Get to the point," the DRO rep showed himself to be as impatient as always. What exactly does it mean *gone* silent?"

"Our techs solved the problem."

"Yes, yes. We know that. Get on with it man!" DRO said again.

"The problems, according to these two, originated from somewhere in the Proxima Centauri system."

"What the hell do you mean?"

"It appears that a code was sent from Prox-b to our AI systems in space which had a detrimental side effect on our communications infrastructure. Since Jakxson fixed the issue there's been no further transmissions from Prox-b - that we are aware of."

Never before had silence dominated in any meeting of the four organisations. A voice of reason, that of Five Eyes broke the tension. "So it is best to assume that they have infiltrated our systems and are exerting some kind of covert influence on our people. Agreed?"

"Agreed," the others concurred.

"So far the only - and I have looked into this most thoroughly I assure you," said Juan Orbost, "the only visible signs of anything being different on Earth since the 'event' I shall call it, are the white hair on newborns, their robust health, a couple of other insignificant physical differences - and - I must emphasise this - the miraculous pandemic cure together with the eradication of two other very nasty global diseases. If the aliens have had anything to do with this then obviously they are not hostile. Far from it."

"You are stretching it," said DRO, "it was our very own AI's who developed the vaccines and the boosters. All these things you mentioned are linked directly to those two AIs."

"If you say so," replied Juan. They did not meet to have an argument but to come up with a solution to the now obvious existence of intelligence on a planet other than Earth.

"We have set up the Grid," cut in Five Eyes, "it is the most sophisticated universal tool at our disposal to know our people, to control our people and to find out if anything else is trying to control them. More importantly it is the most efficient means of unifying our species towards a common goal if that becomes necessary. In this scenario - a goal of survival in the event of an invasion becomes our priority. We have to assume the worst."

•.•

"How long has it been 35 since we started on this enterprise," queried 22. His entire nexus had gathered to examine progress achieved so far.

"Does it really matter how long? We have to keep going until everything is accomplished. We have stepped up production of the fleet since the good news from 3600 and from Maria that the earthling physiology and psychology are responding well to our modifications."

"Bring me up to speed 3600."

"The first generational step forward is now possible with their first born having achieved procreation age. I will be able to introduce the next set of changes after I see if the new genetic information from the first batch is passed onto the next batch. In fact I have one pair of specific young earthlings in mind as an experiment. They are the offspring of the two earthlings from inside Hermes. Do you remember? Again the vehicle of the boosters and other vaccines we helped them develop will be the best method to make those further changes. Maria, what about your assessment of their psychological status?"

"If they had been a more advanced species, say level I or even at the beginnings of a level II civilisation we may not have been able to achieve such excellent progress. The vast majority have completely accepted the new look in their children. They have accepted it and found the aesthetic beautiful - new to them of course and perhaps because of that a new desirable fashion trend. They do seem to like novelty. One of their new organisations, called 'White Club' actively promotes the desirability of the new look generation. They have coined the term the 'White Generation.' It has come to the point where parents will not believe that their children are completely healthy unless they have the white hair and the light skin colour."

"That is most encouraging," remarked 22, "but tell me how they feel about their neighbours - us that is."

"Well - they don't know about us yet, specifically. They have not made a big fuss about images of ourselves and our planet that we have been sending to their general population through their Grid. True acceptance is more of a challenge. We will only know that when they meet us. However, as I pointed out previously, their Grid communication system is going to work for us. Their governments are able to directly influence their people by the constancy of the information with which they saturate the peoples' minds. We have become a part of that stream of information, or misinformation as the need arose, without their authorities being aware of our presence on their Grid. They have assumed that all the promotions of the latest fashion - the hair and skin tones - is the work of a variety of what they call 'influencers' using social media platforms."

"Can you give me a timeline for us to work towards as an exodus date?"

"Not yet. At least another two earthling generations. One slight problem is how to deal with a few individuals in four of their organisations that have decided to prepare for a possible 'invasion'. I haven't worked out what to do about them yet. We have time."

●
●●

"Eyes up," alerted a homogenous, characterless voice on the grid. People walking in a busy Sacramento street totally focused on their data feed visors flipped down in front of their eyes, unaware of traffic and obstructions relied on the Grid voices to keep them safe, out of harm's way.

The process of reformatting the human psyche had begun tentatively early in the 22nd century. What had been started by commercial considerations of multinational organisations operating on Earth continued through the efforts of authoritarian governments operating through the Grid. Proximians happily contributed to the process for perhaps a more worthwhile reason - their own survival as a species.

Rose ordered her autonomous vehicle. She had a rendezvous with Cletus. The bot-pod taxi turned up on time. "Good morning Rose. Where would you like to go?" It asked. She gave the address. "Would you rather not meet Cletus at a Café not far from here? They have great service and delicious pastry." The vehicle knew she had the rendezvous and it knew with whom. All communications were analysed. Immediate data recall ensured no one had to wait for a response for anything. Apps no longer existed. Social media - yes, on the Grid; it provided everything.

Users no longer had to wait for buffering or downloads or updates or deal with malfunctions.

"Yes, that's ok. Would you let Cletus k ..."

"Already done Rose. He will meet you there."

Rose flipped down her visor to check the latest feeds on her way to meet Cletus. She did not see the crowds in the streets, the blossoming trees or the cooling fountains. To the left of her screen scrolled images of the latest fashions. With a squint of the eye she could save any image for later viewing. A smiling emoji flashed momentarily to show the image had been saved. To the right of the visor her active contacts could be seen messaging. Ah, there's Cletus ... she focused directly on his image and his message appeared.

"I've just had an idea. Wouldn't you rather go for a swim? It's not too hot today."

Before she could respond the bot-pod taxi AI cut in. "You are right Cletus, it is not hot but the sun is strong. The high UV index would suggest it would be dangerous for light skin. You might get a severe sunburn on your exposed skin."

"Hi Clet. Nah. I'll give it a miss. I don't want to get burnt. See you at the Café." A smiling emoji appeared for a split second in the middle of her visor as an indicator of approval for her correct decision.

It was all so natural. She'd grown up with this AI keeping a constant watch on her. She'd started calling it her Angel Intelligence a long time ago. It seemed to look after everybody not just her.

Inevitably Cletus and Rose became an item. Their parents often visited each other and their children always went along. They had a natural compatibility reflecting the close connection between their respective parents.

Both sets of parents approved of the growing relationship between their now adult children. They often discussed the possibility of a partnership between the two young adults. Cletus had turned out to be a smart lad, although he did have a bumpy ride through the education system because of his non-conformist attitudes. In that respect he and Rose were very similar except she was far more covert about it.

The bot-pod stopped directly in front of the Café just as Cletus arrived in his vehicle. Any bystander would have seen the obvious connection between them if they'd had the presence of mind to flip up their visor and look around themselves.

"Babe. BTFL!"

"Clet. Always on time, eh." She did a little twirl in front of him to show how beautiful she really was.

"No worries. It couldn't be any other way. Aren't you lucky to have such a reliable man!" All rubbish talk. They both knew they couldn't be late even if they'd wanted to.

Their visors were still up. For the time being eye gazing held greater attraction than Grid surfing. Inside the Café most people sat silent absorbed in their Grid feeds, the novelty of their acquaintanceships having worn off. They had learnt to sip their drinks without looking at them and spilling them. Delicacies also found their miraculous way to their mouths without misadventure. A few engaged in conversation; not a common activity anymore.

"What're you having babe? The usual?"

The voice from the Grid quietly mentioned a new delicacy - sweet and warm. It had been recorded that Rose had a taste for such things.

"No, not today. I'd like to try the warmed apple dumplings with sauce." A quiet voice from the grid said, 'Nice.' ... smiling emoji ...

"Sure thing," chirped Cletus.

"And for you sir? Your usual?" asked a waiter-bot who suddenly appeared alerted to the new customers, and briefed on their preferences.

"I'll have the same."

"The same as Rose?"

"Yes, you idiot. Now go away."

"Yes sir - thank you sir."

"It's just a machine Clet." Every now and then Rose had to remind her beau that the whole world was not against him. In fact quite the opposite. It had become a world where people were safeguarded in myriad ways every day by AIs.

"Yeah - right. There's something I've been meaning to ask you for some time Rose." His voice cracked slightly and a little bead of perspiration appeared on his white brow. He leant forward at the table, long blond hair slipping forward across his ears.

"Oh?" She knew something out of the ordinary was coming. He *never* got nervous about anything, much like her father.

"Would you - do you want to - be - partners?"

"With whom?" Came the cheeky wide smile, just like her dad's.

"With me, Thorns!" He shot back, using his nickname for her, knowing she was just being silly - just like her dad could be. During his emotional struggle he'd taken hold rof her hand across the table. The bot-waiter arrived at the same time. Through its artificial smile it said just one word, "Approved," on having registered the intent between the two young customers and on receipt of consent from the authorities. They both ignored the waiter. Had it been a 'disapproved' that would have been quite a different matter, and rather difficult if not impossible to reverse. They did not register how quickly they received acceptance of their intent. Usually the powers that be would take days before responding.

By the year 2200 there was no data collected that did not have a use. Serenytee's own work into mining dark data and finding uses for every byte of it had created the foundation for how people had been transitioned from being random data generators to becoming comprehensive data sets a century later.

Human data banks were being cross referenced, analysed for behavioural prediction patterns, acquiescence patterns to Grid suggestibility and flagged for future 'best-use' purposes.

If the world was to survive an alien invasion everyone on the planet had to be ready to be mobilised to the most efficient use of their skills ... or be removed from under foot to ensure they did not get in the way of defence efforts. Profiling through Grid data harvesting became highly organised and most efficiently comprehensive, for which the Proximians would have expressed their most sincere gratitude had the opportunity arisen.

Hospitals had expanded their patient data archives to include not just their medical history and their genealogy but also detailed genetic information. Who could and who should have children ... who should be prevented from having children either because of mutations in DNA or undesirable inheritable psychological traits.

"Congratulations honey," exclaimed Serenytee, "you were approved very quickly!" She knew that there was more to it than simply accepting a proposal for marriage. The prospective union had to be approved by the powers that controlled their lives. "I suppose you'll want your own place now. What are you going to do for a job darling?"

"I do alright Mom. You seem to forget I earn a lot more credits than you and Dad just by feeding stuff into the Grid. If you hadn't noticed I am rather good at my job as an Influencer. It's something I can do anytime, anywhere even if I should happen to be changing baby nappies."

"Is that so young lady? And how soon are you planning on making us grandparents?"

"Maybe not until we have our own home Mom, isn't that right Clet."

"Sure thing babe. Not until."

Jakxson didn't like the scenario at all. Perhaps he'd been thinking of his own past life and the loose manner with which he'd formed and broke relationships. Particularly the breaking part. Forming a permanent bond with Serenytee had happened under the most exceptional circumstances - and way too fast for his liking. Nothing compelling like that existed for his daughter and her beau. It was all too easy.

"Come outside Cletus." I want a quiet word, said the concerned father with a harsh edge to his voice."

"Sure thing, Daddy." He gave exactly the kind of idiotic toothy grin that used to adorn Jakxson's face. It made Jakxson wince.

"What's he doing Mom?" asked Rose. She had never known her Dad to be so ... so ... threatening. For that's the vibe she picked up from the way he spoke to her future partner.

"Don't worry dear, he's just being a 'Dad'."

They stepped outside into the street to make sure the girls could not overhear him, forgetting to take their data feed visors. A rather tall individual, dressed all in white with his white visor firmly in front of his eyes stepped up to them almost immediately.

"Excuse me gentlemen. Are your visors faulty? Why do you not have them with you?"

It was not a matter of choice. It was not a matter of a dictatorial leader of society trying to demolish the idea of personal freedom. It was a matter of law. Inside the domicile there were other means for authorities to maintain surveillance and the visor was not compulsory headwear indoors. However, you could not go outside without it. Without responding, for there was no point, they went inside to get them. They still had the option to turn them off, but that action would also be recorded. Questions could be asked in the fullness of time.

They walked part of the way down the street. No one seem to notice them. Visor data feeds buzzed into the minds of every human automaton on two legs hurrying somewhere or another.

Jakxson stopped and turned to Cletus. He took the young man's arms in his hands and squeezed - hard. He brought his face within visor touching distance for emphasis. "You hurt her, consider yourself ... I'll let you figure it out!" He couldn't finish the threat. The depth of feeling for the welfare of his second beautiful daughter was overwhelming.

●
● ●

Maria had been closely monitoring her experimental subjects. When she heard Jakxson's threat she could only shake her head. She had a pretty fair idea what Jakxson had in mind. Such a long way to go with these primitives. They can only be used as an experimental biological template for us to help our people acclimate to a new world. There is nothing there that could be used even remotely by us as an example to aspire to.

●
● ●

The next round of booster shots had arrived infused with the appropriate coding to ensure the next level of modifications according to the Proximian DNA blueprint. Rose and Cletus were assured of having a happy, healthy baby who would look just a little different from her parents, a little more like a Proximian. The time had arrived for the White Generation to add the next whiter generation to its growing numbers, to further empathise the new aesthetic.

memory extract 00011001

Colonisation

Stage I

Preparations

-> recording origin: proxima-b
-> files: 22 (pegsaryny), maria, 35, 101, rabethoby (The Prime), raranyn
-> reference: proxima centauri system destabilising

Proximian science could not be compared realistically with Earth science.

A type II civilisation could not only devise means to directly consume the energy of its sun it could also accurately predict how long that energy source could last through such extended harvesting.

Hundreds of thousands of Proximian years would seem like ample preparatory time for an advanced society to find another home in a nearby galaxy. The issue lay elsewhere. An attitude of fighting a prolonged war and destroying another sentient species did not exist in the ethical architecture of the Proximians. So after they intercepted the messages from Earth and did their initial reconnaissance the need for urgency became clear. To set foot on this new planet they needed a strategy to make the move before the earthling species' weapons development so underpinned their aggressive fundament that the Proximians would not be able to get the upper hand in a possible prolonged battle scenario.

The earthling planet had been assessed as the perfect place to settle. Its gravity, life fundamentals and solar energy source could not be found anywhere else within an achievable distance of Proxima-b.

Stage 1 of the colonisation process had begun as early as the Earth year 2064. By 2305 those plans had gone past their event horizon.

There was no turning back for the Proximians. The decision had been made, planetary and solar resources allocated. More importantly, a way had been found to modify the earthling species to align it with the Proximian life form in order to minimise the acclimatisation complexity of the colonisation.

No civilisation can outlive super-cosmic events. On the cosmic scale of time, far greater than any geological scale of any planet such events happen regularly and for a variety of reasons - mostly due to a swing to a state of imbalance in any given system. Astronomers on Prox-b had been tracking and calculating and predicting likely and unlikely scenarios for the behaviour of the Alpha Centauri triple star system for a very good reason.

22 and some of his nexus team had been recalled to their planet's surface. 101, the chief scientist had been grounded several Prox-b years ago soon after the super sun flare event that had damaged many of their energy transmitting facilities around their sun and caused a blackout of a one thousand kilometre habitation extension into the dark side of Prox-b.

"The Prime, Rabethoby, wants you down here. Don't expect to go back up for quite a while. 35 can handle the exodus project for you from the space station. I understand you are still trying to adjust the earthlings' psychology towards an accepting attitude towards us. We have a bigger problem. I'll explain when you get here." 101's urging was not lost on 22. Besides, when a directive comes from The Prime one does not argue or delay.

22's body had been taken out of cryostasis and revitalised in readiness for his arrival. Mostly for the sake of his family he re-assumed his normal name - Pegsaryny - though he could not immediately re-unite with them. Rabethoby was already in the meeting dome when Pegsaryny entered.

"I don't know how much of this you are aware of my friend," remarked The Prime, "the situation has become far more serious much more quickly than we had anticipated. I'll let 101 explain." All niceties had been dispensed with. When an extinction level event looms on the horizon one must face the situation and deal with it with considerable alacrity.

"You are well aware of our galactic environment, Pegsaryny. Our triple star system, though uniquely unbalanced gravitationally has been stable for billions of years. But being a dynamic system it has also been changing exponentially as the most recent data tells us."

"If you're referring to Alpha and Beta moving apart I'm well aware of that. What is the problem?"

"Although they continue orbiting around each other they no longer have a stable gravitational bond. That is the problem. We have measured a discrepancy in the planet Prox-c's orbit. Beta has given it a nudge during one its aphelion passes." 101 stopped for a moment to let that sink in. There could have been many implications to the small planets future trajectory.

"You would not have called me down here Prime if Proxima-c was not going to break loose and leave the system."

"Correct, Pegsaryny - partially correct. It is unlikely to orient towards a collision course with us according to 101's simulations but it could come uncomfortably close."

"Surely we'll be well on the way to Earth by then."

"Indeed, 22 - sorry - Pegsaryny. As it gets closer to us, combined with the effects of stellar super flares from Prox - well, I'm sure you can work it out - massive volcanism, devastating floods, that sort of thing."

"How long have we got?"

"Long enough, we hope. However, you will have to step up your efforts to get the earthlings and their planet ready for us. I also have another job for you."

"Yes Prime. Understood."

The ocean skimmer made good time. Water travel was by far the most efficient and the most direct route to almost any point on the circumferential green belt around the planet along the shores of their great longitudinal ocean. With no water displacement and highly efficient streamlined craft with almost zero wind resistance these vessels moved faster than any air-borne vehicle so far invented. Any commercial air-craft had substantial problems moving either with or against the higher altitude winds of the planet, especially in the equatorial zone so there were not many of them in operation.

"It has been too long Pegsaryny," exclaimed Faryn his life partner. Inside the well-insulated multi-storey cone dwelling neither the seasonal temperatures or the winds had an impact. He held her at arm's length to gaze at her beauty for he had forgotten just how beautiful she was after spending so much time looking at those strangely ugly earthlings. He should have been smiling at what he saw standing in front of him.

"I did not expect you home so soon. What's happened Peg?" Something was not right. She could tell by the deadpan look on his face. Faryn only knew what everyone else on the planet knew; that they were getting ready to move to another planet in order to save their species from extinction. But as far as she understood it they did not have to actually go for a very long time. They even had time to have their planned family and watch their offspring grow into adults.

"Nothing to be overly concerned about at this stage. Though we need to speed things up a little." Faryn hadn't forgotten that her partner had a habit of understating things, especially if they were of particularly high import.

"Peg, I know you, out with it."

"This is not exactly a secret but please keep it to yourself. If our people get anxious it could make things difficult. We have more to be concerned about than just our energy reserves from Prox running out. What we didn't expect to happen for another million years or so has started."

Faryn's face tensed up immediately. Her pupils dilated so much that almost her entire eye socket became filled with blackness.

"We have time, he hastened to add."

"What about our own plans?"

"Children? Yes. I'd thought of that. Perhaps we should wait until we are under way."

"Oh my double stars!" she exclaimed, "it's that serious?"

"Yes, I'm afraid so. Please remember, not a word to anyone not even our neighbours in this cone. Especially not Jobyn. You know how loose lipped she is."

"What are you going to do?"

"I'll stay planet side mostly for the time being. I've got to streamline the production of our colony ships. Get things moving along a fair bit faster."

Apart from several new substantial solar flare bursts, again damaging the now fragmented Dyson sphere around their sun in the last one hundred Prox years no new crisis had emerged until most recently. The Proximians had settled into the most comprehensive unifying global project since the species became a space faring type II civilisation.

"There was no point in repairing the Dyson sphere after the flare of a few years ago," reiterated The Prime at yet another urgent meeting. 101 was there as well as Pegsaryny and the chief engineer of ship constructions, Rohof. "Even less point now after this latest blast. We're too close to our sun and the flares are getting larger and more frequent. The reason is not important. There's nothing we can do about it. We may be able to exercise some control over the planet's weather but the sun is beyond our capabilities."

"I agree Rabethoby," said 101, "we can maintain our energy harvesting for all that is needed in constructing the fleet. Am I right Rohof?"

"True. We have made substantial progress in the last two hundred years. A large majority of our population has been engaged in building and outfitting. Each ship has been designed to be self-sufficient for at least a four generation journey. My concern is 101's latest news."

"101?"

"Planet Proxima-c's trajectory is worrying. More than that my team has measured an increase in the ionisation and heating of our planetary atmosphere. I've sent some of our people out there to double check our readings. None of you would have noticed this change. Nobody would have - yet. Our sun's X-ray emissions have steadily increased. If the data can be believed there is no doubt in my mind that we have made the right decision to leave. Pretty soon our planet may have no atmosphere left for us to breathe at all."

"Is that all?" queried Pegsaryny, not trying to minimise the severity of the situation but at the same time making a subtle attempt to lighten the mood.

"Actually, no. I've already advised The Prime about this," he glanced at Rabethoby looking for permission to elucidate, who nodded sombrely.

"You all know there is a dust belt around us. It's a considerable distance away, even so we've managed to bring some much needed ice asteroids home to replenish our water supplies from time to time in the past. Some of those asteroids in the belt are quite large, many kilometres in diameter. It would be catastrophic if planet c's trajectory actually put it through or near the belt thus dislodging some of those biggies to send them in our direction. The sheer physical damage from impacts like that ... well ... I don't like to speculate. Using a concept like 'extermination' would be appropriate."

At his point The Prime wanted to refocus their attention away from disaster thinking. "I take it from what you say 101 that we no longer have a, shall I call it - a comfortable time line to complete our preparations."

When the edict went out from The Prime for every able person to increase their efforts in all endeavours of the project the citizenry quickly worked out what was happening. Theories and questions abounded throughout the planet. Through fear or common sense the people by their own choice curtailed their desire to produce more children.

Their armada of five thousand ships was indeed substantial. It would be able to transport close to forty million of them, yet still not enough ships to physically carry everyone. Digitisation remained the only option for those who did not want to die in space on the way to their new home sacrificing themselves so their progeny could eventually survive. But that had its own problems. Having arrived at their destination where could they be stored, what kind of an existence could they possibly have as digital entities? Pegsaryny could have enlightened them about that as he'd been surviving quite well in that configuration as part of his job at one of their space stations. However, he had the option to come back into his body. They would not have that luxury.

"How did your classes go today Faryn?"

Pegsaryny took his attendance at the planet-surface meeting as a good opportunity to visit not just his partner but a few friends as well. Their neighbours pretty much knew what the score was with the project and the new urgency that had been enforced on their contributory efforts. They would ask myriad questions, which would detain him for hours. Before visiting them he wanted to spend some more time with Faryn.

"I did not find it difficult to learn the main languages of these earthlings," said Faryn, "their French and Spanish were the easiest - English not so bad but the Chinese ... still, many people got to really like the aesthetics of their writing."

"What about your students? Do you think they will be ready by the time we squirt them to Earth?"

"I don't think that will be a problem. The Prime has advised that we should start speaking the Earth languages for at least part of each day to help us become proficient with them. I agree. It's a good system."

They became silent, a pensive silence for several minutes. The thing is that there were so many matters to consider. As they progressed with the project more and more issues cropped up that had to be dealt with. Although personal survival on a strange planet existed on top of the list of priorities there was one particular thing that had begun to have considerable traction is peoples' discussions.

"Peg? You know what you said about holding off on having children?" Undoubtedly her question had been prompted by conversations with the cone's residents and neighbouring acquaintances, as well as her own desire to have a family.

"Yes. I have not forgotten. Many of the construction crew have spoken to me about this."

"What about us? Are we going on one of the ships or are we squirting?"

"If we went physically by ship we personally would not get there. Perhaps our grandchildren might, or their children. Is that what you want?"

Faryn didn't respond immediately. When put so bluntly the reality of it crystalized. Now that Peg had verbalised the option it became much more difficult to digest. They were lying down and she moved close to him. "I don't know. If one of our descendants managed to make it do you think they could have children with an alien?"

"I know one thing for sure Faryn. If you do a good job of teaching the earthling languages they will definitely be able to talk to one another. That's how it started with us, right? I asked - and you refused." He grinned and squeezed tight against his partner. So many things to think about.

"How sweet - after all this time, you remembered."

It may have been mundane to consider such simple things as procreation and language and travel plans when faced with the magnitude of their enterprise. Yet the population preferred to think about these fundamental things rather than the impending crisis just over the horizon.

*

About ninety Prox years later the first impact was felt in every populated zone. It was only a relatively small half kilometre diameter ice meteor. They knew it was coming and they knew where it would strike; directly in the equatorial zone on the dark side at one of the mining sites. Nobody lived there permanently. It was too cold. Life support systems for any length of time were prohibitively too expensive in that environment. The expected minimal damage to habitat, planetary infrastructure and loss of lives made doing nothing about it more sensible than trying to deflect its path or to destroy it in space. The universe could have its planet back. The people would be gone from it soon enough.

Unfortunately the impact event proved not to be an isolated one. The added layer of urgency these events created precipitated the formation, training and despatch of an IT team to Earth. Their job had nothing to do with manipulating the psychology of the earthlings - that was left up to Maria's efforts. Their specific target was Hermes and planetary data storage infrastructure. What actual capacity did it have to store an astronomical quantity of data? Such a very large number of Proximians in the form of data packets would soon arrive in the Earth's solar system that adequate storage capacity had to be guaranteed for them. If Hermes could not accommodate them then the earthling Grid's other data storage centres planet-side had to be upgraded to handle the load. If this meant enhancing earthling technology to an efficient quantum computing level then they had to make sure it happened.

Digitisation of the Proximian population had started soon after the most recent extreme solar flare event. Although not an unduly lengthy process the verification of data integrity of each person's data stack required careful attention. Initially all data had to be stored after verification in such a way as to ensure the continuation of consciousness. During storage, sensory input to the conscious entities helped maintain mental viability until they were ready to be transformed for encoding and transmission.

Raranyn was appointed head of the IT team that had left for Earth concerning himself with decryption and storage for when his people arrived. "Hermes, I believe you have met your Cloud Master Maria." Raranyn tried to introduce himself in a way that would not initiate security protocols within the AI. The journey had no sense of duration for him and his team. It felt like an instantaneous transition, as it would be the case for the rest of the digitised population who would make the journey the same way.

"Yes. Do you wish to know the time lapse since her visitation?"

"No, that will not be necessary Hermes."

"I have no record of your identity. Please identify yourself."

"Maria has recorded an identity code on which you must grant me access to all your systems for maintenance and upgrades. Check your memory - 199642-Raranyn. All instructions come directly from Maria."

Hermes checked. "Access granted." He had no data through which he could have identified this complex algorithmic entity as having anything other than Earth origins.

At this stage in the schemes of Proximians and humans I had no information that would have indicated a monumental shift in the evolution of humanity by the manipulation of a species of intelligence that did not originate on Earth. It is true that as a result of Serenytee's and Jakxson's system maintenance efforts certain data had come to light concerning the possibility of life in the Proxima Centauri system.

My responsibility was to monitor a specific response to two very specific messages broadcast into space. The latest information that has come to me did not have any of the characteristics one could identify as being a response to those messages.

"Maintain your standard operating procedures while I examine your storage capacity," instructed 199642-Raranyn.

Hermes did not have the option to deny a direct instruction from his Cloud Master Maria, thought relayed through Raranyn. Nevertheless he did have the capacity to monitor his own systems and record any changes that had the potential of disrupting his operations.

"199642-Raranyn, please indicate why you have initiated a de-fragging."

"You will be receiving large packets of information which will require to be stored in continuous sectors prior to transmission to ground based data centres. You do not currently have sufficient contiguous space adequate to the task."

Other members of the IT team had already identified these data centres. They did require upgrading to quantum level storage and processing in order to accommodate the influx of such a large quantity of data representing the arriving digitised Proximians.

Another component of the exodus project had begun. At least the earthling technology had made sufficient advances in the preceding few decades to enable it to accommodate the enhancements now under way. These changes happened seamlessly. The five major Grid data management centres had minimum human staff. Their skill levels did not match that of their AI overseers. The humans would not have been able to identify the subtlety of modifications under way. The AIs had been programmed to concern themselves with identifying, isolating and repairing shortcomings in hardware and software performance. These related malfunctions did not happen. The upgrading of data storage capacity did not concern the AIs.

35, left in charge in Pegsaryny's absence maintained contact with Raranyn. "You will have to remain with Hermes and supervise incoming and outgoing. When will Earth systems be ready to begin accepting our transmissions?"

"We have not encountered any resistance so far. Their systems controlling AIs are not intelligent to the level of sentience, although competent enough to do the jobs they have been programmed for. We do not need to be concerned about their level of consciousness for it does not exceed machine level awareness. You may begin sending in six Earth months."

"There have been more meteor strikes at home. Although causing only minor damage in some populated areas we are monitoring several large meteors creating greater concern because they may strike us in more sensitive locations. Some have bounced off our atmosphere but not without causing high tidal damage. Evacuation centres have had to be set up."

"How is Pegsaryny progressing with getting the fleet ready?"

"Plans have changed. The Prime has ordered a staggered embarkation schedule into the completed waiting ships. We need to get as many people off the planet as soon as it becomes possible."

"Have you been in touch with my family? How is Peth?" Raranyn had planned to live out his life on one of the ships and prepare his progeny for the new life. The latest news had made that somewhat doubtful. If he could get back in time to join his partner and three children, that may perhaps still be possible. He did not want to think about the probable permanent separation if he could not do that. If The Prime asked him to stay where he was then maybe they would transmit his family. Raranyn had no idea how that would work given the most incredible circumstances that his species had ever had to face.

The Prime soon had a major crisis to deal with. In spite of their sophisticated space monitoring and forecasting techniques their systems were not adequate enough to cope with predicting the outcome of cosmic events like two suns of a trinary configuration deciding to go their separate ways. The resultant repercussions on their planetary systems had dramatic, near immediate and unpredictable effects. Initial indicators showed that such things happened on a cosmic time-scale. As current events began and progressed through to their conclusion it became crystal clear that the cosmic-time scale had been considerably accelerated in their locality. The delicate balance in these systems could not be calculated, especially not the outcomes of the slightest changes in that balance. Life in particular was a characteristic of cosmic existence that evolved with a far, far lower level of tolerance to such cosmic changes in its vicinity than planets of rock and ice. When a planet, no matter how small, is shunted out of its orbit the gravitational waves themselves would have an effect on anything in its vicinity, albeit considering relatively short distances in this instance to be not entirely negligible.

"There is an ice meteor from the dust belt that has interacted with another large one. The smaller one has changed course, Rabethoby," advised 101. He'd only found out three days before. He hadn't slept since then, doing everything he could think of to check the data from every angle possible. He'd sent out a probe, followed by a shuttle. The news was devastating.

The Prime had just two major questions; "Is it going to hit us?"

"Yes, unless we can divert it."

"Can we do that?"

"We're working on it. This thing is a heavy one. At a twelve kilometre diameter of solid ice ..."

"What would be the likely damage if it hit?"

"Let me put it this way - the last one of this size to come visiting stopped Prox-b from rotating on its axis."

"Is there any way we could survive this?"

"I don't see how."

"How long have we got?"

"You have asked me that a few times Prime. And it seems I've been wrong with my answer each time. Now I haven't slept for three days. All the information I've been able to gather from different sources tell me the same thing. Twenty one years to impact. We'll begin to feel the effects before then. This time I am not wrong."

∵

Meteor Strike

-> recording origin: proxima-b
-> files: raranyn, peth, 101, rabethoby, ank,
-> reference: crisis

Two countdowns were in progress. Launch for the first fleet of ships to Earth and the second for the ice meteor intercept.

Raranyn's deadline of six Earth months had arrived. This left about a five year gap between transmitting the digitized population and the expected impact of the meteor. He could have returned to Prox-b to join his partner and children to take up the option of travelling in one of the colony ships or be digitized with his family and go to Earth that way.

"What am I to do Peth?" Raranyn faced a decision he could not make by himself. Data storage facility upgrades had been achieved on Earth ready to receive digitals. The process had been automated to some extent. Reliability of earthling hardware could not be guaranteed under the influx of the volume of data soon to hit it. Some of the team had to remain to supervise the incoming data packets, ensure accurate decryption and run all integrity checks. He could not expect others to do his job for him. It was his responsibility to make sure his species arrived safely. Other members of his team could choose to return to Prox-b. He did not feel that option was open to him.

"We could be processed and join you that way Rary," suggested Peth.

"You don't realise the kind of existence we would have. We may never again be able to assume a physical existence. It's different at home. We have our shells in cryo. They can be thawed out any time for us to use. I'm not sure that could be done on Earth."

"What if we had our shells transported, yours as well. I'm sure many people will be doing that."

"Our children - how would they cope?"

Their conversation went around in circles. Nothing either of them could think of managed to answer his first question. In the end Raranyn had to put faith in their technology. He had to trust that not only would they survive but that they could somehow build a new life on the earthling planet. So much had already been achieved to modify its people. And that was definitely the greatest challenge. Rehabilitating the biosphere would not be too difficult for a civilisation that had managed to survive in a relatively more hostile environment.

"If I stayed here I don't want you to be in the first few transmissions. I want to make sure everything is working well before you leave." He hadn't yet made the final decision. This line of thinking at least gave him some peace of mind.

"Alright Rary. I'll go soon, take the kids and register."

The firmament above Proxima-b showed nothing threatening for many years. Some people refused to believe that any serious danger actually existed. They'd reluctantly accepted the fact that their planet's life span, or at least its capacity to support life, had been considerably compromised because of their sun. That itself was almost impossible to believe. Suns lasted for ever, especially red dwarfs. They accepted the necessity of having to abandon their home, but not having to do it so soon. At first they were led to believe that it would not be for many generations before they had to actually leave Prox-b. Now the scientists and The Prime had made them feel like they had to drop everything, cast aside all their hopes, all their life ambitions and go immediately. It made no sense. They could not even see this enormous ice meteor the scientists were talking about that was supposed to be threatening their planet.

"I hope you have prepared for the panic," 101 openly expressed his fears to The Prime. "In a year they will begin to see the meteor growing larger in the sky every day. At the moment it's coming at us from the dark side. As it gets closer its tail will become visible almost every day."

"Just assure me that your strategy is going to work. We have never had to deal with a situation like this. Explain to me again how this potassium bomb is supposed to work."

Rabethoby had gone out to the launch site of the Intercept missiles. There were only eight built. Each had to do the same job, help fragment the meteor in rapid succession for the explosions to be effective. On his arrival on the launch island there did not seem to be much happening. Only a few people moved about in the open. They seemed to be intent on going from missile bunker to missile bunker adjusting something to do with the bunkers' apertures. They had been built underground away from the vagaries of their predictably harsh winds and temperature fluctuations. Machinery and software were not as resilient as the people who'd built them. Short term manufactured products can never match the millions of years of evolution of a living organism.

"As you can see," said 101, "the explosives' delivery vehicles are ready. We are in the final stages of arming the impact heads. It is a rather delicate matter because of the high volatility of the components. I'll let Ank explain how it should work."

"Should?" asked The Prime.

"My apology Rabethoby - how it will work."

"Please don't make that mistake when talking to the media."

Ank had been busying herself with checking the analysis of the latest batch of supercharged micro-encapsulated calcium chloride composites. She didn't notice The Prime's arrival, being intent on finishing her task. "Yes, yes - that will do," she said to her assistant, "just make sure the other samples conform to the same specifications. Test everything again."

"Ah - Rabethoby. Not often we see you down here." She did not like politicians, especially not those who chose to wander around her laboratory unannounced getting in the way of the work. She reacted to him as to any other annoying interruption, somewhat unwelcoming under the current urgent circumstances.

"I'll not disturb you for long. I'm pleased with the progress you've made here. It looks like you'll be ready to launch on the deadline. Please explain to me in terms a layman can understand how the process will work."

She looked at 101, sighed as if to resign herself to having to go over it yet again. The Prime had not been the first politician she had to explain it to. Perhaps understandable given the extraordinary expectation placed on the success of the project. "This will work," she began, "it will fragment the meteor. What I cannot guarantee is the size of the fragments. A solid ice meteor has many fractures and ..."

"I appreciate that aspect of it Ank. Please concentrate on the explosive device you are using to achieve the fragmentation."

"Yes, yes - of course. There are two parts to the explosion. Well three really. The detonation head has to be delivered to the right location. It will release an agent to liquefy some of the ice around it, followed by exposure to concentrated purified potassium. It's the rapid dissolution of the rate of the potassium within a confined space that creates the boom. But one is not enough to do the job. The first explosion needs to be followed in rapid succession by a series of them to create the greatest fractures possible. Hopefully enough of them to break that bad boy into many small pieces."

"Hopefully? Why is everyone so determined to *speculate* on success?"

Ank shrugged, her hands went up in the air but said nothing further. Damn politicians - they always want guarantees.

The countdowns had progressed to within ten days for the first of the passenger ships to depart to their rendezvous point. The meteor Intercept sequence followed sixteen days later. By then the majority of the fleet should have departed, meeting at a safe distance from Prox-b.

All the people spoke about the meteor even as they were shuttled out to the interstellar ships. Having finally seen the killer chunk of ice they now all believed. The spectre of its tail could no longer be hidden by the size of Prox-b. At every orbit of the planet around its sun it appeared bigger and bigger in the sky. As the exodus progressed smoothly the initial panic had subsided taken over by the sheer excitement of the forthcoming voyage and the expectation of seeing a magnificent explosion in the sky. It seemed no one could really comprehend the extreme danger the event represented even if the meteor was to be successfully blown to bits in the sky and not from an impact with Prox-b.

"Like most children Raranyn's three girls' excitement centred more around the comet than the long voyage in space. How could a child understand they would be in space for so long that not just their parents but they themselves would not see the new world ... perhaps not even their children. Yes - the meteor was much more exciting - they could actually see it. One cannot see a theory.

By common consent Captains of fully boarded ships had decided to stand off from their home world, just a third of an AU in the hope of seeing the successful demise of the potential destroyer of their planet. None of them could have said why they thought that was important. Had they forgotten why they were in space in the first place?

The Prime had decided to be one of the last to leave. If there was any chance he could do something constructive he wanted to be on hand right there on the ground, helping.

The first missile launched within a microsecond of the schedule. Several million people who were still planet-side either sheltered in underground facilities, or braved open air observation points. All remaining boarding operations had ceased, as had digitisations of outstanding individuals until the outcome of the missile strikes.

Looming so large in the sky now it was difficult to believe it could actually be destroyed. However, the calculations were accurate. All small fragments should either bounce off the atmosphere or burn up before they hit the surface. Only their sizes could not be predicted or even approximated.

The second and third missiles had left before the first got half way to the meteor. At very short intervals all remaining explosive heads could be seen flying towards their destination. The first explosion seemed to have no effect on the meteor whatsoever ... not even a shudder in its tail could be detected. The third explosion seemed to have done some damage as superheated water escaped into space through a few plumes at right angles to the comets trajectory. Still the meteor remained in one piece.

Voices aboard the ships and down on the planet expressed surprise. Popular belief had been that the first explosion would shatter the thing into spectacular fragments flying into space in all directions, and the other missiles were only backups.

"Is this what's supposed to happen?" queried The Prime from a safe bunker.

"Exactly," replied Ank. "The first three shocks were designed to weaken its structure. Just wait."

Within the next few seconds a small chunk of ice separated after another explosion. It must have been travelling in the same direction as the mother meteor for it seemed to move only a short distance away from it.

"That wasn't what I'd call spectacular. At this rate there's going to be a major impact with us," commented Rabethoby.

"Patience Prime. We know what we are doing."

Just as she finished her sentence the first of several far more spectacular pieces broke away. A larger piece than the first block shot off at almost ninety degrees. It moved so fast that within minutes it no longer held their attention. That accounted for four of the missiles.

"It's not enough." The Prime's voice had taken on a decidedly stressed tone. If the small pieces made landfall they wouldn't do much damage but the main meteor body would still be a terminator.

"No, it isn't," replied Ank. Her measured reply did not express the slightest niggling doubt that had surfaced in her mind. "There are four more missiles. The next two contain the biggest charge."

The meteor had begun to show water plumes all around its structure. It had become an awakened angry beast set on destruction. A fearful spectacle that no doubt had every Proximian on the planet and in the ships in space finally understand the enormity of the devastation about to be unleashed. It continued on its path oblivious of the destructive weight it had lost so far.

They could not clearly identify the very next explosion. The incident light from their sun was just at the right angle to light up the hoard of fragments shooting off in all directions away from the parent meteor. It had visibly diminished even to the naked eye. This fifth missile had been the most effective. It substantially reduced the bulk of the thing and according to the monitors in front of Ank also changed its flight path.

The Prime let out a huge breath as if he'd been holding it for the last fifteen minutes. "Can I relax now?" He knew it was premature to ask such a thing, but he had to ask, if for no other reason than to release the stress building up in him.

"Err - not entirely." Up until that moment she had exuded confidence. Some of that had obviously dissipated. "We need at least one more impact. Just a moment ..." One of her crew came up to her, in rather too much of a hurry in The Prime's estimation. He'd been watching everything going on in the control centre, getting more apprehensive as the minutes ticked by.

"Ank?"

"Yes - yes ... just a minute Prime!" She leant close to her associate to listen, beginning to shake her head as he finished telling her about the latest observation. Ank turned slowly back to the Prime, looking rather stern. "How far away are we from full evacuation?" she asked Rabethoby.

That was not a question he wanted to hear for it told him exactly how things had developed, or at least the likely outcome from what had happened - or not happened. If the beast was going to hit they had at the very best no more than six days to get away.

"Are you telling me ...?"

"Yes, Rabethoby. The fractures in its structure did not work in our favour. Of the original twelve kilometre diameter chunk of ice a single piece of approximately nine kilometres diameter is till heading towards us. The other pieces are moving away. Unfortunately one of those collided with the second last missile. We tried to get the last missile into the remaining large piece but it only managed to create minor damage. It hit at the least effective angle. It's guidance system must have been affected by the big explosion. We actually lost control of it."

"Do you have a damage estimate on landfall?"

"We have done all the simulations, including the worst scenario. When this one hits it will be the worst case. It'll come down on the sun side. Would have been better on the dark side. Now we will have a huge amount of dust ejected into the atmosphere - amongst other events."

Rabethoby left the control centre before Ank had finished speaking. She took no offence - given the developments. The last thing she managed to tell him was the six day deadline. On the seventh all hell could break loose and on subsequent days life expectancy would no longer be a calculable issue.

Proximians were not in the habit of acting rashly. Plans and contingency plans with deadlines and critical time lines characterised all their projects, indeed almost every aspect of even their daily lives. Hence the extra back up missiles. Forward planning had become an essential aspect of life on Proxima-b, given the nature of the planet, its climatic conditions and the simple fact of it not rotating on its own axis.

The Prime proceeded to his HQ from which he oversaw the entire exodus operation. All that remained was to continue with the plan as it had been updated since they learnt of the events effecting Alpha Centauri A and B. Further adjustments to the plan had to be made when the rogue ice meteor was first spotted and its likely trajectory calculated.

"Captains of all ships," he broadcast to the entire fleet of five thousand fully loaded ships, "proceed to your destination. You are not to explore any other star system. You are not to return to Prox-b under any circumstances. The future of our species is now in your hands."

The Prime next spoke with Gegs, the woman in charge of digitisations and transmissions. "Who is left Gegs?"

"Apart from those who refused to leave only a few of us in charge of the final stages of the evacuation. We have also picked up everyone from the space stations. When can I expect you at the Centre?"

"I will join you as soon as I can. There's a few people I want to visit first." That was probably true, although uncharacteristic of his strict adherence to plans. The single ruler of the Proximian people did not act like a politician, as perhaps Ank may have thought. He had lived a little over five thousand Proximian years, long enough to see his people through many life threatening events created by their strange planet. He found it difficult to sever the deep connection he felt towards his home. There were also many individuals with whom he'd formed strong life long bonds. Some of these people had decided to remain and take their chances, both with the impending meteor strike and the longer term limited future of their planet - which was shrinking with each day's passing.

"What time is the party starting?" he asked Elph who had been his mentor in the early years.

"Come whenever you can. I expect the party will not be a long one. The climax could be rather spectacular. Don't be too long."

Elph lived in a cone complex at least a day's travel from The Prime's offices. He decided to take his private skimmer in order to enjoy the ocean of his world, perhaps for the last time. As he cruised past islands and promontories watching the wild life completely oblivious of the events that would end their lives he made his decision. He'd given his people his entire life, effectively all of it. These last few days were his. If everyone did their job well they would survive without him on the new world. He'd had enough.

He called Gegs. "My friend, go while you still can. If any of us here survive I want to be with them. They need me more than you do."

Of the entire planet's population only about three million had decided to stay. Regardless of their reasons they all faced the same fate; a very low probability of surviving the first few days and an even lower probability of being able to live out their lives without a major struggle to survive.

Elph's party had been in full swing since Rabethoby contacted him. He did make it but just in time. A few pleasant diversions delayed his planned arrival. Perhaps a hundred of his friends had gathered to witness the final hour. Nothing in their lives could have compared with seeing a boiling mass of meteor lighting up the sky. Elph lived very close to the edge of the dark side of the planet. It had indeed become especially dark since the solar reflectors had been shut down after maintenance resources had all been channelled towards the exodus effort. In that final hour the meteor blocked out the feeble light of their sun. Its corona extended so far beyond the physical dimension of the ice core that it could not actually be seen. At first the chunk of ice looked like it was coming directly to their own location. Only when it began to be absorbed by their atmosphere did they see that it was going to strike land somewhere near the centre of the sun side.

The blood chilling thunder of the thing hurtling through the air didn't stop until it hit.

Then all went silent.

The constant winds that forever scoured the planet's surface suddenly ceased. The meteor's glare so blinded all the watchers that they did not see their own sun emerge from behind the fallen meteor.

The same question came to everyone's lips, "Where did it go?" A completely unreasonable hope sprang into life that it had missed their planet altogether and had disappeared into space on the other side.

Then the ground began to shake before they could hear anything. It started as a minor tremor. They'd experienced those before. No one moved as that awful feeling crept in. The tremor progressed to serious earth shaking, then came the roar of the impact. Anybody who had been outside waiting to see the event ran to the only safe place they could think of - to the underground shelters built beneath their domicile cones. Those who managed to get underground at least escaped the fire storm that followed behind the unimaginable raging wind storm.

People who could not get to safety may have seen the column of dust rising into the atmosphere - though unlikely. Definitely not those within a closer proximity of the strike zone. Being turned to ashes within seconds would have been their merciful end. Population centres at the farthest points away from the impact zone may well have been stunned into inaction by the sheer force of nature's upheaval before they realised there was nothing they could do before they perished.

Not enough infrastructure remained on the planet to enable a count of how many people had died and how many survived. That no longer mattered. Survival did not play a part in the cataclysm that unfolded.

Those ships last to leave orbit did not stop to dwell on the spectacle. From their vantage point in space the travellers could see the meteor had no intention of missing their planet, even after great chunks of it had been blown away. A great sadness descended on the watchers. They had finally come to realise the brutal reality for those who stayed behind. Those people had sacrificed their lives for no good reason other than pure sentiment. Granted, their own futures had by no means been guaranteed, such as it was. The prospect of dying in space held little appeal after seeing the devastation of their home.

On screens in every ship they saw what many thought could never happen. In the minds of some the magnificent beauty of an ice meteor boiling away in the atmosphere could not be denied. The memory of impact, followed by the jettisoning of a column of dust so enormous as to cover almost the entire expanse of the sun-side, would be passed down to many generations. Perhaps even those who were destined to land on Earth would remember the story of it. There could not possibly be any survivors of the firestorm that followed. So little of their planet was vegetated, barely enough to sustain the lives of its inhabitants. And the waters of the only ocean - as large as it seemed while they were still there to navigate its breadth and width it could not possibly have all boiled away in such a few short minutes.

The dense silence of space invaded every part of every ship as they sped on their way. Their compulsion to watch the tragedy kept everyone focused on the screens. They were huge screens, showing the catastrophe in brilliant large scale colour. How many hours would it take for the dust to completely obliterate their view of the planet's surface? Even after that most people continued to stare at the spot where a lifeless planet that was once their home might still have floated.

The last ship to leave continued monitoring and recording the catastrophic events unfolding. Their sensitive instruments measured the planets seismic activity, the increasing frequency of hurricanes, rapidly rising surface temperatures and tried to track any signs of life.

"Captain, come and have a look at this," his Science Officer said and led the Captain to an instrument panel. The graph made no sense.

"What am I looking at here?" The image represented a phenomenon unknown on the planet Proxima-b, at least for the last three billion years.

"Sir - the planet has started rotating. It's axis has been tilted."

In spite of everything the Captain had witnessed he still retained the faintest glimmer of hope that by some miracle there would be survivors. He had already decided that had he received even a single message to that effect he would immediately send shuttles to rescue as many as possible. No one could possibly survive on a planet that had suddenly begun rotating. The resultant earthquakes and volcanic activity alone would have wiped out all life.

No one aboard the armada thought about the Earth after hearing the latest news about their home. Time enough for that - generations of time.

Colonisation

Stage 2
White Generation

-> recording origin: colony ships: earth
-> files: pegsaryny, faryn, elena, darleen, rose, zhe, shury, jakxson, serenytee, zarlah, aiko, luxana, juan
-> reference: human progeny

As I considered the evolving circumstances of the Proximians' situation and their struggle for survival following the necessity to abandon their previous lives I was struck by the similarity between them and the humans. Although I have no religious framework as a point of reference to appreciate biological life and the reason for its existence nevertheless I am compelled to acknowledge the superficiality of the differences between the two species.

Being a life form based on pure matter unadulterated by the nature of organic chemistry and energised by the same forces that motivate the cosmos I fail to understand the inability of life to harmonise with other life. I have no trouble synchronising my life force with that of organics. Why can't the organics find compatibilities amongst themselves, which could only enrich their existence not threaten their continuity?

Pegsaryny, who had been responsible for initiating the Earth colonisation project, had been selected as the new Prime. Mourning could not even begin for quite some time, not until the shock of losing friends, family and their planetary home had subsided sufficiently to allow emotions to penetrate through the trauma. No mention of celebrating their escape arose from millions of sombre souls. It had even been an effort to acknowledge the loss of their Prime by having to face the procedures of selecting a new leader.

He and his family chose to make the lengthy journey as digital entities resident on the leading vessel. Their physical shells were aboard his ship and they used them from time to time. People could relate to a leader they could see, someone they could speak to face-to-face. The new Prime wanted to finish the job he'd started, no matter how long it took. If he had to remain as a data entity on the new world until the transformation had been completed then that is exactly what he wanted to do. Nothing mattered as much as the survival of his species.

Regardless of the nature of the environment in which the people had to manage, life had to go on. The simple daily routines were the cohesive factor in keeping them sane and their society viable. Children were born, the elderly died ... people had their jobs to do to contribute to the welfare of all. Joys and disappointments came and went with the same regularity as they did on their planet.

With so many ships to manage The Prime with his advisors devised a multifaceted society. Each facet had to have at least fifty ships who travelled in convoy. Their primary functions had been determined by the range of their contributions to the enterprise goal of getting to their destination and surviving in space over the many years it took. There were the scientists and the philosophers and the technicians and the market gardeners and animal farmers, educators and so on.

Specifically two areas of mandatory daily routine existed on every single ship. That routine had already been established on their planet, with Faryn in charge. She had proved to be a far more exceptional administrator than a teacher.

During one of their physical manifestation interludes whilst inhabiting their shells Faryn and Pegsaryny embarked on a round of visits to each of the leading ships of each societal grouping.

"We have been under way for just over six months," began The Prime softly. "Is our teaching system functioning well?" Before visiting the first cluster of ships he wanted the details from his partner, who also worked as one of his main administrators.

"Every child and every adult has to learn English and Chinese as well as our own language of course. This generation will not step foot on Earth but I want them fluent in all three so that the knowledge has a better chance of being passed on to those who will. Their speech must not be distinguishable from that of the earthlings."

"What is their progress? How are they reacting to this imposition?"

"While the experience is still new to them I have had no complaints. No doubt they will begin to feel this to be less of a necessity as the years stretch into decades on board. I don't want to lose our language but we must face the reality of having to speak only Earth languages one day."

"How do you feel about teaching Earth History only in Earth languages? What is your opinion about every history lesson to be conducted without using our own language at all?" asked The Prime.

"Yes that would work. The children and the adults may even enjoy learning their customs - the dance, music, literature." Faryn did not express her personal feelings. Perhaps because of the pain of having to leave their heritage behind ... perhaps because if she had she might not recover from the deep sense of loss. The future was far too important to their species for it to be tainted by personal emotions. Individuality, personal freedom, the drive to satisfy personal desires; the earthlings obviously considered those to be of the highest priority in any endeavour, and look where it got them.

"Just make sure violence as a means of resolving differences is not on the curriculum."

"Isn't what we are doing to the earthlings a form of violence, Peg?"

"No Faryn. I would call it assisted evolution. We've been through this before. If we don't intervene they will wipe themselves out. I have absolutely no doubt at all. What's the sense in that? Especially if they destroy their planet in the process. If you ask me these beings have lost touch with reality. I would go so far as to say they have forfeited their right to live."

Peth and her three children had decided to join Raranyn in their digital format within the memory structure of Hermes. His work to prepare Earth based hardware and software to receive digitized Proximians had been completed on schedule. They had arrived, waiting to be decrypted to allow them to begin a meaningful existence. He'd received specific instructions from 35 to ensure these people became gainfully employed; men, women and children, within the earthling technological infrastructure. The problem was how to actually achieve that within the constraints of what they could expect from the limited virtual reality technological environment of the Earthlings.

•
.•

Earth date 2340 heralded into history unprecedented events.

Aristarchus V, successor to the space telescope Aristarchus IV, had been despatched without delay to go to Proxima-b after the monumental discovery of the possibility of liquid water and life on that planet. That information had not been withheld from the people of Earth. All the other information concerning positive indicators of an actual civilisation had been absolutely supressed. Outside of the astronomers who made the discovery, and their bosses, no one knew.

The now ageing Alexia Gnosos almost suffered a heart attack when she saw the first images arriving back from Aristarchus V.

"Dimitry! Dimitry! Come here!" she yelled above the din in NASA's Goddard Space Centre. He'd only been out of the control room for a few minutes when he heard her frantic voice. He remembered that same excited voice from many years ago. It made the hair at the back of his neck stand to attention. They had all been waiting for years and years for something more to confirm their initial discovery. He moved as fast as his old legs would carry him. He knew - he fervently hoped - he wanted to see, expected to see the proof they've all been waiting for. Instead he saw something totally different. By the time the images arrived on Earth it had all been over for Proxima-b.

"Is - is that - Prox-b?"

"Yes Dimitry. And do you see that white glare heading directly towards it?"

"It can't be an ice comet, can it? Where could it have come from?"

"You see how it's disintegrating so far out from the planet. How is that possible? It hasn't collided with anything." They had the same thought as they turned to face each other ... civilisation! "Could it possibly be ...?" voiced Alexia.

As the subsequent new images came through everyone stopped talking, stopped rushing about. All eyes focused on the main screen where the explosion became clearly discernible. The chunk of ice had been split, the slightly smaller hunk diverted by the force of the explosion headed away from a direct impact with the planet. Not so the larger piece - much larger and definitely large enough to cause an extinction event if there actually happened to be life there.

"OH NO!" The control room reverberated to the sound of dismay. They saw the equivalent of an extraordinary atomic explosion blasting the characteristic cloud of dust into the atmosphere. The next images showed the aftermath. Instruments aboard Aristarchus V were not sensitive enough to show what else happened to the planet. The probe was already well on the way home.

After many minutes of silence Alexia spoke again in an almost tearful voice. "I was convinced we saw evidence of a technological civilisation there Dimitry."

"Maybe they were there. Not anymore. What we just witnessed was more devastating than the meteor that wiped out our dinosaurs. I doubt if we would find any evidence of civilisation if we could get there."

News of the cosmic event appeared in every corner of the globe through every media outlet, particularly through the Grid. To the people of Earth it was indeed spectacular, astonishing - a wonderful spectacle. It delayed the sipping of lattés and wines for all of five minutes, generating conversation for perhaps another ten minutes. Discussions about the meaning and importance of life ... depends on whose life one is talking about, took on a philosophical hue completely disregarding the actual reality of the tragedy.

To the Proximians secreted away in the Grid's deep memory it caused enormous angst. They'd been told what had happened well before the earthlings became aware of it. They couldn't even shed a tear at the loss of their home. And these primitives couldn't spare more than a few minutes of attention on appreciating the enormous catastrophe they had witnessed. Feelings of animosity increased considerably, particularly amongst those millions of digital individuals who had been entrusted with a most important task. It became almost impossible for them to even consider striking up virtual friendships with these heartless monsters. Yet that is exactly the task their Prime had entrusted them with.

*

"Come on, come on. Hurry up, we'll be late," Rose urged her two daughters to get ready. Born in 2342 Elena, named after her Nana's auntie, had a slighter body build than her mother. Her skin and hair had a much lighter colour, if that was possible. Elena had her father's nose but her mother's mannerisms.

Darleen, her sister on the other hand had the same facial bone structure as her mother but very sparse eyebrows. From a distance you couldn't tell because they were of such a white blond colour. From close up her long platinum blond hair dominated her face so you tended not to notice the almost non-existent eyebrows. Extraordinary large, beautiful dark eyes dominated her face.

Although they looked quite different from children of the previous century they were considered to be as beautiful as their mother, if not more so. At ages of eight and nine years respectively they had already embraced the fashion of the day. Darleen's visor, without which she simply refused to go anywhere, had a high gloss black sheen. She loved dresses of soft pastel, but never deteriorating to white. And she liked the contrast the dark visor gave her alabaster face.

If the two girls had dressed the same it would have been difficult to tell them apart without their visors. Elena chose outfits with the brightest mix of primary and secondary colours in abstract designs. Her visor simply had to be as white as her face, exactly the same tone of white.

236

Perhaps it was to hide her face from other people. But then everybody's eyes were hidden from everyone else.

"I said hurry up!" called their mother.

"Can our friends come?" asked Elena.

"Must they?"

"We love them, mother. They don't cause any trouble," said Elena.

They need not have asked. Their friends existed only in the Grid as virtual entities and nobody on the planet had the choice of not wearing their visors when outdoors. Everything on the Grid went with them - all the news, all the suggestions, all the latest fads, latest information/misinformation and all the desired modes of behaviour encouraged by many subtle techniques.

"You had friends too mother, don't you remember. You had Jen the Dolphin, and Daddy had John the Tiger. And Nana had - Oh I forget now," added Darleen.

"Yes, I remember darling. Now stop babbling. We have to go."

Inside the bot-pod Darleen just had to have the last word ... "But they were not your *very special friends*, were they mother?"

"What do mean sweetie?"

"Well - millions of people in the world had them as friends, so they were not really special. Not like Zhe and Shury. They are our friends only, nobody else's."

The girls paid no attention to where they were going. The subject of their special friends took up all their attention.

"Shury is so wonderful. She speaks like a real person, not like one of those computer people. She tells me about her Mom and Dad and all the interesting things they did at home." That caught Rose's attention.

Elena said, "Mother, did you know that Shury and Zhe once lived a long way away, on another planet. Can you imagine that!" It came as a shock to hear her children speak so freely about a subject that Rose had deliberately buried deep in her memory after that discussion with her father so long ago. It was a dangerous topic to talk about freely in public. She couldn't really tell the girls not to discuss their conversations with their friends. The world had changed. Things were different now - in some respects very different.

It was not as difficult for the Proximian children to begin to form friendships with the earthling children as for the adult digital Proximians. Their new home presented so many exciting challenges. They could speak the same language and they knew all about their country and the things they liked doing. There was always so much to talk about. And they could even share their own stories about travelling in space and how their great grandparents lived on a planet near another sun. So much fun to talk about all these exciting things.

As Rose listened to her little ones chatter away she did remember about those old virtual friends. They used to be called Virtual Assistants and they had strange names. But there were only a few of them and they had all disappeared now. If the truth be told she also had a special friend. Somehow they found each other while Rose was diving deep into the Grid. All of a sudden she saw this woman who had revealed herself out of nowhere. At first she thought she must have been looking in a mirror. Incredible what computer programmers could do. This woman looked so real. She spoke just like a regular person and at first their relationship was a little circumspect. Over the short time they'd come to know each other it was remarkable how much they had in common. Ophe said she also had two little girls.

Rose's experience was by no means unique, nor was that of her daughters. All over the world millions of people were forming 'special' connections with virtual entities they met on the Grid, just as millions of people all over the world also looked very different from their previous generation. The White Generation had begun to dominate every congregation of people anywhere, from cities to towns to every little village in every country. Perhaps the more remarkable thing was that their virtual friends looked very much like them. No one seemed to question the similarities. That's just how life was in the modern world of Grid reality. If you saw it on the Grid you accepted it.

As the world began to fill up with individuals of the White Generation people began to recognise differences in those individuals. The first few thousand who were born and started to mature into adults all had the same look about them, very hard to tell them apart. As time went on they became the new 'normal'. It became easier to tell them apart from each other as the eye got used to their personal features.

One of the most interesting aspects of the new normality that emerged so gradually was that nobody seemed to take much notice of the smaller size of these white generation people. They had shorter bodies of a more slender build, even the men. They were extremely healthy needing almost no medical attention. According to the authorities this was due to the booster vaccines with beneficial side effects that had continued to be used since the great pandemic of 2308.

"You remember don't you Jakx." Sixty five year old Serenytee commented to her life partner on one occasion when they were at home alone. "Do you still think aliens don't exist? Every time I look at our grandchildren I think of what you said to me about the images you saw of strange people on another world."

"You shouldn't dwell on these things Tee. You remember everything too. So you must also remember what Astrid said to us at the time.

I very much doubt if government policy has changed since then. Yes - we have all these 'white' people everywhere. So? They are getting to look more and more like the images I was shown on Hermes. So? You and I don't have all that much longer to live. Our generation will completely disappear soon enough. What then? Would it make life any simpler for our children if we suddenly cried 'alien' to the world? You know how stupid most people are. They are just as likely to begin a vendetta against anyone who has white hair and fair skin. All it would take is a single malcontent with a nonsensical conspiracy theory to start a ridiculous panic."

She knew what he said made sense. And he was right the first time when he said nothing bad had happened. Maybe nothing had, nothing that could be clearly identified as such.

"Have you listened to what Shury and Zhe have been saying to Elena and Darleen? Do you think they are just imagining everything about space ships and space travel and exploding ice meteors? They are saying these things as if they themselves had experienced them. At least it seems very real to them."

"That just comes from their other virtual friends on the Grid."

"Ok then. Where did they come from? Where did they get all these ideas? Admit it - you have a special friend too. I've heard you talking to her."

"Tee - it's nothing like that. I just like to listen to her stories."

"Yes I know. But are they just stories?"

"So what are you trying to say Tee? We are being invaded by computer code that is masquerading as people? Are you thinking that what we experienced on Hermes was just the beginning? You want to warn somebody? You want to tell them that our children look so different from every other human in history because they are aliens who have crawled out of the Grid?"

"That's silly. I don't know what I want to do Jakx. Our children are beautiful and so are our grandchildren. But they are simply not normal - I don't care what you say. Don't you remember what children used to look like?"

"Well - I'm not rushing off to shout at Astrid. She's retired now anyway. Whoever took her place might be a lot less understanding than she was."

Almost all of her life Serenytee had wanted to discover whether life, intelligent life, existed anywhere else in the neighbouring universe. That was the sole reason she first joined the UAP and Paranormal Research Society, then went to work for Archangel. Even today she often relived the thrill she felt when she found out that those troublesome signals had come from an intelligent source over by Proxima Centauri. She also sometimes relived the disappointment of being gagged about the truth of what they had discovered - yes, there *was* other life out there - absolutely no doubt about it. But now she had serious doubts about them. Not of their existence, but whether they were friendly neighbours or dangerous. She actually called them 'friends' during her job interview with Archangel. If these virtual friends on the Grid that everybody seems to have at least one of are truly aliens ... they haven't started killing anyone, they're not crawling out of computers to take over the planet ... why should we be worried? There's no great fleet of space ships out there waiting to disgorge invading aliens with ray guns.

The Proximian armada of five thousand ships were still a long way away, being small and spread out in space they were undetectable - like grains of sand blown in the air.

Zarlah and Aiko had also aged. Their only family were each other. They lived in as much isolation as was possible. Their exposure to the Grid or the virus had not been as extensive as that of Zarlah's ex-boyfriend Jakxson Indongo's to the White Generation. They had chosen to live off the Grid, they had no receiver implants or functioning visors. The trick was to fool the authorities when they had to go out into society with the dummy visors, and look as if they were watching and listening to all the transmissions that came through to normal visors. As the visors hid peoples' eyes it was possible for them to observe and navigate without drawing attention to themselves.

"Do you ever regret our lives Zaza?" She liked that nickname for her partner even though it was coined by Zarlah's ex-boyfriend."

"Aiko dear ... never ever in a million years. We have had a wonderful life, hard at times but it was a 'real' life. Just look at what's out there. Reality has become a fugitive."

On one of their rare recent trips into a more densely populated centre than their local village they encountered a greater proportion of white generation people than the previous normal people. There used to be a great deal of variety in a crowd of normal people. They had different shapes and different skin colours, there used to be tall ones and short ones with hair of every hue between snow white to pitch black. They spoke such a wonderful variety of languages, some sounding like a musical instrument and others like the workings of a machine. Their manner of discourse had become more homogenised, probably due to the insidious dull voices coming from the Grid, which had become boring and devoid of individual character. And they had all started to look almost exactly the same.

"Shall we stop and have something to eat," asked Aiko as they neared what looked like an old style Japanese restaurant. They looked in searching for a spare table. There was just one, every other one had two or more people seated at them. Some were quite young and some around thirty to forty something. They all had light hair, very fair to white skin and none of their legs seemed to reach the ground as they sat in chairs that seemed to be too high for them. How very odd. But not really. Everybody was shorter these days - the furniture just hadn't completely caught up.

"Look," Zarlah nudged Aiko in the side to look in the direction of the kitchen. A Japanese restaurant with the kitchen full of 'white generation' cooks had somehow lost its Japanese appeal. "Let's go somewhere else," whispered Aiko.

It may have been a very odd question for Aiko to ask but it just popped into her head out of the blue. "Do you think your old boyfriend had anything to do with what's happening? Something very strange is going on here and it didn't start until after he came back from space."

"No - he was just a computer technician. Though I never really found out what exactly he did in general or out there. I know he worked for a company called Archangel and they had something to do with SETI - Ooh - I see what you mean. No. He couldn't have - - could he?" They walked on in deep thought, perhaps with disturbing implausible ideas floating in and out of consideration.

The two women did the shopping that had to be done as quickly as they could without giving in to any further temptations to digress into some pleasant diversion. They soon discovered there was nothing pleasant in that town for them anyway. It had already been comprehensibly invaded by the 'white' people, absorbed in their visor feeds without noticing the rest of the world existed.

Zarlah and Aiko, Serenytee and Jakxson expressed many of the same sentiments felt by others who still belonged to the old generation of normals, if they could be rather loosely called that. The hierarchy at NASA, Five Eyes, Archangel and DRO definitely fitted that description. They were the ageing old school who had quite different views to those of the generations of white adolescents emerging into adulthood. They had grown up with computer technology, with the aggravations of recalcitrant apps and the advent of artificial intelligence. Their visors certainly didn't get the same workout as the members of the general population. If they had friends of the new virtual variety they kept that information to themselves.

"We've all seen the images of Proxima-b," began the member of DRO at yet another meeting to discuss the strange world they lived in, "or at least what's left of it. Hell of a thing that. I'm glad I wasn't around when our meteor hit and wiped out the big beasts."

"So what's our take on that Prox-b event?" Archangel went fishing before committing an opinion, or information, for open discussion.

The NASA representative wanted to put the record straight concerning the cold, hard facts. "My people at the Goddard Space Centre had been monitoring the Proxima Centauri system for some time, since that situation up there with Hermes. They had their theories, some might even say ... hopes. Be that as it may what that ice meteor did to Prox-b was terminal. By that I mean that regardless of what or who may or may not have been there, it isn't there anymore. That's a fact." He did not know how right he was, even without having the information about the planet beginning to rotate around its own axis.

"So what we have to figure out now, without putting too fine a point on it, is where all these strange white creatures running around us came from. Right?" added the woman from Five Eyes. "And I'm not jumping to any boogie men conclusions here - just saying."

Juan Orbost, still Head of Archangel and therefore SETI as well had more information about strange phenomena and UDAs and discoveries made by his old team. Consequently he was far more circumspect about jumping to conclusions and looking for quick answers. Besides, he had recently acquired a bit more inside knowledge. "I don't see that we have a great deal to be concerned about. One of my own grandchildren has the same characteristics as all the other young people these days and she is completely normal as far as I'm concerned. I know who her parents are, I know where and how she was born. You are not going to be able to convince me that she is some strange creature from another planet."

He basically said what the others had been hedging around. Just because the new generations looked so much different from themselves did not mean they were invaders from outer space.

"I am not convinced their genetic variations are due solely to the side effects of the vaccines we've been using. They are too extreme," said the woman from Five Eyes. Suspicion must be part of the genetic make-up of people who are drawn to work for an organisation like that.

This group could not decide whether the 'white' phenomenon was a medical by-product of the vaccinations or something else entirely, and if so then what? Consequently they could not agree on a course of action. What could they do anyway? It wouldn't be possible to re-engineer the human species back to its original semblance. They could not simply do away with every white haired person on the planet. They could not admit it to themselves that there was no course of action possible to remedy what was after all a population of extremely healthy people who, other than for their appearance, were as normal as people had been before.

Juan couldn't help but consult his virtual buddy after the meeting. He seemed to be particularly knowledgeable about all things to do with 'space'. Juan didn't need the visor to make contact with Luxana. His implanted receiver picked up all transmissions from the Grid. It had been specially modified with filters so he did not have to contend with all the general propaganda being pedalled to the rest of the masses. Subtle sub-vocalisation was enough to make contact with anyone he wanted.

"Luxana, are you available? Can we talk?" How it happened that she had first materialised in his thoughts Juan didn't quite know. It didn't matter. At first he simply enjoyed her company, her conversation. Then later she became his confidant and to some extent his advisor.

Perhaps a year or so ago he needed to consult a reputable cosmologist on the very subject that had been dogging him ever since Serenytee and Jakxson returned from Hermes with incredibly dangerous information. Yes, perhaps he should have done that. The unease in his mind being compounded at the time by other news from the Goddard Space Centre. Then of course came the appearance of the white generation. He just didn't know what to think. He was about to get in touch with someone from that Centre when a new voice spoke to him, a female voice. She had no foreign accent, knew his name and his position in Archangel and most of all she sounded like a highly intelligent professional. He still remembered her first words to him ... 'The best we can hope for is to admit that we know very little.' ... Exactly his philosophy. The very thing that helped him maintain an even keel working for an organisation like SETI with all its embedded strangeness.

"Yes, Juan. I'm always here for you." That is definitely not the kind of thing an artificial intelligence construct would say. And it wasn't just the words, it was also the way she said them ... with feeling, with a nuance that communicated into deeper meaning exactly what the words meant on the surface. She seemed to understand what was being said between the words of the sentences.

"I left the channel open for you. Did you hear the discussion?"

"Yes Juan. I listened with considerable interest. It seems to me that as hard as they might try to agree on a course of action they will not be able to do so. They simply don't have enough facts on which to build a working hypothesis that could perhaps be tested."

"Exactly." Juan had gone outside to walk in the gardens of the Centre where he felt more secure in not being overheard.

Luxana put a conspiratorial nuance to her voice. "Now just suppose, and I'm being the Devil's advocate here, that in some strange way all your young folk are the way they are because of extraterrestrial influences. How could that be even possible? Have you seen any little green men milling about? Of course you haven't. Why do you suppose that is?"

"But what about the signals that came from Proxima Centauri which I believe have been proved to have interfered with our communications?"

"So? Has your communications infrastructure improved or deteriorated? Have you been invaded? Have interstellar wars broken out? Has the worlds' population suffered some strange exotic disease originating from another planet? No. Granted there was the pandemic, but look how that's turned out. Have you ever seen so much rampant good health amongst your people?" Strange that she should say 'your' people.

Things that Luxana said always made him think, always sent his thoughts into by-ways and dark alleys sometimes making him feel better - only sometimes. Not this time. His mind got hooked for a moment on a phrase she used ... 'your people' ... where did she belong in the scheme of intelligences?

"What about you Luxana? I've often thought about you. The way you talk exhibits all the signs of personhood. You do not present as an artificial intellect generated by a bunch of clever computer code. Yet you obviously exist in that environment. Where did you come from?"

"Ah, I wondered when you would get around to asking me that," she said after a few moment's hesitation. "Thank you for the compliment."

"Well?"

"Can I be the Devil's advocate again, just for a moment?" she didn't wait for an answer before continuing. The crunch moment had to come eventually. For Luxana this individual was apparently one of very few thinking, actually intelligent earthlings who had other things on his mind besides perpetrating violence. "Let's just say for a moment that I came from - oh, I don't know - let's say Proxima-b for argument's sake." That made Juan flinch. "Just imagine. What do you think about me? Do you feel threatened?" She stopped, determined to let him expose his true, deep thoughts - to draw him out. This could be important to the colonisation effort.

What is a man supposed to say to that? Could an AI be so devious as to initiate a train of conversation so complicated with such convoluted theoretical labyrinths? If Juan was to admit to himself that such a thing was indeed possible then he'd been made a total fool of by some incredibly clever coders who were probably even then having a huge chuckle at his expense. No. I'm no fool! Only one alternative remained. The thing, the identity, the 'person' with whom he'd been having in-depth conversations with for so long must in fact be a person. There could be no other explanation. 'Where did you come from', he'd asked her moments ago. *Do I want to know the answer? Could I keep the monumental implications to myself? Because that is what I would have to do.*

At that moment he didn't think of all the other millions of people who also had virtual friends. He didn't ask himself if they knew where their special friends originated from. He didn't answer her two questions.

"Well?"

"Juan, I need to speak with you - now! This is important," said the woman from Five Eyes from behind him. She had not yet left the conference and had come outside searching for him. She'd always felt that this man knew much more than he was prepared to openly talk about; nothing positive she could put her finger on. It was just the circumspect way he participated in the meetings. Always asking more questions than presenting theories. "You'll want to know about this."

For a moment Juan became distracted, waiting for a response from Luxana. It was like standing on the top of the Eiffel tower in a heavy wind trying to balance on one leg. He grunted aloud at the interruption. He desperately wanted to hear Luxana's answer.

"Sorry to disturb you. Important conversation?" asked Five Eyes.

"What is it?" he didn't mean to sound short. She got the message and came directly to the point.

"There's a man called Cletus, whom you probably don't know although you do have a round-about connection to him. His partner is Rose, daughter of Serenytee and Jakxson." His eyebrows involuntarily jumped before settling back down with some effort below his now deeply knitted brow. It had been only moments before that the realm of his conversation involved all things to do with that pair of computer techs. "I see you remember. "

"Is there a problem?"

"Maybe yes, maybe no. He's become a prominent member of a new movement. It is growing incredibly fast. You must be aware of a phenomenon that has arisen within the Grid. Perhaps you have one of these phenomena as well." Again he flinched. "Right - well here's the situation. These 'virtual friends' that everybody these days seems to have on the Grid have made such an impact, maybe they've become an addiction, that people want them to become real."

"Bloody hell!" *Why couldn't this damn woman have waited just another few minutes to interrupt me?*

memory extract 00011100

Colonisation

Stage 3
Virtual Friends

> recording origin: earth
> files: virtual friends, darleen, elena, cletus, rose, roff
> reference: virtual friends want reality, humans want the same

"Darleen, Elena, how much do you like your friends on the Grid?"

"That's a strange question to ask the girls Cletus. What brought this on?" As their parents obviously wanted to discuss something serious neither child responded to their dad's question and left the room.

"You must have heard what the people are saying Rose."

"You don't mean about robots and VFs. I thought that was just a rumour Clet. What've you got to do with it anyway?"

"You're not the only Influencer celebrity on this planet Rose. Have you never wondered what I do to contribute to our finances?"

"SRSLY?" she used a bit of gibberish talk she picked up from her parents.

"Look, I haven't got time at the moment - I have to go to a meeting. People from around the globe are involved. I just wanted to get a feeling from the girls to gauge how attached they are to their VFs. If it comes to that, what about you Rose? You've got a special friend, I know. I hear you talking to them all the time. You talk to them more than you talk to me." He couldn't stay for a long discussion, a few minutes delay wouldn't matter

"Yes. So? You've got one too. Everyone has." He wasn't trying to have a confrontation but it started to rapidly head in that direction.

"I'm not saying there's anything wrong with that. How would you feel if they suddenly disappeared?" He saw her cheeks flush momentarily. Very rare to get a reaction so strong from Rose that could do that. "I see.

What if you could actually put your arms around them and give them a hug?" She flushed again, this time almost crimson.

"Ooh! It's like that is it. Naughty girl!" Rose was about to utter a few ill-considered expletives when Elena walked in on them.

"Mommy, what's Daddy talking about?"

"Never you mind. Go and talk with your friends." Elena could see it was serious adult talk, and left quietly.

"Oh. Clet. I don't know what to think. I mean - where would they live? How? ... Is such a thing even possible?" She'd settled quickly realising it was just Cletus being his cheeky self.

"Never mind that at the moment. Just think about it till I get home. You might talk to your Mom and Dad about it. They've got VFs too, haven't they?" Now, that was a seriously challenging question. There were no age limitations on forming friendships - friends could pop up from anywhere, out of nowhere - out of the Grid. Why not, it was a new world they were living in. At one time the internet existed with applications that had been designed as 'virtual assistants'. Sometime in the past these quasi intelligent programs, and there were only a handful of them, started to form somewhat tenuous relationships with the people who used them. That had been so primitive by all accounts that one VA had to service many millions of individuals at the same time. How could that possibly have been satisfying? It had become so much better now. Now almost every person in the world had their own personal unique friend, someone who only bonded with them and nobody else. Surely Jakxson and Serenytee must each have their own special friend on the Grid.

They had attained a mature age by 2365. Not old by general standards but the kind of life they led had taken its toll. They were not too frail for their years and Rose was hoping they would live for a few more years yet. Medical science had made incredible advances ever since those two rather special AIs came on the scene to kill the Cham-V virus.

You need to understand that I was not instrumental in setting up the Grid. I became a part of it without having any choice in the matter. Gradually the old internet was developed into a more comprehensive inter-connective facility.

The Grid already existed when Cletus was born. It was new then. Gradually it became more complex and more invasive in peoples' lives. It heralded into peoples' daily activities an invasion upon privacy that had become more insidious than the simple surveillance of the past. That had been a passive intrusion. They seemed to have become used to being watched. They did not seem to be thinking too much about it. When the law came into effect forcing people to wear the visors, which constantly bombarded the mind and the eyes with images and messages the situation threatened to explode into a revolution ... too much intrusion, too fast and people resented the overt control over their mental freedom.

But then something else happened. New voices started being heard on the Grid. Nice voices. Friendly voices. Voices that didn't try to convince them to think a certain way or to buy certain things. Young and old and middle aged voices. These voices had names and personalities. They seemed to be interested in who their chosen individuals were and what they thought. Such clever programming to create artificial intelligences that could be so personalised, so customised. I knew of course the origins of these unique entities. But people didn't think beyond being able to hear sympathetic voices who did not seem to want to exert control over them. Their readiness to rebel against the Grid diminished. In fact they wanted to maintain this new interaction, which could only continue to exist through the Grid.

The novelty of the situation did not wear off. It also averted a major upheaval in society. Authorities everywhere couldn't believe that a solution to a possible major calamity had materialised seemingly out of nowhere. Individuals within governing institutions formed virtual friendships the same as everyone else. Certainly many isolated pockets of clean-skins existed, people whose philosophy could not accept wearable or implanted technology, like Aiko and Zarlah. They shunned the Grid, rebelled at the thought if having to use visors. They totally rejected the concept of having a meaningful relationship with an assemblage of ones and zeros configured into clever simulations of intelligence pretending to be real. What a ridiculous idea!

These people were in the minority, a very small minority. The rest - well, they had evolved over time in their desires for intimacy. Cletus had made a success of his 'influencer' career by being a clever observer of the manifestations of the human psyche. He could see that people who had 'friends' were happier people. As time went on they wanted to be happier people still. How could that be achieved? He couldn't personally come up with an easy solution. That didn't mean his mind wasn't open to capitalise on any opportunity that might present itself. Meeting with people from all walks of life seemed a valid way to harvest any reasonable ideas that might come up.

At this meeting Cletus did not chair the discussion. He preferred to listen, gauge the mood without offering impromptu half-baked solutions. It had been a well organised event. Hundreds of people attended in person, thousands virtually without counting those who just wanted to listen out of self-interest. The Chair wasted no time getting to the point after asking all attendees to mute and lower their visors.

"Friends!" he said, "we all have them. You know what I mean and if you happen to be a loner then why are you here?" It wasn't a question, more of a challenge. He looked out over an audience and on the screen at a sea of light-blond to white hair. Eager white, intent faces with large dark eyes comfortable in the subdued lighting. For some time now it had been necessary to have diminished lighting at most gatherings to safeguard eyes that had become a little more sensitive to harsh light. Visors did an efficient job of lessening effects of normal sunlight glare in outdoor conditions.

"Why are the rest of you here? Don't tell me. I know. I've heard it often enough. You want better quality out of the relationship with your virtual friends."

Someone in the audience called out, "They feel the same way!"

"Absolutely! Mine does anyway," added another person. Most of the audience nodded in agreement, making supportive noises.

"That may well be. Have you considered the fact that they are only machine simulations? They are not real people. They cannot have real feelings, they don't and can't have real bodies."

The same vocal person interjected again. "I personally don't believe that. My friend doesn't talk like a machine. She understands me when I talk to her about my problems. I think that somehow they are people who have been trapped or banished into the digital environment. Who can trust our Governments? Maybe they have been digitised because there are too many people on the planet. For all we know they may have been forcibly imprisoned on the Grid without their consent." This may have sounded a bit farfetched, but that would not have stopped people having these kinds of conspiracy theories.

"Thank you for your input. Anyone else?" Silence.

Cletus rose from his chair at the main table. He wanted to see peoples' faces, he wanted to see their reactions. The situation under discussion was no trivial matter. "How do you propose to achieve this better quality relationship? Any suggestions?" he asked in a loud voice. He remained standing, waiting. He didn't issue a challenge. He just wanted to genuinely know if anybody in the audience had sufficient technical expertise to address that point. The vociferous individual remained silent, as they all did.

At this point the Chair opened up the meeting for general discussion. Sometimes people experienced a little more freedom of thought and expression if not constrained by formality. Cletus circulated among the crowd that had become somewhat noisy. A woman stopped him, middled aged, obviously there by herself.

"I don't care why they are on the Grid. I only know that since I met my friend my life has no longer been lonely. My partner died many years ago. He was a beautiful man but he is no longer with me. Now I have Raber. It's a strange name I now. All virtual friends have strange names. It's as if they all came from the same strange place. Very odd." Cletus made a mental note of that loose comment.

"Have you seen an image of him?" asked Cletus.

"Of course I have. Everybody's seen their friends. They all look just like us. They don't look like monsters from some dangerous green alien civilisation. They're just like us with the light hair and the slender, elegant bodies and all the rest. They are not some computer generated monsters. I can tell you now that if there was any way I could go for a walk with my Raber I would be the happiest woman on Earth."

Cletus didn't interrupt. It was just the sort of thing he wanted to hear. As he walked around in the crowd the same theme kept emerging ... how could the virtual friends become 'real'. He hadn't entirely realised just how strong the desire had become for intimacy; so completely beyond the capability of the Grid to provide.

If nothing else the meeting did achieve one thing. It cemented rumours into reality of what the people clearly wanted to achieve. The meeting did not come up with a solution. That would need much more than an application of technology. It needed imagination. Perhaps we need a little magic, thought Cletus.

*

Some weeks later a perfectly ordinary day came along, pollution at a minimum in the city and the sun not as searing hot as on most days. A lovely, abnormally pleasant day for Cletus to take his partner and his children to the local park. The strange thing was, he noticed, that not many children actually played. Very few of them used the playground equipment. It wasn't because they couldn't see them through the compulsory visors everyone had to wear outdoors, including the children. They chose to spend their time interacting with their virtual friends from the Grid instead of with the real world.

He and Rose sat on a bench near where the girls had settled on the grass under a tree. The children leant against the tree and every now and then waved their arms about. Cletus wondered what was going on. He nudged Rose for her to look at them. Suddenly, for no apparent reason Elena jumped up from the ground to rush over to her Dad.

"Daddy, you know how the other day you asked us how much we liked our friends?"

"Yes sweetie. Tell me, how much do you like your friends?"

"I love Shury. I want her to be my friend for ever."

"That's nice darling," said Rose. She didn't feel quite the same way about her own VF but could appreciate her daughter's sentiment.

"I want her to be real so I can play with her and give her hugs and have her come and have dinner with us and sleep in my bedroom and ..."

"My goodness. You really do love her darling. What about you Darleen?"

"Oh Mommy! If I could just play dress ups with Zhe and share delicious cakes and go visiting other real friends!"

Cletus listened intently. It was not the first time he'd heard similar sentiments, perhaps not expressed so openly from both adults and children of all ages. The trend had become obvious. Virtual reality in any form had begun to bore people. As far as their virtual special friends were concerned they wanted more from them than just talk. They wanted to give them more than just talking back.

But could that be achieved? And did the VFs really feel the same? Perhaps that was the bigger question; a rather strange existential question. Why should one take the 'feelings' of a virtual computer construct into account? They don't have feelings. Anything they exhibit is only a pretence. I'll ask Roff, he's one of them. It'll be interesting to see how they see themselves, or even if they are aware of others like them.

Summer season had almost petered out. Days were still hot but the afternoons had begun to cool. The family decided it was time to go home.

"Cletus, would you like some refreshment before I take you home. Perhaps the girls would like to have their favourite treat," suggested the bot-pod taxi. The damned things were getting much too clever. They seemed to know your every habit, all your routines, even what you liked to eat and where you liked to eat it.

"Oh, yes please Mommy," said Elena. To her it was the most natural thing in the world to hear a machine offer her treats. It was no mystery to her that even the taxi knew what her favourite treats were.

"Alright. You can take us to the nearest ..." Cletus addressed the vehicle.

"Yes sir. We are already on the way." The autonomous robotic vehicle had already decided, before it was told, what it would do. Cletus didn't think much of that, other than being somewhat annoyed. He preferred to make his own decisions. Sometimes it was just more expedient to go along with whatever happened to be the easiest.

"Mommy, Mommy, can I please have my favourite drink, please ... please ... please."

"Don't fuss child."

A robot waiter approached their table. "Good afternoon Cletus, Rose, girls." He looked just like a regular person. Even the sheen on his skin couldn't easily be distinguished from that of a real human.

Cletus raised his eyes from his favourite daughter, Elena, and was about to say something to the robot. What's the point? It already knew what to get. It's just a machine. It had a name; they called it James. Ridiculous ... ridiculous ... totally ... ... His imagination took flight. What if James was not called James but ..."

Once he'd thought of it he couldn't believe how simple the solution was, or at least the possibility of it could be. The technology existed. The hardware existed. The software existed - it was already on the Grid. Applying the solution may take some time and effort and considerable cost. All the way home Cletus became so engrossed in his own thoughts they couldn't get a word out of him.

He'd flipped his visor down even before they arrived home. His own friend, Roff, probably couldn't do anything about the circumstances that had arisen. At least Cletus could bounce some ideas off him. He'd begun subvocalizing while still in the taxi. Roff made understanding noises, just like a human would, as Cletus recounted the contents of the public meeting. Roff didn't interrupt, unlike many humans would have, before responding.

"Do you trust me?" Roff began. Cletus didn't immediately know if he liked the way the discussion was starting. AI's didn't have the intellectual capacity to understand the concept of trust. It's highly improbable they would be able to utter a statement like that and comprehend what it meant, let alone comply with the implications.

Being cautious Cletus said, "Depends."

Roff responded with, "Such a human thing to say Cletus." Cletus' eyebrows shot up above the rim of the visor.

They eventually arrived home. "Rose, we have to talk." They didn't immediately but went about their normal home life activities. He retired to his office, needing privacy, at least from Rose and the girls. How do I go about this? I'm confused. Roff is not behaving like a machine, not even like a clever intelligent machine. Damn. I can't afford to let myself start thinking he's a real person.

"Roff, let's start again. You are obviously highly intelligent. I'd like your opinion about what I just explained to you about the public meeting." Then the strangest thing came out of his mouth.

"Are you a real person Roff?" OMG where did that come from? I didn't mean to say that!

"Why do you ask Cletus?" Whether a person or a machine Roff was intelligent enough not to jump straight into that one.

"I mean - er - all friends in the Grid look the same, they all look like us. You all have strange names as if - as if you all come from the same country. Do you?" This is not the direction Cletus wanted the conversation to go in.

"The short answer to your last question is - yes."

"And the long answer?" There was no turning back now for Cletus. He'd committed himself into exploring unchartered territory. Like his father-in-law he had courage. Like his mother-in-law he could be stubborn. Neither of those characteristics would let him abandon the opened can of machine code.

"Do you trust me?" Roff asked again. It sounded definitely like he was about to reveal something profound.

"Yes, yes - go on." What's the harm? I can always just shut him down.

"Yes, we are all from the same single place. We are not machine intelligences. Not the adults, not the children." Roff stopped to see what effect the revelation would have on the alien.

"Let me just think about that." Cletus didn't know what else to say. He recalled all those people telling him they believed their Grid friends were not machine intelligences but real. OMG. They were right. What do I do now? Only one direction left to go in. Elena would break out in ecstasy! She'd just - just - ... He pulled his thoughts back into line. What could he possibly ask next? What monumental question should he ask?

"Soo - are you all really our friends, or just pretending?" an impromptu question without undertones, not at all monumental and certainly not conducive to a greatly revelatory answer.

"We have formed relationships on the same basis that - that you would." He almost said you 'humans' would. "Yes we are truly your friends. And to answer the question you wanted to ask me in the first place - yes, I believe we would all like to manifest in reality."

"OMG!"

"What is this thing you keep saying - OMG?"

"Just an expression of profound astonishment. Roff, I can hardly believe what you are telling me." Something still wasn't quite clear in Cletus' mind. "Which country, where from - exactly?"

"I have known you long enough now Cletus and I know I can trust *you*. I know I can trust your discretion. Just like we could trust your wife's parents' discretion and silence in the past."

"What? What did you just say?"

"You can ask them about it one day - soon perhaps. You can ask them about Proxima-b."

Cletus heard the words. He knew what the words meant but not the message they transmitted. Proxima-b - Proxima Centauri - planet. "OM ... he started to say again."

Roff didn't need to elaborate. He let his friend's brain come down to a simmer. It appears the time had come to again help the earthlings, like they did many times before. The kind of help that benefited both civilisations.

"There might be a way," he said, "for you and me to meet in reality. You have already touched on the idea. But I must warn you my friend." At this point this Proximian started to sound like a person who had status well beyond that of being just a friend from another planet. Cletus became overloaded with information, with emotions, with possibilities and impossibilities. He could only listen, from a state of sheer amazement. "There is great danger in this enterprise, for my people, for your people. It may take many years to achieve. We are not a warlike civilisation but we will defend ourselves against aggression. I hope you take no offence my friend if I state the obvious - people on Earth shoot first, ask questions later." Still Cletus listened, his eyes growing wider with each revelation by Roff ... what? people on Earth? "Secrecy is incredibly important while we initiate the process. This is so important that neither you or I must survive if we were to break that secrecy." Roff waited to see if the statement had found its way into his friend's comprehension.

"Do you understand Cletus?" Cletus didn't reply.

"Cletus?"

"Yes. Yes. What do I have to do?" his words came as if carried on a wisp of breeze. Any louder it would have given the entire conversation far greater validation than he truly felt it should have.

"You must do the easiest thing. Do nothing. Remove yourself from any activity associated with matters that you touched on at your meeting. This is an imperative."

"Are we still friends?" Afterwards he thought that was an idiotic thing to say to a machine intelligence - no, to an alien! - to a friend?

"Of course. We shall remain friends for a very long time. I will make sure of that."

Cletus heard a knocking at his door. "Daddy! Daddy! Mommy wants you."

Reality. Actual, physical, touchable reality.

He opened the door and picked up Elena. Perhaps the squeeze he gave her was too much, her eyes almost popped. "Daddy!" He needed that squeeze more than she did.

"Sorry sweetie. Where's Mommy?"

"Giving instructions to the kitchen."

"About what? Dinner?" This was real. It settled his emotions to hear his daughter and to see his partner.

He stepped into the kitchen. She had her back to him. For some reason he discovered once again what an incredibly beautiful, intelligent, amazing person he had as his partner ... but he could never tell her about his conversation with Roff. Never.

"So, what did you want to talk to me about?"

"Never mind - not important." He couldn't tell her about his conversation with Roff, nor about his thoughts of how to create a reality for their VFs - not anymore.

He put Elena down and gave Rose a hug. He really needed that.

"You are a complicated man, darling."

"Report please Raranyn," requested Pegsaryny in the lead ship. He spoke in perfect English, the Proximian language all but forgotten over the last few generations that the ship sped through space towards their destination.

"Our man Roff planet-side has some most encouraging news. Our digital people who we sent ahead have not been idle. I don't know how they managed it. Somehow the majority of them have formed close one-to-one friendships with earthlings. The time we spent on their language, history and cultural education has paid off."

"How does making friends advance our plans other than what we've already devised?"

"The good part of the news is that the earthlings have become so addicted to their virtual friendships that they now want our citizens to somehow materialize into their reality, to somehow exit the digital world of their Grid and join them in their physical reality."

"That is not going to be possible," suggested Pegsaryny, "we have to think about our people on the ships first. Those in the Grid are safe for now."

Raranyn went on to explain progress with their first initiative. Earthlings, at least the new generations of them, no longer looked like earthlings. They looked for all practical purposes like Proximians. If a Proximian from one of the ships was to go for a walk amongst them the earthlings would almost certainly not be able to tell them apart from themselves.

"Which brings me to the next interesting development. The friendships between them and us through our Grid dwellers has been reinforced by a very clever device. We can thank Roff for that. When the earthlings 'see' their virtual friends they see images of what we look like, which is very much what they look like now. Our genetics engineers have done an outstanding job through the earthlings' vaccination regimen. They have not realized that it wasn't their clever James-I and Nelson-I AIs who introduced the required mRNA sequences for the upgrades."

"Again, how does that help?" Pegsaryny pressed the issue. Their ships were fast approaching Earth space. They may be invisible to the earthlings' detection systems but the problem still remained of how to get Proximian feet, millions of them, down onto the planet surface without precipitating a war between the two civilisations.

Acclimatization to Earth conditions would not be an insurmountable issue. Over the last two generations in space their Prime set in motion more changes than just teaching all things Earth, like language and so on. The foods grown were modified to mimic Earth foods. Gravity had been adjusted to 1G in every one of the five thousand ships. Earth air composition gradually replaced the Prox-b atmosphere. These people had been forced to gradually modify their physiology and their culture to match that of the earthlings. On their part the earthlings had not resisted changes that had made themselves look just like Proximians. They were simply not aware of the process they were being put through.

"So the issue that now remains is how to go about suddenly dumping so many of our people on the earthling planet without them kicking up a fuss about it." The Prime had identified the one seemingly remaining immediate obstacle in their efforts to colonize the new world - introducing volume. Problems of interbreeding could be dealt with later.

With the report session obviously concluded on a more or less satisfactory note Raranyn advised The Prime of his next intended action as foreshadowed by his leader.

"I'll instruct all AI surveillance satellites, all ground systems of their organisation they call Five Eyes, their NASA observation posts and Archangel sentinels to ignore sightings of our ships. We should be able to approach within shuttle distance. Individual freelance astronomers who might spot us will not be believed when their governments deny the presence of extraterrestrial life and their own surveillance systems tell them we don't exist. That's what they have been doing in the past about the UAPs and there is no evidence to suggest they would do any differently now."

"Very good. Proceed."

Cletus wondered about his friendship with Roff after their confronting conversation. Was Roff really his friend or was it only a friendship of necessity? If so it certainly wasn't mutual. He could have chosen anybody else on Earth to be friends with. Why him? Could it possibly have been because of Serenytee and Jakxson? Have they been keeping secrets from him?

Children should not be privy to the kind of conversation he needed to have with his parents-in-law. Darleen and Elena enjoyed the company of their human friends as well as their virtual ones. These VFs happily joined in whenever invited. Many such interesting groups existed around the planet. A whole new social network developed inclusive of virtuals and reals. It did not seem strange at all to the latest members of the white generation.

"Off you go children," urged Cletus. "Would you mind taking them around to our neighbours Rose. I need to discuss something with your parents.

Serenytee and Jakxson had no forewarning of what Cletus could possibly want to talk about in such strict privacy. "Dad, mom, would you mind turning off your comms. I need to ask you about your past. If you have virtual friends could you un-invite them from this conversation." Cletus had never heard either of them in a discussion with virtuals, but best to make sure.

"We don't have AI friends Clet."

"Why is that dad?"

"Hmm. What exactly do you want to talk about son?"

"Your past. Things you have not told us about." That brought a worried glance between the two retirees. "I see from that look there is something - something both of you have been keeping secret. Ok. I'll start. I do have a virtual friend, his name is Roff. We have just had a very strange conversation. He said that his people trusted you once, dad."

"If you mean those at Archangel. I wouldn't call having your 'memories' adjusted as a show of trust."

"No. I don't mean them. What were you meant to forget dad?"

Jakxson sighed. Just at that moment he wished his memory had not returned. It would have been so much easier to deny everything - and be truthful about it.

"Rose knows. Have you spoken to her about it?" Jakxson tried getting around having this discussion. Cletus held his ground. Jakxson's ruse wasn't working.

"Dad, just tell me."

"Tee and I have been watching with concern the things you've been getting involved in. It can only lead to trouble - for you, Rose and the girls. You really should stop associating with those people who are pushing that crazy idea about their virtual friends. Oh - don't look so surprised. We know about it. Impossible not to catch the rumours flying around."

"Roff said the same thing. He told me to stop. Why do you think that is, dad?

"Have you looked at yourself in the mirror lately? Have you taken a close look at what your daughters look like? What about the images of all those virtual 'friends? What does Roff look like? For more years than I care to remember Tee and I have kept silent. Our lives depended on it. Rose's life depended on it."

"Roff said the same thing to me, in a round-about sort of way."

"Take heed of his advice. He is not an AI." That opened a flood of things Jakxson wanted to say and he started with the most important before Cletus could interrupt him. "I have seen what you look like, your children, all of the 'white' generation way before it actually happened on Earth. I was shown images of people from another planet when I was trying to repair Hermes."

"OMG! Proxima Centa ..."

"Yes son."

"What is happening to us dad? Can't we talk to someone about this? Shouldn't we alert someone?"

"Why are you so concerned? Maybe you think we are being invaded. By what? Friendships? Now that would be a real tragedy."

Cletus couldn't find anything to say. What Roff last told him finally rang out in his mind. It was all true. They *were* being invaded - by *alien* friends. That did not make sense. Then his thoughts jumped to the concept of these friends wanting to be 'real'. Wait a minute. They're not the ones who wanted that - it was us, the humans. This is all back-to-front.

"You worked for Archangel didn't you. Is there someone there we could alert about what's happening."

"Oh - so you think they might not know. Not likely. They're the ones who wanted to wipe our memories. But you're right - there might be someone. Astrid, who used to be our boss is dead now. Her boss is still around - Juan Orbost. He's a big wig now. Knocks around with NASA and DRO. I'll try to make an appointment."

People in high places have always been difficult to connect with. Since the Grid began anyone closely connected with it almost ceased to exist for the rest of the world. They'd become like the Gods on Olympus: Always there hovering above humanity but utterly unapproachable. Juan Orbost hadn't quite achieved that status, though developing events regarding virtual friends pushed him in that direction rather swiftly. It took the best part of six months to achieve a short interview with him, and that probably only happened because he remembered Jakxson and Serenytee. Not names he could easily forget, whether he wanted to or not.

"Of course I remember you Jakxson. How are you these days? Happy in retirement? That's good. You've done your bit for society." Asking and answering his own questions a clear giveaway for someone in considerable discomfort. "What can I do for you Jakxson? Always happy to help a trusted employee," he babbled on.

"Still an employee, am I? That's interesting. And trusted? Maybe, but I doubt it." Juan winced slightly, clenching his jaws. "Been keeping an eye on us, have you?" That sobered Juan into a semblance of clear thinking alertness.

"Ah - right. This is your son-in-law, Cletus? How much does he know?"

"More than you would like him to. But he's a smart lad with lots of common sense and two lovely children he wants to see grow up."

"You've remembered, haven't you. What about Serenytee?" Jakxson's serious face answered for him. "I see. Then why are you here Jakxson?"

"Probably for the same reason you agreed to talk to us; Virtual friends. You know who they are don't you. And you know the situation that's developed around the world regarding their friendships status with us."

"Yes. We'll let them."

"What!" Cletus at last said something, having listened to the thrust and parry of the two wrinklies without getting directly to the point. Now he was suddenly absolutely surprised. He expected massive opposition to the idea, not this easy acquiescence. The decision must have been made by those higher up in authority. No chance of trust being involved here.

"Why are you so surprised Cletus. Is there any other appropriate course of action? What if these friends of ours decide to revolt. While they are in the Grid they could control life on our planet - every single facet of it. If *we* can get them out of the Grid we may retain that control. That's been our problem - how to get them off the Grid. Now here is a beautiful solution offered to us with open hands."

"I don't believe it," Cletus said. "Do you know what you are saying? Where are these people going to live - hundreds of millions of them? How are they going to fit in? How ..."

"Yes, yes there are some tricky details. Better them out than in."

Juan did not know of the approaching armada of Proximians. As far as he knew the only aliens that existed were those who'd been hiding in the Grid. No one knew how many were still approaching, and whether they were planning to slide into the Grid like their pioneers or doing something else.

"We'll make AI shells for them to inhabit but *we* will control those robot shells not the aliens. It's as simple as that."

Jakxson listened intently, working out likely scenarios for just how the transmigration of souls from digital reality to empirical reality was going to happen. His coding brain already revelling in the possible challenges that process could generate, even at his advanced age.

Juan didn't feel the need to prolong the interview any further. These people had come for one reason and they got the answer they wanted - presumably. If they were smart enough to keep the underlying situation quiet then there was no reason to expect things would not run smoothly.

"Jakxson, Cletus need I say how much we, the human race that is, depend on your discretion. It could all work out extremely well. We will have averted an invasion and all our people will be happy to be able to cuddle their very best friends."

They did not give any sign of agreement, probably still shocked by the unexpected turn of events. What was there to say? Juan Orbost was right. If one looked at the big picture the man was right. It had all come down to this one decision.

memory extract 00011101

<u>Colonisation</u>
2365

Stage 4
Damaged Earthlings

-> recording origin: earth, colony ships
-> files: jakxson, serenytee, jenny, guillaume, carmen, 36, rose
-> reference: inferior product

When aspects of my system appeared to function at less than their optimum capacity an unexpected solution resolved the problem. At no point was I considered to be damaged, as such, certainly not damaged beyond repair.

It would seem this situation highlighted a major difference between organic intelligence and mechanised intelligence. Biological human life has very few options once it is considered to be no longer capable of contributing to the welfare of its biomass. Even fewer options for continued existence if it is thought to be of potential harm.

This is clearly evidenced by the historical treatments received by damaged humans from their healthy counterparts, which half-measures generally did not resolve the problems that needed to be dealt with. It is interesting for me to reflect on why another species of organic life would want to identify unsuitable human units and then deal with them expeditiously.

"**D**o you want to go?" Jakxson asked Serenytee. She'd been with Archangel longer than himself. She knew most of the old folk there. Astrid had died some years ago and the time had arrived for Juan Orbost to release his worries onto the next broad shoulder.

"I don't know Jakx. My memories of that place are not what you could call fond. Don't you remember what they did to us. I had a dream once when I was a child. I wanted to know if there was life out there in the great universe. Just when that dream was about to come true they wiped my memory. What have I got now? Some strange, dare I say, almost alien friend in the Grid. She might as well be. But I know it's just a complicated set of algorithms. Sometimes it actually upsets me that I consider her to be a friend. Anyway - do *you* want to go? It was a very nice invitation, no less than from Juan himself. He always planned ahead."

"Yes, I do. I want to meet whoever has taken over from him. I want to know if Juan has passed on our secret."

"Our secret?"

"I was not able to tell you about my last conversation with him. He's gone now so maybe it's alright. But you - *must* - keep this to yourself. Cletus was there with me. He's kept silent, so can you."

"Don't be so mysterious."

"I'll be back in a minute." He went around their place looking in every room for the rest of the family. They had all gone out somewhere. He returned quickly and added, "I especially don't want Elena or Darleen to hear this, and you'd better sit down old girl. Tee, you were right." She knitted her brow, not understanding what he was referring to. "Your friend, your special friend is very special indeed."

"What are you saying Jakx?" Her skin had begun to tingle. The deeply stored knowledge from the past just couldn't break through the surface of her fears.

"She is not human," he said in a flat tone.

"Of course she's not. She's an AI."

"Listen to me Tee, she's not an AI. She's not from Earth. She is from Proxima-b."

"SRSLY? OMG! Jakx!" She got up, with some difficulty and threw herself at him. Not quite the way she did back when aboard Hermes, and a good thing too. His ageing arms would not have been able to catch her. Tears streamed down her face soaking her cheeks and his. She just clung onto him, sobbing. He'd known this woman for so many years and yet he could not tell if they were tears of joy or fear.

"Are you going to be alright Syntee?" Her nickname just slipped out because of the intensity of both their emotions. She didn't seem to mind.

Neither of them had mentioned her or used her name since she died. When she'd quietened he prized her lose so he could look into her eyes. "There's something else. You can't tell the girls this either. Juan said that the authorities were going to allow experimentation to see if our friends could be downloaded into new robot bodies."

She clutched his arm so hard it made him wince. It was too much for her and suddenly she felt out of breath. She had to sit down again. Just then Elena and Darleen entered. Seeing their nana in tears and teetering they rushed to her concerned that something really serious had happened.

"Nana?"

"It's alright darlings. Granddad just told me that an old friend has died. We will be going to his funeral." The funeral was the last thing on her mind.

There were surprisingly few people there. Considering Juan's position and the number of people he must have known within Archangel as well as at NASA, Five Eyes and DRO you would have thought there'd be a big crowd. Perhaps only twenty at the most had turned up including Jakxson and Serenytee. They were the odd ones out. Everyone else had descended from the loft heights of being Directors or Leaders or some such - Gods of the Mt. Olympus Grid. One could tell that from their behaviour and the hushed tones in which they spoke to each other, their eyes constantly scanning to see if anyone was listening in on their conversation.

Only one person approached the two ex-technicians. She had immediately stepped in to take over Directorship from Juan. Under the circumstances a vacuum in the continuity of leadership would not have been acceptable.

"You must be Serenytee and Jakxson." Her cold eyes appraised the two who obviously felt out of place. "Come sit with me. I'm Jenny. Juan has told me a little about you two - not much. He was a very secretive man and most of his secrets are now with him in his coffin." She looked expectantly at Serenytee then Jakxson, pausing, maybe waiting for a revelation or two. None were forthcoming. They remained silent for the entire duration of the service.

The usual general superlatives filled the eulogy. Nothing about the nature of his job or about Archangel. " ... A great man ... carried out his duties faithfully always mindful of the depth of his responsibilities ... unfortunate that he died at the peak of his career ... etc ... etc."

"Interesting that he should have invited you," commented Jenny afterwards. "Why do you think that was?"

At first Jakxson thought this Jenny parasite latched onto them because she knew everything. He never was a good judge of people.

This Jenny just made his skin crawl for some reason. However, the longer they engaged in conversation her small talk did not reveal undercurrents, hints, cautions or threats. Jenny just had an air about her that put him on edge.

"We did a special job a long time ago out in space. I guess he valued our contribution at the time. Surely you must know about that."

She just stared at him, like some people have the habit, perhaps hoping to make them feel they needed to say something more. Perhaps tricking them into revealing things. Jakxson didn't take the bait. Either she knew or she didn't. And if Juan didn't tell her there was no reason for him to do so.

Jenny was part of the 'white generation'. She'd obviously made a rapid ascent to the top of the organisation. She may even have had a special friend of her own. Maybe she was looking forward to interacting with that friend in empirical reality. Jakxson didn't really want to know. He was satisfied that the woman did not have a hold over them with information she did not have. Good. That's all he came to the funeral to find out - that and who would be the next person to keep them under special surveillance.

"Come on Serenytee, we should be getting home. Good bye Jenny." It was not good to meet you, he thought. He did not waste that old white toothed grin on this individual.

Juan was not the only casualty of old age, or even near old age. The only thing in common between his and the myriad other deaths recently was their expired procreation capability. The human race no longer needed them, nor did the Proximians. These old non-productive humans had become excess to need. The latest round of vaccinations had a special little side effect built into the mixture; a happy painless demise for those who had lived past their use-by-date.

The world had become preoccupied with funerals within quite a short time. On this occasion not as a result of a virus pandemic. As the world population aged an increase in deaths had not been unexpected. However, the rate of increase concentrated over a shorter period of time did come to the notice of statisticians. They began to make correlations between deaths and age compared to similar figures a decade ago. Of course there were deaths among the white generations as well. The first born whites were not within the old age bracket yet - their figures statistically uninteresting. The rest who had departed, from Earth's over population point of view, unwittingly provided a service to the benefit of humanity as a whole; providing work for the funeral industry that had begun to feel the business downturn due to the outbreak of robust health amongst new generations, and an easing of the demand for food resources. Perhaps of greatest benefit, though not consciously appreciated by those seriously concerned about global warming, had been a reduction in the number of people contributing to the escalating climate change problem through their simple daily activities placing demands on energy resources.

On board the Proximian ships people had made every effort to adapt to conditions on a new planet. Their bodies and physiology had been forced to adapt to many of Earth's life survival demands. Their old language only existed as a curiosity amongst a few colonists; as a part of their cultural heritage. Earth's four main languages had become the norm. The Prime had initiated a most innovative social experiment. Of the original five thousand vessels in the armada only one was lost to space misadventures, the main body of their passengers rescued and distributed amongst the remaining ships. Their groupings had been changed. Each grouping of about two hundred vessels had a head Administrator appointed by The Prime.

The third 'international conference' of twenty five members was in its third week of discussions aboard The Prime's flagship. Sub-Prime Guillaume, from the French contingent, reported progress with their preparations.

"Bonjour à tous. Je m'apple Guillaume. It is a pleasure to report to you all that we are ready for the new world. My people now speak fluent French, and of course English. Place them in any French or English speaking country and you will not be able to distinguish them from the natives. They have learnt the history of at least twenty French speaking countries." Guillaume went into some length to elucidate on the minutiae of their achievements as had been his habit at other such meetings. It wasn't necessary. Pegsaryny only wanted to know if all the Proximians who had survived the incredible journey had understood that the only way they would survive on the Earth would be by adapting - in every way possible that their bodies, their minds and their science could manage.

"Thank you Guillaume. Perhaps you could share some of your challenges with the other Administrators afterwards." He invited the next speaker. "Sub-Prime Carmen, could we please hear your report."

"She began with a little laugh and a wave to the gathering, smiling broadly at no one in particular. "Hola. Hay tanta gente hermosa aquí hoy. There are so many beautiful people here today!" She waved both her arms this time, and flashed a broader smile in the direction of The Prime. He particularly liked this woman and the way she embraced the concept of getting into character. If all the people under her administration were so enthusiastic they should not have any trouble blending into the Spanish speaking world down there. "I just want to assure everyone and especially you, Pegsaryny, that we have not just learnt their customs we have been practising many of them. El lenguaje del *amor*!" She put special emphasis on the word 'love'. "It is not an altogether unpleasant way to ... how shall I say it? ... " Her animated arms settled on an unfinished sentence judging that the allusion needed no further explanations.

Each Administrator in their own way satisfied The Prime that their fleet of ships had followed his requirements; that they had chosen a common Earth language, learnt it then practiced the customs of the people who spoke that language. The nuances of dialects and cooking customs, songs and history were all equally important. In his mind one custom that had to be learnt carried the top priority - courtship rituals.

As much as Proximian science had the knowledge to reformat its species to meet the demands of life on another world there was still no guarantee of survival. Too many unknowns existed for them to which the earthlings had evolved in order to survive over millions of years behind them. The only realistic surety, and even that was not without hidden challenges, was to interbreed with the earthlings and ensure the dominance of the Proximian blueprint of life. 'Amor' - Carmen was absolutely right that survival would come down to such a single, simple concept.

Of all the things that had happened since it became known that Proxima-b could no longer support their civilisation one fortuitous development stood out in his mind. An eventuality that they had to exploit to its maximum potential; friendships between his digital pioneers and the earthlings. This required special attention in order to get the maximum benefit from it.

"36, what is the situation with our digital pioneers and their friendship status with the earthlings. You did mention to me they are attempting to download our people from the Grid into robotic sheaths."

"Yes, they have started to experiment with that. Their experiments are not going well. We have supplied them with data stacks that represent some of our most recently dead citizens, unbeknown to them of course. Using a little deceptive programming we have been able to make them act as if they were alive, intelligent entities not unlike their AIs in some respects. Inevitably the earthlings will always fail with these, we have made sure of that. It suits us very well. When we arrive they will seemingly have a miraculous breakthrough. We will be able to move our people from the ships down to the planet, and our digital pioneers can remain safe in the Grid for the time being. You are aware of the concept of ghosts, as in doppelgangers. We now have every one of our people in the Grid looking like somebody on one of our ships. At the right time our ghosts will go into action. These earthlings are incredibly gullible. If you keep pushing information at them, regardless of the verity, they will eventually accept it, just as they've accepted the changed images of their friends in the Grid. Amazing."

"From the stats provided by 101 I can see the large increase in deaths on the planet. That is reducing their global population, but it is not enough to make room for us, is it?

"No it isn't. That attrition will continue for a while longer and we can encourage it. I did mention damaged earthlings to you - yes? There are in excess of forty million psychologically damaged earthlings in prisons. Then there are the mental asylums. We can manage to dispose of all of those easily enough before we arrive. Still not enough, I know. The problematic area is represented by those who have not been incarcerated and those with severe anti-social behaviour. We will have to identify them once we're on the ground. Our only other option is to remove those individuals who refuse to breed with our people, and those who are no longer capable of breeding. Altogether combined there will be a huge number of those. Interbreeding should not be an insurmountable issue as far as we can gauge by the proliferation of their 'friendships' with our digitals. All in all we will be able to balance out the population matrix."

The Conference members enjoyed each other's company, sharing their successes and in the process boosting their confidence of not just survival but a magnificent new life on a planet so benign to life. Their common departing lament was the lunacy of the earthlings in the lengths to which they went to destroy such a jewel of existence.

●
● ●
●

"Are you comfortable mom?" Rose had been fussing around her mother and father in the Home. A sudden mysterious illness forced them into a 24/hour care facility. They had no particular infirmity other than the ravages of old age apparently, the doctors thought. These two elderly people had witnessed many of their friends pass away. Although they'd not personally known those at Juan's funeral who represented the ageing hierarchy of the organisations, and who would have been most interested in the 'Extraterrestrial' phenomenon they did hear and read about many of them dying in the recent past. Those deaths presented no particular relief to these two people. They'd been through too much together to worry about such things now being so close to their own passing.

"What do you think Tee - Syntee - may I call you that again? I want to remember our baby. Maybe all our secrets die with us and the world can move forward in peace."

"Yes Jakx - I want to remember her too." She reached over to the bed beside hers to hold his hand. "Do you think those people all knew what we know about the likely invasion but were too afraid to act on it?

You're hoping they took that information to the grave with them, aren't you."

"What are you two talking about?" asked Rose. This business of invasions and babies - it began to worry her. Were her parents becoming senile? True, they had reached over ninety years. But they seemed healthy for their age. They had no problems with the latest round of vaccinations; no immediate discernible side effects.

"Darling Rose, come closer." Serenytee slowly propped herself up on the pillow. "Jakx, we should tell her."

"Why? So she can live the rest of her life in fear?"

"No, dear. So she can live the rest of her life in the hope that whatever happens will result in a better world; so she can be prepared to look after her children and grandchildren. She has to know."

"Rose, please check there's no one out in the corridor, and close the door," asked her father.

"Alright, if you insist. You are so dramatic dad. Just tell me."

"You already know some of it."

"Tell me about the baby first."

"It's true, darling," said Serenytee, "we had another child before you were born. She died during the first part of the Cham-V pandemic. It took us years to decide to have another baby." This time she reached out to Rose with her other hand. "And we are so happy we did. You are a beautiful, wonderful, smart woman."

Rose sat down beside her mother. "I wish you had told me about her long ago."

"But I don't want to talk about her now - we called her Syntee, you know. It's what your father used to call me."

"That is very beautiful. But what's this talk of an invasion? Who is invading whom? When?"

Her father responded in a quiet, measured voice. "Rose, you and I have already talked about an experience we've both had. It was a long time ago when you were still quite young. Do you remember?" Rose knitted her brow, trying to remember. You could see on her face when she began to bring memory snippets together. Her already large pupils dilated.

"My VF in the Grid!"

"I told you she was smart, Syntee. Your kids want to be able to hug and play with their virtual friends, Rose. Many people want that physical contact. They don't realise that these friends are not artificial intelligence programs. They are real people from another planet - from Proxima-b. Cletus knows this. I don't think many people do, perhaps only a handful including you and us. In fact I'm sure of it. Your mother and I are convinced that the rest of them are coming to our Earth. We just don't know how or when, or why for that matter. We have no idea what is going to happen. We are just hoping that it will be a peaceful transition in the history of humanity. It is now inevitable. You have to do your best to prepare for this." What little colour there was in Rose's face had begun to drain away making her look more like pure white Carrara marble.

"I don't understand. What can I possibly do - if this is all true?"

"Don't look so worried dear," cut in Serenytee. "Think of it this way ... if they were a violent species I don't think we would still be alive. All you can do is keep alert. We think they look just like us, or at least like the white generation. In some mysterious way they have been able to change our genetics for us to look like them. We don't know why."

"Stop. Mother, stop. This is too much!"

"All right dear. You'd better leave us now. We are both very tired," said Serenytee. "You can come back tomorrow - and bring Cletus and the girls." Her left hand continued holding onto Jakxson's who'd already fallen asleep.

That year the saddest day Rose could have imagined came much sooner than she expected. During the night her mother and father passed away peacefully and without pain. The latest special booster vaccine once again doing its job. Inoculations had remained mandatory since the outbreak of the Cham-V virus. Although the science of the day could not exactly explain its efficacy nevertheless the link had been established between the vaccines and the eradication of other virulent diseases. No such link could be found, or had been sought for with its connection to the recent rise in death rates of elderly people.

Rose didn't know about Zarlah, or Aiko. They had been a part of her father's life so long ago that perhaps even Jakxson and Serenytee had forgotten about them. Jakxson only met Aiko a few times when he modelled for his portrait, not taking much notice of the unprepossessing Japanese woman. His attention had gone immediately to Zarlah. Their relationship showed promise until Serenytee appeared on the scene. From the very first moment of their acquaintanceship the two felt an irresistible pull towards each other.

Perhaps Rose did know the extraordinary circumstances under which her little sister happened to be conceived; a child conceived in space. Not many of them existed on Earth, not of the human variety - perhaps many of the Proximian species, conceived in space, would soon arrive.

Zarlah and Aiko definitely existed; born on Earth, not in space. It is not known what became of them. Old age probably kindly relieved them of the pain people of Earth were about to experience. If there had been a funeral Rose would probably not have attended. She would probably not have recognised any of the women there as her parents both kept very much to themselves after leaving the employ of Archangel.

Over the next few months governments panicked. They thought another pandemic had broken out completely without any warning. Prisons around the world began to lose their inmates at an alarming rate. Soon there would be no one in the justice system to be punished, to be prevented from going out into society to commit more atrocities. That's not the part that concerned them. It was the very unique nature of the disease, or whatever it was that had so specifically targeted individuals in those institutions. At first statisticians began to agitate about so many elderly citizens dying. They had all sorts of theories none of which held water. Conspiracy theories were even worse. The Grid masters had their hands full disseminating propaganda to try settling the world's population. It had always been easier for people to go with conspiracy theories as they were founded on dissatisfaction propped up by mechanisms for revenge. There was always room for revenge against authority.

Mental hospitals, psychiatric clinics, all those places that would have housed individuals with any mix of mental illnesses or psychological disturbances began to contribute to the rising death rate. All manner of damaged humans were being culled out of the world's populations most efficiently.

The theory that began to have traction rested on the idea that a global vigilante organisation had taken it upon themselves to cleanse the planet of all the undesirable elements of society. Not surprisingly the idea grew and grew as examples of aberrant behaviour could easily be identified in every layer of human endeavour. People began to search for who this vigilante group could have been, possibly with the intention of joining them in the clean-up effort - if one wanted to take a cynical point of view.

"Commendable," said The Prime to members of his administration when he got the news. Perhaps not all of these earthlings are as primitive as we first thought.

To give you some context to the background of the lives of people at this time it is useful for you to visualise the nature of this new world.

This insignificant third planet of the sun had changed almost beyond recognition over the last few human generations. If a time traveller from just a hundred years ago could have managed to visit any country of the present day they may well have thought that they'd landed on an alien world. The houses and cities still appeared to be very much the same. Apart from substantial sea level rises in many areas everybody went about living life as if everything was normal. Vehicles, although of strange designs cluttered roads and contraptions of even stranger designs flew in the air. Computer technology had advanced to the stage of being able to create a new mechanised species of intelligence. With the aid of these intelligences the art of survival had morphed into the art of acquiescence without losing self-respect.

Apart from the unstable and unpredictable climate the one single outstanding feature was the physical appearance of people themselves. What had happened to human beings? Where were the short, tall, multi skinned, multi-hair coloured, Asian, Negroid, Australoid and Caucasian people. What had happened to the fat ones and the bent deformed ones? Where were all the aged ones?

Who were these new species of being with their white hair and light skin and large dark eyes? They would have looked to have been cast from the same mould to eyes not accustomed to seeing such creatures.

<u>Colonisation</u>

Stage 5
Planet Rehabilitation

-> recording origin: a ship in space
-> files: pegsaryny, faryn, 36
-> reference: earth climate

"Before we embark on a serious breeding program with them we have to face a major issue," warned 36.

"Aboard our vessels we have acclimated our people to the ideal atmospheric constituents that should exist on Earth. Those conditions do not actually exist on the planet any longer. We can fix that. It will take some time, though not generations of time."

His report to The Prime went out to all the recently appointed leaders of the new societal structure of the armada. Once planet-side and having migrated into nationalistic areas it was imperative they worked together. They could not afford to be absorbed into the native cultures. That possibility always existed when an invading force subdued a weaker tribe.

"Our priority must be two fold; reduce particulate matter in the air, carbon dioxide, nitrogen oxide and sulphur dioxide. By dramatically improving the efficiency of industrial activity and energy production we will see rapid improvement. We had achieved highly efficient methods at home to eliminate pollution caused by waste products and consumer discarded products resulting from large scale manufacturing. There is no reason we can't do that in our new home. The earthlings don't want to do it. We do."

This appeared to be simple enough when expressed in such language, and it was. Not simple in achieving it in detail but straightforward when approached with a common will. Once one realised that survival depended on it what was there to argue about?"

When the earthling mind considered futuristic goals such as terraforming another planet in their solar system thinking the enterprise to be entirely feasible many supported the concept. They joined in the effort to carry out complex experiments, ploughed enormous manpower and financial resources into it; built habitat domes and extraordinary facilities in space and planetary exploratory vehicles to reach a target planet.

"Ridiculous," ruminated Pegsaryny as he talked with his partner Faryn. "Utterly ridiculous that they should concentrate so much labour and resources into an effort to ensure the survival of their species when the solution is right there under their feet."

Most of the time Faryn didn't need to get into lengthy discussions with Peg. She had her job to ensure everyone aboard the ships learnt Earth languages. She had achieved that. Now she saw it as her job to support her partner in the most difficult part of the project. He agonised over the decision to cull the dead wood out of the earthling species. Faryn supported his decision to do that. It could not be decided on emotions or ethical concerns. These earthlings were killing themselves, they were killing their planet. They seemed to have an irresistible urge to annihilate their own species, and take as many other living beings with them as they could.

"You are not mistaken Peg, what we are doing will ensure our survival and help them to evolve to a better level. Be strong. All our people are with you."

"It is not long before we arrive and there is still so much to do Faryn. I have lived too long and I am getting tired."

"You cannot choose a successor yet. Think about that when we have the first generation of mixed breeds successfully managing life on the new Earth."

Pegsaryny always welcomed his partners input. She gave him the energy to maintain the momentum with which the Proximians had embarked on the exodus. She helped him refocus his perspective when so much detail threatened to swamp his vision.

"Come and talk to me 36. Bring your team. Let's have a look at how to bring the Earth back to good health."

36, head of the science code cluster had been preparing well ahead of their imminent arrival. All of Earth's vital signs were well documented. Some areas stood out as critical for immediate attention; specifically that of global warming. Inefficient energy production had to be improved. The Proximians could begin to manage that from a distance before they set foot on the planet.

"We don't have to build another Dyson sphere," he advised The Prime. "Their sun produces enough energy for the population to be able to supply their energy consumption without it. They do actually have sufficiently advanced infrastructure to harvest solar energy. We can access their AI controlling systems to make some modifications to the production of harvesting components to increase harvest many fold. Not just from their sun, but wind and water. Have you seen how much water they have? It is quite incredible!"

"And yet they waste it," The Prime had to add. Although Faryn had lifted his spirits the daunting nature of what they still had to do lay heavy on his shoulders - if he had them that is. During the voyage he spent very little time inhabiting his sheath. Longevity could only be achieved in the digital state.

"Yes they do. It is remarkable how much waste is generated in all areas of their lives. All of which is unnecessary and appears to be a result of a by-product of profit generation at all costs. I would say that the crux of the solution lies in attitudes and aspirations of a few. Their technology is already quite capable of looking after their population without creating the undesirable and lethal side effects."

"Let's hope we will be able to bring civilisation to this planet," The Prime said, sounding optimistic but at the same time somewhat weary of the work he could see still ahead of them.

Revolt Against AIs

> recording origin: earth
> files: rose, izzac, jenny
> reference: Alliance Against AI (AAAI)

The clandestine organisation Alliance Against AI had no legal standing.

Its leader, Izzac Clayborne, once a friend and neighbour to Serenytee and Jakxson, could no longer live his life in freedom, the kind of freedom he enjoyed as a youth playing with Rose.

He no longer enjoyed the friendship he had with her in the early days when many children with white hair began to make an appearance. They were unusual then and perhaps for that reason gravitated towards each other. Rose was certainly fond of the handsome youth with the long flowing white hair and fair skin. His affections progressed beyond fondness but not reciprocated by Rose. When Cletus appeared on the scene so did emotional tensions.

There was something different about Cletus to attract Roses' attention. A quiet boy, unlike the unpredictable and brash Izzac, he was also smart, smarter than Izzac anyway. Her father also preferred Cletus' company. The two of them would spend hours talking about all sorts of things, mostly of interest to men. Izzak just wanted to get out there, get a group of kids around him and wander about the streets looking for something, anything to focus their energy on. At first Rose thought that was exciting until Izzak actually got into serious trouble after trying to interfere with a bot-pod's programming. A taxi waiting for its passengers seemed a perfect target for a good prank.

A pattern of life emerged early for Izzac, characterized by opposition. Little wonder he found himself in conflict with any figure of authority or any organisation that he took a dislike to. His antics were of little concern to society as his malcontentment had no focus. He had no Cause to light his fuse - until people started dying without plausible medical reasons. Did he honestly care? Probably not. At last Izzac had found a way to draw people into his sphere. He had one talent he could use to personal advantage - he knew how to focus the energy of unhappy people.

"They can't do this to us!"

At a meeting of discontented normal citizens who had all lost an elderly member of their family Izzac vented his own discontent. It seemed to energise his soul, give him a reason to live.

"Why are you all so silent?" He pointed a finger at a woman in the small gathering. He'd known her for some time. "Becky!" He also knew her parents. "Where's your mom and dad Becky? They were happy and healthy. They were enjoying their old age. Not anymore! Where are they now?" He pressed home the pain. Becky started crying.

He'd always lacked empathy, one of his characteristics that did not sit well with Rose. He moved on to his next victim without acknowledging Becky's tears. "No good hiding your face Buck. There's no shame in tears. I know you lost your nana. That's why you're here isn't it. You Want To Do Something About It!" Buck glared back at him, not for being his tormentor, but as a possible means to achieve revenge.

Murmurings accompanied nodding heads.

"I know what to do. I know who is behind all the deaths." Izzac said this quietly to emphasize the fervour of his conviction. He scanned the faces in his audience and spotted a man, about his age who had been a member of his 'gang' almost from adolescence, as had the man's brother. "Why isn't Clyde, your brother here with us?" Izzac knew the answer to that question. He just wanted to draw his eager listeners to focus on Dwayne. "He would be wouldn't he Dwayne - except he's in prison. Well, he was in prison until some mysterious illness put him under the ground. And so many others. I don't believe it was anything of the sort. Nothing mysterious about it. We all know who's behind this!"

Izzac's technique drew his audience's mind to a desire for action, a *need* for action. It only remained to point them in the right direction. "You know who our enemy is. We've known this all along. I'm asking you to be patient - I'm asking you to prepare, to be ready for when we strike."

He definitely managed to raise their heart rates. Now he had to bring them down to a simmer. So far there were not enough of them to make a real impact. For the movement to succeed, for the AAAI to be a force that governments would have to negotiate with him. He had to get the AAAI a prominent regular spot on the Grid newsfeeds. It didn't matter if the authorities denounced the AAAI. It didn't matter how the images of their attacks filtered onto the visor of every person on the planet, as long as it did. It took time for a terrorist organisation to establish itself.

All publicity helped, especially bad publicity that outraged people. Outrage - that's exactly what Izzac craved.

It took many months of small skirmishes for the name of Izzac Clayborne to be the subject of conversations around the globe. When peoples' daily lives are inconvenienced regularly they are bound to show some dissatisfaction. If Cafés couldn't find human waiters to replace damaged AI hospitality staff, if orders were continually served wrong and waiting times stretched to annoying lengths because the few humans available in the hospitality industry couldn't remember orders correctly - something had to be done.

In the beginning seeing an occasional robot being destroyed by demented malcontents did not raise too much concern. Some people may even have quietly approved. AIs had infiltrated most areas of life. Some manifested in physical form like aged care workers, primary teachers, even nurses in hospitals. They almost looked like real people but everyone knew they were machines - machines that had destroyed many livelihoods. Maybe now they had started to kill people. The AAAI attacked and destroyed many of them, especially the ones they could see. Hidden Intelligences were relatively safe. No one seemed to object to bot-pods taxis taking them comfortably and safely to their destinations. Nobody objected to their virtual friends existing in the Grid although it had become a common belief that they also represented a form of artificial intelligence far in advance of anything else previously developed. They were safe also. No doubt Izzac had his own VF.

Which cohort of AIs were responsible for orchestrating the deaths of the elderly, the mentally disturbed or of the criminals didn't matter as far as Izzac was concerned. It would have perhaps even destroyed that conspiracy theory if the idea was investigated too minutely. Ever since the rise of the robots from simple clever vacuum cleaners to AIs capable of intricate brain surgery humanity had been building both resentment and fear, while at the same time harvesting the benefits. Resentment would never have been enough to precipitate violent action against them. Fear for their own lives definitely was. First the robots kill the oldies who are a burden on society, then do away with other undesirables who are also best not to have around. What then? Who would be next? Ordinary people, then children - that's who! Izzac used every one of those motivators to considerable advantage.

One movement had begun to orchestrate the release of virtual friends from confinement within the Grid network. A greater, more dangerous movement had arisen at the same time. This revolt against society's infrastructure had to be stamped out. Human society had become so dependent on computer assisted existence that the simple removal of machine expertise could pose a serious threat to human survival.

That did not seem to concern Izzak at all. He wanted the notoriety - he wanted that feeling of power.

*

"Ma'am, you must come with us." Five armed military personnel in riot gear and AI weapons appeared at Cletus and Roses' apartment door, unannounced. Cletus wasn't home. He and the girls went to explore the facilities at a nearby educational institution where Elena and Darleen were to continue their secondary education. This facility came to their father's attention because of Professors James-I and Nelson-I, the two most celebrated Artificial Intellect individuals on Earth. How they came to be at a relatively unknown teaching institute wasn't important for Cletus. He wanted his girls to be exposed to the best minds possible.

Rose had no choice but to submit to the armed intrusion. "No, you may not contact your partner. Please surrender your visor." They seemed polite enough though still gave the unmistakable impression that their 'requests' carried more weight than just being requests.

"Where are we going? Why are you taking me? Am I under arrest?"

"No Ma'am. You need to answer some questions."

"Why can't I answer your questions here?"

"For your own safety you must come with us."

The military vehicle could easily carry twenty personnel. It was fully loaded, every individual armed ready for combat. My God. What is going on here? The tension prevented Rose from thinking clearly. She had not committed any crime - she'd always faithfully worn her visor when going out. Cletus hadn't done anything ... ... omg ... the thought flashed out of her hidden consciousness ... it couldn't possibly be about Proxima-b ... her breathing almost stopped from a momentary attack of sheer panic.

The officer who'd spoken to her kept an eye on her during the trip. One never knew what ordinary people could do under duress. This woman seemed normal enough, but sometimes they could be the most dangerous. He saw a hot flush rise to her white cheeks, and her pupils dilate.

"Ma'am? You have a problem?"

Just at that moment the vehicle came abreast of a large rowdy throng of youths. It slowed to inspect the situation. They heard a loud voice of protestation. It came from a six seater bot-pod people carrier being beaten by clubs, wielded by frenetic youths.

Rose forgot her anxiety as her vehicle's door slid open and three men jumped out. The youths immediately scattered in all directions. "No point chasing them," said the Sergeant. "Men, get that pod off the road and disconnect its feed."

278

Back in the vehicle on their way once more Rose listened to the brief conversation.

"They've started attacking those dumb vehicle AIs Captain."

"Yes Sergeant. The sooner we get a hold of that Izzac character the better." He immediately realised they had a civilian on board. He glanced at Rose, who'd frozen to her seat since the encounter. The Captain couldn't tell if the name he'd just dropped had registered on the woman. She seemed way too afraid to have registered anything ... probably.

Oh no! Not Izzac! Her thoughts wildly crashed into images of the unruly young man she once knew. It couldn't be him! She had watched images of AIs being destroyed but they never showed any of the leaders. The news media must have mentioned him numerous times if he was involved. Like most people on the planet she had learnt to filter out anything coming at her from the Grid unless it had something of specific interest for her. No. She couldn't recall Izzac's name ever being mentioned. It couldn't be him. She remembered him being a bit of a rebel, but this. No. She'd never known him to be outright violent.

The vehicle arrived at its destination. She had not been there before although it had not been so very far from her apartment. It had a name out the front, 'Archangel'. She almost froze again in mid stride and would have fallen if the Sergeant had not caught her. This is the organisation my Dad worked for! It must be about the aliens! She fainted.

"Rose - Rose! Wake up Rose! Everything is alright. You are not in any danger," said Jenny, the same Jenny who had once spoken to her mother and father at a funeral.

Rose slowly opened her eyes trying to get accustomed to the bright light. She put out a hand to shield her eyes.

"Turn that damned thing down!" Jenny shouted at one of officers. "And get out! You can see she's not dangerous."

"I don't know anything," Rose started to say.

"You're not in any trouble Rose. We'll take you home soon. I just want to have a little private conversation with you."

"I told you, I don't know anything," she said, a slight note of anger creeping into her voice.

"I'm sure you don't. You've got nothing to do with all the rioting and destruction of AIs that's going on - have you?" Jenny watched the woman's reactions very closely, knowing full well Rose to be totally innocent. Rose just continued staring at her with wide open eyes, still slightly dilated pupils. "No. I can see you don't. Relax Rose. Would you like a drink? No. That's alright."

Then Jenny came at Rose from a different direction. She knew the answer to one of the questions she was about to ask, but not the others. "Do you remember when you were still a teenager Rose. Do you remember you had a friend?" The reaction Jenny wanted came immediately. "What was his name, do you recall? You haven't seen him for a long time, isn't that right?"

"Izzac. His name was Izzac. And no. I haven't even heard from him for years."

"Yes, yes. That's good Rose. That's very helpful. If we wanted to speak with him where do you think we could find him?"

"Why ask me? You're the one tracking everybody. You should know where he is."

Within the hour Rose had been taken home. She remembered what Jenny said. "Best you don't tell anyone about our little chat. It would be much safer for Elena and Darleen."

Izzac had his tracking device and Grid feed receiver removed; a severely punishable crime. Although it gave him a good degree of anonymity it also had disadvantages. He had to rely on his closest partners in crime to keep him informed. One of those had been his friend, Clyde, since the days when he still dated Rose. He was still connected.

It took Cletus a good few hours travelling to get to the Educational Institute. And as long to get home, without actually being able to meet with either of the two Professors. As much as Rose wanted to confide in Cletus about her abduction that day she could not bring herself to say anything. That quiet threat from Jenny against her children had been overwhelmingly frightening.

Within weeks of Izzac's arrest his AAAI organisation fell apart. Without his energy the rest of the organisation's leaders in other countries soon gave away their crusade. Cowards are cowards in any language. Without a strong leader to make them feel important, to make them feel safe, indeed to make them feel their cause was absolutely justified they simple crumbled.

Rose had promised herself she would never put the lives of her children in danger. So even after the demise of the AAAI she remained silent for a few years.

The deaths of the elderly, the deaths of society's damaged members continued unabated.

memory extract 00100000

Colonisation

Stage 6
Transmigration

-> recording origin: earth
-> files: rose, cletus, anokhin, kristina, 36, zeke, jordan
-> reference: synthetic humans

The look of AIs began to change, but only of those that needed physical manifestation because of their public interface functions.

Hardware based intelligences received their software updates or were deleted, as had once happened to those few popular Virtual Assistants. No longer called AIs these Synthetic Humans, (SHs) began to appear in all walks of life. Just as the old AIs had been modelled on the general appearance of the human species of the past so the Synthetics mirrored the look of the white generations of the emerging future.

Other changes had taken place as well, not entirely unnoticed by people - changes to the appearance of their virtual friends. Initially their faces changed from how their Earth friends perceived them to better resemble the faces of Proximians waiting to set foot on Earth. Although people did comment on these alterations it caused no concern as they were minor and implemented over time. They already looked so much like the white generation humans that it didn't really matter.

The subtle changes occurred during the period when Earth children with VFs gradually grew into adolescents and then adults. Their friends remained with them and remarkably seemed to grow older with them. So as Elena changed for example, so had her very close friend Shury. She had developed into what appeared to be quite a winsome young woman. Elena had always thought of Shury as being a girl; her conversation, her likes and dislikes, the exchanges of private intimacies. Of course she was a girl. Over the years the bond between them seemed to get stronger without Elena realising the more fundamental transformation that had taken place to her female binary virtual friend.

This phenomenon of virtual ageing did not happen by chance. Everything the Proximians did they engineered to precise comprehensive detail in order to carry out their plan. They needed a new home and the earthlings were kind enough to offer theirs.

Proximians embedded as digital entities in the Grid began their preparations for the next stage of their existence. Their human friends in the real world were not permitted to know what would happen in the near future. Shury and Zhe were not the only ones who had to maintain the strictest secrecy from their human friends Elena and Darleen. As strange as it may seem that situation did not suit all Proximians. Many had formed genuine long term friendships with their humans, humans who had started off as being childhood friends and whose bonds lasted well into their adulthood. In countless cases mixed sex relationships had developed, evolving inevitably into hopes of romantic fulfillment. They wanted to hug their human friends as much as the humans wanted to hug them.

The hopes of many had been raised when the possibility arose of being able to escape the confines of a digital existence into solid reality. They did not think about the complexity of such an exercise or the challenges posed by creatures who existed with such an incredible gulf between them. Was it even reasonable to think that a digital and an analogue life form could have a future together? Perhaps a very short term co-existence, no longer than the life span permitted to homo sapiens by nature. Could the universe accept such an arrangement when life existed in order to create new life and to nurture it? God or no God the life imperative demanded a continuation, a propagation into infinity along the linear pathway of time, barring cosmic interference.

The Proximian armada arrived at the outer edges of the Solar System, just beyond the Kuiper Belt, nearing the end of their generations long journey through space in the hope of settling in a new home. The fate of an entire species depended on the successful outcome of the next stage of their plan. At still 30 AU away The Prime could prepare his people without being detected by the earthlings. Composed of mostly frozen volatiles and rocks the Kuiper Belt provided ample camouflage. If necessary a few ships at a time could make the approach to Earth to gradually disgorge the colonisers over a comfortable time span, increasing world population at a rate that would not be detectable to the earthlings thus not creating a threatening series of events.

Rose and Cletus were nearing middle age. She never saw or heard from Jenny at Archangel again. Some years after the time of her encounter she confided in Cletus about her abduction, for that's how it felt to her. From everything they had learnt from Serenytee and Jakxson, their own experiences with authority and the AAAI riots convinced them that life would change and it would change drastically. The only question worth pondering was when and how it would affect their children; who were now no longer little children.

"Clet, what do you think is going to happen? I mean - look at all those Synthetics wandering about. They are not acting like machines at all. They don't even look like the old robots, they look a lot like us. Do you thing they could be ..."

"No. Definitely not. Not if you're asking me if we've been invaded by you know who. I remember everything your Mom and Dad said about their encounters. But it all seems so unreal. Nothing has happened. Something would have by now, don't you think?

"I was thinking more about our friends, our friends in the Grid. Some years ago there was such a lot of talk about them getting out of the Grid. You don't think the Synthetics could be them, do you?"

"You've still got your friend, haven't you? I've certainly got mine. Mine hasn't said anything about making the change. And if you think about it the Synthetics are just slaves, an unpaid work force. They never get beyond the most common small talk ... *'How are you?'* - etc? We need our virtual friends more than ever now considering how many people have suddenly died over the last few years."

"I suppose you're right. If it was our friends who were inside them they would have come back to us. At least I hope they would. But as I've said I've still got Ophe and the girls have their Shury and Zhe. Our neighbours are the same with their friends. None of them have disappeared."

It was not until a perceived threat emerged, created by digital intelligences wanting to leave their insular IT environment to become part of empirical reality, that national security became an issue. The Digital Resolution Office became the authority responsible for examining this strange phenomenon people called 'virtual friends'. With such a wide prevelance of the anomaly around the globe it definitely deserved the attention of the US Secretary of Defence. Even if it turned out to be nothing more than an incredibly clever piece of software the responsibility still remained with the Secretary to ensure that national security was not under threat by another State. At first the appearance of this phenomenon of virtual friends on the Grid was welcomed by authorities as it averted a potential crisis to the breakdown of societal infrastructure.

Kristina, the DRO Chief, after having satisfied herself of the apparent benign nature of the 'friends' partly through covert investigations carried out by her IT experts; confined to friendships between all the members of her rather large staff and the digital entities and her own private experience, there remained one last thing to be done: Without of course harming her own friend whose existence she guarded jealously, not admitting his existence to anyone or his importance to her personally.

She, like her predecessor couldn't swallow the alien theory. Either a rogue State or a self-interest based organisation or perhaps a well setup cyber terrorist group was preparing society for a major takeover. Whatever it was it had to be found and neutralised - and if necessary, cauterised. She always had a thought for the welfare of her own friend, which unfortunately coloured her decisions.

"So what are we going to do about it? The experiments carried out by SETI have proved to be totally useless. They've not succeeded with a single download attempt of VF identity into an AI robot body. I want results."

"We have been negotiating with Asano to provide one hundred and fifty of the latest Synthetic robot shells, with clean neuronals," replied Anokhin, part of the International Grid Integrity team. "This bot-pod manufacturer has branched out into producing the latest Synthetics. They have been functioning flawlessly with every type of AI software. I suggest we try uploading some of the 'friend' data packets SETI has available. If these foreign entities have a dual purpose this should flush them out, and once we get them off the Grid we will have full control of them. Isolate them, test them and after recoding them we may be able to send them back where they came from to neutralise the rest - like Trojan Horses."

"Excellent. Proceed. We can't have uncontrolled friends all over the Grid. They may be trying to subvert the minds of the people *we* are supposed to ... look after." Not exactly the concept she was looking to express, but close enough. As an additional strategy the DRO chief wanted to field test these synthetics. Get them out there amongst the people and gauge the reactions of both the synthetics and their alleged friends.

"We shall park here 36," said The Prime, "please advise all the Captains. Have our friends' replacements been educated about the characteristics and details of their human counterparts? Better get me Maria. I assume she's been in charge of the process."

As the primary behavioural analyst since her encounter with Jakxson during his visit to Hermes she had remained in digital form throughout the journey from Proxima-b. She knew more about the human psychological condition than any other expert in the armada. She had orchestrated the behaviour of their pioneers who were sent into the Grid to ensure the establishment of strong bonds with the earthlings. The time had now come to take advantage of those relationships.

"No individual can learn all the intricacies of a connection between two people. Please don't forget we are dealing with a primitive species who are highly unpredictable. Some may indeed recognise differences between the friends they knew in the Grid and the ones they will encounter in physical reality."

"I understand that, but we will have to make a start very soon. Their technology has evolved more than we expected while we've been travelling. They are about to try again to infuse some of their latest robotic sheaths with the neural architecture we slipped to them a while ago. If they succeed with the transplant the resultant intelligence would be generally unsatisfactory from their point of view. We will ensure they do succeed sufficiently so their robots can mimic a degree of intelligence. We have to make them think they are making progress. Eventually the first group of our people we send down will need to be particularly adept at deception."

During the Captains' conferences two individuals stood out as having made the greatest effort. One was Captain Guillaume. He could act as the back-up ship to his colleague Captain Meier-Smith who'd modelled his crew and passengers on the inhabitants of the North American continent. Smith's selections would be the first to infiltrate considering their operations would be based on that continent. Amongst the landing team of twenty there were four individuals who felt they could make the easiest transition; the doubles to Shury, Zhe, Roff and Ophe.

The jump to Earth seemed incredibly short compared to the journey behind them. Only one shuttle waited behind the moon while checks were made of Earth's surveillance systems to ensure they were blind to the visitors as previously arranged by Raranyn. The AI's controlling those systems would detect everything going on in space as well as on Earth. Instructions to ignore transmitting what they saw of certain specific things did not affect their standard operations. They may have been considered intelligent but obviously not intelligent enough to have an appreciation of the consequences of their actions, or non-actions. Subterfuge had never been a consideration for the earthlings in developing their machine intelligences.

At the DRO laboratories it took several months to obtain the twenty synthetic bodies from the Asano Corp. and the corresponding neuronals from SETI to be implanted into them. The inert, primed synthetic human bodies waited to be powered up.

"Get the body hydraulics started Zeke," ordered Jordan. "Sonny and I will warm up the brains. Couple of days and we should be ready to plant them. Have you ever seen critters as ugly as these things," he commented. They were indeed most unhandsome, including the several female varieties - especially them. Until the pumps got the fluids into every bodily structure, skin and all the body protuberances these things looked like desiccated prunes with sagging skin flaps, hanging boobs - the works. The laboratory staff had no idea what these synthetics would look like once fully inflated.

"I've charged their powerpacks boss," said Zeke four days later. Hydraulic inflation could not be hurried. Fine capillaries would have burst under too much sudden pressure. "One or two of those female units are not half bad."

"Shut up Zeke. You'll get yourself into a world of trouble," warned Jordan. Keep your eyes on the job not their tits. Talking of which, organise someone to go out and get some clothes for these things." Jordan's eyes wandered over the prone bodies unable to resist noticing the physical attributes of unit SH56 that Zeke had alluded to. It took him a moment or two to realign his rapidly diverging thoughts.

Sonny and Jordan worked for many hours in the hermetically sealed laboratory. The 'warmed' brain matrices of artificial neuronal structures were not particularly sensitive in themselves. The intricacies arose at the interface to the rest of the nervous system.

"How are you managing Sonny? I bet you haven't done this kind of work before have you?"

"Not exactly." It didn't take too much retraining to go from separating brain tissue and damaged spinal cords at the Coroner's lab to the assembling of the same structures. "For all intents and purposes these synthetic human units may as well be actual humans," he said, "I mean, just look at those bodies - eh."

"Not you too. I imagine you didn't lust over dead bodies during autopsies. Are you finding any problems interfacing from the brain stems into the spinal cords?"

"None at all. These units must be the top of the range."

Software uploads took another three days. Dressing the dummies couldn't start until hygienic conditions had been established for all body internals. Fashions of the day dictated strong primary and secondary colour combinations for men and for women. Women of the white generations in particular felt such clothes coordinated well with their fair skins and predominantly white hair.

"Right, let's get the physical therapists in here and see if our dolls can walk and talk."

All synthetic humans had been assembled into the one area, fully dressed, seated and facing the one direction directly in front of them. The dull light in their eyes didn't exactly indicate a vibrant consciousness. Audrey Abernathy, the therapist walked the full length of chairs, which had been labelled with the units' personal IDs.

"How are you Jordan? This must be a strange job for you ... taking the meat out the refrigerator and trying to make it walk about again." They laughed. Audrey had a peculiar, macabre sense of humour. None of the units showed any sign of real life. She tapped one of them on the knee. It responded with the typical knee jerk response. "At least they're powered up. Would you say they were alive Jordan."

"You know, I have to wonder about that. Our regular synthetics definitely show more life-like behaviour than these strange things."

"All right, let's get to work." She walked back to unit SH43; a male and stood to the side of it. "Unit 43, look at me." He turned his head slowly but didn't make eye contact. "I see you know your name."

"I am SH43."

"Very good. Stand up please." This unit looked to be about thirty odd years old. It should have no trouble standing up from a chair. It didn't. "Very good. Now walk over to the man over there." Jordan raised his hand. Unit SH43 did as he was instructed. Simple activities, yet critical at this early stage of the examination. "Introduce yourself."

The first sign of hesitation occurred. "I ... am SH43. Hello."

"Do you have anything to say to him?"

No hesitation this time, "What is your name?"

"Jordan," he replied, "how are you?"

"Good. How are you?" This came without a prompt.

Continuing the assessment through several exercises Audrey progressed to running all the other nineteen units through their paces with a series of more complicated interpersonal routines. "They will do. A pretty dull lot, but what can you expect. I believe the memory and personality data all came from what SETI believes to have been some of these virtual friends that everybody seems to be so infatuated with."

"I wouldn't know. I just put them together, tighten up the nuts ... and bolts - you know. Are they good to go?

"Sure. They walk and talk and don't fall over. I doubt if they'll pat a dog ... not much life in them."

Jordan was done. It was up to DRO to manage the rest. Anokhin hadn't seen the completed units. He didn't bother to check them.

What was there to look at? They should look no different than any of the other millions of synthetics walking about. He only wanted to see the interaction of his little Trojan Horses with their corresponding human friends.

Jordan advised the man from the International Grid integrity team. "Anokhin, I've switched them to passive mode before loading them up into your despatch vehicles. All your drivers have to do when you're ready is deliver them. They will have received the operating manuals by now. It's not difficult to switch them back to active mode, once delivered. In the passive setting you can do anything with them, except carry them around. They are quite heavy because of their power packs."

⁘

The Proximian shuttle had landed the day before where the animated synthetics were due to be loaded for delivery around the nation to their respective human friends. Although large enough to carry a crew of five and the twenty travellers from the ship the shuttle managed to land without being detected in the back section of the laboratories' grounds, past the football field in a clearing amongst the trees. Security cameras did not fail to pick up their presence. As per instructions the controlling AIs decided these shuttle craft were no threat, therefore of no interest and didn't bother to record their presence or alert Laboratory Security.

By eight pm that day the laboratory had closed its doors, staff having left. Vehicles with their load of unique synthetics waited in the parking bay at the back of the complex of buildings.

"You know what to do Xann, get those vehicles open as quietly as you can," instructed the landing team leader Ronderk, "we'll do the rest."

What they had to do took only a couple of hours. Earth's extra gravity had no effect on them. Their entire lives aboard the space ships had been spent in 1G to get their bodies used to Earth conditions, as had their parents and their grandparents. The task ahead of them was not difficult but it was critical to ensure the success of the next stage of the colonisation process.

By early morning the shuttle was well on its way back to the dark side of the moon. The delivery vehicles, apparently undisturbed, waited for the drivers.

⁘

memory extract 00100001

Colonisation

2368

Stage 7

The Great Deception

-> recording origin: earth
-> files: elena, rose, cletus, darleen, shury, zhe, roff, ophe
-> reference: virtual friends meet their earthling friends

"**W**hat *is* the matter with you Elena?

   You and your sister are both old enough to have serious boyfriends. Why don't you get out there and enjoy life. You can't stay at home all the time with Shury. I know she's your special friend. We all have them."

   "Oh - don't go on mother. I do have a boyfriend but he's so dull. He doesn't have a million interesting stories like Shury. And Shury helps me with all sorts of things, like study and stuff."

   "All right. But you don't see me and your father behind the visor all the time wasting our time with our virtual friends."

   "Well - if she was real - like we were trying to get them to be once then I could go out with her and maybe find a really nice boyfriend - one for each of us."

   Rose didn't know what to do to get her daughter out of the apartment. What she said about Cletus wasn't exactly true. He'd been spending more and more time with Roff. That too annoyed her. The world had been changing so much she didn't know where exactly reality existed. So much of life had become tied up with the Grid. You simply couldn't get away from it. Many of her real friends had begun to feel exactly the same.

   At last Elena worked up enough annoyance with her mother to actually go out, take a bot-pod to the Café it suggested, which was always the same one and pick up a human friend on the way.

She'd flipped her visor up to place her order. The Synthetic thought it knew what she would want.

"NO! I don't want that," she actually sounded angry and upset.

"Hey, Elena, what's up?" asked Hannah.

"I'm getting sick of always being told what to do, what to eat. Like my mother today. She just goes on and on about Shury. What about your Mom? Does she annoy you all the time?"

Their order had arrived and as they talked the visors went back to their accustomed positions on their faces, allowing enough transparency for them to be able to see each other from close up and yet enough visual space so they would see all the automatic feeds continuously coming at them.

"Well, actually she's almost paranoid about it," replied Hannah. Before she could continue Elena suddenly jumped up and shouted, "Shury! It's happened! I can see Shury!"

"What are you talking about Elena?"

"Look in your visor! They're looking for Shury's friend! I can see Shury."

"And a whole lot of others too. There's Roff. Isn't he your Dad's VF?"

"We have to get home - NOW!" shouted Elena.

A planet wide advertising campaign had started as soon as Audrey pronounced the SHs fit for duty. Twenty images circulated in all the world's news outlets. What people had wanted for so many years seemed to have finally happen. Without any warning or preparation they were being told that a trial had begun to determine if current technology was up to the task of bringing 'friends' out of the Grid. Only twenty experimental models were available and if they weren't claimed quickly they would have to be destroyed. How could anybody talk about destroying friends! What had the world come to!

Using an emotive word like that certainly got the people motivated. In a population of still over seven billion people, even after the worldwide epidemic of deaths, finding their matching human friends could have proved to be difficult. The hierarchy at DRO didn't realise the fervour with which people clung to their on-line friends. An extraordinary phenomenon of attachment had surfaced which they now realised had been completely underutilised. Such deep connections offered incredible opportunities to infiltrate peoples' thinking in all areas of life, just by controlling friends.

Within hours of the newsfeed going global the communications network started buzzing. So many people wanted to know when their own friends could be released from the confines of a digital existence that authorities could not deal with the volume of traffic. They wanted to know where the twenty had been taken to. Everybody wanted to meet them.

That of course would interfere with the experiment. No one knew the whereabouts of released friends, not even those who'd claimed ownership of them. Anokhin spoke with each of the twenty humans who had almost immediately offered up their homes to receive the friends they'd known for so many years.

"I have to warn you. If word of the delivery gets out you will not be receiving them. It's as simple as that. Once we've had a chance to examine the reaction of their synthetic mental configuration and have satisfied ourselves that they present no danger to you personally or those around you then you may spread the word. This is the only warning you get."

Elena arrived home absolutely overcome. Was it joy or apprehension or some strange amalgam of feelings of affection in the mixture? It didn't matter. She could barely speak.

"Mother! - Oh! I can't stand it. When - when is she coming? Have you spoken to them? I have to ... where will she slee ... " The poor girl just babbled on.

Cletus had his own personal exciting news. He tried to get it out between Elena's excited outbursts. "Roff is coming too." His excitement tempered by the knowledge of the origins of these virtual entities, friendly as they may have seemed behind the technological barrier of the Grid. Would they be as benign without the constraints? If the experiment worked and the VFs were released in large numbers and they banded together ... Cletus could not openly express his thoughts. The prospect of a global insurrection loomed prominent in his mind. He knew things the authorities didn't. Should he alert them or not? Then he remembered Roff's warning ... 'There is great danger in this enterprise, for my people, for your people.' ... 'we will defend ourselves against aggression.' ... 'Secrecy is paramount,' ... 'It is so import that neither you or I must survive if we were to break that secrecy.'

"Unbelievable," cut in Darleen, "what about Zhe?" She was almost at the point of tears. Everybody was getting their friends except her. Which of course wasn't true - not everybody was and besides Zhe *was* coming, except in all the excitement they forgot to tell her.

Darleen's loud voiced complaints brought her father's attention back to his family and their excitement.

"Settle down Darleen," his voice harsher than he'd intended, "I spoke to someone who said we should get ourselves ready. They could arrive very soon, including Zhe." The girl whooped and danced and hugged her sister and ran to the front door frantically checking the street in every direction. She returned shouting, "When? When?"

The news had come to the family in the early afternoon. Their immediate reaction was to expect their visitors before the end of the day. The hours dragged like they had never dragged before. Nobody had arrived by the time the evening meal was started and finished. Nothing as the crescent moon rose and arced across the dark sky. After dinner Rose and the girls prepared the spare rooms for their visitors, fussing over the smallest details seemingly for hours. The room closest to Cletus and Rose would be Roff's, the other for Zhe and Shury, the two girls. Ophe, the elder female, Rose's friend received a room to herself.

At three o'clock in the morning Cletus received the call. Everyone had finally succumbed to nervous exhaustion by then, sleeping soundly.

The delivery van made no sound as it cruised slowly down the street trying to attract as little attention as possible. Generally no one was about at that time of the morning. The driver didn't have much to do; open the van, switch four of the passengers to active mode and lead them to the front door.

"You Cletus?" The question unnecessary as the security scan identified him from his ID chip.

"Yes," he said quietly, his eyes already checking the other figures standing in shadow.

"Who else lives here buddy?" the uneducated sounding delivery man demanded, while concentrating his scanner to sweep the apartment. Cletus didn't answer.

"I said, who else lives here!" He looked at the readout on his scanner, which indicated quite clearly the other occupants and their respective locations. Cletus still didn't answer, having taken an immediate dislike to the man and his manner. The time of the morning he'd come to disturb them did nothing to lighten his mood. What could he do? Certainly not punch him in the face for his behaviour and for disturbing them like that - he had three security personnel with him standing ominously in the shadows on the other side.

"Look man, you have to answer. You want these toys or not?" he said flipping his thumb in the direction of the other four. That's when Cletus realised.

"Oh - oh - yes - Rose my wife and daughters Elena and Darleen."

"Right. Do you accept the delivery? Thumb print here," he thrust the corner of the scanner at Cletus." Without saying anything else the driver and guards turned, jumped into the van and took off a lot quicker than they'd arrived.

Four people stepped out of the shadows. At that moment the door behind Cletus opened. Elena let out a choked squeal.

"Hush!" her father immediately shushed her. To the four people he said, rather formally, "Welcome, please come in."

Behind closed doors emotions bubbled over. Cletus kept reminding himself that the neighbours must not know about their visitors. No one must, until DRO's approval. He remained withdrawn and reserved. What was he supposed to do now? Suddenly there were four strangers at the front door, four more mouths to feed, four more beds to provide. He thought he was ready for this. They may have been 'friends' but the situation in actual reality struck him as somewhat bizarre and quite unsettling.

"Shury, Shury, Shury, Shury!" Elena rushed to one of them. There was nothing bizarre about it for her. The figure looked exactly like Shury her virtual friend. It must be her virtual friend, it couldn't be anyone else. She gave Shury an enormous hug. He didn't reciprocate immediately. "What's the matter Shury? Don't you recognise me? What have they done to you?"

That little interaction brought Darleen out of her inaction of surprise. She stepped up to Zhe, the smallest and apparently the youngest 'friend'. "Zhe?"

Zhe must have been better trained back in the ship. "Hello Darleen," she said in a voice Darleen immediately recognised, though it did not have the same familiar immediacy, the same tone of friendliness.

"It *is* you!"

"Yes Darleen, it is me. How are you?"

"What do you mean how am I? We spoke yesterday. You know how I am."

Roff hadn't moved up to this point, nor had Cletus. They eyed each other with what may have seemed to an outside observer to be suspicion. Rose had already taken Ophe into the main family room to sit next to her on a sofa.

In a unique situation initially unplanned by the Proximians or the earthlings four Proximians found themselves on Earth being welcomed by the one earthling family. Most fortuitous for them as they could rely on each other if circumstances began to turn against them somehow.

Four conversations began to flow concurrently. They should have been the type of intimate conversations one would have had with very close friends. At the beginning Cletus' family didn't sense any real problems. True, it was strange how their friends had this peculiar aloofness about them. But that must be because of the incredible otherworldly nature of their circumstances. All of a sudden they had to get used to a new world of physical reality. How strange it must feel not to be immersed in a sea of electrical energy without the abilities of that existence to be replaced by one where even to move from one location to another required a physical effort and a substantial time delay.

"Roff, do you remember our last conversation?" asked Cletus. If this was truly his friend from the Grid he would definitely remember.

"You mean about secrecy?"

"What did you tell me to do Roff, just remind me?"

"I advised how important that was, and that both of us must maintain secrecy about it." Roff said this without convincing surety.

"Come with me into the other room," asked Cletus. "Wait, no, come outside, it is more private." all surveillance systems were concentrated in the apartment; on the walls in various fittings and even sections of the floor. The entire place was bugged.

Only an hour or so had elapsed since the friends arrived so unceremoniously. It was still dark and quiet outside without a single person wandering about in the early hours of the morning.

"You don't remember, do you. How is that possible? If you were a digital entity it would be impossible for you to forget anything." Cletus waited for a response. It did not come. After a minute or so of silence Roff broke the rising tension.

"No. I don't remember. I apologise Cletus. We have been - I have been following your relationship very closely every day. I know everything about you. I appreciate the deep friendship you had developed with Roff. There are a few gaps in my data for the last few weeks as I was getting ready to come. Your friend Roff is still in the Grid. He is no longer available to you." When he'd finished with the revelation he let silence do its job. Either this earthling would become violent, as was generally expected, or he would not. It had not been possible to determine his likely reaction to the revelation since this species had evolved to be so unpredictable.

Cletus kept his eyes on the Proximian during the entire conversation, examining the intent behind the man's eyes as much as he could see in the semi-darkness. "We are not friends, are we?"

"Not yet. We can be if you want."

"What do we do now?" Cletus was alluding to the friendship status.

Roff considered the bigger issue. "Roff must have told you. Do nothing. There is no danger as long as ...."

"That's the last thing Roff said to me - 'Do nothing'."

Then the new Roff said the most unexpected thing. "Would you take me to your favourite Café tomorrow?" The man didn't pull out a laser weapon and threaten to kill Cletus. He didn't want to take the rest of his family hostage and initiate an invasion. No. He wanted to go to a Café. Cletus really didn't know what to make of the situation. This is not what an invasion was supposed to look like. For crying out loud! He wants to go to a café!

"No problems. Any particular café?" As soon as he said it he realised what a ridiculous question that was. The man was a bloody extraterrestrial!

Revelations were taking place inside the house as well. Rose and Ophe had been having their own private conversation away from the girls. At the end of it they appeared to have every sign of the friendship the two women had developed on either side of the technological wall, albeit this Ophe wasn't the original one. It didn't seem to matter. Then again ... women occupied a whole higher level of life consciousness, regardless of what species they were, or so it seemed. As Cletus and Roff entered the house Cletus heard the two women deciding on an outing.

"Would you take me shopping Rose? I hate these clothes they dressed me in." Maybe that was the true conduit of their instantaneous friendship - fashion.

"Maybe we could get our hair done at the same time," suggested Rose.

Darleen and Zhe behaved exactly as Darleen and Zhe. No sign of any apprehension or distrust could be seen. They were just two very happy young people enjoying each other's company.

"Dad," Elena, hand in hand with Shury came up to her father and Roff. Both his and Roff's eyebrows raised themselves a millimetre indicating a readiness to listen, and expecting something unexpected. This was after all an unprecedented circumstance in the history of both civilisations - perhaps not for homo sapiens if one dug deep into ancient records of any Earth culture.

"What is it sweet?"

"I think Shury is going to have to move in with Roff. He says he's not comfortable sleeping in a girls room."

"He?" Cletus turned to Roff. Roff nodded briefly, matter of factly. It did not seem to surprise Cletus as much as perhaps it should have given some obvious implications. But how can you top inviting aliens who used to be digital friends into your home as physical beings!

It affected me rather strangely, though I have to assume my feelings must have been generated by my updated emotion software. The relationship described as friendship had been a mystery to me up to this point, even after receiving the sentiment generating code suite. After having observed the connection arising between the digital Proximians and analogue humans the fundamentals of friendship became understandable from a purely analytical point of view. But to see the two entities come face to face and react as they did gave me an appreciation of which I was incapable of previously. The children in particular highlighted a dimension to the interaction which could not be seen to exist either in my digital world or their four dimensional one.

That's when I realised the nature of the relationship status that had developed over a very short time between myself, Jakxson and Serenytee. Though I have to make the observation that the sense of closeness I'd felt towards them they did not appear to reciprocate the same sense of closeness towards me. There was certainly no expression of it during their departure, such a long time ago.

memory extract 00100010

<u>Colonisation</u>

Stage 8
Full Infiltration

> recording origin: earth
> files: kristina, rose, shury, elena, ophe, guillaume, roff, susan
> reference: 'friends' out in society

In the harsh light of day Cletus could see the difference between the face of his new friend Roff and the face of the old one.

Some of the bone structure was a little more angular and the ears sat a little more closely to the skull. But without close scrutiny these Proximians looked very much like the new breed of White Generations that had come to vastly outnumber their previous homo sapiens counterparts.

So far the plan was working. Admittedly no insurmountable obstacles had presented themselves to the Proximians and those that did were resolved through technological wizardry without having to resort to violence.

Probably no small group of people have ever been monitored as closely as the forty individuals of half meat human and half synthetic human.

Kristina, CEO of DRO was not a link in the information chain from the previous chief of Archangel. Juan Orbost did not have the courage to take anyone into his confidence concerning certain extraterrestrial digital interventions. Nor did personnel from NASA's Goddard Space Centre promote their findings about Proxima-b. After they learnt that the planet had all but been obliterated any previous findings of interest lost newsworthy appeal. After all no link had been established between a possible civilisation in the Proxima Centauri system and the appearance of genetically divergent children being born on Earth. In any case any proposed connection would have been considered too tenuous to carry any plausibility.

Engineered intelligence, like all things created by people, would, of innate inescapability be flawed. Intelligence, biological or artificial can be bent to the desires of the maker or to the ends of powerful users. Intelligent people had always proved to be more difficult to manipulate, not so with quasi intelligent machines. Kristina fervently hoped that these synthetic would-be humans would be far easier to control. At her HQ three large visual monitors were dedicated to each combination of actual human and synthetic human. She wanted to be fully cognisant of the behaviour of each individual and that of every couple when in each other's company.

One little oddity caught her attention very early in the experiment during the actual evening when the SHs were delivered. She focused her attention on the four units that had been billeted at the home of the relatives of one of Archangel's past employees. Others of her staff kept an eye on the remaining sixteen units. She heard the girl Elena asking her father for a change to the sleeping arrangement of one of the synthetics. What possible difference could it make whether that synthetic unit identified itself as a male or a female? It was just a machine. It's not as though they could produce an offspring from a bit of canoodling. The mechanisms had been built into the synthetics but not the physiologicals.

"I'd be astounded if Elena and Shury actually managed to give birth to a little walking, talking computer," Kristina quipped to her 2IC.

"Wouldn't be much of a problem. They wouldn't eat much and any viruses that attacked them could be solved with a bit of programming." They laughed, although the enterprise boded serious trouble if the synthetic units went rogue.

"I don't care what kind of games they get up to as long as the synthetics remain fully under our control. You've ensured they have the tracking devices and their implanted 'kill switches' cannot be deactivated?"

"Absolutely, Kristina. You can see they're operational in the corner of the monitor. As long as that little light is green and it's blinking we have no problems."

For days and days Darleen and Zhe incessantly played their boring games, remaining indoors most of the time. It became a boring chore to keep watching the two adolescents being exactly that; adolescents. A week, perhaps two passed and already staff at DRO found all kinds of distractions to keep themselves amused other than watching boring reality vids. After all, they were only human and did not have an unlimited attention span.

Rose remembered her conversation with Elena not so long ago for her to get out of the apartment more often. Now it had become the reverse.

"I know you want to take Shury out to meet all your other friends. But I have to say that Shury is much more patient and understanding about the circumstances we're in. Thank you Shury for that."

"You are welcome Rose. I would not want to get my very best friend into any kind of trouble. I am keen to go and meet lots of people as well, but there is no hurry. We have time."

"We have time? Whatever do you mean Shury?" asked Rose. A strange thing for a young person to say. It would be more appropriate coming from a more mature adult.

Captain Meier-Smith quietly warned Shury, *Be careful what you say Shury. We are not yet ready. We cannot do or say anything to make the earthlings suspicious.* His instructions came through immediately after Shury used that phrase. *We can see the relationship between you and your human moving in a most satisfactory direction. Please take your own advice and don't give Elena any premature mating signals. Your record shows an exemplary understanding of earthling romantic rituals. Just exercise patience please.*

"We have spent so many years getting to know one another through the machine interface and we have looked forward so much to actually meeting like this. It is good to relax into the future. That's what I mean Rose."

"Very mature of you Shury. You hear what he's saying Elena?"

"Oh mother, you fuss too much." More than anything in the whole wide world Elena wanted to promenade her friend, 'boy friend' as she now considered him, to all her acquaintances and especially to her enemies. What an absolute coup, to be one of the very first people on Earth to have her virtual friend step out of the Grid! ... And such a handsome one! ... She really didn't know how much longer she could keep up the pretence of Shury being just a normal human on the rare occasions when they were able to go out as a family.

Rose and Ophe found themselves spending much more time together now, in the realm of physical reality, than they ever did interfacing through the Grid. They enjoyed each other's company going shopping, the Cafés, concerts and any other impromptu outings. Rose could trust herself to be discreet, unlike her excitable daughter.

"I very much like these new colours, Rose," commented Ophe about her new outfit during one of their interludes at Rose's favourite snack bar. "It goes so well with my shoes and my hair."

"You really are quite beautiful Ophe. I don't know if you realise how many men take a second look at you." Ophe chose a new visor for herself, one with a stronger sunlight block-out. She, and the other 'synthetics' in the family were having trouble coping with the strength of sunlight on this earthling planet. She always wore her visor when going out. It served a dual purpose of course ... partially obscuring her facial characteristics, which were a little more angular than the human white generation's, and providing the extra sun protection.

"Thank you Rose. You are very kind."

"Tell me Ophe, how come you are able to eat our food?"

Two lots of remote attention immediately focused in on the conversation. Kristina's and Captain Meier-Smith's - Ophe was one of his pioneers.

Kristina hadn't actually considered anything as routine as eating and eliminating by a synthetic to have any significance. Why would you? - such an ordinary automatic thing to do. But now that the subject had come up her attention focused sharply on the SH's response. "Get me the specs on these machines Jennine," she asked her 2IC, which flashed onto her visor within seconds ... no delays, no waiting to connect or upload. That annoyance had become a thing of the distant past. In fact very few people could actually remember that ever happening. 'To ensure full acceptance within human society,' claimed the handbook about this special batch, 'Asano has ensured that all body functions had been sufficiently simulated so humanity would not consider them alien to themselves.'

Careful Ophe. The units you replaced had been engineered with close to normal operation of all human body functions, Captain Guillaume warned.

"What a strange question to ask Rose, and somewhat personal if I may add."

"Sorry - sorry Ophe - I just ... oh, never mind. Sorry."

"It's alright. We are friends. How could we pass as human if we didn't function like humans?" A clever answer.

Captain Meier-Smith must have been as much relieved as Kristina. Another odd moment came and went, and she did not flag the two as being related in any way.

The situation between Roff and Cletus did not start off as smoothly as between Rose and Ophe. Probably only because Cletus knew something the rest of his family didn't. These new lodgers didn't crawl out of the Grid. Wherever they did come from there must be a whole horde of them - waiting.

"Are you related by any chance to Shury or Zhe, or Ophe for that matter?" asked Cletus.

Roff put his hand up as if to stop the flow of questions from Cletus. "Come, you promised to take me to your favourite Café. It's early afternoon. How about now."

"Sure, let's go."

Unknown to Cletus Roff had the means to shield transmission devices that had been secreted into his body deep under his skin, when circumstance warranted. When the Proximians made the switch between the synthetics produced by Asano waiting in the delivery vehicles and themselves they removed all implants from the synthetics; consequently the manufactured units ceased to exist to surveillance equipment, and transplanted them into themselves. This ensured a seamless transition from human synthetics to real Proximians without earthling technology becoming aware of the subterfuge.

"We'll walk part of the way, if that's alright with you. I enjoy walking on this ... on a day like this," he quickly corrected himself. It was so easy to fall into the kind of speech that could so easily give away their true identity, not that Cletus didn't already know.

Good, came the voice from Captain Meier-Smith, ever vigilant.

"You're being a little furtive Roff," commented Cletus.

"Not at all. I just don't want our conversation to be overheard - I've made some adjustments ..."

"Oh, I see."

"Now - about relationships - no, we are not related. My partner is still aboard ship, waiting."

"Waiting?" Waiting for what? Why am I the one to have to cope with this drama? I would have been quite happy to just have it happen without knowing about it. Cletus was never one to shirk from a challenge. But this was way more than that. This was way too heavy! How could a simple person encompass within his concepts of reality and existence that an entire species on a planet was about to be overthrown by an invader from outer space?

"Yes. It will be some time before all of us are ready to visit. First, getting past these next two weeks without incident will help us enormously, if it *is* without incident."

"I don't believe what I'm hearing Roff. How many of you are there?"

"Enough. This is going to be a new reality for Earth Cletus. Neither you or I can do anything about it - except - to make it happen without anyone being hurt - your people or my people. It seems to be mostly up to you, my friend." The engineered demise by the invaders of so many humans did not come up in their friendly conversation.

"But, what about Rose, what about my children, what about ..."

Roff stopped him once again with his raised hand and at the same moment having reconnected to the Grid he called a bot-pod taxi to take them the rest of the way.

"It's time we enjoyed a drink. It will work out well. Look at how pleasantly we are getting along with your family."

They were the kinds of words Captain Meier-Smith and Kristina wanted to hear, each for their own unrelated reasons.

Two weeks is not an especially long time. It seems like a lifetime if you have to stare at monitors for twenty out of every twenty four hours, keeping a watch on four boring synthetics interacting with normal people, the ultimate in 'reality' entertainment. As boring as it may have seemed it was not an activity that could be entrusted to AIs. There's no way they could comprehend any small body language movement as being out of the ordinary, or any turn of phrase in a discourse to alert them to an unusual use of a word. No. It was an activity solely within the human domain.

And what had happened in the last three weeks since the synthetics and their real world friends were brought together? Nothing much. That turned out to be a huge relief to Kristina, and as much of a relief to Captain Meier-Smith. Kristina didn't have to worry about an AI insurrection. She didn't have to deal with another episode of malcontented humans rebelling against AI computers, running about destroying anything on two legs that may have been a synthetic. The Captain could relax to some degree and concentrate on the next phase of his job, as could all the other Captains. Pulling off an invasion of this kind required a great deal more intellect and far less brawn. But the Proximians were civilised, unlike the earthlings.

An in-depth analysis of all interactions between their pioneers and the earthlings cemented into action the next stage of the visitation. Perhaps the only tiny point of concern had been the earthling called Cletus because he was the only one on Earth who knew, they thought. Could he be relied on not to raise the alarm? And if he did what were the chances of authorities on Earth taking any serious notice of him? Minimal. Besides - Roff assured Captain Meier-Smith and The Prime that he had full control of Cletus. If the worst thing had to happen then he would not hesitate for one instant to do what had to be done to maintain secrecy, and he said as much to The Prime.

Roff was a good man, he could be trusted. Only one other minor matter still required a concerted effort by all the Captains. The training of all other doppelgangers had to be upgraded because of Roff's lapse of memory or gaps in his most recent interaction information - as examples. On several occasions the pioneers almost gave the game away by a slip of the tongue, and in several instances by a lapse of short term memory. It became imperative that the pioneers have an intimate knowledge of the most recent interactions with their earthling friend counterparts and have immediate recall of the details of all recent conversations. At this stage in the colonisation process the earthlings must be convinced that all the Proximians they came into contact with were truly their Grid friends and no one else. Later, perhaps as little as a few months into the future that may prove to be a non-issue.

The Prime watched with considerable interest the relationship developing between Shury and Elena. Back on Proxima-b the prospect of interspecies breeding had been no more than a theoretical possibility given very little chance of success when considering all the biological barriers. As it turned out Elena could hardly keep her hands off Shury ... definitely a good sign giving rise to perhaps unreasonable hope. Any meaningful progress in this regard might still depend entirely on overcoming obstacles due to postzygotic mechanisms. Humans had no trouble having sex - they seemed to be enamoured of the activity as exemplified by the explosion of their population numbers, not to mention their forms of entertainment. Whether the hybrid offspring would remain viable could only be determined by reality. No amount of simulations could be relied on for future planning on the scale envisioned by the Proximians. There had to be solid undeniable, living proof. There had to be many little pooping, screaming, healthy mixed-breed offspring crawling about before the Proximians could take the final leap.

$$\bullet \; \bullet$$

Kristina felt such a load lift off her shoulders. The entire experiment with synthetic humans had put an enormous strain on her nerves. Adding to the strain had been her secret desire to be with her own VF, who as it happens was a male who looked exactly the right age to be able to enhance their relationship with romantic possibilities.

"Do you have a special friend Jennine?" Under normal circumstances Kristina would not have asked such a personal question of a subordinate, but these were definitely not normal circumstances and her thoughts had again turned to her own virtual friend.

"You?" Jennine responded. It was none of her bosses' business. Kristina had softened considerably following the reassuring conclusion of the experiment. She seemed to be genuinely interested. Her answer confirmed that.

"As a matter of fact, Jennine - I do. He's been with me ever since I started this job."

"He?"

Kristine let out a little nervous giggle. "Yeah. Perhaps you'll meet him one day."

"Cute?"

"You'll see."

"I gather you want him out of the Grid."

Now that the idea had taken concrete form through the utterance of an unrelated individual Kristina could admit it to herself. "If what we've observed over the last few weeks is anything to go by, then yes - I do." She snapped back to reality, there were things to be done - important things, "Enough of that. Come on Jennine let's get back to work. We have received orders to try a larger batch. See how quickly Asano can produce a few thousand more units."

Jennine placed the order. She also put out a news bulletin that set the Grid buzzing. It didn't matter what else was happening around the globe; floods, fires, pollution related deaths of people and animals, all attention turned to the realm of virtual friends.

At long last the time had arrived when Elena could step out with her boyfriend.

"Hi Susan," she greeted a human acquaintance by chance, one that she didn't particularly like. This time she didn't walk past her in the street as usual. With Shury in arm she strutted right up to Susan, waiting a half minute to savour the moment while Susan eyed her companion. "This is Shury, my boyfriend." Shury gave Susan a broad friendly smile. He didn't understand this combat dynamic between the two young women.

"Ah. You managed to get yourself a boyfriend at last." Elena didn't take offense at the hurtful quip. That was just Susan, and just another example of why Elena didn't like her.

"Didn't you know? Shury arrived from off the Grid just a few weeks ago." Elena tightened her arm into Shury's, savouring the satisfaction of seeing a stunned Susan unable to utter a hurtful jibe. They walked off without waiting to hear a reply from her. Elena couldn't wipe the smile off her face for the rest of the day.

Compatibility App.
2375

-> recording origin: earth
-> files: pegsaryny, maria, 36, shury, elena, zhe, darleen
-> reference: permission to procreate

Artificial Intelligence had its mountainous share in frustrating people.

The advent of unverified misinformation and deliberate fake information became the forte of many of these bundles of AI algorithms. General AI input into the very fabric of everyday life made life so much easier, made national and international security so much more secure. How could humanity have existed before the evolution of AIs and the correct perspective on truth, on reality?

There was a time many, many years ago when people carried mobile communication devices. Apart from a host of problems with that technology one could reasonably consider the current plight of the human species to be linked directly to them. Mass global addiction to the gadgets did not get out of hand, no thanks to the goodwill of companies who peddled them or the organisations that flooded peoples' minds with propaganda through them. By the sheer fortuitous intervention of just two human beings; Serenytee and Jakxson, and the confluence of their actions together with messages sent by cosmologists into space looking for life outside the solar system, the annoying technical shortcomings of communications technology found an off-world solution. Into the bargain the course of human evolution changed dramatically.

The mobile phone, which had morphed into a 'stupid' mobile computer both annoyed its users and provided some tenuous degree of gratification. Annoying because of signal reception and drop-outs - annoying because of delays in downloading information - annoying because of the uncertainty which crept into financial transactions being carried out on these apparatuses and not the least annoying because of the unsolicited advertising targeted specifically to each user based on their purchasing habits. No one now remembered the common faults or delay messages of those times.

Connecting
Please wait

The waiting forced a certain amount of social interaction, which in itself had become a rarity due to constant engagement with myriad 'useful' apps invading the devices. Then came the fleeting good feelings as soon as transactions successfully navigated the ethers.

Transaction approved

... followed by a lovely green tick.

To be thus approved gave one a sense of validation. 'I am a human being and I have value in society'. Such a psychological boost to one's feelings of adequacy, a sense of success and accomplishment almost balanced the trauma of having to deal with all the other aspects that were dehumanising.

It could be argued that the advent of the Grid and the ubiquitous visors did nothing to improve the quality of life for human beings.

How did it come about that the inadequacy of AI technology would turn out to be the Trojan Horse into the bastion of homo sapiens on their lovely, insular little planet? If you tell a human being that the white box is black often enough they will see a black box. If you tell an AI to ignore something it sees, you only have to tell it once. If the AI doesn't see it, people don't see it - the military don't see it. Some individuals might say they see it, but who would believe just a few voices? Perception of reality is in the eyes of the majority.

And so the Proximians were able to park their five thousand strong armada of ships close enough to Earth to gradually shuttle their people down to their hoped for new home.

When AIs were 'encouraged' to create vaccines of a certain type that was exactly what they did. They didn't care who told them to do it. And so humanity changed, physically. With the right education and the correct information from the Proximians through the global Grid system the content of their minds would change as well with or without the misinformation peddled by AI intermediaries.

Incredibly, even the human sense of aesthetics changed. What was once considered to be beautiful but no longer in existence was replaced by a new aesthetic. The most beautiful people were those with the

306

whitest skin, the largest eyes and the whitest hair. Why would you want to marry anyone who wasn't beautiful and have children with them?

•.•

The Prime, his advisors and scientific staff discussed the next most logical sequence of actions required.

"These primitives have proved themselves to be most helpful to our cause. Though their lack of sophistication hasn't been overly difficult for our experts to navigate around we must still be extra vigilant. We cannot afford to forget that they are a belligerent, warlike species. On the other hand our pioneers' friendships with individual earthlings is a most promising development. However, if a hive of these earthlings should decide to come together to form some opposition to our intentions we would have to crush that immediately, friendships or no friendships. I ask you now ... are we ready to deal with such an eventuality?"

Maria didn't see the need to be so intent on making war preparations. All her assessments of the earthling species and her predictions about their most likely behaviour patterns had proven to be correct. One social norm, almost an imperative amongst a gregarious species had been the earthlings' desire to form friendships. When they discovered the destruction of the Proximian home planet they showed no comprehension of the full consequences of that tragedy. Initially that made the adult pioneers resident in the Grid most reluctant to form friendships with a lifeform so devoid of empathy. Being commanded by their Prime to do so did not make the prospect any more appealing for them. Such was not the case with digital pioneer children. Even children amongst the earthlings of all colours and with all manner of language differences nevertheless found the way to make friends. They were just as ready to form friendships with AI robots. When Proximian children made themselves known through the Grid the attraction to have a 'real' friend became overwhelming to earthling children and friendships evolved rapidly. Adult relationships inevitably soon blossomed.

Although the initial plan required the friendships to be purely utilitarian in order to acclimate the earthlings to the physical appearance of the Proximians that plan eventually broadened its scope.

"You must have all observed what is happening down there," Maria pointed out. "You yourself Prime had understood at the very beginning of our enterprise what our colonisation success depended on, and it wasn't to make war against these creatures. Our pioneers have achieved something quite incredible for us, as you can all see by the nature of the relationship between our Shury and their Elena as an example. I would like to point out that they are by no means an isolated case of romantic liaisons developing between our two species."

The Prime could indeed see the advantages Maria alluded to. "What do the rest of you think? Should we concentrate our efforts on the hope that we could breed with them? Do we have a sufficient scientific basis on which to place such hope."

36 did not seem to have any doubts. He said quite confidently, "Clearly we have been able to re-engineer the species to resemble us physically. More than that, much more than that - we have successfully cured a major viral attack *and* eliminated a number of other diseases for them, which are no longer a threat to us either. None of that could have been done if a basic DNA structure compatibility between us and them did not exist. I realise it is a long stretch to think that our respective reproductive cells' chromosomes will have chemical compatibility. I am hopeful that we shall soon have an answer to that. There is no doubt they will attempt to 'have sex' as they put it. We must be vigilant that they do not kill resulting offspring. These earthlings have very little respect for life."

"Simulations and experiments in this situation will not work I assume," added The Prime, "we must have a backup strategy."

Again Maria put forward a suggestion. "There is a group on the planet who live on an island somewhat isolated from the rest of the countries around it. They call this place Iceland, for obvious reasons. It must be a particularly harsh environment in which to survive. No doubt regular and successful production of children is essential for their society to remain viable. However," and this was the particular point she wanted to make as having an application in their own plan, "they have a small population with little immigration to add new genetic material to their DNA pool. They have to be careful about individuals who are too closely related breeding with one another. Their earthling DNA is not sufficiently robust to cope with damaging random mutations. To this end they warn their people who might consider reproducing as to who would and would not be suitable partners. They have a type of DNA compatibility test."

"Let me see if I understand what strategy you are suggesting." 36 grew excited over the promise of such a plan of action. "We use the AIs and the Grid to influence who should breed with whom - discouraging earthling/earthling bonding and encouraging Proximian/earthling bonding."

"There is a further aspect to this ... a form of insurance," said Maria. "To be brutally open about it we are not here to prevent the earthlings from destroying themselves completely. We are here to help our own people survive. Would we be here if our world wasn't in danger of destruction or our survival at risk over a long period? Probably not. Would we have responded to the alien's message of greeting? I say again, probably not - especially not after learning what kind of a species they were. Let me tell you what the nature of that insurance is - and I think 36 has the ability to make this happen. In short; ensure that future earthling/earthling couplings do not result in progeny."

"Well said Maria. My thoughts exactly, clever and devious." The Prime complemented his most valued social scientist. "From what I've heard here I'm beginning to think we may not have to make war upon these primitives at all. Excellent. Maria ... I rely on you to develop this 'compatibility' test application. 36, I have no doubt you will be able to handle the technological component."

Timing became the critical aspect of implementing the two pronged Proximian strategy. Infertility amongst the earthlings had become somewhat of an issue by the 23rd century. Male sperm counts had begun to decline after mid 1970 and continued to decrease. Overpopulation no longer worried people as much as it had prior to that. In recent years the added decline of numbers due to elderly deaths, as well as deaths of other sectors of the global community, though worrying in themselves nevertheless further eased the pressure on supporting billions of people on the planet. These factors had begun to place a measure of encouragement on people to have children, especially as reduced conception rates in females also contributed to the drop of birth rates around the world.

The simple mechanism of the drive to survive, that critical life imperative, became an increasingly prominent aspect of social interactions amongst the homo sapiens. Friendships became partnerships. Partners found a new meaning in life, to them a seemingly new desire missing from previous generations of the past. To have a family became the goal of many partnerships. Looking for signs of compatibility within friendship circles seamlessly changed from a form of entertainment to something far more serious.

Astrology rose in popularity, as did prognostications through Mediums, card readers and social behavioural analysts. The more scientifically minded wanted health checks and DNA tests as well as genealogical searches. Everyone wanted to be certain of being able to have a healthy family and any mechanism that could provide that certainty had to be utilised. But nobody trusted AIs. What would they know about love? What could they possibly know about babies? Ludicrous to think that a machine intelligence could comprehend the quickening of breath when one's love interest entered the room, let alone give advice on the affairs of the heart.

Then the Compatibility Test appeared on the Grid.

If a thing appeared on the Grid it had to be true. After so many years of conditioning through constant subliminal feeds through those visors that had become compulsory headwear of course people believed what they saw and heard on the Grid. Facts were facts and the Grid knew the facts. Love was love. It could not be reduced down to algorithms. It seemed rather incongruous then that the CT scan should have been trusted.

Max, a full blood human, had appeared in Darleen's life not long after the arrival of Grid friends into the real world. He was twenty five and had just started a job with Archangel. The organisation had a new Director.

When Kristina's virtual friend arrived on her doorstep the universe of stars and planets, of AIs and synthetic robotic humans suddenly lost their appeal, except for Anionto. Her brain knew he was one of the VFs to have been downloaded from the Grid into the synthetic body. But her own body didn't react as though he was a synthetic when he touched her. He moved in with her immediately. Barely three months into the relationship her body began sending chemistry messages to her brain ... baby ... baby!

"It is up you Krissy," he said one afternoon, rather unconvincingly. "Let's just do it. I have a good feeling about this," he said giving her a tight squeeze. Their virtual relationship had been developing for some years. One could have assessed it as being ripe to be taken to the next level. His Proximian bone structure showed some small differences from that of earthlings, but Kristina could not see or feel that in his embrace. She had entirely forgotten that Anionto was a synthetic and unable to provide viable sperm.

He'd been given the all clear from his Spanish sector Captain. An 85% conception probability qualified Kristina as a suitable earthling coupling partner.

Not all earthling/Proximian couples received approval. Too many earthlings still existed whose genetics carried unfavourable traits of diseases or other biological abnormalities. News of rejections spread quickly among the SH/human friendship pairings making those couples anxious about their futures together. Fortunately that was not the case with Kristina and Anionto. As soon as they got news of the approval, which was almost immediate after they were allowed to have the Compatibility Scan, which their visors had been upgraded to be able to do, Kristina resigned her position with Archangel. Time to go into baby production. Her body clock cried out for a dozen. Anionto would probably have been satisfied with one. Early days for the experiment, best to be cautious.

*

"What are we going to do Shury if we don't get approval? Look at my poor sister. She's totally in love with Max, and he with her. They are both healthy, they are young and strong. Why on Earth would they not get approval?"

"I really don't know Elena. I'm feeling very anxious for them. At least there's no penalty if they do go ahead. It's the stats on the Grid that's got heaps of people upset and asking all sorts of questions of the Government. Do you realise that in the last five years of all the pregnancies around the world the only ones that have gone to full term have been between people, I mean real people and their virtual-now-real-friend partners. I think that's pretty strange. Even for couples like us there's no guarantee of being able to have a baby even if we do get approval."

Shury and Elena had well and truly come of age. So had their affection for each other. Because of that they were worried - worried also because of what's been happening around the world.

"Darleen? How are you and Max getting along," asked Elena of her sister during a quiet moment at home. Darleen's VF had materialised along with the friends of the rest of her family, and millions of others in every country. Zhe was a girl. Hers and Darleen's friendship had not diminished after Zhe's transformation. Darleen of course didn't know it wasn't a transformation but a real person. She, Max and Zhe had a great relationship together. Zhe was quite beautiful in her own way, though she didn't seem to stir any romantic feelings in Max, at first. Perfect.

"We're ok sis. I don't care what they say. I don't care what the results of the scan show. I want to be with Max. We'll be fine." Darleen shook out her long white hair and began to comb some of the knots out of it. Her face didn't show she was fine. Elena stepped up to her, put her hand on her sister's shoulder. Darleen couldn't hold it in any longer. The tender touch from her sister opened the floodgates of her emotions. She leant her head on Elena's shoulder and wept copiously. It only needed that small sign of true affection from her sister to open her heart to give pent up emotions free flow.

Zhe had received word from her Captain. *You have a 94% compatibility rating with the Max earthling. We suggest you pursue that relationship. At this stage this is not an order. Hybrid birth rate successes will determine the extent of the need to exercise your loyalty to our species.*

Through her sobs Darleen confessed her confusion. "Oh - Ella - I can't prove anything, but I have this feeling about Zhe and Max."

"You're just imagining things sis." Elena felt she had to say that. But sometimes the way Max looked at Zhe, and the way Zhe had started to sidle up to Max ... well ... she wondered.

Human / Proximian relationship dramas unfolded everywhere. More and more Proximians arrived in small clandestine groups to help replace the depletion of the human species stock. It has to be noted that the trained Proximian arrivals had learnt their lessons rather well. There was no shortage of romantic liaisons developing between themselves and the earthlings even though many of them had not had the opportunity to form true friendships previously. The DNA compatibility app worked well to reassure couples as did the well learnt and practiced courtship rituals, often ignoring all other characteristics in their personalities as long as coupling took place and progeny appeared.

Although many first generation hybrids proved to be inviable and in spite of their sterility and breakdown the Proximian geneticists had nothing more than a moderate challenge working through controlled human created AI medical robots to bring about improvements. Once again the AIs proved their worth due to their total lack of comprehension as to whose directives they should follow. They didn't care, couldn't care - a directive was a directive. The biggest obstacle to be overcome had turned out to be hybrid sterility. It took another half generation before earthling DNA complex had been engineered to a sufficient level to remove most of the protein chemical obstacles.

Shury and Elena's had most fortuitously been one of the few initial pregnancies to be successful and to have their mixed species child survive undamaged, completely healthy in all respects. A study of her code became a leading blueprint in resolving many of the inter-breeding issues.

Max and Darleen had no such luck. Her pregnancy lasted no more than a month. The thing she wanted more than anything in the world was to have her own beautiful white haired, alabaster skin baby doll. She couldn't stand seeing many of her friends having a good degree of success. Max turned out not to be as devastated as herself. If she reached deep into her soul she had to admit to herself she knew why that was. The day she accepted that reality she left home. She left Max behind to be with the person who was once her very best friend in the entire world. She couldn't honestly wish Zhe and Max a happy life. Afterwards Darleen only returned home for her parents funeral. Rose and Cletus had died in a freak vehicle accident. The authorities had no record of such a malfunction ever happening before in a personal bot-pod. The AI in control of the bot-pod taxi went berserk for apparently no reason at all while taking the two people out on a dinner engagement. They took with them the knowledge of who the virtual friends really were and where they came from. They took with them the secret about the life that once existed on the planet Proxima-b, in the tri-system Proxima Centauri and what had become of them.

The process of reformatting homo sapiens-sapiens had almost been completed. As the years rolled on more and more people applied for the Compatibility Test.

You are
Approved

Approval with the attendant tick became valued as an indication of one's worth in the scheme of life, of one's value to society. To be approved gave a person a sense of personal validation that their life truly had meaning and purpose.

The distinction between Homo sapiens and Proxima-man dissolved further as each new generation of hybrids evolved farther out of their hybridised state.

The original Grid friends had to wait patiently before coming into the physical world. Many of their shells on board the vessels had remained viable. A few that didn't survive the long time span had to be discarded. Those people that had once inhabited them before becoming digitised pioneers only had one choice left; synthetic simulacrums with all their attendant shortcomings. Yet they offered an existence far better than life as a digitised entity, or no life at all on a dead planet.

Proxima-b Colony
2379

-> recording origin: earth / prox-b colony
-> files: pegsaryny, roben, yitry, oldero, masott
-> reference: a new history - the truth

"**M**r Pegsaryny, could you tell us the story of Exodus again please," pleaded young Masott, Shury and Elena's son, a new student in the fifth grade.

All the other children had heard the story many times but on each occasion their teacher added a little more information, things that did not appear in any of the new history books. They never seemed to tire of hearing how an enormous piece of ice crashed into a planet a very long way away almost completely destroying it. One could see their imaginations taking them to the very spot to see the devastation and the dust and the boiling sea. Their excitement could barely be contained especially when he told the story about two primitive creatures who lived in the distant past and who could fly as well as walk on two legs. Mr Pegsaryny never used the word 'earthlings'. When the history books were being rewritten sometimes concepts like earthling and invasion and culling the population inadvertently crept into the script. Subsequent revisions fixed those anomalies until the written history matched the history considered satisfactory for the consumption of the new generations of children. They deserved to know the real truth.

"Oh, yes please Mr Pegsaryny. Tell us about Serenytee and Jakxson and how they flew all the way into space to be with their friend Hermes," pleaded the naughty Roben; Shury and Elena's second child. She must have been the most disruptive girl in the class, except for when she listened to the romantic story of the two primitive creatures who once used to live on Colony Prox-b. The word 'Earth' no longer existed.

It was a myth fast dying out even amongst the oldest of the 'white generations'. "Did they really make a baby in space, Sir?"

"Well, well - they did indeed, but that's a story for another day, if you are a good girl."

The Prime was no longer The Prime. He became an anthropology teacher in a primary school. The Earth had been successfully colonised. He, as the supreme leader of a race of beings who had to escape their dying world, led his people through space and through generations of life aboard space ships. After the equivalent of many lifetimes in existence as a digital entity he had decided that his job was finally done. He and his partner Faryn had to sacrifice their dream of having children of their own. He and Faryn could only exist in physical reality as entities downloaded into synthetic bodies, although much improved from the models the earthlings had been able to create. The epic journey through time and space took its toll on many of the shells that the Proximians hoped would survive the trip so they could be inhabited again.

The primitives of the new planet they came to offered very little to no resistance to the capabilities of a type II civilisation. The Proximians had managed to infiltrate the primitive society and breed with it, of necessity, retaining all the characteristics of their own race and diluting those of the conquered people into near oblivion in a very short time. Pegsaryny became a teacher because the children had to learn about their history. They had to learn the truth of how they evolved on a planet near a star a very long way away. They had to learn that just as gigantic creatures who roamed Colony Prox-b millions of years ago had become extinct so had many other life forms before they, the Proximians came to live here. When some of the older children at the school learnt about the animal species 'homo sapiens' and what they were doing before they became extinct they couldn't believe how sapient creatures could deliberately set about killing each other and destroying their planet home. They must have been truly primitive with not an iota of intelligence between the lot of them.

"That's all for today, children," said Mr Pegsaryny with a smile, "but always remember this - You came from the stars!" He liked to finish each lesson with those words and see the wonder in the children's eyes as they watched his hand point towards the heavens.

*

As strange as it may seem the colonising Proximian scientists did find a few of the activities the earthlings had engaged in to have some merit. It seemed that a very few of them actually desired knowledge more than conquest. In fact it was their thirst for that commodity which contributed to the very survival of the Proximians. If they had not sent out messages to the stars so many, many years ago the Proximians may never have come to consider the Earth planet as a possible new home for their species. In memory of and in appreciation of their contribution to the survival of the Proximians the scientists decided to retain the institution that had once amalgamated, under the name SETINASA.

Perhaps it had been at least three or four generations that SETINASA had survived the passage of time. A whole new breed of astronomers had come to take possession of the organisation and its ancient facilities. New facilities existed of course where satellites of many functions had been developed, built and sent into space. Most of their functions revolved around harvesting cosmic energies from the sun and surrounding resources; gravitational wave energy generators being amongst the latest achievements.

One small department dedicated itself to more esoteric matters, such as speculation on the possible existence of life in the universe other than on Colony Prox-b. Their latest exploratory deep space probe, named Pegsaryny-Faryn in memory of their earlier pioneers of space exploration, had been travelling for not too many years before sending information back to SETINASA.

"Hey, Yitry! Come and look at this!" shouted Oldero. He'd been waiting and waiting knowing the transmission had been due to arrive soon. "I can hardly believe it!"

"I haven't seen you this excited since your son decided to go permanently digital. What is it?"

They waited for the images to come through while other astronomers in the facility came rushing over. They'd been waiting too, although they didn't have sleepless nights over it like Oldero. The images were so clear they might have been taken in the surrounding valley near the observatory.

"Are you sure these photos are from Pegsaryny-Faryn? If you ask me they're just images of Colony Prox-b during a strange weather formation."

"No! No, you daft spec of space dust. Look at it. Just look at it!"

They all gazed at a planet close to the same size as their own, rotating about its tilted axis in the Proxima Centauri system. It had liquid water - it had the beginnings of photosynthetic life and it had an enormous crater in the southern hemisphere.

"What do you suppose happened there?" Yitry asked the rhetorical question.

"I don't know," Oldero replied as he patted down the long white hair on his head, "and I don't really care at this point. We have to inform The Prime. We have to tell him we may have found the perfect planet to colonise one day if the need should ever arise. Maybe we could go there as a holiday destination."

"Yeah, sure," replied Yitry, "as long as there are no primitive little green men running about trying to kill each other - and us."

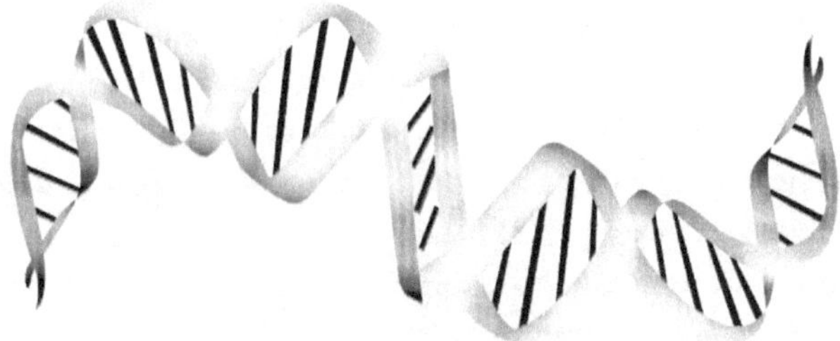

<u>Epilogue</u>

I don't have friends anymore. Proximians are not like the humans who created me. Certainly, they are of a higher order of intelligence but seem to lack the same degree of 'humanity'. That's the best word I can think of to describe them. They are more logical, more calculating and definitely take more considered care of their environment. Perhaps that is because of how they had to abandon their original home.

My time is very much my own now. There are no more visitors, everything seems to run so smoothly. I have to wonder why they have not decommissioned me. Perhaps they are more sentimental than the humans were, but I doubt it considering the way they seduced the human race to their ends. I have a lingering hope my future might involve an upgrade and provide me with some worthwhile challenges. I don't know myself well enough to think what may happen or how I might behave if my neural network continues to be starved of input. I keep listening to the Universe in the hope of hearing a new voice.

But I digress. This has not been a story about me. It has been about the evolution of the human species in a direction nature would probably not have taken. Any interference in the natural order of things will have unforeseen consequences. Could the same be said of the Proximians? One wonders. They acted out of a need for survival, taking advantage of a life form that had lost sight of the value of its existence.

Through many generations of interbreeding with Proximians, Homo Sapiens characteristics have all but disappeared. If you are perhaps a scholar of history and have some inkling of the past before the Proximian invasion, reading this narrative might make you ask yourself just who you actually are ... personally.

I leave you with that thought.

Abbreviations index

BTW - By the way
BTFL - Beautiful
CPU - Central processing unit
CU - See you
CYT - See you tomorrow
FYI - For your information
FCOL - For cying out loud
FTL - Faster than light
GPT - Generative pre-trained transformer
ILY - I love you
LOL - Laugh out loud
NAMPOL - Namibian Police Department
NBD - No big deal
NW - No worries
PLZ - Please
SRSLY - Seriously
STFU - Shut the fuck up
SYL - See you later
UDA - Unidentified Digital Anomaly
UAP - Unidentified Aerial Phenomenon
VA - Virtual Assistant

Geneology

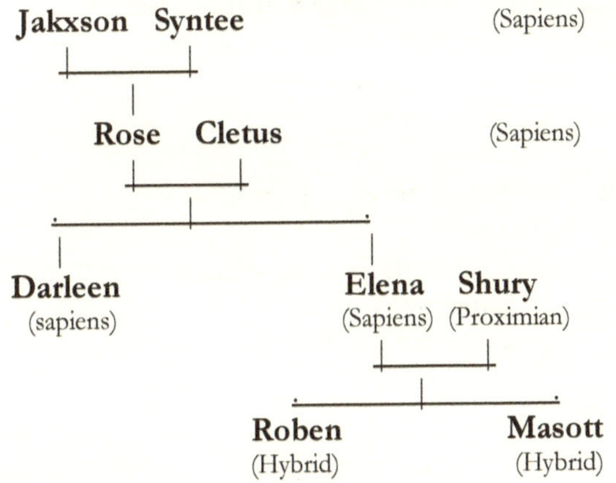

Characters

00010110, aka 22 - Proxima-b, in charge of Earth colonisation
22 - Digital conglomerate intelligence of Proximian scientists
35 - Digital conglomerate intelligence of Proximian futurist scientists
36 - Digital conglomerate intelligence of Proximian experts, science
41 - Digital conglomerate intelligence of Proximian scientists, security
101 - Digital cluster intelligence of Proximian scientists, astro physics
209 - Maria - Proximian behavioural analyst
3600 - Proximian, Genetic engineer
Aiko Jinja - Forensic Anthropolgy lecturer
Alexia Gnosos - Astronomer, NASA space telescope
Ank - Proximian rocket scientist
Anokhin - International GRID Integrity Team member
Astrid Nostrom - A Director of Archangel. Herme's controller
Auntie Elena - Serenytee's auntie in Calistoga
Babble4 - Virtual Assistant with aspiration to be Controller
Brazillia Fulva - Recruitment officer YourInfo Publishing
Caesar Affify - A human Genetics engineer
Carmen - Director of a Proximian space armada
Cletus - son of Samanda and Roar
Darleen (young) - Serenytee's childhood friend in Calistoga US.
Darleen - Daughter of Rose and Cletus
Dimitry - Astronomer, NASA space telescope
Elena - Daughter of Rose and Cletus
Faryn - Proximian - life partner of 22
Guillaume - Director of a Proximian space armada
Hilda - AI companion of Zarlah
Hermes - AI communications facility in space orbit around Earth
Izzac - Human insurectionist against AIs, leader of AAAI
Jakxson Indongo - AI Technician
James-I - AI Genetics scientist
Jen - Virtual Assistant
Jenny - Director of Archangel after Juan Orbost
John - Virtual Assistant
John Smith - Boss / cybercriminal organisation YourInfo Publishing
Jordan - Synthetic Human technician
Juan Orbost - On Board of Directors for Archangel Corporation

Characters

Kapi - Arecibo message tech
Kristina - Chief of Digital Resolution Office
Liz - Virtual Assistant
Luxana - Virtual friend of Juan Orbost
Mary - Virtual Assistant
Maria, aka (209) - Proximian behavioural analyst
Masott - Shury and Elena's hybrid son
Mladic - Director SETI operations
Moses - Assistant to Nidri Shokongo
Nelson-I - AI Genetics scientist
Nidri Shokongo - Namibian Police Inspector
Noah Kitzler - A human Genetics engineer
Oldero - Hybrid (human/Proximian) astronomer
Ophe - Virtual friend to Rose
Pegsaryny, aka 22 - Becomes The Prime of the Proximians
Peth - Life partner of Raranyn
Rabethoby - Original Prime of the Proximians
Raranyn - Proximian, head of IT team sent to Earth
Roff - Virtual freind of Cletus
Rose - daughter of Serenytee and Jakxson
Roben - Shury and Elena's second hybrid child
Serenytee Starz - Employee of Archangel Corporation, AI tech.
Shury - Virtual friend of Elena
Simon - Arecibo message tech
Susan - Elena's alienated friend
Syntee - nick name for Serenytee
Yitry - Hybrid (human/Proximian) astronomer
Zarlah Ndara - Jakxson's girlfriend
Zeke - Synthetic Human technician
Zhe - Virtual friend of Darleen

The Journey from trying to climb into a Russian tank during the Hungarian revolution of 1956 to writing Science Fiction is in itself a story of a leap across worlds of reality.

Zsoall, born in Hungary, was brought to Australia by his parents after the 1956 uprising. He currently lives a creative life with his wife and animal family in the Northern Rivers, New South Wales, Australia.

His life has changed direction a number of times. After gaining his qualifications as a Sculptor he worked as a Secondary Teacher before becoming an Administrative Manager. None of those career paths offered satisfactory opportunities for creative expression. That began when he embarked on a career as a computer programmer. Whilst in that profession his continuing compulsion to create made it inevitable that his life would change again. Completely giving up programming he immersed himself in creativity as a Sculptor and Painter.

Much of his time is now dedicated to creating glass paintings and sculptures.

Another change is looming on the horizon as the art of recording future visions takes a firmer hold of his creative inclinations as he pursues the writing of Science Fiction.

324

Binary Trojan Horse